Hot desert nights…
with the sheikh!

Powerful passions…
Sensual delights…

Two fabulous bestselling novels
from favourite authors
Sharon Kendrick and Susan Mallery

100 Reasons to Celebrate

We invite you to join us in celebrating Mills & Boon's centenary. Gerald Mills and Charles Boon founded Mills & Boon Limited in 1908 and opened offices in London's Covent Garden. Since then, Mills & Boon has become a hallmark for romantic fiction, recognised around the world.

We're proud of our 100 years of publishing excellence, which wouldn't have been achieved without the loyalty and enthusiasm of our authors and readers.

Thank you!

Each month throughout the year there will be something new and exciting to mark the centenary, so watch for your favourite authors, captivating new stories, special limited edition collections…and more!

THE DESERT

Sheikh's
P A S S I O N

SHARON KENDRICK
& SUSAN MALLERY

M&B™ and M&B™ with the Rose Device
are trademarks of the publisher.
Harlequin Mills & Boon Limited, Eton House,
18-24 Paradise Road, Richmond, Surrey TW9 1SR

THE DESERT SHEIKH'S PASSION
© by Harlequin Books SA 2008

The Desert Prince's Mistress © Sharon Kendrick 2004
The Sheikh & the Princess in Waiting
© Susan Macias Redmond 2004

The Desert Prince's Mistress and The Sheikh & the Princess in
Waiting were first published in Great Britain by Harlequin Mills &
Boon Limited in separate, single volumes.

ISBN: 978 0 263 86682 7

10-0908

Printed and bound in Spain
by Litografia Rosés S.A., Barcelona

The Desert Prince's Mistress

SHARON KENDRICK

The Desert Sheikhs
COLLECTION

August 2008
THE DESERT SHEIKH'S VIRGIN
Penny Jordan

September 2008
THE DESERT SHEIKH'S PASSION
Sharon Kendrick & Susan Mallery

October 2008
THE DESERT SHEIKH'S BRIDE
Lucy Monroe & Alexandra Sellers

November 2008
THE DESERT SHEIKH'S MARRIAGE
Jane Porter & Sarah Morgan

Sharon Kendrick started story-telling at the age of eleven and has never really stopped. She likes to write fast-paced, feel-good romances with heroes who are so sexy they'll make your toes curl!

Born in west London, she now lives in the beautiful city of Winchester – where she can see the cathedral from her window (but only if she stands on tip-toe). She has two children, Celia and Patrick, and her passions include music, books, cooking and eating – and drifting off into wonderful daydreams while she works out new plots!

Sharon Kendrick has a new novel, *Sicilian Husband, Unexpected Baby*, published in November 2008 in Mills & Boon® Modern™. Don't miss it!

To Sarah and David Nicholson,
Wilf and Hubie,
who always provide a place
of chaos and fun in Winchester!

CHAPTER ONE

IN HER hands she held dynamite.

Not real dynamite but something equally explosive, and Lara's fingers trembled as she looked down at the letter.

Above her head, the magnificent and ornate chandeliers of the Maraban Embassy threw glittering diamonds of light down onto the sheet of paper, and Lara stared at it, knowing that this letter held information which could change the lives of so many.

If it was true.

Lara swallowed, wondering if she should have opened it in the first place—but wasn't that part of her job, as demanded by her temporary role as secretary, to open the post? A job which up until about ten minutes ago had seemed as perfect as a fill-in job could possibly be. Her recent appointment had been a blessing for the Embassy, because their usual employee was off sick, and a blessing for her, too—since work hadn't exactly been thick on the ground recently. As a model and actress she had been 'resting' so much that lately she'd wondered why she even bothered getting out of bed in the morning.

The letter was written in a slightly wavery style, though whether that was due to the age of its author or to the emotional impact of the contents, Lara didn't know. The letter was also dated over two years ago, but somebody had obviously only recently posted it for it to have arrived just this morning.

Could it be a forgery? She supposed it could.

She read it again, slowly, taking in each incredible word.

5

To whom it may concern.

I wish to inform you that my son, Darian Wildman, is the progeny of the late Sheikh Makim, Monarch of Maraban. The Sheikh was unaware that he had a child outside wedlock, and indeed Darian himself has no idea of the identity of his true father. By the time you read this I will be dead, but I could not go to my grave taking with me a secret as powerful as this.

Below is my son's address. I therefore give you this information with my blessing, to do with what you will.

Yours

Joanna Wildman.

Beneath the woman's signature was the name 'Darian Wildman', and beneath that an address. A business address in London.

Shakily, Lara put the piece of paper back into the envelope. This was dramatic stuff. But then she had learned that drama and intrigue were part and parcel of anything to do with Maraban. Her best friend Rose had married Prince Khalim of Maraban, and through her Lara had caught glimpses of a life so very different from her own.

If someone else had opened such a letter what might they have done? Destroyed it and then forgotten about it? For didn't the existence of an unknown brother pose a threat to Khalim and his country? He might be older than Khalim and try to overthrow him.

Even thinking such thoughts they sounded far-fetched inside her own head, but they were not—they were true. For the mountain kingdom of Maraban inspired deep and dark passions which went hand in hand with its beauty and its turbulent history.

Slowly Lara rose to her feet, startled by her reflection in the beautiful looking-glass which hung over the huge fireplace. She looked so pale. Almost frightened. As if she had seen a ghost. But in a way maybe she had. Not *seen* a ghost, but learned about one.

Prince Khalim had a brother!

Oh, *why* hadn't someone else opened the letter? Then she would not have found herself in this awful dilemma of having information and not knowing what to do with it.

It would be so simple if the Prince wasn't married to Rose, but he was. Whether or not she liked it, she was involved, and that involvement had begun the moment her startled blue eyes had alighted on the stark words contained in the letter.

Lara stared out at the grey autumnal day, at the London traffic which moved slowly by, its sound muted by the thick bullet-proof windows, and thought once more about her friend.

Sometimes it still seemed incredible that Rose was now a princess and living in Maraban, with Khalim ruling at her side. Rose had been an ordinary girl, just like Lara herself—and yet look what had happened to her. Even now it still seemed like a fairy story that hadn't really happened.

Except that it *had* happened.

Just as this letter had been written and Lara had opened it.

It could be a lie. It could be a forgery. The author of the letter could be completely mad. A blackmailer. A potential assassin. Anything.

So what did she do?

Did she get on the phone to Rose and tell her that her husband could have an illegitimate brother?

But Rose was pregnant again. Think what the shock might do to her.

Should she go to the Ambassador? But surely that would

amount to the same thing—the first thing he would do would be to contact Khalim and tell him.

Still the thoughts continued to spin round and round in her head, unchecked until a solution occurred to her which was so blindingly simple she wondered why it had taken her so long to think of it.

What if *she*—Lara—went and found this Darian Wildman and sussed him out for herself? Almost as if she were sounding out the suitability of a would-be boyfriend.

Lara tucked the envelope into her handbag. If he was a good man then she would feel duty-bound to tell Rose and Khalim about him.

And if he wasn't?

Then she could destroy the letter and no one would be any the wiser.

Her heart pounded. Maybe she was being too simplistic, and playing God with information which had fallen into her hands quite by chance. And yet Khalim himself always said that nothing in life happened by chance, that everything happened for a reason. Only he called it something else. Lara racked her brain while she tried to remember what it was, and then she nodded.

Predestination. Yes, that was it. Predestination. Perhaps she had been *meant* to open the letter and to take the matter into her own hands.

Her mind drifted over the name. Darian Wildman. An intriguing name and an intriguing situation. She would find him. And see for herself just what kind of man he was.

But Lara's heart was beating very fast as she picked up the telephone and asked for Directory Enquiries.

Her thoughts were still reeling when she let herself into her apartment that evening to find Jake, her flatmate, cooking a fiery-looking concoction of curry.

He looked up and smiled as she walked into the sitting

room and threw her coat down on the sofa. 'I was about to ask if you'd had a hard day at the Embassy,' he joked. 'But judging from the look on your face I'd say it was a pretty redundant question. What's up, Lara? Has someone threatened to overthrow the Prince?'

'Shut up, Jake!' Lara bit her lip as the tight knot of tension somewhere in the pit of her stomach made itself known. 'Any chance of a drink?'

'Coming up—though I must say it's a little early for you, isn't it?' He slopped red wine into two glasses and handed her one, a slight frown creasing his brow. 'So what's up really?'

Lara sipped her wine thoughtfully, feeling the warmth flood through her, momentarily dissolving the sense of panic and trepidation she felt. Jake Haddon was the perfect flatmate—indeed, to almost every woman with a pulse he was the perfect man, full-stop. The darling of the British stage and screen, with his long legs and lazy charm and the lock of hair which flopped so endearingly over one of his soulful eyes and which had women itching to smooth it away for him. She had worked with him once but had never fancied him, which was fortunate given that he was now sharing her flat. He had moved in as a temporary measure, when he had been between homes and then had liked it so much that he'd never bothered moving out again. It felt like home, he told her.

And Lara didn't mind a bit. He was sweet and intelligent and trustworthy—even if he did sometimes tease her about Maraban and her friendship with its ruling family—yet, deep down, she knew she could not possibly confide in him about the letter, or her worries about the effect it might have on Khalim. He simply wouldn't take it seriously. In fact, sometimes she wondered if he ever took *anything* seriously.

But he was resourceful, she knew that—far more resourceful than she felt in this weird, jittering state of having discovered something momentous and not having a clue about what to do with that discovery.

'Jake?'

'Lara?'

'Just say…just say you wanted an introduction to someone and all you knew was the place where they worked—how would you go about meeting them?'

He batted his outrageously long lashes. 'This is a man, I take it?'

'Er, yes. How did you guess?'

'I know women,' said Jake smugly. 'And you have that kind of secretive, bursting excitement kind of look which immediately tells me that it's something to do with a member of the opposite sex. Am I right?'

That might be the easiest way to explain it, surely? Jake wouldn't ask too many questions if he thought she had a simple crush on a man.

'Sort of,' she prevaricated.

'Another actor?' he hazarded.

Lara shuddered. 'You know I'd sooner walk into a pit of deadly snakes than get involved with an actor!'

'Why, thanks,' he said wryly.

'You know what I mean, Jake.'

'Yeah, sure. Feckless commitment-phobes with fickle hearts—that's us actors!' He drank some wine and then gave the pot another stir. 'So who is he?'

Lara had been doing her homework. 'A businessman.'

'Successful?'

'I…think so.' The company was in Darian Wildman's name, which meant that he was successful, surely?

Jake's eyes narrowed. 'You haven't met him?'

'Er, no.'

'Curiouser and curiouser. What happened? You saw him at a party and were smitten, decided he was the man for you, but before you could do anything about it he'd left, yes? So you asked around a bit, found out his name, and now you're hot on his heels, pursuing him?'

'It was nothing like that,' Lara said weakly. 'And it's far too complicated to explain. I just want a chance to meet him, that's all.'

Jake threw a handful of coriander into the pot. 'Phone his office.'

'On what pretext?'

'Make something up! You're an enterprising woman, Lara—and you're an actress! Play it by ear—and once you're standing in front of him I am sure he will be completely dazzled by your wild dark hair and amazing blue eyes. The rest, as they say, is up to you!'

Lara finished her wine and held her glass out for a refill, studiously ignoring Jake's look of surprise—she rarely drank more than one, but tonight she felt she needed it. Could it be that simple? But why not? After all, what did she have to lose? She wasn't saying that you could know everything you needed to know about a person in one short meeting, but surely it would tell her whether he seemed a decent kind of man. And it would make up her mind whether she told him what she had discovered.

Or whether Khalim should hear about it first.

'That's very good thinking, Jake,' she said slowly. 'Very good thinking. I'll give it a go.'

'I don't know why you should sound so amazed!' he said drily. 'Just because I'm known for my boyish good looks doesn't mean that I don't have a few brain cells rattling around inside my head. Now, stop acting like I'm your servant and go and measure out some rice—that's if you want to eat this side of Christmas!'

She laughed and began to help him—he was so easy to get on with, but she knew deep down that was only because she didn't fancy him, nor he her. If she had, or he had, then their no-effort compatibility simply wouldn't exist. It wasn't that Lara was a cynic where men were concerned; she just preferred to think of herself as someone who was realistic.

They ate supper and watched a video of one of Jake's films, while he tore his own performance to pieces. In fact, Lara's resolve not to think any more about the situation lasted all the way until bedtime, but then she lay sleepless, looking at the ceiling for a long time, while moon shadows danced before her eyes and doubts began to creep into her mind.

She had the strangest feeling she was courting danger, as if she was standing on top of a high cliff and preparing to walk over the edge into the unknown—an unknown far more scary than just her usual uncertainty about the future. But that was just her imagination, she told herself as she finally drifted off to sleep. All actresses were cursed with an excess of imagination.

And in the morning everything looked different—as it so often did. It was funny how daylight seemed to put everything into perspective. She told herself that she was being stupid and ridiculously melodramatic—as if unable to separate her working life from her real life. Except that when she stopped to think about it 'real' life had taken on a very different meaning ever since her friend had married into Maraban's royal family!

Even Lara's mother had been taken aback by it all, and she was fairly used to the bizarre. In the past, if Lara had telephoned blithely to say that she was appearing as a tomato on a commerical for a new brand of soup, her mother had been merely interested. Yet for once she had been lost for words when Lara had announced that she was being Rose's bridesmaid when she married her prince, and would be wearing cloth of gold and a fortune in ancient jewellery for the day.

It had been easy enough to find the number of Wildman Phones, but not so easy to find the courage to dial the number, and when she did her nerve nearly failed her. But her drama training saved her. Pretend it's a job, she told herself—and maybe in a way it was. If not a job, then a mission—to be a good friend to people she cared about.

She drew a deep breath. The only way to get past receptionists was not to sound nervous or diffident but to brazen it out. 'Darian Wildman, please,' she said smoothly, as if she had known him all her life.

'I'm afraid that Mr Wildman is out of the office all day.'

Damn! Lara gave an exaggerated sigh. 'That man! Why the hell didn't he bother telling me? And he's left a whole stack of important papers behind,' she said, half to herself, then sighed and adopted a confidential one-woman-talking-to-another tone. 'Do you know where he can be reached?'

There was the briefest of pauses. 'Sure. He's out casting all day. Let me see…yep! Hold on, I've got the address here—do you have a pen?'

The receptionist obviously wouldn't have won any prizes for maintaining the privacy of her boss, thought Lara.

'Fire away,' she said calmly.

The receptionist rattled off an address in Golden Square, which Lara knew was right in the centre of London, just a breath away from Nelson's Column.

'What's he doing there?' Lara asked casually.

'Oh, he's been there all week—they're casting to find the face of Wildman Phones,' said the receptionist chattily. 'Why? Are you an actress or a model?'

Lara's heart gave a great leap in her chest, but she tried to keep the excitement from her voice. 'Well, actually,' she said, 'yes, I am.'

CHAPTER TWO

THE taxi drew up outside a tall building which looked like an old warehouse—and that, thought Darian wryly, was precisely what it was. It was a dark, monstrous shell of a place which now housed the most modern of photographic studios.

'Shall we go in now, Darian?' asked the man by his side, his voice touched by a slight edge of anxiety.

Darian's eyes had been shuttered, but now they widened by a fraction so that just a glint of gold light gleamed from between the thick black lashes. He turned to look at Scott Stratton, the head of an advertising agency known to be one of the best in the business—famous for its slick, award-winning campaigns and its ability to match client needs with consumer expectations. Or at least it had been up until now, when casting after casting had so far stubbornly refused to find the new face of Wildman Phones. Maybe Darian was being too choosy—an accusation which had been thrown at him often enough in the past—but he was certainly uncompromising, and he would not be satisfied until he found exactly what he was looking for. He just wasn't sure quite what that was.

Or who.

'Sure, Scott,' he murmured. 'I'm ready.'

Scott glanced at him. 'Need anything? To make notes?'

Darian gave a glittering smile. 'No, thanks. I won't need them. I'll know her when I see her.'

They walked into the building together, and stood in the chrome-walled reception area.

'They're all up there?' asked Darian, jerking his dark head towards the spiral staircase which led up to the studio.

He spoke softly, but even so the two women who were busy flicking through the models' cards at the far end of the room immediately stopped what they were doing and turned round to look at him, as if awaiting a command. But then, people always did that when they encountered him. Darian was used to it. They seemed to shrink to his will whenever he exerted it—and even when he didn't.

'Yeah,' answered Scott. 'Ready and waiting.'

'Then bring on the parade,' said Darian mockingly, putting his foot on the bottom rung of the staircase, faded denim straining over one taut, muscular thigh as he did so.

'Er, not *parade*, Darian,' corrected Scott. 'If you say that they *parade* then that makes them sound a bit mindless, doesn't it? Makes them sound as if they're taking part in some second-rate beauty contest, and models are very sensitive about that kind of thing. Particularly in these politically correct days.'

Darian laughed and turned his head, and as he did so he heard the faint but unmistakable intake of breath from one of the secretaries as she looked at him. He was used to that, too. He guessed it was because his eyes were not run-of-the-mill that the fairer sex always seemed to get transfixed by them. When he was younger he had found the effect a little disconcerting, and later he had rather enjoyed it, but now he was so used to it as to feel nothing more than faint amusement. Another man might have used the power of those eyes more ruthlessly, but Darian did not. He had no need to.

'Far be it from me to contradict you, Scott,' he said, choosing his words carefully. 'But, putting political correctness aside, surely a casting session is exactly like a beauty contest? Though admittedly not a second-rate one—not in this case—not if they're going to be representing Wildman. Twenty females about to be assessed on their looks and their sex appeal—how else would you define it?'

'But it isn't just looks and sex appeal we're searching for, is it?' questioned Scott seriously. 'Otherwise someone we've shown you already would surely have come up to standard?' He sighed. 'You've seen loads of beautiful women this week.'

'You think I'm being too choosy?' asked Darian.

Scott shrugged and then shook his head. 'I admire your perfectionism, if you must know. Your search for that indefinable something or someone—a person who will embody everything you want to say about your company. I guess that's the secret of your success. Am I right?'

Darian shrugged. 'That's part of it.'

But only part. Darian put a lot of his success down to a restless and relentless seeking nature. He never did anything long enough to get bored, because when you were bored all the freshness and enjoyment simply vanished. It was the same with relationships. Familiarity, in his experience, bred a tedium far more deadly than contempt.

He glanced at his watch. 'Come on, then—let's go.'

They made their way up the winding staircase towards the studio.

None of the people who worked for him knew yet that this advertising campaign was to be Darian's swansong. First he would choose the perfect woman and with her face bombard the country with the name of his mobile phones to ensure maximum publicity.

Then he wanted out. He was planning to sell the company and walk away. To take the money and add it to the pile he had already made by selling previous successful companies, and look for yet another new challenge.

And then what? prompted a little voice in his head. Is that going to bring you happiness? Darian's mouth curved into a sardonic smile, and he batted the thought away as if it had been a mildly troublesome fly. Men who sought happiness were doomed. Women, too. Success and achievement were far more tangible concepts than happiness as far as Darian was concerned.

They were almost at the top of the flight of steps when he heard Scott's slightly muffled voice from behind him. 'We should announce you, really, Darian—shouldn't we?'

'Well, you could, I suppose,' said Darian lazily, but then he shook his head. 'No, on second thoughts—don't. Let's surprise them.'

'Sure?'

Unseen, Darian smiled. 'Oh, perfectly sure,' he said softly. 'Women are always so much more *interesting* when you catch them unawares, don't you think? You see them for what they really are, rather than what they want you to see.'

'That sounds like a pretty harsh judgement,' observed Scott. 'I didn't have you down for a cynic.'

Darian smiled again, but this time it barely curved his lips. 'Not harsh at all,' he said softly. 'Nor cynical. Just an accurate assessment. Now, come on—let's go.' And as his dark head appeared in the lighted studio the whole room fell silent.

Lara was out of breath, her unruly hair looking even more tousled than usual. The denim jacket she wore was making her much too hot, but she didn't want to spare the time to take it off. She waited for the bus to swish its way through the puddle past her, and then made a run for the door of the studio, glancing at her watch as she did so. Damn, damn and damn!

Her agent had been doubtful—sniffy, even—about putting Lara forward for the casting, but frantic questioning had assured her that, yes, there was a last vacant slot in the day's casting for Wildman Phones.

'Why the hell didn't you put me forward for it in the first place?' she had wailed.

Her agent had sounded incredulous. 'Lara—the last time I saw you your hair was cropped and dark.'

'But I was appearing in a Russian play!' she'd protested. 'It's back to normal now!'

'How normal is normal?' her agent had enquired patiently. 'You're a brunette, lovie—and they're looking for the archetypal English rose!'

'Archetypal, not stereotypical!' Lara had retorted. 'There's nothing in the rulebook to say an English rose can't have dark hair!'

'I suppose *not,*' her agent had responded doubtfully.

Lara pushed the studio door open and a brief feeling of irony washed over her. English rose indeed! Clad in denim and a clinging black tee-shirt, anyone less fitting the description she had yet to see. But she reminded herself that she wasn't really here to get the job. She was here to see the great man himself, that was all—and what better way to do that than legitimately?

The two women standing in the foyer looked her up and down.

'Which way's the casting?' Lara squeaked.

One looked uncertain and the other gave a slightly smug smile as she jerked her thumb in the direction of the spiral staircase. 'Up there. And you're late,' she added bluntly.

'I know I am,' moaned Lara, as she legged it up the steps.

The room was stifling, reeked of lots of different clashing perfumes, and was full of women. Correction—beautiful women. And every single one of them had taken to heart the English rose theme in a big, big way. Despite her nerves, Lara bit back a smile.

Some of them wore lace-trimmed blouses; others were resplendent in flower-sprigged high-necked dresses. There was even one woman clad in floor-length muslin who looked as if she would be more at home eating cucumber sandwiches on a quintessential English lawn, instead of packed into a crowded studio with a load of competitive peers.

And every woman in the room shared one unmistakable characteristic.

They were all blonde!

'S-sorry!' gulped Lara as each sleek golden head turned in her direction.

Then, just as quickly, the women turned away from her again, and it took a moment or two while she caught her breath for Lara to realise that they were now all looking at one person. Or, rather, one man.

Lara hadn't noticed him at first, because he had been standing in the shadows in one corner of the room, but once she had seen him she wondered how on earth he could have escaped her attention—because he seemed to radiate a vitality which made everyone else in the room look as though they were only half-alive. She narrowed her eyes in his direction and felt her heart clench in her chest, as if an iron fist had crumpled it between cold, hard fingers.

'I—I'm l-late,' she stammered.

'Damn right you are,' he agreed, in a silky murmur.

She kept her face composed—she never quite knew how she did it—not when she was feeling this faint and dizzy and weak—and surreptitiously snaked her tongue out over lips which had dried so thoroughly that she felt she would never be able to speak again.

Sometimes you knew the truth about something by in-stinct alone, and if she had ever doubted the claim made by the writer of that letter then that doubt was vanquished instantly as she stared across the room at Darian Wildman.

Was it just her imagination working overtime—fuelled by the information she had received—or was everyone else in the room, Darian included, blind to what was as obvious as the blazing glare from one of the studio lights?

This man had royal blood running through his veins, setting him apart from everyone present. Marking him out as a different breed altogether—as different as a lion standing amid a group of mewing kittens.

He was tall—impressively tall—even taller than Khalim—yet his skin was not so dark as Khalim's. But then this man was only half-Marabanese, Lara remembered. His flesh glowed gold and tawny and his eyes were gold, too. She had never seen eyes like them—they were like shards of golden glass, deep and gleaming, except that gold was a warm colour and this man's eyes were cold.

His hair was very dark—though not quite black—and was shaped to a head which was held with confidence and a certain arrogance. And pride. And irritation.

'Do you make a habit of turning up late for jobs?' he questioned tersely.

Lara was having to fight an uncomfortable desire to run over to him, whisper her fingertips wonderingly down the side of his hard, beautiful face and tell him that she alone had the secret of his ancestry.

With an effort, she pulled herself together. 'Of course not!'

Her complete absence of an apology made Darian tense, and he narrowed his eyes, feeling the tiny hairs prickle at the back of his neck as he looked at her. Her rain-sprinkled dark hair was awry and her cheeks were flushed. And her eyes were the bluest he had ever seen. They made him think of summer skies and cornflowers and Mediterranean seas. Momentarily, and inexplicably, he was sucked in by the sheer beauty of those eyes and the distraction irritated him.

'And are you in the habit of poor time-keeping?'

Be bold, Lara, she thought. You don't need this job.

She shrugged. 'Not usually.'

Not *usually*? It was not the reaction that Darian had been expecting. Didn't she care that there were women in this room who looked as if they would kill to get the job? And, judging from some of the shameless glances they had been directing at him, they would also offer far more sensual incentives if they thought that might work.

'Looking as if you've been dragged through a hedge backwards?' he continued, in an acid tone.

'So much for the tousled look!' retorted Lara flippantly. 'Actually, the reason I'm late is that my agency nearly didn't send me.'

He met the challenge in her gaze, and something about her directness made him carry on staring at her. He wasn't used to a challenge—and certainly not from a woman.

'I'm not surprised,' he said softly.

She arched her brows, hot and bothered and not just from her hurried journey. Something in the way those gold eyes were studying her made her wish that she was looking as cool and unflappable as every other woman in the room. But Lara knew that nobody could guess what you were feeling on the inside; it was what you projected from the outside that counted. Which meant that her one-word reply shot back at him sounded cool, and only just on the right side of insolent. 'Really?'

'Yes, really,' he mocked. 'The brief was to look like an English rose,' he added impatiently. 'Since when did that entail looking as if you're in the middle of hitching a ride to a rock concert?'

Lara heard a little buzz from the other models, and she

guessed that they were enjoying seeing the delectable Mr Wildman losing his cool with one of the competition. She glared at him.

'Do you want me to ask her to leave, Darian?' murmured Scott, in a low voice.

'No, I don't,' demurred Darian. 'I asked a question and I'm waiting for an answer.'

She felt like asking him sweetly if he always got whatever it was he wanted, but she refrained. It was neither the time nor the place, and she suspected that the answer would be yes anyway.

'It depends what your interpretation of an English rose *is,* surely?' she answered confidently. 'Even *they* have to run for taxis or buses sometimes, don't they? They can't spend the whole of their lives sitting on pretty wicker furniture and fanning themselves! Not modern English roses anyway!'

There it was again, he thought, with a cross between grudging admiration and irritation. She was talking to him in a way which he could have confidently predicted no one else in the room would have *dared* try! And she did have a point, he conceded. Modern was what he was really looking for. A modern look for modern technology.

Ask for someone who summed up everything that it was to be English, and everyone immediately jumped back a century or two! He glanced around the room at the lace and the flower-sprigs and the muslin and he frowned. Modern and English—surely the two weren't completely incompatible?

'You do have a point,' he admitted grudgingly.

Lara lifted her chin, telling herself that she definitely wasn't going to get the job now, so what did she have to lose? How far could she push him? She had seen for herself that he was grumpy—as well as successful, powerful and devastatingly attractive—would his temper really turn ugly if she challenged him a little bit more?

'Tell me, how do *you* see the woman you're looking for?' asked Lara calmly.

Scott bristled. 'I think you've said quite enough, don't you?'

But Darian shook his head. 'No, let her speak.'

'Gosh...*thanks*!' said Lara sarcastically.

Darian knitted his brows together, wondering if this rather unusual tendency to answer back at what was essentially a serious job interview was simply a way of getting herself noticed. Didn't people sometimes act outrageously in order to detract attention from their glaring faults? And did she have any?

He let his eyes travel from the top of her head to the tips of her pointed leather boots. If you discounted the fact that her hair looked as though she had spent a large part of the morning being pulled through a particularly thorny hedge it really was the most glorious colour—the deep, burnished mahogany of a lovingly polished piece of furniture, touched with deeper, brighter shades of gold and amber. Dyed, most probably. All women dyed their hair these days. His mouth twisted. He had yet to meet a *natural* blonde!

But her brows were beautifully shaped and arched, and her skin looked soft—all roses and cream—like petals in the early morning when they had been kissed by the dew. It was skin that made her look as though she'd been brought up in the fresh air, raised on nothing stronger than milk and honey.

She had answered her own question, he realised. She was exactly the woman he was looking for.

'Take your jacket off,' he said slowly.

For a second Lara's sang-froid almost deserted her. It was a perfectly normal request to make in the circumstances. It wasn't as though he was asking her to perform a striptease. But that was exactly what it felt like. Inside, she was suddenly overcome with a bubbling mass of insecurity, which was crazy—*crazy*—and yet there was something about this darkly golden man which made his request seem like an intrusion. She didn't move.

Darian raised his eyebrows questioningly, ignoring Scott's frown and the indignant glances of the other women.

Lara flashed him a cool and professional smile and slid her jacket from her shoulders with hands which were miraculously steady. Then casually slipped her finger through the loop of the jacket and stood before him, feeling a little as she imagined the favoured member of a harem must feel. All the women vying for one man's attention and only one of them receiving it. Her heart was beating fast. You're concocting fantasy, she told herself sternly. That's all. Just because you think he's the brother of the Sheikh you're attributing to him all those kind of primitive man-woman things which you wouldn't dream of doing if he was any average man.

'How's that?' she asked, in a voice which she hoped didn't betray quite how unsettled he was making her feel.

'That's fine,' he said evenly, trying to be objective, but for once it wasn't easy. Her body was good. Very good. She was tall and slender, and yet curved in just the right places, and her breasts were quite simply perfect—not too full and not too small, the white tee-shirt emphasising their shape and not quite disguising the pinpoint thrust of her nipples, which made him tense in desire even though he tried not to.

Darian looked around at the others. In terms of beauty there was not one woman present who could be faulted. There was every variety of womanhood represented here today. Most were slim—too slim, in his opinion, but that was the fashion. True, there were a couple whose curves were more luscious than slim, but the camera didn't flatter real curves; he knew that.

Leisurely, he ran his eyes over each and every one of them, until they came back to rest and stay on the girl in the jeans. She looked normal and healthy and glowing and...and something about her was still making his skin tingle.

He nodded and turned to Scott. 'Can I have a word, please? In private?' he asked him.

'Sure,' Scott replied.

The two men moved to the only vacant corner of the studio. 'I think we've found our English rose,' Darian said slowly. 'Don't you?'

Scott turned to him. 'But she's a *brunette*!'

'So? I don't remember specifically asking for blonde!'

Scott lowered his voice. 'We haven't even tested her yet, Darian,' he said, a touch anxiously. 'In fact, we haven't tested any of them.'

Darian gave an arrogant shrug. 'There's no need. She's the one I want.'

'But she might project completely the wrong image.'

Darian studied the varying blondes in the studio, who were all looking at him hopefully. They looked...they looked...*bland*, he realised impatiently. He flicked another glance at the brunette, who seemed so full of life and vitality in comparison, and a steady pulse began to beat at his temple. 'She won't,' he said steadily. 'Trust me.'

'The place will erupt if you don't test the others, too,' protested Scott.

Darian shrugged. 'Then test them.'

'And show you the results?'

'If you want. I'll see them, but I won't need to.'

'How can you be so sure?'

Darian gave a slow smile. Instinct. Simple as that. She had what he wanted. 'I just am. She's the one.'

The atmosphere in the room was electric, and Lara felt decidedly odd. This wasn't like a normal casting at all. Everyone was staring at her, and she wondered if the composition of her body had undergone some remarkable transformation, whether her blood could suddenly have become jelly. Because that was what she felt like—that was the way *he* was making her feel.

The man with the golden eyes had turned back and was staring at her, and Lara felt as though she was helpless, caught in the honeyed intensity of that gaze. Like a rabbit hypnotised and blinded by the glaring headlights of a car, or a snake lured and seduced by the sound of the charmer's pipe.

'What's your name?' he asked softly.

Lara took a deep breath. She just knew that he was going to offer her the job! This couldn't really be happening. It shouldn't be happening. She had turned up late, looking scruffy, and been rude to him—he should be sending her packing, not seriously entertaining the thought of employing her! But she kept her voice steady—as steady as his golden stare. 'Lara. Lara Black.'

'Lara Black,' he repeated thoughtfully. 'Yes.' He gave the room a cool smile. 'Well, I'll leave you all in the capable hands of Scott.'

He moved away, and Lara watched him as he placed one foot on the staircase. He glanced up at that moment and their eyes met, and she was suddenly filled with an inexplicable feeling of disappointment and stupidity.

Was that it, then? She bit her lip distractedly. What had she expected? That he would suddenly announce to everyone that she had got the job without bothering to test the others? As if that would happen! Especially to someone who had behaved with such utter disregard for professionalism.

She felt a stupid sense of loss as she watched his dark, lustrous head disappear from view. He had gone and she had blown any chance of getting to know him better. But she knew one thing for sure.

He was Khalim's brother. The resemblance was unmistakable.

So what was she going to do about it?

CHAPTER THREE

LARA put the phone down and stared at Jake. 'I've got it,' she said slowly.

Jake looked up from the script he was studying. 'Got what?'

'That job I went for. You know—I told you.'

Jake frowned. 'Something about a mobile phone company? You turned up late, looking ghastly, and the owner was there and subjected you to a grilling?'

It was still taking a moment or two to sink in. 'That's right.'

Jake elevated one brow in a manner which would have caused almost any other woman in the country to swoon, but not Lara.

'Does this guy have a death wish?' he joked. 'Or does he just like a challenge?'

Lara didn't say anything. She suspected that Darian Wildman *did* like a challenge, and something about that worried her—though it now appeared that her gut reaction had been the correct one, after all. She had *thought* that he was going to offer her the job, but then he had just disappeared and left them all to be photographed. Still, when she mulled it over now, he couldn't possibly have done otherwise, could he? Not employed her without testing her and, more importantly, without testing all the others—otherwise he would have had a small riot on his hands.

Yet she had sensed that he was about to do so. He looked like the kind of man who broke all the rules and made his own up. The word autocratic might have been invented with him in mind. It had probably been the other man with him, she reasoned, who had persuaded him to adopt the usual method of casting.

She should have been overjoyed. This was *work*, after all, and she needed to work—especially as the person she'd been covering for at the Embassy was now much better and ready to go back to her job. And she was supposed to be finding out more about Darian Wildman—so wasn't this a heaven-sent opportunity to do just that? To work for his company and to become the face which symbolised that company.

Except it didn't feel like that. It felt uncomfortable. Wrong. As if she was doing something that she shouldn't be doing. And coupled with that was the burden of the knowledge she possessed.

Or maybe it had something to do with the fact that Darian had excited her in a way that no man had excited her for longer than she could remember. And that in itself was a *bad sign*. One which made her feel gloomy about him in general. If she was attracted to him then he was *bound* to be trouble, because Lara's track record with men was nothing short of abysmal.

She didn't fall for men very often, but when she did it was always for the kind of man your mother warned you to stay away from. Philanderers and cheats. Good-looking, weak, shallow men. The sort who promised you the earth and a little bit more besides, and then were busy glancing over your shoulder to see if someone more attractive had just walked in. In fact, she had sworn off men altogether— at least until she had worked out what was the basic flaw in her character which attracted her to the wrong type of man.

Her friend Rose had a few theories of her own. She said that it was because Lara yearned for excitement and was looking for it in the wrong places—but how on earth could

you go looking for it in the *right* places if solid and decent
men—the kind your mother *would* approve of—left you
cold?

'Oh, you need a sheikh, like Khalim,' Rose had laughed
on the eve of her wedding.

At the time Lara had been struggling into a dress which
weighed almost as much as she did. 'Don't be so smug!'

'But I'm not,' Rose had protested, and had laid her hand
on Lara's shoulder, her voice gentling. 'I'm serious. It's
just a pity that Khalim hasn't got any brothers.'

Lara chewed on her lip. Oh, Lord—she had completely
forgotten that conversation until now! But that was the
cleverness of the mind, wasn't it?—It dragged things up
from the hidden corners of your subconscious when it
thought they might come in useful. If only Rose had
known how eerily prescient her words had been.

If it had been anyone other than Khalim then it might
have been easy to pick up the phone and say, Hi, guess
what? I've discovered you have a secret half-brother! But
Khalim was no normal man. He was Sheikh of a vast kingdom, and if another man was related to him by blood, then
couldn't he lay claim to that kingdom and jeopardise the
livelihood of all of them? His and Rose's and their son's,
and the child soon to be born? How could she knowingly
endanger all that until she knew something of the man
himself?

'Lara?'

She looked up to see Jake staring at her with concern.
'What?'

'You've gone as white as a sheet.'

'Have I?' She touched her cheek and found that it was
cold, and suddenly she began to shiver. 'We shoot on
Monday,' she whispered.

On Monday she would see him again. Those strangely
cold golden eyes would pierce right through her and see...

Would they sense that she was not all she seemed? And how would he react if she told him that *he* was not all he seemed, either?

Jake frowned. 'Lara, what *is* the matter? You've just won a fantastic contract—why aren't you cracking open the champagne?'

She forced a smile. Why not, indeed? Perhaps she was simply guilty of inventing problems where there were none. 'Coming right up,' she said brightly, and headed for the fridge.

The winter sun streamed in through the glass, warming his skin as Darian slowly buttoned up his white linen shirt and watched an aeroplane creeping across the sky in the far distance. Outside, the clouds were tinged with pink and gold, contrasting with an ice-blue sky which made the world look as perfect as it was supposed to look. But then the views from his penthouse apartment were always matchless and magnificent and never the same. It was one of the reasons he had bought it—that and its inaccessibility to people in general and the world in particular.

The phone rang, but he let it ring. Most phone calls, in his experience, could be usefully avoided, and he hated having to make small-talk—especially in the mornings. Which was one of the reasons why it was a long time since he had stayed overnight with a woman.

He listened to the message on the answer-machine, to hear the voice of the travel agent telling him that his flight to New York was confirmed, and smiled. If he *had* picked it up then he would have had to endure all kinds of bright and unnecessary questions about the state of his health!

He picked up his coffee cup and sipped thoughtfully at the strong, inky brew, glancing over at the mirror as he did so. There was no sign of blood. Not now. He gave a tiny grimace. What was going on? He had cut himself shaving that morning—lightly nicked the skin around his jaw—something he could not remember doing since he was an adolescent boy, when he had first wielded the razor with uncertain fingers.

In his gleaming bathroom mirror he had stared at the bright spot of scarlet which had beaded on the strong line of his jaw, disrupting his normal, ordered routine, and it had taken him right back to a place he rarely visited.

The past. That strange place over which you had little control and yet whose influence shaped the person you would be for the rest of your life.

He had never been one of those boys who had shaved before there was any need to. It was simply that he had seemed to develop way ahead of anyone else, with a faint shadowing of the jaw when most of his peers were still covered in spots. He had shot up in height, too, and his shoulders had grown broad and his body hard and muscular.

Such early maturity had set him apart—especially with the girls—but then, in a way he had felt set apart ever since he could remember. He had never looked like anyone else, even though his clothes had been no different. His skin had always had a faintly tawny glow to it, and his golden eyes had marked him out as someone different.

The girls had loved it and the boys had tried teasing him because of it, but he had quickly learnt that his height and strength could intimidate them enough to stop the insults almost before they had started.

So his childhood had been lonely. The only child of a single mother, bringing him up in a seedy apartment in one of the wastelands of London where tourists never ventured. That in itself had not been unusual—poverty had brought with it all the casualties of human relationships, and Darian had known only a couple of sets of parents who had still been together—and they had fought enough to make him wonder why they bothered.

He guessed it was that at least other kids had *known* who their father was. Whether it was the father who had run off with a younger woman, or the father who would appear threateningly drunk on his former family's doorstep, or the father who refused to pay money the courts had told him he must pay. These were fathers it was easy enough to hate, but Darian's own paternity had been one big secret. He would rather have had someone to hate than no one at all.

He had tried asking his mother about it, but even broaching the subject had made her mouth tremble, as if she was about to cry—and she never cried. He had learnt only that some questions were better left unasked...

The doorbell jangled, disrupting his thoughts. His driver was here. Darian picked up his jacket, feeling an almost imperceptible glow of subdued excitement as he sat back in the soft leather luxury of the car. He told himself it was because they were shooting the photos today, and that something which no longer challenged him was coming to an end, but he knew that was not the whole story.

The truth was that he wanted to see the model again. What was her name? Lara. Yes, that was it. Pretty name and a pretty girl. Fearless and spiky. He rubbed his eyes and closed them as the car began to accelerate, stretching his long legs out in front of him and yawning lazily.

He was tired. He had sat up until the early hours, sorting through his accounts and feeling bored—with pretty much everything. Appetites which were fed with everything they needed tended to become jaded, he told himself ruefully.

He wondered when his life had become like a game of Monopoly—just a load of numbers that were so big they didn't seem real. But that was the way of money—too much and it almost seemed to get in the way, not enough and it dominated your whole life and all your thoughts. Was there no simple in-between way?

He guessed there was—the way most men chose. Marriage and babies and a house in the suburbs. Daily train journeys and home for supper and a drink. Weekend barbecues and driving out to pretty country pubs.

But to Darian it sounded like a lifetime's incarceration. A cell padded with sofas and chintz curtains. Maybe that was why he had never even come close to commitment, because commitment carried with it the price of settling down and raising a family. That was the way of things. In fact, no one had ever stirred his blood enough to make him even *think* of committing, or to make him feel a pang of regret that he was unable to.

You will be a lonely old man, taunted a little voice inside his head, but even that didn't bother him. Lonely and alone were two entirely different concepts, weren't they? He felt as if he had been alone for all his life, so why change now? Even if change was possible, and Darian didn't think it was. That was the mistake that people always made— women especially. They thought that a person could change the habits of a lifetime and become the someone they wanted you to be.

The driver turned his head as Big Ben loomed up magnificently in front of them. 'Do you want me to wait?'

Darian shook his head. 'No, thanks. I'll ring when I need you. I may hang around for a while,' he added casually.

He told himself that he liked to be in control—which was true—and that he liked to be hands-on—which was also true. If there was going to be an advertising campaign then he wanted to have some input into the final images which would represent his company.

But most of all he wanted to watch Lara at work, to see

her thick dark hair blowing in the autumn breeze and see the sky reflected in eyes which echoed its hue.

Lara Black.

The English rose.

Lara noticed him before he saw her. The heavens themselves seemed to be conniving in his entrance, because just as his long legs began to emerge from a seriously luxurious car a shaft of pure golden sunlight chose that very moment to spear its way through the fluffy clouds. And he chose just that same instant to look up, his eyes vying with the sun for brilliance.

Lara shivered.

'Keep still, Lara,' said the make-up artist patiently as she dabbed on another stroke of pink iridescent lipgloss.

Lara couldn't reply, not with her lips half open to deal with the lipgloss, but she was aware of him approaching, silent and stealthy—like a natural predator. The sharp colours of the autumn day seemed to emphasise his strong features—etching shadows which fell from beneath the high cheekbones and the firm, luscious mouth.

He wore linen, which managed to be both casual and smart at the same time. Yet somehow it looked all wrong on him, and she wondered what he would look like with the fluid, silken robes of the Maraban aristocracy clinging to his lean, hard frame.

She could hear the chatter lessening as the make-up artist turned her head to see what what was happening and whistled softly. She gave Lara's lips a final blot with a piece of tissue.

'Oh, *wow*,' she whispered fervently. 'I wouldn't mind getting my hands on *him!*'

Lara gave her chin a welcome stretch, but her heart thudded painfully in her chest. 'You mean from a professional point of view, of course?' she joked.

'Yeah, sure.' The make-up artist gave a rich and fruity

laugh. 'One look at him and all I think about is work, work, work!'

Lara watched him while the stylist fussed around with her dress. Little clusters of people had stopped to stare at the proceedings, alerted to the possibility of excitement by the photographer and his acolytes and the sight of a woman wearing a floaty, filmy dress on a blustery autumn day.

'Are you making a film?' she heard one middle-aged shopper ask.

'A photo-shoot,' drawled the photographer's assistant, with a shake of his long hair.

But Lara felt as though they might have been aliens from another planet—she felt disconnected and oblivious to just about everything except for him, which was more than a little bit scary. She tried to tell herself that *of course* she was going to be interested in him—that was the whole point of her presence here. But surely that wouldn't account for the pounding of her heart and the silken throb of her blood which seemed to strike soft hammerblows at all her pulse-points. Not by anyone's standards could *that* be described as professional behaviour.

Maybe the make-up artist had put it in a nutshell. Think Darian Wildman and the last thing you felt was professional.

She turned away, breaking the spell with an effort. The last thing she needed was for him to look up and see her staring at him like some kind of starstruck adolescent. There were enough people already doing that.

'We're never going to keep your hair under control with this breeze!' grumbled the stylist as she pushed a wayward strand off Lara's face.

'Looks perfect to me,' came a slow, deep voice from behind her.

Lara tried to count to ten, but the numbers became jumbled in her mind as she turned round. At least the half-smile on her lips was appropriate, as was the polite, almost deferential raising of her eyebrows. After all, he was the boss and she the model.

'Hi,' she said.

'Hi.' He found himself mocking her, enjoying the brief moment of discomfiture which allowed itself to break through her cool little smile, but then his eyes narrowed. Maybe she was used to men coming onto her. With looks like that she was bound to be. He saw her shiver. 'You're cold,' he said softly.

Lara looked down at the goose bumps on her arms, which was infinitely easier than meeting that clear golden stare, and composed herself enough to look up again, a rueful smile playing on her lips. 'Well, yes,' she agreed. 'Silk chiffon is a wonderful floaty fabric, but it wasn't exactly designed with warmth in mind!'

'No.' He forced himself to be objective. He had sat in with the creative team while they thrashed around the kind of image they wanted to project. Delicate and ethereal had been the objective—an objective achieved perfectly on the mock-ups they had shown him.

But reality, in the flesh and blood form of Lara Black, had an impact he had not been expecting. A bone-melting, sensual impact. Maybe that had been the subtle difference which had marked her out from all the others, Darian thought—that understated but persuasive femininity which could overpower men by stealth.

'Do you want a jacket or something?' he asked suddenly.

The question took Lara off-guard, and for one mad moment she thought he was actually going to take off his own jacket and offer it to her! As if! Lara pointed to a soft pink wrap which lay draped over one of the canvas chairs.

'I have a shawl. I'll—'

'Here—let me.' He bent and scooped the garment up, and draped it around her shoulders, feeling her shiver as he did so. 'You really *are* cold,' he observed, feeling the smoothness of her skin through the fine cashmere.

'Yes.' But that was not the reason she had shivered. She knew that, and she suspected he knew that, too. It seemed like the most deliciously old-fashioned and chivalrous act—a disarming act—to put her shawl on for her like that. A man like Darian Wildman would be aware of that. Talk to him, she told herself. This is your opportunity!

'Do you…do you often go on shoots like this?' she ventured.

The lips curved into a cool smile. 'Is that a take on the "do you come here often" line?' he mocked.

At that moment Lara hated him for making her feel so unoriginal, but she didn't show it, shrugging her shoulders instead. 'Don't answer if you don't want to,' she murmured. 'I'd hate to think I was straying into unprotected waters!'

He laughed. This was better. He liked her spiky better than he liked her soft. Softness made women vulnerable, and vulnerable women weren't equals. They got hurt, and then they made you feel bad because of it. 'Was I being rude?' he mused.

'Yes.'

He raised his eyebrows fractionally, taken aback by her blunt reply. 'The answer to your question is no—but then I rarely conduct advertising campaigns.'

'So why this one?'

He wasn't about to start telling *her* about his plan to float Wildman on the stockmarket—she, like the rest of the world, would find out about it soon enough. 'Because I want the name Wildman to be synonymous with mobile phone technology.'

'You mean it isn't already?' she teased. 'Shame on you!'

He allowed his mouth to curve into a small smile. 'I know. Shocking, isn't it?' he questioned gravely.

'Utterly,' she agreed, realising that he was flirting with her and that she was flirting right back.

Their eyes met and he regarded her thoughtfully. He wanted to take her out to dinner, he realised, not exchange snatches of conversation while the crew ran around, shouting and disrupting them. And just then, as if echoing his thoughts, someone shouted her name.

He frowned. 'Sounds like you're needed,' he observed.

'Sounds that way.' She hugged the shawl tightly around her as the stylist beckoned, hoping that she didn't sound reluctant to leave. 'Excuse me,' she murmured, glad to get away because nothing seemed to be going according to plan—although when she stopped to think about it what plan had she actually made, other than to somehow get to meet him? And now that she had managed to do that, all she could do was fantasise about his golden eyes and his lean, hard body. It just wasn't good enough.

Darian watched while the stylist fussed around with Lara's hair and then the photographer moved over, whipped the wrap away and began to coax her into position, prowling around in front of her, crooning directions.

'That's right, baby—smile! Not too much—just a kind of cool, thoughtful smile, as if you're deciding whether to dump your lover or not!'

Lara smiled.

'That's good! Now half close your eyes—as if you're trying to drive him wild with jealousy! You're thinking of another man—and you want him more!'

Lara did as she was told, her eyelashes fluttering down, finding it remarkably easy, picturing golden eyes and tawny skin and a dark, burnished head of royal descent...

She snapped her eyes open, startled as the bright flash exploded, staring into the eyes of the man who was fantasy and yet real, and for a moment the rest of the world receded.

Darian stared back at her, and for the first time in his life he recognised the intrusiveness of the camera and despised the intimacy it created between photographer and subject. For a moment there she had looked so sexually excited that it might almost have been for real. His mouth tightened. What a way to earn a living, he thought in sudden disgust. Yet it was what he wanted, wasn't it?

No. It was what his *company* wanted. And this was an assignment, he reminded himself. A professional assignment. He hadn't been introduced to her at a party—maybe if he had it might be different. Instead, he had run across her in the course of work, and he kept the line between work and pleasure strictly delineated.

Lara saw his face harden and wondered what had happened to the courteous man who had wrapped the soft wool around her shoulders. The golden eyes had darkened, a flush of colour was running along the high, aristocratic cheekbones. For a moment she saw the glimmerings of a hard, almost cruel contempt, and his expression filled her with trepidation even while something feminine ached at the very core of her, revelling in that cold look of mastery.

With an effort she tore her gaze away from him, staring instead at the phtographer, giving the shot everything she had and suddenly wishing that she was a million miles away from that hard, glittering scrutiny.

She held her arms aloft and the silk chiffon twirled and clung to her thighs. Abruptly, he turned away, and she forced herself to concentrate on the job in hand, losing herself in it because that seemed infinitely easier than losing herself in the gaze of Darian Wildman.

But when the photographer had stopped shooting there was no sign of him.

'Where's Darian?' she questioned casually as she pulled the wrap back round her shoulders.

'Gone,' said the assistant.

She hadn't even noticed him leaving, and she was surprised by a great, swamping feeling of disappointment. Gone! There were five other London locations to get through and suddenly the day seemed to stretch away endlessly in front of her.

Had she thought that he would be accompanying them to Tower Bridge and the Mall and Leadenhall Market and the other places which had been carefully chosen each to reflect a different mood of London life?

But perhaps this was best—he was a distracting man in anyone's book.

Lara channelled all her frustration into getting exactly the poses which the photographer demanded, and tried not to think about whether she would see him again, and where she went from here if she did not.

It was dark by the time she arrived back at the apartment and Jake was at home, all dandied up in a stunning black dinner jacket, swearing softly as he attempted to subdue his bow-tie.

'Do this for me, would you, Lara?'

She put her bag down, knotted the black silk into a neat bow, and stood back. 'How's that?'

'Perfect.' He made another small, unnecessary adjustment. 'Someone rang for you,' he said casually as she flopped onto the sofa with a heavy sigh.

'Oh?'

'A man.'

'Oh, again,' said Lara uninterestedly. But something about the amused curiosity in his voice made her sit up. 'Did he leave a message?'

'He did.'

'Jake—stop playing games! Who was it and what did he say?'

Jake enunciated his words carefully. 'His name is Darian Wildman and he says he'll call you tomorrow.'

CHAPTER FOUR

WHY was it, Lara wondered, that whenever you wanted someone to telephone you, they didn't—and the opposite was always true?

And why had he rung at all? Had he already seen the finished photos and decided he didn't like them?

Making up her mind that there was no point wasting time wondering what he wanted until she actually heard from him, Lara spent a frustrating morning deliberately doing much-needed chores around the flat—which would give her a legitimate excuse to stay in while not looking as though she was deliberately hanging around waiting for Darian Wildman to ring.

He didn't.

By nine o'clock that evening she was feeling pent-up, frustrated and angry with herself, telling herself that it shouldn't matter. Of course it shouldn't. But Jake had gone to stay with his parents, so she couldn't even drag him out for a pizza, and it was too late to ring anyone else. Instead she had a long, scented bath, taking care to leave the bathroom door open just in case the phone rang. And of course it did, just as she was up to her neck in jasmine-scented bubbles.

Leave it on the machine, she told herself sternly. If he really wants to speak to you he'll ring back.

But she found herself clambering out of the bath, dripping water all over the bathroom floor, and depising herself for doing so.

'Hello?'

'Lara? It's Darian.'

She knew that; he had one of those voices which, once heard, was never forgotten. Briefly she wondered whether to play the game a little and say, Darian *who*? but decided against it. A man like that would be used to the pointless little games that some women played, and he would like her no better for it.

'Hello,' she said.

'I haven't disturbed you?'

There were games and there were games, and half-truths were sometimes necessary—especially if you wanted to avoid looking like a fool.

'Not really.' She watched the water running down her bare legs to form a small puddle on the bathroom floor. 'I was just...relaxing.' Which didn't have even a grain of truth to it, because she had never felt less relaxed in her life. And there seemed something slightly decadent about talking to him while she was naked, so she injected a brisk and professional note into her voice. 'What can I do for you, Darian? Have you seen the photos yet?'

'That's what I've just been doing.' He allowed himself a brief half-smile. It seemed that his instincts had not failed him—because Lara looked nothing short of sensational. Some of London's most stunning backdrops emphasised her bewitching looks as she stood holding a variety of his company's phones in her hand, a dreamy, thoughtful little smile on her face. She looked as if she was talking to her lover. Beneath each one would be printed the single shout-line: *Wildman: Presses All The Right Buttons!*

He had felt the unmistakable tremorings of desire as he had studied them. But, having seen them, had wondered aloud to Scott whether the final images weren't just *too* sexy. Scott had shrugged and given him a knowing look.

'Oh, come on, Darian—you don't use a young and beautiful model to do anything *but* sell sex,' he had pointed out. 'Do you?'

Selling sex.

Put like that, it sounded off-putting, and Darian had grimaced with a slight element of distaste—but that hadn't stopped him finding her number and ringing her, had it?

'They're terrific,' he said softly.

'Good. I'm pleased.' She waited. She knew that she wanted to see him again, in fact she *had* to see him again, but she was perceptive enough to know that she was dealing with a man who would always be pursued, and natural predators did not *like* to be pursued.

'I wondered if you'd like to have dinner with me?' he asked. 'As a kind of thank-you for turning in such a fantastic job.'

Lara very nearly asked him whether he always asked people out to dinner on the strength of their having done a good job, but she knew she couldn't risk scaring him away.

This, after all, was precisely why she had fought to get the job in the first place. To get closer to Darian, to find out as much as she could about him before she told Khalim what she knew.

'I'd love to,' she murmured. 'When?'

Human nature was a funny thing, Darian decided as a contrary feeling of disappointment washed over him. He hadn't expected it to be quite so easy, but why on earth should it make her seem marginally less desirable because she had not played games with him?

Because women always made it this easy for him, that was why. Had he hoped that her spikiness and spirit would make him have to battle for a bit to get her to agree to have dinner with him—and hadn't there been a part of him which had been anticipating that battle?

'I don't suppose you're free tomorrow night?'

Lara heard the slight cooling of his voice and knew

immediately that she had been too eager. 'Not *tomorrow* night, I'm afraid.' She paused, waiting.

Darian relaxed. There was nothing more off-putting than a woman who dropped everything because she wanted to see you—or, worse, a woman who had a social diary with great yawning gaps in it. But then he thought about her sparkling blue eyes and her perfect figure and guessed that Lara Black would not suffer from a lack of anything to do.

'Thursday, I'm flying to Paris for the day,' he mused. 'And I'm back late. How about Friday?'

She paused for just long enough to sound as though she was consulting a diary—after all, he wasn't to know that she was standing dripping in the bathroom, with her body tingling not just from the cold but from the effect of that rich, deep voice and the thought of seeing him again.

Because you *need* to see him, she reminded herself firmly. 'Friday's fine,' she said calmly.

'Shall I pick you up?'

To her horror, she felt her breasts tighten in response to the sudden softening of his voice, and the face which looked back at her through the blurred and misty mirror was startled. And confused. She didn't want to be attracted to him—certainly not *this* attracted. So she'd spend one evening with him, she told herself. That was all. 'Okay,' she said slowly.

'Good. Give me your address, and I'll see you around eight.'

Darian parked the car, expertly edging into the tiny space available at the address she had given him, and as he switched the powerful engine off he registered that he was surprised.

So she lived in Notting Hill, did she?

Which meant that she was successful. Property in this part of West London was astronomically expensive these days, ever since it had become 'the' place to live, with rock stars and Hollywood actresses swooping in to buy up every graceful house available.

Except that no one had heard of Lara Black—not really. So how come all the outward trappings of success? Scott had told him that she had done a few forgettable plays and a couple of television commercials where she had either been playing a vegetable or lost in a crowd of people drinking cola. But she'd been in nothing major to date.

He climbed the elegant steps to the house and pressed the button for Flat B. She probably rented, he reasoned. Or shared with a group of other impecunious women, pooling their resources so that they could live in an area with a prestigious address.

The door opened and Darian's eyes narrowed as he was greeted by a tall man with a lock of hair flopping into his eyes. Darian was rarely taken off-guard, but this time he was—amazed to be staring into the face of a stranger who was instantly recognisable. You would have had to have been living underground not to have recognised the star of the film which had broken all records at the international box-office last year.

What the hell was Jake Haddon doing *here*?

'I'm looking for Lara Black,' growled Darian.

Jake smiled. 'I know you are, but she's having one of those dress crises that women are prone to. The last thing I heard was a squeaked request from the bedroom asking me to answer the door! Come up and have a drink,' he offered easily.

'Thanks,' said Darian shortly.

He followed Jake up the stairs, his mind buzzing. What had Jake said? *A squeaked request from the bedroom.* So what kind of bedroom was that? A *shared* bedroom? And if that were the case then why had she agreed to have dinner with him tonight? Unless she had thought it was business—that he wanted to discuss the shoot with her.

Darian was unprepared for the overwhelming sensation of irritation and—*disappointment*.

He walked into the flat, which was huge—but at least now the up-market address became understandable. Of course she could afford to live in a place like this if Jake Haddon was footing the bill!

'Drink?' asked Jake.

'I'm driving.'

'Something soft, then?'

Darian forced himself to be pleasant, though he most decidedly did not feel it. In fact, he was feeling at a distinct disadvantage—a situation which was both novel and unwelcome.

'No, thanks. I'll just wait for Lara,' he said, and summoned up a brusque smile from somewhere.

'I'd better go and hurry her up, then.'

Darian nodded and watched the actor as he disappeared out of the room with a familiar loping stride. Funny, he thought, how celluloid could make you feel you knew someone—the way they walked and the way they spoke.

There was a tap on the bedroom door. 'Lara?'

Lara looked up. 'Oh, Jake! Come in! Do I look okay?'

'You look gorgeous, darling—but why go to so much trouble to date a man with a face like thunder?'

'Is he cross?' she asked, and flicked a glance at her watch. 'I don't see why—I'm only a couple of minutes late!'

Jake shrugged. 'It might be me—you know the effect I have on boyfriends.'

This was true. 'He isn't a boyfriend,' she protested unconvincingly, and then stared at herself in the mirror. She had chosen a cream silk dress with hundreds of tiny little buttons down the front, worn with black knee-length boots. 'Do I *look* as though I've gone to a lot of trouble?' she moaned.

'As if you've tried on a hundred dresses and then a hundred more? Stop frowning, darling—I'm only teasing—and run along and greet him. I think I'll go and hide in my room in case he decides to take a pop at me!'

Lara's fingers were trembling as she picked up her bag, and her heart was crashing against her chest as she walked into the sitting room to see Darian Wildman studying all her books in the manner of a detective on the lookout for pornographic literature!

He must have heard her, for he turned round as she walked in and she couldn't mistake the inky dilation of his eyes as he saw her. She wondered whether her eyes were doing exactly the same thing, because the sight of him made her knees go weak.

He looked all predator again—the cool and uncluttered clothes doing absolutely nothing to detract from his potent masculinity. His tawny skin gleamed as though it was lit from within and the golden eyes seemed to look at her too long and too hard. Too everything, really, because when he stared at her like that it was difficult to remember that this was not a normal man and this was not a normal evening.

'Hello, Darian,' she said, in a voice which sounded surprisingly calm.

Darian sucked in a breath because she looked utterly...not quite beautiful, because the term implied a set of criteria which needed to be filled and her looks were much too distinctive for that. But she had a definite head-turning quality which was difficult to define. Gorgeous, yes. And sexy, too—in a simple little cream dress which fitted her much too well and high-heeled black boots that made his gaze want to linger on her legs for ever.

Distracted, he broke a lifetime's rule and spoke without thinking of the consequences. 'You didn't tell me you lived with Jake Haddon!' he accused silkily.

And a very good evening to you, too! thought Lara. 'Why on earth should I have done? And, anyway, I don't *live* with him—I share a flat with him!'

Darian had been unaware that he was holding his breath until it was expelled in a long, low rush. Well, that told him something! When a woman said she shared a flat, it usually meant that she *wasn't* sharing a bed. He looked around the room and then back into her eyes. 'Lucky you,' he said softly.

'Or lucky him?' she countered sweetly.

'I should think that ninety-nine per cent of the female population would give anything to trade places with you.'

'Which presumably is why *I'm* sharing a flat with him— since I'm in that incomprehensible one per cent to whom it doesn't really matter that he's a handsome film star— just that he's a very nice person!'

Jealousy was not an emotion that Darian was used to feeling, and he was not enjoying it. With an effort, he glanced around the room, reluctantly acknowledging its style and taste. 'Pretty nice place he's got!'

It was with indignation that Lara opened her mouth to demand how he dared jump to that conclusion—even though it was the obvious one to reach. But to do that would be to tell him that the apartment belonged, in fact, to her—and then she would also feel duty-bound to explain why, and risk arousing his curiosity.

He seemed such a judgemental man that he would prob-ably conclude that she was running an escort agency—or something equally wicked!

'Yes, it's beautiful, isn't it?' she agreed conversationally, because this really was straying into dangerous waters.

The apartment had been given to her by Khalim, after his wedding to Rose. He had been concerned for Lara's welfare, unwilling to see her living in a crummy little place after he whisked her best friend and flatmate off to live in Maraban.

He had handed her a ribbon-tied envelope before he and Rose had flown off for their honeymoon and Lara had waited until they had gone before she opened it.

She'd only ever been a bridesmaid once before, and then she had been given a sweet gold St Christopher to hang around her neck. She had almost fainted with shock to find inside the envelope a set of deeds which showed her to be the owner of the most gorgeous flat she had ever seen!

'I consider myself very lucky,' she said truthfully as she gestured to the high ceilings and the elegant dimensions of the room.

Darian watched her, unable to deny that his interest in her had increased, due as much to her modesty as anything else. Most women would have boasted of their connection to such a high-profile star, not played it down. It was the last thing he had expected, and surprise was such a rare commodity that it would have set his pulses racing.

If they hadn't been racing already.

'Shall we go?' he said evenly. 'My car's outside.'

'Okay.' Only now her voice didn't sound so calm. Could he hear that she was almost breathless with anticipation and apprehension at the thought that they were now to leave the safety net of her home, with Jake lurking comfortably in the background?

Soon she'd be alone with this handsome, exotic stranger in his car, nursing a secret she didn't know how she dared tell him.

CHAPTER FIVE

DARIAN'S car was predictably powerful, Lara reflected as she climbed into the low seat with an agility which made her grateful she had done all those ballet classes when she was younger. And suddenly she felt as unsure of herself as that young girl had briefly been—out of her depth and scared.

'Where are we going?'

In the semi-darkness Darian gave a grim little half-smile, realising that Lara was not a woman who would be impressed by status for status's sake. Why, Jake Haddon had probably taken her to every single famous restaurant in London!

'It's a surprise,' he murmured softly.

'Oh, good. I like surprises,' she said—because what else could she have said? That being alone in a confined space with him was making her aware of all the wrong things? Like his powerful, brooding presence and long, long legs, which were affecting her on a purely personal level, and being personal was not supposed to be on the agenda. This was not an expedition to discover their compatibility or to acknowledge the bone-melting effect he had on her, but to find out more about him. She half turned in her seat, looking as a passing streetlight flickered golden highlights across the hard, sculpted profile. 'So where do *you* live, Darian?'

He opened his mouth to answer immediately, and this, too, was a new sensation. Normally he played down his home because of its unmistakable luxury, but for once he realised that he didn't have to! 'I have an apartment over-looking the river.'

'Let me guess—big and stark and minimalistic, with huge windows which look out all over London!'

He shot her a sideways glance. 'Are you a mind-reader, or something?'

'You mean I'm right?'

'Yes,' he growled suspiciously. Frighteningly and accurately right. 'How did you know?'

'Because I'm an actress and we're very perceptive, or at least we're supposed to be—it goes with the job!'

'So it was a guess?'

'An informed guess,' she corrected. 'I could tell the kind of place you definitely *wouldn't* live in.'

'Oh?' He changed down a gear as he cut through a backstreet. 'Enlighten me.'

This bit was easy. 'You wouldn't live in a cosy family house,' she said confidently.

'Because?'

'Because you haven't got a family.'

'How do you know that?'

Lara turned her head back to glare straight ahead into the darkness, her heart leaping with something which felt very like fear. That was a factor which hadn't even entered her head. She hadn't considered that he was a married man, and she didn't want to question why the thought of that should upset her quite so much. 'Well, if you *do* have a family, then you shouldn't be in the habit of taking women who might jump to the wrong conclusion out to dinner!' she said crossly.

'And what conclusion would that be?' he murmured.

That this was a date. Lara suddenly realised that she *wanted* it to be a date. Oh, *why* did he have to have a damned connection to Maraban—and when was she going to get around to broaching the subject?

Not yet, she told herself.

Not yet.

'And where else wouldn't I live?' he asked softly, changing the subject back because she seemed to have lapsed into a thoughtful kind of silence.

Lara settled back in her seat, relieved to discover that, like all men, he wanted to talk about himself. And wasn't that good, in the circumstances? 'Nowhere there are lots of houses all the same,' she said firmly. 'And nowhere that's fussy or predictable—the kind of place where people always do the same thing, day in, day out—you know, like catching the train at the same time every morning and washing their car before lunch on Sundays!'

Unseen, he narrowed his eyes. It was uncanny. Disturbing. How had she managed to echo the very thoughts he had had the other day?

Any minute now she would be telling him what colour boxer shorts he was wearing—Darian regretted that thought instantly, as it was met with an answering jerk of desire.

With a small sigh of something like relief, he drew into the parking lot of the restaurant and Lara peered through the window, interested to see where he had chosen. She had been so wrapped up in him that she had barely noticed where they were going, and this was an area of London she realised she didn't know at all. Had she been half expecting him to opt for some glitzy place right in the centre of the city?

Because this was the very opposite. It was a small, unpretentious building with fairy lights strung outside, making tiny blurry rainbows through the misty autumn air, and as she opened the car door she heard the sound of music. It conjured up memories of days when money had been tight, days when people were happy to eat simply because they were hungry, and not because a restaurant was *the* place to be seen. A little sigh escaped from her lips. Nostalgia could be very powerful.

'Where's this?'

In the circumstances, Darian didn't think it pertinent to tell her that it was a small, noisy, family-run Italian restaurant that he had stumbled on by chance years ago. And that, apart from the food, one of its main attributes was that he was never recognised in there by anyone remotely connected to his business life.

Jake Haddon probably took her to places where *he* wouldn't be recognised all the time, he thought, again with that infuriating shaft of something very like jealousy.

The owner and his wife greeted him warmly, and that, too, took Lara by surprise. Had she thought that he would be aloof—one of those men who swanned into places as if they owned them? They were shown to a table in an alcove—private, yet managing to provide a good view of the rest of the restaurant. It was as if they had been saving the nicest table just for him, and that *didn't* surprise her at all.

As they settled into their seats Lara thought that perhaps this was the best way of all of finding out what the real man was. A one-to-one dinner where she could discover as much about him as possible. It would be like taking an inventory.

'You were miles away.'

His voice was a velvet murmur which nudged into her thoughts, and Lara blinked to find the gold eyes trained on her, piercing through her as if the light which shone from them was the precious metal itself. And for a moment she felt uncomfortable, as if what she was doing was somehow furtive. Well, when she stopped to think about it—it *was*.

'W-was I?'

He gave a wry smile. He didn't usually send women off into a trance! 'Drink?'

Lara nodded. 'Please.'

'What?'

'Whatever you're having.'

He raised his eyebrows fractionally and ordered wine. 'Shall I choose what you're eating, too?' he questioned sardonically.

Lara nodded, enjoying the confounded look on his face. 'Please.' She smiled. 'You've obviously eaten here plenty of times before—I'm happy to take your recommendations.'

'Are you always so delightfully acquiescent?' he questioned, in a voice of silky provocation.

Lara didn't react to the not-so-subtle implication. 'Only in matters concerning my stomach,' she said. 'I'll eat whatever is put in front of me.'

'You don't survive on cigarettes and black coffee, then?'

Lara shuddered. 'You're joking!'

He studied her. A small moonstone necklace gleamed against her pale skin, and it took a supreme effort not to be completely distracted by the soft shadows of her cleavage. She wasn't all skin and bones, like a lot of actresses and models.

'How come you stay so slim?' he questioned.

'I only eat when I'm hungry, and I walk wherever possible.'

'Even in London?'

'Especially in London—it's the best way to avoid the traffic and to see the city properly!'

He ordered, waited until red wine had been poured for them, then sat back in his seat, his fingers caressing the deep bowl of the glass.

'So.'

Lara took a mouthful of wine, needing something to help her relax, to take her mind off the fact that his mouth had softened and she was wondering what it would be like to kiss it.

She smiled. 'So.'

'What shall we drink to?' He raised his glass, his eyes questioning. 'The new face of Wildman?'

'Why not?' Her heart was beating very fast as their glasses touched.

'Soon to be emblazoned on posters all over the country,' he mused. 'How does that feel—knowing that your face will be everywhere?'

'I'm not sure,' she said slowly. 'I've never done a poster campaign before.'

'But you've done other kinds of advertising—television, magazines.'

'A bit.'

'And does it feed the ego?'

It was a mocking challenge. A faintly hostile question. 'Not really. Actors are notoriously insecure,' she said, taking another sip of wine. 'Didn't you know that?'

He shrugged. 'That's the theory, but if that's the case, then it strikes me as an odd type of profession to choose.'

'Maybe the two are inseparable. Maybe it's *because* they're insecure and don't feel comfortable in their own skins that they're able to inhabit someone else's so easily.'

The curve of her breasts gleamed softly beneath the cream silk. 'I can't imagine that *you* feel uncomfortable in your own skin,' he observed quietly. 'When you're so very lovely.'

Lara quickly put her glass down before he could see that her hand was shaking. The compliment warmed and yet alarmed her. This wasn't supposed to be happening. Her body was not supposed to be tingling and glowing and basking in his approbation as a cat would contentedly lap up the warm rays of the sun. This was not a date, this was a fact-finding mission, pure and simple.

If she wasn't careful then they would spend the whole time talking about her, or, even worse, his wretched company, and then, before she knew it, the evening would be gone and she might never have this opportunity again.

The waiter came over, and she waited until he had deposited two dishes of steaming prawns before them.

She speared one uninterestedly. 'Anyway,' she said brightly. 'You know something about me, but I know absolutely nothing about you.' Other than that your contained and watchful silence makes me feel as jumpy as a cat on a hot tin roof.

'But I thought that all actresses were self-centred and like nothing better than to talk about themselves?'

'It's very insulting to continue making those sweeping statements.' Lara narrowed her eyes. 'Though I suspect that's why you said it—to try and stop me asking you questions about yourself.'

The golden eyes bored into hers. 'You're very persistent,' he observed.

'I think persistence is an undervalued quality.'

His voice was cool. 'What do you want to know?'

'Where you were born.' She chewed a mouthful of bread, as if she was just thinking the questions up as she went along. 'Where you grew up.'

Darian went very still, his antennae on alert. 'How very curious,' he murmured. 'Why?'

And Lara realised that she wanted to know in spite of everything, that even if she hadn't opened that letter and needed to find out then she still would have *wanted* to find out more about Darian Wildman. He fascinated her; he was an intriguing man. But he was also a perceptive and intelligent man, and doubtless one who was used to women clamouring to know all about him. And if in the process of finding out about him she appeared like one of many, then that was just too bad. 'I'm interested,' she said. 'That's all.'

He twirled the stem of the wine glass between his long fingers. 'Why do women always want a history?'

'Because we like to know what makes people tick.'

'And men don't?'

'Not really. Men are more interested in the here and now—women like to discover how we got to it.'

'Because?'

Now she spoke from the heart. 'Because our history is what defines us all and makes us who we are.'

Darian's senses would usually have been put on alert at the turn the conversation had taken, but he was lulled by the sudden passion in her voice, by the blue fire which sparked from those long-lashed eyes. She was thoughtful and insightful, not what he had been expecting at all, and the unexpectedness coupled with the novelty made his habitual guard slip a little.

'My history isn't a particularly exciting one.'

She heard the brittle note which edged his voice, and part of her wanted to back off. But she couldn't. This wasn't just some prurient interest, some woman on the make, chipping away at the formidable exterior to find out what had made the man beneath. This was serious stuff.

'Isn't that subjective?' she queried. 'Everyone else's past always seems more interesting than your own—just like other people's relationships always seem to be made in heaven. When you're looking from the outside you don't see all the imperfections; you just get an idea of the bigger picture.'

She was right, of course—and her reference to relationships didn't go unnoticed, either.

'There's no man in your life?' he asked suddenly.

Lara stared at him. 'No.'

'Why not?'

'That's a very personal question,' she protested, feeling her cheeks grow pink beneath the piercing scrutiny of his stare.

'You think you have the monopoly on personal questions, do you, Lara?'

'Of course I don't—and the reason there's no man in my life is simply because there isn't.' She threw him a challenging look. 'I don't need a partner to define me!'

'How very refreshing,' he murmured.

Lara's fork chased a piece of rocket round the plate. 'So, where were you born?' she questioned casually.

'London.'

'Big place.'

'Nowhere you've probably ever visited.' He named one of the city's most run-down areas and watched carefully for her response, noting the instinctive little frown which pleated her forehead. 'You're surprised,' he observed.

'Well…' For once in her life she was lost for words. 'I guess I am, a little.'

'Because it's reputed to be the birthplace of gangsters?' His words were dipped in caustic irony. 'Or maybe you think that if someone's born in a place like that then they stay there—is that it?'

She shook her head a little. 'No…no, that's not what I meant at all. It's just difficult to imagine you being…poor, that's all.'

'Is it?' The dark lashes came down to shutter his eyes. He looked like a lion, Lara thought. The way a lion looked when you thought that it was asleep, only to discover that it was garnering all its energy to pounce. Lots of men tried to pounce on her, and usually it made her recoil, but Darian Wildman was a different propositon entirely. The lashes parted again and the golden light from his eyes washed over her.

'For a woman who eats whatever is put in front of her, you aren't managing very well tonight,' he mused.

'I'm not very hungry,' she confessed, wondering if this deliberate change of subject meant that she should now withhold her line of questioning. But somehow the questions no longer seemed important—not when he was looking at her like that.

'Me neither.' He wondered if her lack of appetite was rooted in the same reason as his own. He held her gaze, saw the way her lips parted, and knew that she didn't want to be here any more than he did. He felt another short stab of desire. 'Which makes ordering pudding a complete waste of time, don't you think?'

She nodded, but a feeling of disappointment threatened to well up and spill over. Was he bored and wanting out? Had she overstepped the mark with her intrusive line of questioning? And where did she go from here?

The golden eyes glittered and his dark, lean body was very still. 'Are you tired?'

Lara stared at him as something in his voice told her that the evening was not yet over. Yet the implication behind his question made her tense just as surely as it made her body begin a slow, irresistible flower into life.

This is dangerous, she heard a voice inside her head warning her, but she ignored it. 'Not really,' she said, as though she couldn't care less one way or the other.

'Then why don't we continue this fascinating discussion back at my place? You can enjoy one of the finest views over London while I give you...' He paused, his voice lingering deliberately. *'Coffee.'* The golden eyes glittered, and dazzled her with their precious fire. 'What do you say, Lara?'

It was what they called a loaded question, and the unmistakable air of sensuality he exuded warned her that a wise woman would thank him politely and say no. If lion he was, then why be foolish enough to walk meekly into his den?

But she might not get this chance again, and here he was offering opportunity on a plate. She reassured herself that he was far too sophisticated to do something as crass as leaping on her if she didn't want him to. The only thing she had to fear was the fact that she *did* want him to.

Miraculously, she kept the excited tremor from her voice. 'Sounds good,' she said carefully.

'Then I'll get the bill,' he said, equally carefully, and his eyes narrowed.

For once, he hadn't expected it to be quite so easy.

CHAPTER SIX

'OH, IT'S beautiful,' said Lara softly. She leaned over the balcony and gazed out. The mist of earlier had cleared, and now the lights of the city sparkled like precious gems against the navy velvet of the night sky. 'Just beautiful.'

Darian eased the cork from a bottle of wine and watched the way the breeze ruffled her dark silken hair, so that it fluttered behind her like a banner. 'Yes,' he agreed slowly.

For once he had been wrong—imagining it would take more than a little persuasion to get her to come back here with him tonight. The prickle of anticipation he had felt—that here was a woman who might make him fight a little—had been replaced by the much more familiar feeling of slightly jaded anticipation, but not jaded enough to stem the rising tide of desire.

'Some wine?' he drawled.

Lara turned round. He had removed his jacket and he looked relaxed, almost domesticated. Behind him, the brightly illuminated room looked like the stage-set of a play, with he the hero of the piece.

Or the villain.

Her heart thudded. 'I thought you promised me coffee?'

'I did. But how about a little wine first? You hardly drank a thing in the restaurant.'

A faintly bored note came into his voice, as if her inference that he was trying to push alcohol on her was offensive.

'But I'll go and make coffee if you'd prefer.'

'No. Actually, I'd love some wine,' she said truthfully. Perhaps wine might make her stop feeling like a woman who had never been invited into a man's home before. She wasn't such an innocent! She crossed her arms over her chest and rubbed them up and down her bare arms. 'Brrrr! It's freezing.'

'Go inside. Make yourself at home.'

She felt his eyes on her as she made her way back into a sitting room which was a byword for luxury. This was crazy, she thought. She had spent her life being watched, sometimes on stage and sometimes by the camera, and usually she managed it with aplomb—easily becoming the person the director wanted her to be.

And maybe that was the problem here—that she was being herself. Only she was discovering an unwelcome and unfamilar nervousness in the company of a man who intrigued and attracted and disturbed her, compounded by what she had read in the letter.

Darian followed her into the room, tipping just a tiny amount of the rich red wine into two crystal glasses while she sat down primly on one of the giant leather sofas.

He noticed the way she pressed her knees tightly together as he handed her the glass. Did she always do this? he wondered. Send out such beguiling and conflicting messages? She had agreed very quickly—too quickly—to come home with him, and there was a not-so-subtle subtext to deals like that. If you didn't want a man to make a pass at you, then you did not go back to his apartment late at night on a first date.

Darian was used to knowing the score. To women quickly and blatantly letting him know that they wanted him. It happened so frequently that it was just par for the course, as natural as breathing for him—he had never had to fight for a woman in his life, though sometimes he had idly wondered what it might be like to have to do so.

He was instinctive enough to know that the attraction between he and Lara was mutual, but only up to a point.

Because now there was a wariness about her, almost a shyness, which seemed to contradict her innate sensuality. And mystery and contradictions were always fascinating, he acknowledged with a slow ache of awareness as he sat down on the sofa—just far enough away not to threaten her, but close enough to smell the soft scent of lilac which drifted from her pale skin. Close enough to touch...

Lara sipped her drink, but her throat felt tight and she had to force down a mouthful of the smooth, rich wine. 'Lovely,' she remarked politely.

'So where were we?' He put his glass down on the coffee table and half turned to look at her, a small smile playing around the edges of his mouth. 'Ah, yes, your tender heart was melting at the thought of my underprivileged upbringing.'

With a shaky hand she put her glass down next to his. 'Don't make fun of me.'

'Is that what I was doing?' he murmured.

'That or patronising me,' she answered quietly. 'You don't have to talk about your childhood if you don't want to.'

Liar! Liar! But her words had exactly the desired effect. By telling him he didn't have to talk, he immediately began to relax—although had she known that on some deep, gut-level? That here was a man who would not be forced into telling anything about himself—and the only way to get information about him was to appear not to care?

'And poor doesn't mean unhappy,' she continued coaxingly.

He gave a low, mocking laugh. 'That's the fairytale version, spoken with the voice of someone who has absolutely no idea what material deprivation is like.'

'You can't know that!' she protested.

'True,' he agreed. 'But I'm right, aren't I?' The golden eyes flickered over her lazily. 'Let me guess—you grew up in the country? A stable family life with brothers and sisters? Fresh air and exercise and three meals a day? A pony in the stable and dogs barking when you came home from school?'

Lara froze, then swallowed, and the tiptoeing of fear began to shiver its way down her spine. 'That's…that's bizarre. Well, except for the brothers bit—I have two sisters and they are much older. And my father was away a lot. But the rest is correct.' Her blue eyes were as big as saucers as she looked at him. 'How could you possibly have known?'

'About the country?' Some things you didn't need to be told. He reached his hand out and lightly touched her cheek. 'It's written all over you. Skin like this wasn't made in a city.'

Was that a trace of wistfulness in his voice, or was she imagining it? 'W-wasn't it?'

'No.' He let one of his fingers drift over skin that felt like satin. 'You're a real milk and honey girl!'

Lara found the compliment shockingly satisfying—almost as gratifying as the all too brief contact when he had touched her, making her want him to touch her again. She shook her head slightly, trying to remember why she was here.

'Very good. Ten out of ten,' she said lightly. 'Your turn now.'

'Isn't this supposed to be a guessing game?' he mocked.

'Well, I know you grew up in the city.' Lara drew a deep breath and decided to go for broke. 'I'd say that you are an only child and that your parents were…separated.'

There was an odd pause. 'Is it really that obvious?' he questioned, and a slightly bitter note came into his voice. 'Do I have one-parent family written all over me?'

Lara felt guilty, but she managed not to show it. 'Not at all,' she said hastily. 'It's more a case of working things out from the information available. Putting bits in, like a jigsaw. The area you mentioned doesn't really conjure up a cosy family scene, with roses round the door.'

'As opposed to the image of a mother who was hard-pressed to put food into her hungry child's mouth?'

'Is that what it was like?' she whispered, horrified.

'Not quite,' he commented sarcastically. 'But I should hate to puncture the little bubble-picture you've invented in your head!'

'Now you *are* making fun of me.'

'I thought that all women liked to be teased?'

He was making her feel gauche and unsophisticated. And she didn't like his constant references to what 'women' liked—it made her feel one in an endless line of them—which, when she stopped to think about it, she probably was. But this isn't about you, Lara, she reminded herself—it's about him. And Maraban. 'But you *were* poor?' she questioned bluntly.

His eyes grew flinty. 'Do you want me to give you a breakdown of our weekly finances?'

She heard the distaste in his voice, and she didn't blame him—her questions were crossing over the line between good taste and bad, and unless she gave him some kind of explanation she couldn't possibly keep on asking them. What on earth was she going to *do*? Tell him, or tell Khalim first?

'You're right. I'm sorry—I was just being nosy. Don't worry, I won't ask any more.'

Darian studied her, noting the way her blue eyes were suddenly looking haunted. The vulnerable little tremor of her lips made him want to kiss them. 'You know, you really are very sweet, Lara,' he said softly.

A pain stabbed at her heart. What would he say if he knew? And how could she suddenly just blurt it out—

Darian, I am almost certain that you are the illegitimate brother of the Sheikh of Maraban?

'I am not sweet,' she contradicted, and bit her lip.

'And so modest, too,' he teased. 'Now, don't frown. Relax.' Casually, he reached out to capture a handful of her hair, and began to trickle his fingers through the silky curls so that they touched and tickled the back of her neck. 'Relax,' he whispered softly.

'Darian, don't,' she said weakly.

A woman didn't cross and uncross her legs in quick succession and then wriggle her head back into your hand if she meant *don't*.

'Don't what?' He moved closer, moved his hands from her neck to her shoulderblades. 'You're tense,' he exclaimed softly, and began to gently massage the tight flesh. 'Very, very tense.'

If only he knew why! 'This…this isn't such a good idea—'

'What isn't? A simple massage? I'm very good at it, you know.' His fingers continued to knead away, lulling her into a dreamy and hypnotic state. 'Relax, Lara—if you don't like it, then I'll stop.'

Which made it even worse. He was giving her a let-out. The decision was completely in her hands. She could stop him whenever she wanted to, and she should stop him now. Except that she *did* like it; that was the trouble. She liked it a lot. It's only a massage, she told herself dreamily.

'Is that good?' he whispered.

Helplessly, she closed her eyes. 'I, oh…yes.' The decision wasn't in her hands at all, she realised—he had all the power.

'Why not lie down?' he suggested. 'You'll be more comfortable that way.'

It was, after all, only a massage. She tried to tell herself that as he was gently pushing her back against the sofa.

But the word 'push' implied force, and there was no force involved—merely a delicious compliance as she sank down onto the leather, her cheek resting on its soft surface, her eyelids fluttering to a close.

Darian worked on her neck and her shoulders, gradually feeling some of the tension released by the rhythmical movement of his fingertips. 'Is that better?'

'It's...heaven,' she mumbled.

It felt pretty good from where he was sitting, too. A little too good. Darian shifted his body slightly as the tightness easing away from her body was replaced by a growing tension in his own.

Lara's limbs felt as fluid as water, her blood as thick as warm honey, and the pulse-points around her body began to deepen and speed. She could feel their slow and relentless pounding in her temple, her wrists, and somewhere deep in her groin. This is sheer craziness, she told herself. But she couldn't move; she didn't want it to end.

He heard her sigh, and his hard mouth glimmered in a brief smile, his eyes drifting over the tight, firm curve of her bottom.

'Am I sending you to sleep?'

'Well, yes,' she murmured drowsily, knowing that was only half the story.

'Then I'd better stop. We can't have that.'

He took his hands away. 'Oh!' Lara whispered disappointedly.

'Turn over,' came the soft command.

Somehow she managed to, even though her body felt so deliciously lethargic that it took all her energy.

Her hair was all mussed, her cheeks pink and flushed, and behind her half-hooded eyelids her blue eyes glittered hectically. He read in them self-doubt and utter confusion and, almost without intending to, dipped his head and brushed a featherlight kiss over her lips, felt her shiver in response.

'Darian—'

'Shh.' He kissed her again.

This was dangerous. The brush of his lips was barely there and then gone again, only to return. Tiny, butterfly kisses which coaxed and maddened. 'Oh,' she murmured instinctively.

His mouth smiled against hers, and this time his lips stayed longer, teasing and caressing until hers opened beneath his and her arms came up to wind around his neck, like tendrils of ivy clinging to sun-warmed brick.

'Darian—'

'You don't like it?'

She grazed her lips over his, unable to stop herself. Just once, she told herself. She would kiss him just once. But she kissed him again, and again, and then again, and his low laugh of delight made her want to do it some more.

She tried to speak, but her lips were so dry and her head so spinning that the words came out as a parched kind of whisper. 'It isn't a question of not liking...'

'But that's the only important question, darling. Nothing else is worth asking.' He drifted his mouth along the line of her jaw. 'Is it?'

Her head fell back and his lips moved immediately to her neck. Lara shuddered. In her befuddled state of desire his words seemed to make perfect sense, and this was dangerous indeed. Very dangerous.

She should pull away and ask him to take her home. If he wanted her that much then he would be prepared to wait—and wouldn't that be what any woman in her right mind would do? Wait at least until she had told him the momentous news she had?

So why were her fingertips running over the back of his head as if learning him by touch? Why was she doing nothing to stop him when he ran the flat of his hand down over one breast and then back again, where it lingered, and she could feel it growing tight and hard against him.

Because she couldn't, that was why.

She lifted her head, which felt as if it was weighted with some heavy metal—like the gold which matched the hot, molten colour of his eyes. Two flares of colour ran along each aristocratic cheekbone, and at that moment he looked like a pure Marabanese, with all the accompanying pride and arrogance that went with that ancestry.

Yet his hard mouth had been softened by her kisses, so that for one second he looked unexpectedly vulnerable. It was like having a curtain twitch and seeing behind it a glimpse of a man you dared not dream existed. A man with softness beneath the hard, polished exterior, making him utterly irresistible. And with something approaching shock Lara realised that she wanted him now, no matter what the consequences.

She remembered the first time she had seen Khalim and had almost melted into a puddle on the floor. Was she just one of those women who were suckers for arrogant and exotic-looking men who seemed to make most normal men look like a pale imitation of the real thing?

Darian sensed her reservations melting away and smiled lazily as he ran his hand down over her stomach, which curved faintly beneath the clinging cream fabric of her dress, and then down further still, until it edged up beneath the thin material. He splayed his fingers with arrogant possession over the space of cool flesh above her stocking top and Lara felt her thighs part, as if no power on earth could have stopped them.

'You *do* like it,' he purred approvingly, and the pad of his thumb stroked the silken flesh there. He felt her squirm, enjoying the look of helpless pleasure which made her lips form a disbelieving little Oh!

She tried one last, futile time. 'We shouldn't be doing this,' she protested half-heartedly.

'Want me to stop?' This as his fingertips floated tantalisingly close to the moist, filmy barrier of her panties, and she shook her head distractedly.

'No!'

He kissed her, and his words were muffled against her lips. 'You just want me to know that you aren't in the habit of leaping into bed on a first date, is that it?'

Lara felt her cheeks grow hot. 'Well, I'm not—'

'And neither am I,' he murmured silkily. 'So we're equal, aren't we?'

If only he knew!

'And now that we've established that...' He pulled her into his arms and began to kiss her—only this time he *really* kissed her, deep, searching seeking kisses, which dissolved away everything but the need to be joined with him.

'Darian,' she moaned weakly as he started to unbutton her dress, little by little, bit by bit, lowering his head so that where his fingers led his mouth followed, annointing her skin with gentle kisses which made her squirm with pleasure. He slipped the dress from her shoulders and it slid away unnoticed, so that she was lying there in a tiny cream bra and knickers, her stockings and black leather boots.

Darian sucked in a hot, ragged breath. Women only ever wore undergarments like that if they were expecting to be seduced. This was what she wanted. What she had obviously expected. The heat built up inside him. 'Undress me,' he urged. 'Take my clothes off, Lara.'

But Lara felt almost kittenish in her helplessness. Her fingers fumbled at the buttons of his shirt until he made a low sound that was halfway between a groan and a laugh and tipped her chin up with his fingertip, unbearably excited by the beguiling contrast beween wanton abandon and a kind of sweet shyness.

'Your hands are shaking,' he said gravely.

Her whole body was shaking—surely he could see that? 'Yes.'

He pulled at his shirt with a hunger so sharp he scarcely recognised it. What invisible buttons was she pressing? he wondered distractedly as he yanked it off and impatiently threw it aside.

She saw the tension on his face and managed to undo his belt, but he unzipped his trousers himself, as though not trusting her to do so. Her lips were parched with both fear and excitement as the last of his clothing was removed, and she gave an instinctive sigh as she feasted her eyes on him.

His body was as beautiful as she had known it would be—his skin the colour of deep honey, his limbs long and lean and strong. And he was very, very aroused...

He ran a slow finger over her leather boot and up along her thigh, and felt her shudder in response. 'Do you want to wrap these round my back?' he whispered.

It was one of those questions which told her exactly what the score was. A deliberate and studied celebration of sensuality and nothing more than that. But Lara was too much in thrall to back out now—and what reason could she possibly give? That she was afraid he was going to hurt her as no man had ever hurt her before nor would again?

Instead, she reached her arms up to pull him close, and as he lowered his body down onto hers she had the strangest feeling of inevitability—as though this moment had been determined from the first time she had set eyes on him, as though her life would somehow be incomplete without this.

'Wait!' he commanded, and reached down to pull a packet of condoms from the pocket of his trousers.

'I'm…I'm on the Pill,' she said, her voice shy, which in itself was madness in view of the intimacy of their naked bodies.

Golden eyes glittered. 'Let's just be sure, shall we?' he murmured, and slid one on.

Lara felt heat suffuse her cheeks. He was only being safe and sensible, the way she would have wanted and expected him to be, but it made her feel as if this was just…mechanical instead of special. Part of her wanted to pull her clothes back on and run away, but he had started to kiss her again, and the sweetness of his lips made flight impossible and unwanted.

'Lara!' Darian groaned as the hard, flat planes of his body met her moist and giving heat, bending his mouth to hers. Their lips met and fused and a strange warmth filled him. What the hell was she *doing*? What game was she playing that could have him feeling like this?

All she was doing was holding him in her arms, her hips rising up as if to invite him inside, and suddenly he knew he could wait no longer.

The last of her doubts fled as she felt him tremble because helplessness in such a strong man could be very potent. 'Yes,' she whispered, as if she had read his mind. 'Oh, yes.' But he was already entering her, plunging deep, deep inside her, and she gasped with delighted pleasure.

He heard the sound she made and felt a wild and exultant kind of joy, steadying himself as he began to move. She moved in harmony with him, and he watched the rapture flower and bloom on her face.

Lara's breath caught in her throat. It had never been like this. Never. So… Her eyes snapped open and she saw the dark and golden man who moved above her with such sweet and piercing precision. How could she be this close? This soon? This…?

'Darian!' It was a sigh and a cry laced with a sense of wonder.

But he was a silent lover. There was no response at all bar the silken touch of his skin and the feel of him moving inside her—the sudden brilliant gleam from his eyes was the only sign that he had heard her. She had to bite back words of passion, because even though they were joined so intimately there were some things you didn't do. And telling a man like Darian that you thought he was the most wonderful lover was one of them. And then she was past thought…past caring…

Holding back until he thought it might kill him, he looked down and watched her until the instinctive and frantic arching of her back set him free. He let his seed spill into her with a spasm of pleasure which seemed to go on and on and on, and when it was over he felt as though she had robbed him of something. Taken something from him which he had not been ready to give.

They lay there, spent, in shuddering silence for a moment or two, and a tiny sigh escaped from her lips.

'Oh, Darian,' she whispered, and, turning her head, she kissed his shoulder. But he didn't move, didn't answer, just lay there like a statue made of flesh and bone and blood—and that was when the doubts came flooding back, startling her out of her post-coital haze, and she closed her eyes in despair.

What had she *done*?

Lara knew that regret was a waste of time emotion, but it washed over her in a great wave, leaving her shivering and cold in its wake. What in God's name had she been thinking of? To have sex with a man so quickly—and not just any man—*this* man. And she still hadn't asked him the most important question of all.

She licked her dry, parched lips. 'Darian?'

Darian gazed at the ceiling. Usually he felt restless, not dazed like this. He would jump up, make coffee, perhaps play a little music. Indulge in physical activity which put a distance between him and a woman, and that was the way he liked it. A bout of sensational sex should be seen in context, as nothing more nor less than just that.

But tonight felt different. His limbs didn't want to move and sleep was tempting his heavy eyes as his heart slowed into a regular pounding beat. It was as if he'd landed in a warm, safe place and didn't want to leave it.

He fought it, and yawned. He would offer to take her home now. It was always the acid-test—how the woman reacted. Like a cool, emotionally independent woman or like a clinging little girl. The moment you let a woman stay the night she started moving in her toothbrush and leaving pairs of panties around the place—marking her territory. Though when he stopped to think about it he wouldn't mind the tiny little scraps of nonsense which Lara wore lying *anywhere*. In fact, he'd preferably like her wearing them, so that he could slowly remove them and...

'Darian?' Lara said again, as she felt him begin to harden against her, and she wondered if he could hear the worry in her voice.

'Mmm?' He had been about to pull her into his arms again, but something in her question, something in her body language made him tense, and instinctively his features became shuttered. 'Yes, Lara?'

She sensed just as much as she saw his mental retreat. It was there in the yawn, the way he hadn't been tender, or kissed the top of her head, or told her that it had been amazing. But there were still things she needed to know. She had allowed herself to be seduced, and in so doing she had momentarily veered off course, but she needed to know one thing above all else.

'How old are you?'

Darian was rarely surprised by a woman, particularly after he had just had sex with her; women tended to be predictable in their reactions to fast physical intimacy— they either acted as if you were about to start choosing the ring, or they started asking unanswerable questions like, Do you still respect me? But this was the last question he had been expecting.

Was it a Why aren't you married yet? kind of question? And would other inevitable questions follow—like why had he never settled down before and didn't he ever want children? The last drop of pleasure evaporated in an instant, like rain splashing onto a sunbaked pavement. 'Thirty-five. Why?'

She felt the walls close in, and it had nothing to do with the odd, cold note which had entered his voice.

Thirty-five!

Which made him exactly the same age as Khalim. Or, rather, it probably made him *older*—because surely Khalim's father would not have had a lover straight after he was married? And the repercussions of *that* just didn't bear thinking about.

Suddenly something which had been almost abstract was brought into harsh and painful reality, and she knew that this was a responsibility too much to bear alone.

She had to tell someone, but it could not be Darian.

Not yet.

She ran her fingertips over his chest, her blood running icy-cold in her veins.

'I think I'd better go home now,' she said.

He only just resisted a sigh of relief. 'Okay,' he agreed. 'I'll get dressed and then I'll drive you.'

'I can get a taxi.'

'I *said* I'd take you,' he said, in a tone which broached no argument.

Lara thought that she would have preferred to take a cab, alone with the reality of what a huge mistake she had just made.

Because the fact that he hadn't tried to talk her out of leaving told its own story.

CHAPTER SEVEN

THERE was a click on the line and Lara waited, as she had been waiting on and off for the past two days—but of course it was never going to be an easy matter to get through to Prince Khalim of Maraban. Despite the fact that phone lines to the mountain kingdom were notoriously unreliable, and the fact that she counted herself as his friend, Lara was pragmatic enough to realise that no one ever really became close to such a powerful and enigmatic figure. Certainly not close enough to just pick the phone up, get connected immediately and say Hi!

And she still hadn't worked out exactly what she was going to say to him when he finally answered anyway.

'Hello?'

It was unmistakably Khalim's voice—deep, with the slightest accent. And—Lara didn't know whether she was being simply fanciful—didn't its deepness and richness remind her of Darian's voice?

'Khalim?'

'Hello, Lara.'

He sounded wary, and Lara couldn't blame him. He was married to her best friend Rose, and loved her with a fierce and unremitting passion, but he had spent his life being propositioned and pursued by countless other women. Why wouldn't he be suspicious that Lara had decided to contact him in a way which had been specifically meant to exclude Rose?

'I know you're probably wondering why on earth I'm ringing you, and I hardly know how to begin.'

He made no helpful sound. There was merely silence

from the other end of the phone. It would have been better to tell him this face to face—but he was hardly going to jump on a plane to England on her say-so, just as she was hardly likely to fly to Maraban at a moment's notice.

'Khalim, you know I was working at the Embassy while someone was off sick?'

'Yes, of course.'

'Well…well, one morning this…this letter arrived.' Lara began to speak, scarcely knowing what it was that she said, because the words seemed to come tumbling out of their own accord and she realised just how much she must have bottled it all up. It was incredible, but as the story unfolded it began to sound more real. She told him that she had found Darian, and that she had met him, deliberately and blushingly skating over the graphic details of their meeting.

'And that's it, really,' she finished, and the sense of a burden shared gave her a brief feeling of lightness. 'I'm sure that this man Darian Wildman is your half-brother.'

There was a short silence. She could imagine Khalim turning the incredible words over and over in his mind, choosing his own answering words carefully, as he always did—because men like Khalim could not risk misinterpretation, not even by friends.

When he spoke there was no emotion in his voice. 'You cannot be certain of this, Lara.'

'I know. I only know what I've found.' She paused. 'He…he looks like you.'

This time there *was* a reaction.

'But he is half-English, you say?'

'Yes, he is.' Lara closed her eyes as she remembered the golden eyes and the dark and tawny body, that autocratic air and undeniable sense of solitude which Khalim always carried about him, which Darian shared. 'But he is unmistakably related to you,' she finished softly. 'I am convinced of that.'

Khalim said something rapid in Marabanese.

'He could be a clever fraud,' he bit out. 'An impostor.'

'How can he be? He knows nothing of the claim,' argued Lara. 'Nor anything of the letter.'

'You hinted at nothing?'

'Not a thing.'

'Why, Lara?' asked Khalim softly. 'Why did you say nothing to this man of such a momentous discovery?'

'Because...because...' Her words trailed off as she recognised that a kind of betrayal had occurred—but surely an inevitable one? 'Because my first loyalty is to you.'

'Thank you,' he said simply. 'The question is what we do about it now.'

'Some people might ignore it. Throw the letter away and pretend it never happened. Carry on just as before.'

'Could you ignore it, Lara?'

Doubt and uncertainty prevailed. Her body still ached from Darian's lovemaking, her senses were still full of him, her mind unable to banish the image of his hard, mocking mouth softened by her kisses.

'If you asked me to, then I suppose—'

'No!' He cut into her troubled words. 'Your hesitation does you credit. I would not ask you to ignore it, nor could I ignore it myself—for the hand of fate is at work here. Predestination,' he mused. 'Sometimes friend and sometimes foe, but unable to be ignored or avoided. We cannot pretend something has not happened because something has—and because of it—things are for ever changed.'

'Y-yes,' said Lara falteringly, and she felt the strangest feeling of foreboding tiptoeing its way up her spine as she repeated his words. 'For ever changed.'

There was a short silence, and then, unexpectedly, he asked, 'Do you like him, Lara?'

Lara stared straight ahead. 'Like' him? Like did not seem to be a verb that one would apply naturally to a man like Darian Wildman. It seemed much too bland an assessment. And how could she possibly be objective about a man who had been the most wonderful lover she had ever encountered and yet also the most unsatisfactory? But it had only been unsatisfactory from an emotional point of view, and she had only herself to blame. You should not fall headlong into the arms of a man if you could not cope with the fact that he might reject you.

For there had been no word from Darian—not since he had dropped her off at her apartment two nights ago and dropped a perfunctory kiss on her lips that had felt as cold as ice, as different from his hot-blooded kisses when he was making love to her as it was possible to imagine.

But he wasn't making love to you, said that same, cruel voice which had been tormenting her non-stop. *He was simply having sex with you.*

'I'll give you a ring,' he had said, but it had sounded casual, and she suspected that he had intended it to do so. He had waited until she was safely inside her front door and then driven off, his powerful car sounding like a fighter jet as it had roared away.

Lara had hoped—like a foolish holder-on to romantic dreams—that perhaps he might have rung her first thing the next morning, told her that it had been beautiful and that he wished he was waking up next to her. Except she suspected that both those things would have been a lie, and something deep down told her that Darian Wildman might be all kinds of things a woman should steer clear of, but dishonest was not one of them. He would speak the truth, she recognised painfully, no matter how much that truth might hurt.

'I hardly know him,' she answered now, and her own honesty had the power to hurt, too.

She still didn't quite believe that she had let him make love to her so quickly. Lara was no prude, but she worked in an industry which was notorious for its fickle sexual values, and up until now she had always fiercely guarded her reputation. Her lovers had been few, and not one of them had lived up to her unrealistically high expectations—until now. But there again never before had she allowed herself to be seduced with such ease, and then to experience such intense and unforgettable pleasure in the arms of a man she barely knew.

So what did that say about *her*? Maybe she was one of those people who could only be physically fulfilled if there was no true and lasting intimacy. Just like Darian, she recognised, with a sudden sinking sense of insight.

'Lara,' said Khalim urgently, 'I will have to meet him.'

'But how? And, more importantly, where?'

'Rose is pregnant,' Khalim said thoughtfully. 'And must not be worried. If Darian were brought out to Maraban—'

'Khalim,' Lara interrupted, completely forgetting that he was not used to being interrupted, 'I don't think you quite understand—he isn't the sort of man who could be brought anywhere, not unless he was in full agreement.' A bit like you, she wanted to add, except that it was glaringly obvious. 'And what are you going to do? Ring him up and mention that you might be related and would he please fly out to Maraban so that you can check him out?'

'Then I will have to come to London,' said Khalim slowly. 'And you must arrange for me to meet him, Lara.'

But how? thought Lara as she slowly put the receiver down.

Especially if she didn't hear from him.

Which was kind of defining her as a self-made victim, surely? She had been intimate with the man—didn't that give her the right to telephone him?

She knew that in situations like this there were subtle

games played between the sexes, and that the man always liked to feel as though he was the one doing the hunting, but wasn't she in danger of forgetting the bigger picture?

This wasn't about her and Darian and a relationship which seemed to have started and ended on his leather sofa—it was about his ancestry, and Khalim's. *She* had been the one to let her emotions get in the way, to fall for him, but none of that was relevant.

That was when she realised that she didn't have his home telephone number, nor even his mobile—which left his business. She was going to have to ring him up at work.

And what if…what if he didn't want to speak to her?

You cross that bridge when you come to it, she told herself, though her heart was beating frantically as she dialled the number and asked his assistant if he was free.

Another click.

'Darian Wildman.'

Her heart began to pound. 'Darian? It's Lara. Lara Black.'

Darian raised his eyebrows fractionally when he heard her voice. He had been thinking about her and deciding when to call her again. In fact, he had been thinking about her a lot. It had been a pretty amazing evening all round, but something about it had made him wary. And so had she.

It had all been too…too easy, in a way. That wasn't unusual, but it had not been what he had instinctively expected from Lara. Something about it had not seemed all it should be, and he couldn't put his finger on what it was. But it seemed that Lara Black was liberated and bold enough to ring *him*.

He gave a faint smile. 'Hello, Lara,' he said smoothly. 'How are you?'

'I'm…' I'm almost spitting with rage at such cavalier treatment after such an intimate evening, if you must know—but you won't know, because I would never give you the pleasure of telling you, and if it weren't for this whole Maraban business I wouldn't ever see or speak to you again, that's how I am.

That was what she *felt* like saying.

'I'm fine,' she murmured instead. She paused, hating the words she knew she must say next and giving him the opportunity to say them first. But he didn't. 'I was wondering whether I could see you.'

Frankly, he was surprised. She was far too lovely to be chasing after men. Yet he could hear some suppressed emotion in her voice and knew he wasn't being fair to her. Nor, he thought, with a sudden aching memory, to himself. 'That would be lovely.' He paused and his voice softened just as his body began to grow hard. 'I enjoyed our evening together very much.'

Lara felt indignant, filled with a sudden sense of impotence that she was having to put herself in the humiliating position of ringing *him*, seeming as if she was desperate to see him. And aren't you? mocked a voice inside her head. Aren't you?

She set her mouth into a determined line. No, she wasn't. She rated pride far more highly than desire, and this incident with Darian had taught her a salutary lesson. Never again would she allow herself to be carried away by the needs of her body, allow herself to believe that they were the clamourings of the heart.

But she had to see him. This wasn't just a boy-meets-girl scenario; it was a whole lot more. She had set into motion a chain of events, and now it had gathered momentum and taken on a life of its own. She had no part in all this now other than to set up a meeting between Darian and Khalim.

'Yes,' she said softly, closing her eyes and imagining that she was playing the part of a sophisticated woman of the world, used to dealing with the fallout from such casual, passionate dalliances. 'I enjoyed it, too.'

He pictured the soft rose-white skin and the sparkling blue eyes, the gentle swell of her breasts, and all his vague misgivings fell by the wayside as he experienced an overpowering urge to see her again. He felt the hot, hard physical jerk of desire.

'So when?' he asked huskily.

She opened her eyes and glanced down at what she had scribbled on a piece of paper. The times and the dates when Khalim could practically and realistically be in London in person. 'Next week?' she questioned. 'Say, Friday?'

Darian's eyes narrowed at her unexpected response. Friday? He hadn't imagined that she would be so upfront as to say tonight, or even tomorrow night—but next *week*?

The instincts of the hunter in him were aroused. 'You can't make it any sooner than that?'

She knew that she was playing this game well—too well, she thought bitterly—and that if she had suggested sooner then a bored note would have entered his arrogant voice.

'I'm afraid I can't,' she said regretfully.

'So where shall we meet?' he demanded.

'Would you like to come to the flat? Say, lunchtime?'

Lunchtime? Maybe she would be alone in the flat, with Jake Haddon away somewhere. A small smile of anticipation curved his lips as he flicked a glance at his diary and saw that he was busy. He scored through the appointments with a single stroke of his pen and added the words 'cancel them' for his secretary. 'Sure,' he said smoothly. 'That sounds okay. About noon?'

'Noon is fine.' Lara swallowed, suddenly feeling assailed by nerves. 'I'll see you then.'

The week passed by in a curious state where time seemed either to be suspended in a state of utter unreality or to pass in a flurry of high-level communication with Maraban. Lara had the letter itself flown out to Khalim, and he acknowledged it in a telephone call, his voice sounding cool and thoughtful.

She half imagined that a small contingent of his armed guard might accompany him, but when the Prince arrived on Friday, just before midday, he was alone. Lara opened the door to him and blinked in surprise.

'No guards?' she questioned softly, once he had greeted her and she had closed the front door.

Khalim gave a brief smile. 'My emissary and two others are waiting outside. They have orders not to disturb us.'

'Would you like tea?' Lara questioned shyly. 'Mint tea?'

Khalim smiled. 'You remembered!'

'How is Rose?' she demanded eagerly.

'Rose is complaining that she is the size of an elephant! And I have photos to show you of my son.' A frown crossed his dark face. 'She does not know that I am seeing you. For if she did she would ask questions for which I do not yet have any answers.'

'Oh,' said Lara.

It seemed all so incongruously suburban. Khalim sitting on her sofa, drinking tea and proudly showing her photos of his wife and son. He was wearing Western regalia—a beautifully cut Italian suit in charcoal-grey, snowy shirt and a silk tie the colour of an emerald—and he looked just as much as ease in it as he did in his flowing garments of soft gleaming gold.

Outwardly, he seemed relaxed, but Lara could see the faint lines which fanned out from the jet-dark eyes. She wondered if he was worried about problems at home or simply about meeting Darian—but it seemed impertinent to ask.

She found herself comparing him to the man she was certain was his half-brother. Darian was taller and broader, his skin not so dark as Khalim's, and his eyes were golden, not black, and yet there was an unmistakable similarity between the two men. You could see it in the firm and unblinking gaze, and in the almost tangible strength of character which emanated from them. What would happen when they met?

She shivered, and Khalim looked at her.

'You are nervous, Lara?'

'A little. Aren't you?'

He shook his head. 'In Maraban we have a saying: Life is like a narrow bridge—the most important thing is not to be afraid.'

'He's…he's the same age as you, you know.'

'And?'

'What if he's older? Won't that make him the legitimate heir?'

'But he is *illegitimate*, Lara,' Khalim reminded her gently. 'If indeed he *is* my brother.'

So he wasn't taking her word for it, realised Lara—but who could blame him when something so important was at stake?

The doorbell rang, and her eyes opened very wide. 'He's here! What shall I do? What shall I say?'

'Bring him to me,' commanded Khalim sternly. 'And do not worry, little one,' he said, his voice gentling a little.

Lara's heart was beating so fast that she could barely breathe as she walked to the front door. And when she opened it her feelings of apprehension only increased.

For Darian was standing there, looking impossibly gorgeous and so tantalisingly touchable. The breeze had ruffled his hair, so that all its gleaming darkness was emphasised, and the soft, dark cashmere sweater provided a perfect foil for the living gold of his eyes and the tawny glow of his skin. His lips were soft, and so were his eyes.

Without a word, he pulled her into his arms and stared down at her. Did he have some crazy, masochistic instinct which might have denied him such exquisite pleasures when they were here for the taking? She was beautiful.

The other night had been beautiful. He wanted her again and he wanted her right now.

'Lara,' he murmured.

She knew what he was about to do, and knew that she ought to stop him, but she was powerless to resist.

He drove his mouth down on hers, like a hungry man who had just seen food. The touch of her lips brought memories of her body crashing back into sweet, sharp focus and he gave a little moan of pleasure.

Instantly Lara felt herself responding to his kiss, her body beginning to ache and to dissolve into a hot, moist heat, and as he tightened his arms around her she could feel his taut, shivering tension which matched her own.

She splayed her fingers over his back, feeling the hard muscle contrasting with the softness of his sweater, and made a little sound of pleasure as his thigh nudged its way between hers. She felt her own thighs part instinctively, a hot flame of desire shooting up her as he ran his fingertips possessively down over her hips.

And Khalim was waiting next door!

She tore her lips away and opened her eyes to him, startled by the look of naked need on his face. 'Darian, we mustn't!'

He gave a low laugh of pleasure. 'Afraid that I'm going to take you here, standing up in your hallway?' He stroked her trembling mouth. 'You'd probably like it if I did. Come to think of it, so would I.' And then he frowned. 'What's the matter, darling—is Jake around?'

His words brought her quickly to her senses, for they were nothing more than an arrogant sexual boast. An acknowledgment of how easily and how quickly he could make her melt in his arms. And, dear Lord—he was right! If Khalim *hadn't* been here then she probably wouldn't have stopped him at all!

She reminded herself that if Khalim were not here, then he wouldn't be here, either.

She shook her head. 'No. Not Jake.'

How did she say it? She didn't want to anger him, because what was about to happen was going to affect him pretty deeply on some fundamental level, and she didn't know how he was going to react.

'I've got someone I want you to meet,' she whispered.

'Oh, Lara, no,' he groaned. 'Not now! What did you do that for?'

'Come with me.'

Aching, Darian had no choice but to follow her, but he was irritated. He didn't want to meet her friends—not at this stage, and certainly not now!

Lara threw the door open and Darian froze, his instincts immediately alerted to the fact that the man who stood beside the huge marble fireplace, his dark face so cool and expressionless, was no ordinary man. And it had nothing to do with the costly clothes he wore—for many men wore those.

No, it was something in his eyes and in his posture, something which transcended the mundane and the everyday—he wore an air of comfortable superiority, which silently sizzled out across the room and struck an answering chord in Darian himself.

Darian narrowed his eyes, knowing somehow that conventional conversation was both irrelevant and inappropriate. 'Who *are* you?' he demanded softly.

There was a silence which seemed to go on and on. Lara looked at Khalim and saw him give an odd, brittle kind of smile which was tinged with a sadness.

'I am Prince Khalim of Maraban,' he said slowly. 'And I believe that you are my brother.'

CHAPTER EIGHT

DARIAN kept his face poker-straight, not a flicker of emotion crossing his features. He had always been a past-master at keeping his feelings hidden. As a child he had learnt not to react, and it had stood him in good stead through his life.

He let his mind assimilate the incredible words that the man had just spoken, then gave a brief, dismissive smile.

'You are mistaken,' he said flatly. 'I have no brother. I have no living relatives at all. Explain yourself.'

Lara gasped, shocked—and so, judging by the look on Khalim's face, was he. She doubted whether he had ever been spoken to like that in his life—except perhaps by his wife, but that was different.

Khalim gave a small nod, as though an unasked question had just been answered, and gestured towards a chair. 'Should we perhaps sit down?'

Darian shook his head, and then slowly turned his head and looked at Lara. For the first time it dawned on him that this man was in *her* apartment. He glanced at the way she stood there, so wide-eyed and expectant and...yes, there was definitely an air of apprehension about her. What the hell was going on?

But Lara was a distraction. He concentrated instead on one overriding fact, and that was the claim which had just been made.

'I think I would prefer to stand.' He looked at this man Khalim, and a vague memory of something he had once heard on the news came drifting into his memory.

A country. Where had he said? Maraban? Yes. Maraban.

91

'You are the Sheikh of Maraban?' he questioned.

Khalim nodded. 'I am.'

'And why are you here?' asked Darian quietly.

'Because a letter arrived recently at my Embassy in London—a letter from a woman purporting to be your mother—'

'The woman's name?' snapped Darian.

'Joanna Wildman.'

Darian's eyes narrowed and he felt the sudden acceleration of his heart. 'That was my mother's name.' His voice sounded like grit being poured onto melting snow. 'Let me see the letter.'

It was a definite command, thought Lara, wondering how Khalim would react. But he simply nodded as he withdrew the letter from the breast pocket of his suit, almost as though he had been anticipating this request.

Darian's eyes scoured over it disbelievingly, but there was no doubt that the words were written in his mother's hand. 'She died two years ago,' he said slowly.

'Yes. As you will read, the letter was not intended to be opened during her lifetime.' Khalim's black eyes glittered. 'And, as you will also read, she claims that my late father, Makim, was indeed *your* father, too.'

His eyebrows were elevated in question, and the statement he had made was so utterly bizarre that Darian wondered if perhaps he was in the middle of one of those dreams which were so real that you mistook them for reality. Maybe in a minute he would wake up.

But even as he answered he was aware of the first glimmerings of unease. 'I know nothing of my father. Absolutely nothing.'

'No.' Khalim paused for a moment. 'Your mother was an air stewardess?'

'Up until I was born.' Darian's mouth twisted in derision. There had been no mention of her employment in the letter. 'You've had me checked out!' he accused softly.

Khalim nodded. 'But of course.' He paused. 'She flew to the Middle East regularly.'

And the missing piece of the jigsaw which had always eluded him began to hover tantalisingly over the gap in Darian's memory. His mother had spoken of his father maybe once, perhaps twice. He had been a good man, she had said, but a man who was not free and was certainly not in a position to support them. Darian had assumed that his father was married, had noted his mother's reluctance to talk about him and her distress whenever the subject was brought up.

Children soon learnt to make life easy for themselves. When to pry and when to leave well alone. He had accepted her reticence, just as he had accepted that he looked different from the other children. Darian had been focused on the future, on getting out of the poverty of his upbringing. Whoever his father had been he was not a real figure, not in terms of having any influence in his life, and so Darian had simply closed the door on all his questions.

There had been nothing about him in the papers his mother had left after her death, though at the time it had crossed his mind that now he was in a position to seek out his father without causing his mother distress. But Darian had decided to let sleeping dogs lie, asking himself what end it would serve if he went on such a quest—other than to unsettle him. Why pursue a man who had never felt the need to know his son?

But now the past had been dropped before his eyes, falling like a heavy pebble into a pond, its ripple-like effects spreading down through the ages—and for the first time a very important question *did* occur to him.

He turned again to look at Lara, where she stood as still

and as frozen as a statue. 'So what does Lara have to do with all this?'

She had been wondering when he would get around to asking. Lara spoke before Khalim had the chance to defend her. She would not shrink from the truth, not any more.

'I was the one who first read the letter,' she said quietly. 'I was working at the Embassy at the time and it came into my hands.'

'When?'

She heard the raw anger in that one stark word, and flinched. 'Almost a month ago.'

A different jigsaw now, and these pieces slotted into place with insulting ease. He looked directly into her blue eyes and gold accusation flooded over her in a hot, sizzling shower. 'You came looking for me,' he seethed slowly.

'Yes.'

'You chased the job as the face of Wildman.' His dark lashes shuttered by a fraction. 'Didn't you?'

'Yes.'

The lashes moved again, and now there was an odd expression in the strange and beautiful eyes, the cold, cruel smile which glittered over her. She knew what the next accusation would be almost before he had a chance to form the words, and her gaze begged him not to ask it—not here and now and in front of Khalim. But he ignored the silent plea, his voice taking on a bitter, hard timbre she had never heard before.

'Is that why you slept with me, Lara?'

Lara glanced at Khalim, who was observing and listening to the fraught interrogation session in interested silence. Only the faintest elevation of his eyebrows indicated that he had registered Darian's final damning question, but Lara knew that Marabanese men knew the value of silence. He would not interfere in something which did not concern him. She was on her own here.

'I don't think that now is an appropriate time to discuss this—'

'Oh, *don't* you?' His sarcastic words sliced through her half-formed sentence like a knife through butter. 'I don't really think that you're fit to be the judge of what is or is not *appropriate*, Lara!'

He remembered the way her vulnerable blue eyes had made him soften and melt, and then made love to her in a way which had blown his mind, and he cursed silently at his blind stupidity. Of *course* she would be adept at pulling heartstrings—she would know every trick in the book, about how to behave and how to manipulate. She was a god damned *actress*, wasn't she?

He sucked in a deep breath. His rage and his retribution with her could wait. He turned his head towards Khalim again.

'So why are you here?'

'To see you,' said Khalim simply. 'To see whether it was true.'

'But you can't, can you?' drawled Darian. 'You can't tell just by looking?'

'Oh, yes, I can,' demurred Khalim quietly. 'I saw it as soon as you entered the room today. You have the blood of a true Marabanesh running in your veins.'

Something in the way he said it made a small shiver of something unknown snake its way down Darian's spine. Not fear—no, he had never felt fear, nor would he ever give in to the false and futile pressure of fear. Something else—something which momentarily made him feel as if things were edging out of his control. But he deliberately blocked the feeling, substituting it instead with the strength and single-mindedness for which he was known.

'Even if I have—so what?' he challenged, in a low, deep voice. 'It doesn't change my life—how can it? So do not worry, Sheikh—the secret will remain just that. You can go back to your kingdom safe in the knowledge that my life is fulfilled and complete. I have no need of your wealth or power and I will make no claim on it. I give you my word.'

Khalim's eyes narrowed into icy black shards. 'You have no wish to see Maraban?' he demanded, as if Darian had raised a fist and hit him.

Again that tantalising feeling. As if some scarcely heard and hypnotic music were luring him to run away and dance. Darian shook his head, furious with himself for such a bizarre flight of fancy.

'You must come as my guest,' continued Khalim.

The two men stared at one another.

'Why?' demanded Darian simply.

Lara thought again how peculiar it was to have Khalim spoken to like that, and for him to accept it.

'I should like to get to know you better,' answered Khalim. 'Man of my blood.'

If Darian had heard a statement like that even an hour ago he would have given a sardonic laugh. It was not the kind of thing men said to one another—not in his world. But something had inexplicably changed. This whole crazy and bizarre situation was linked to a past of which he knew nothing, and it was that fact which troubled him.

His past.

But the past held no interest for him, he reminded himself. Life lay with the present and the future. His life was here, and it was good.

He shook his head. 'No. I can't see the point.'

Khalim smiled then. 'Can't you?' he questioned softly. 'Can you just let me walk away today, Darian, and turn your back on the opportunity I am offering you? To discover Maraban and in so doing perhaps discover a little of yourself?'

It was a tantalising proposition, and Darian felt the hard,

pounding beat of excitement. He was not into the 'self-discovery' so popular in the modern world. He considered such things an indulgent waste of time. And yet...

Would he be left with a whispering feeling of regret if he turned this opportunity down? He turned his head slowly to look once again at Lara. Her face was pale now, all the roses fled. All he could see were the twin sapphires of her eyes, sparkling blue but wary, almost afraid.

And afraid you should be, he thought grimly.

His lips curved into another slow, cruel smile as a plan began to form in his head, and he nodded. 'Very well,' he said slowly. 'I will accompany you to Maraban—but on one condition.'

There was silence. And when Khalim spoke it was as soft as the hiss of a snake. 'You dare to stipulate a condition?' he demanded. 'Of *me*?'

'If I am your brother—or half-brother,' retorted Darian, 'then some kind of equality must exist. I am neither your subject nor your inferior—am I, Khalim?'

'No,' answered Khalim, and a reluctant smile nudged at his lips as he looked at the man with the golden eyes and the tawny skin. 'Then name your condition, and if it is within my power it shall be met.'

Darian savoured the moment as his eyes captured hers and held them, hard. 'I want Lara to accompany me.'

Khalim nodded, as if he understood perfectly, and turned also to look at her, a silent question stilling the dark features.

Lara's heart pounded with something very like fear. She loved Maraban, and in any other circumstances she would have been overjoyed to be given the opportunity to go there again. But these circumstances were different. She knew without being told that Darian Wildman was not asking her to go with him because he still thought that she was 'sweet' or because he enjoyed her company so much he couldn't bear to be without it.

No, the sudden hardness which had made the golden eyes look so cold filled her with a foreboding that made her skin grow chill, and in that moment she wished she could just close her eyes and be a million miles away from here, and then return to find that none of it had ever happened...

But it had happened.

And didn't she owe it to him—in some strange kind of way—for the way that she had deceived him? And to Khalim, too—who had been so generous to her in the past?

If Darian visiting Maraban was all down to whether or not she would go with him, then how could she possibly refuse?

Her skin felt icy-cold as she nodded, lowering her lashes so that she didn't have to meet that mocking gold stare. 'If that is what you want, then I will comply.' Comply! She sounded like some little subordinate now! Lifting her chin, she turned to Khalim, trying to keep her voice steady. 'Wh—when did you anticipate us leaving?'

Khalim smiled. 'My jet is on the runway. We will leave for Maraban just as soon as you have both packed sufficient for your needs.'

CHAPTER NINE

DARIAN sat back against the leather seat of the car as it silently and powerfully sped towards the airfield, his mind spinning with thoughts which seemed just too incredible to be true.

Beside him sat Khalim, and in the front, next to the driver, a burly man whose bulk made his position as bodyguard to the Sheikh unmistakable.

Lara had elected to travel in the second car, hastily reassuring Khalim that she would be happy to do so. I bet she is, thought Darian grimly. Deceiving and conniving little Mata Hari! He had read of women who used their sexuality to try to get close to a man, to sensuously make them let their guard down before blowing their lives into smithereens, but he had foolishly imagined that kind of woman to have no place in the contemporary world.

How very wrong he had been!

He felt the jab of fury combined with the hot thrust of lust, but he steadfastly put all thoughts of Miss Lara Black out of his mind. She wasn't going anywhere—or at least nowhere that he wasn't going—and he would deal with her when the time was right. For now, his head was too full of thoughts which sounded more like the plot for some fantastic story. But facts were facts—however incredible—and this was no story, it was his life.

He was going to Maraban! To a mountain kingdom to which, it seemed, he was linked by birth. And through all his anger and confusion he felt the stir of something within him, some soft blaze of an emotion he did not recognise.

He turned to look at Khalim, who had been sitting si-

lently at his side, managing to be both alert and yet relaxed—as though there was little in this world which surprised him, and maybe there wasn't. For wouldn't life as
ruler of a country such as Maraban present all kinds of
dilemmas and problems which a normal man would never
encounter in his lifetime?

'You don't seem angry,' observed Darian quietly.

Khalim turned to him, a wry look on his dark and shadowed face. 'Why would I waste my time being angry about
what exists?' he murmured. 'That would be like being angry because it was raining, or because…' He seemed to
search for some analogy which the Western man would
understand. 'Because the horse you had placed your last
dollar on had broken its leg before the big race!'

For the first time Darian smiled. 'I am not a betting
man.'

'No? You do not gamble on luck and on fortune?'

'I don't gamble on anything.' And it was true. Gambling
was precarious, and Darian had spent his life avoiding the
precarious. He made things certain wherever it was possible, and for that you needed something far more tangible
than luck. Simple, really. If you worked hard and used all
your brains and initiative and imagination then you would
reap the benefit of that.

Yet Khalim possessed untold, almost unimaginable
wealth, Darian acknowledged as he glanced around the car.
This vehicle was bullet-proofed, he recognised, and mod-
ified for the man it carried—as different from even a rich
man's car as cheap plonk was from vintage champagne.

'We're here,' said Khalim shortly, as the car pulled into
the airfield, and Darian saw a gleaming jet sitting there,
the tiny emblem of a small flag on its tail golden and rose-
pink and a deep sapphire-blue. Blue, like her eyes, he
thought bitterly. Like her lying and cheating eyes.

Lara stepped out of the other car, seeing the two tall,

dark figures emerge. Already she felt an outsider—she, who had known Khalim for years now, felt peculiarly isolated as she saw the two men standing together. As if they belonged and she didn't. Or was that just her imagination working overtime, as usual?

But then Darian turned to look at her, and she felt her heart sink. How could such a warm and rich and vibrant colour as gold be transmuted into something so cold and threatening? But gold *was* like that, she reminded herself. The colour was warm, but the metal itself was cold—and since time had begun men had died in the pursuit of the costly and elusive treasure.

She shivered, hugging her coat tightly around her, though she knew that the garment would be redundant once they were in the soft, scented heat of Maraban.

As she stared back at Darian, a wave of longing and regret washed over her. Except that she had nothing to regret, did she? Not really—for the man she yearned for was nothing more than an idealised figment of her imagination. True, he had been passion personified...until afterwards... Remember *that*, she told herself fiercely. Afterwards he had been as cold as the gold of his eyes.

She had lost nothing because there had been nothing between them to lose, other than a brief and beautiful encounter on his leather sofa. A man who respected you and had feelings for you did not take you straight home after such an encounter and then not bother ringing you!

Darian was smiling at her now, but it didn't seem like a smile at all—more like a grim declaration of intent to pay her back for what he undoubtedly saw as her deceit and betrayal.

And Lara had a pretty good idea of how he was intending to extract that payment.

Well, tough, she thought, with a defiant return of some of her fighting spirit. If you think you're going to repeat that physically satisfying but ultimately soulless encounter, then you can think again, Mr Half-Brother-to-the-Sheikh.

So why was it that her stupid heart ached with sadness for what might have been?

Yet the reminder of his cavalier behaviour made her feel better in some perverse kind of way, and she even managed to flash a friendly smile at him as they made their way up the wind-buffeted steps to the aeroplane, only to be met with a tight-lipped glower in return.

The flight was long, but supremely comfortable, and Lara unexpectedly found her eyelashes fluttering to a close. Oh, thank heavens, she thought muzzily as she drifted off to sleep. The last thing she could have endured was Darian's simmering disapproval for six hours!

Darian watched her, saw the way her breasts rose and fell, outlined by the soft pink silk dress that she had changed into. She had been wearing jeans and a tee-shirt, but once the decision to fly to Maraban had been made she had opted for flowing, flattering, more feminine clothes—and she seemed to look at home in them, even here on the aircraft.

He glanced around him. He had flown by private jet a couple of times in his life, but nothing to match this; this aircraft was a curious mixture of the very modern and the very old.

Inside the state-of-the-art plane there were lavish silken cushions to recline on, and mint tea and and sparkling water flavoured subtly with oranges was brought to them by two very beautiful stewardesses who were unmistakably Western.

Khalim waved his hand towards the proffered tray. 'You would prefer whisky, perhaps? Or wine? My culture forbids the use of alcohol, but you are my guest and you must choose what you will.'

Darian shook his head. 'No, thanks. I never drink when I'm flying, and I've made it a rule always to follow the customs of wherever I happen to be.'

'When in Rome?' Khalim laughed softly.

Darian laughed back. 'Or when in Maraban, in this case!'

The joke broke some of the tension and an air of ease settled down between the two men.

The blonde stewardess offered Darian a small dish of pistachio nuts.

'Thanks,' he murmured as he took a couple, automatically registering the sideways glance she gave him, and the way that her uniform clung to her tight and luscious curves.

As she wiggled her way out of the cabin Khalim turned to him. 'She is very beautiful, yes?'

'Very.'

'Her name is Anastasia. You would like to meet her later? When we land?'

Angrily, Darian crushed the empty shells between his fingers. 'You offer women to your guests as you would a dish of nuts?' he demanded. 'Is that another of your customs?' His voice lowered to a hiss. 'Is that what your father did to my mother?'

Khalim appeared unperturbed by his reaction. 'I can assure you that Anastasia has a mind of her own, and would never deign to be offered as you would a bowl of nuts. But she is young and healthy and beautiful—is there such a crime in introducing a woman like that to a man like you? She is a strong woman.' He paused. 'Was your mother not similarly strong?'

Darian nodded. It was not his way to discuss such matters, but this was an extraordinary situation, and for some reason he found himself answering Khalim, wondering if he had been deliberately provoked by him into doing so.

'Yes, she was strong,' he said. 'Necessity made it so.' Hard and proud and strong. Her remarkable beauty had made men flock to her, like moths to a flame, but she had rebuffed them almost coldly, as though she would never again allow herself to fall for a man.

But how deeply had she fallen for Khalim's father? Had it simply been a one-off? A brief passion with unexpected and unwanted consequences? And even if there was any way of ever discovering the truth did he really want to know—or was it better to let things lie?

His golden eyes grew flinty as he gazed into the unfathomable stare of the man who it seemed was his relative, the only person connected by blood to him in the whole world.

'So was that just some kind of crude test?' he questioned softly. 'To set me up with the stewardess? Or merely an attempt on your part to get me to talk about my mother?'

Khalim shook his head, and now his expression looked pained. 'Never a crude test, Darian,' he said sincerely. 'Though perhaps subconsciously I did wish you to speak of your mother. But my primary motive was altogether more straightforward than that. I know the appetites of men, and by your lack of interest it would appear that your appetite has already been satisfied.' He flickered a glance over at the sleeping Lara. 'By Lara,' he said softly.

Darian saw the direction of his gaze and again experienced that potent cocktail of rage and lust. He knew what Khalim wanted to know. Lara was his friend, and he would automatically wish to protect her. But it was none of Khalim's damned business what went on between him and Lara! He would give him the bare facts, nothing more. 'Yes, by Lara,' he said shortly, hastily averting his eyes from her moving silk-covered breasts.

'You are lovers,' Khalim observed.

'Yes.'

'And it is serious?'

'She lied to me,' answered Darian stonily.

'She lied because she was trying to protect me.'

But in so doing she had betrayed him. Surely Khalim could see that? 'Perhaps.'

'You didn't answer my question,' persisted Khalim softly. 'I asked you whether it was serious.'

Darian gave a lazy non-committal smile. 'I don't do *serious*,' he said truthfully.

Through the light mists of her snatched cat-nap, Darian's words came drifting into her subconscious, and as she allowed them to register Lara was filled with a sick, cold feeling. Had he said that deliberately—hoping that she would hear, and hear very clearly in just which category he had placed her? And wasn't it better to know, to hear the truth that she had instinctively guessed at spoken out loud?

She pretended to sleep, but in reality she was listening to their conversation. Darian did not come out with any more comments like the preceding one. Instead, he asked Khalim questions about Maraban, and Khalim began describing the history and the culture of his people, his rich voice softening with innate pride. Now and then Darian prompted him with an insightful question, and once he made Khalim laugh. Lara didn't know why this should surprise her so much, but it did.

Until she reminded herself that Khalim was intimate with few; his position as leader isolated him from confidences and shared jokes.

After a while she made a great show of stirring, and when she opened her eyes it was to find that unforgiving gold stare trained on her. She found herself in the infuriating position of half wanting to go over and slap him and half wanting him to come over and kiss her.

Just reaction, she told herself. He could not be faulted

as a lover, and her body was simply reminding her of that—it didn't mean she had to act on it. She yawned, and the two men turned towards her, but all Lara could see was that burning golden gaze.

Khalim smiled. 'You are rested now, Lara?'

'Thank you. Yes.'

'You will have some refreshment? You have eaten nothing.'

Lara shook her head. 'Thank you, Khalim, but, no. I am not hungry.' She glanced down at her watch. Not long to go now. 'When do we land at Dar-gar?'

Khalim hesitated. 'We are not going to Dar-gar.'

Lara frowned. 'Oh?'

'I am flying us to the western province instead,' he said smoothly. 'To Suhayb.' He saw her look of consternation and his voice softened. 'Rose is pregnant, as you know,' he explained gently. 'And such an unresolved development as this would merely trouble her. I am needed in Suhayb, and it is as good a place as any in Maraban for Darian to see a little of how we live.'

Lara nodded. She had heard of Suhayb, of course, which was Maraban's second city. Rose often wrote long and chatty letters about the country so that Lara felt she knew it well. She was aware that a second palace was sited there, and that the region was fringed by beautiful mountains from which crystal streams flowed to bring life to the parched earth.

'Sounds wonderful,' she said.

As if this was some kind of damned holiday she had booked, thought Darian furiously—until he was forced to remember that she was here solely at his behest! But then the engines of the plane changed sound, giving the signal that they were about to land, and he leaned over to look out of the window, his heart beating with an odd kind of excitement as he stared down into Maraban.

Beneath he could see mountains, snow-capped and gleaming in the late-afternoon sun, so that they looked as if they were lit from within by a copper-red flame. As the plane descended he could see the silver glint of water. His first impression was a land of light and fire. It looked, he thought, like a picture from a child's book.

A child's book. Like the kind he had chosen to escape into, to blot out some of the harsh reality of his upbringing. His mouth hardened as the plane touched down. How different his life would have been if his father had stood by his mother!

Lara stood up and saw his face, and suddenly and inexplicably she felt nervous.

'The cars are waiting on the runway,' said Khalim. 'They will drive us to the palace.'

CHAPTER TEN

THE palace at Suhayb stood in an oasis of green as verdant and as manicured as the garden of a large English country house. Bright flowers, mainly roses, mingled in riotous and scented glory, and in the centre of a large square space of water a fountain sprinkled, catching the light in rainbow rays, the sound soft and soothing against the occasional cry of some unseen and unknown bird.

The palace itself was fashioned from mosaic in every shade of blue imaginable—from pale sky to deep ocean and a hundred shades in between—and Darian was reminded with an unwelcome pang of how the blueness of Lara's eyes had impressed itself on him the very first time he had seen her.

Damn! He didn't want to remember that—he didn't want to remember anything other than the way she had deceived him.

But as Lara gazed in wonder at the palace all she saw was the gold, which picked out the varying shades of blue, as deep and as rich a gold as the eyes of the man who walked slightly ahead of her beside Khalim, their voices speaking in a low tone, so that she didn't have a clue what they were saying.

Khalim turned, the dying embers of the sun beating down on his head, and Darian turned also, in a disturbing mirror image of the Sheikh. Despite the cool linen trousers he wore, and the fine shirt which hinted at the lean, muscular torso beneath, he looked...

Lara swallowed.

He looked as if he *belonged* here—and she didn't, she

thought, with a slight touch of hysteria. But wasn't that what he was intending her to feel? With that stern and icy demeanour and the cold look of distaste? Didn't he want to make her feel an outsider? To marginalise and isolate her? And you would not need to be a genius to work out why he should wish to do that...

A veiled female servant stepped silently out from the shadows of the magnificent entrance hall and Khalim smiled.

'Latifah will show you to your room, Lara,' he said. 'And Darian will accompany me. You will find there all you need, and later someone will come to collect you for dinner. Is that to your satisfaction?'

What could she say? That she felt as though she was being edged aside, cast in a secondary role by these two powerful blood-brothers? And wasn't it ever thus in Maraban? The men ruled and dominated—certainly in the external world, outside their homes.

Rose at least had the protection of being married, surrounded by the invisible aura which was part and parcel of being loved so fiercely by the Sheikh.

But what was Lara? A second-class citizen who could not even draw comfort from speaking to her friend, pregnant and far away in the capital of Dar-gar. Commanded here by Darian and not knowing his motives—though having a pretty good idea, she thought, with a sudden leap of her heart.

She smiled at Khalim, determined that neither man should see her spirits flagging. She was tired; that was all.

'That sounds perfect,' she said softly. 'I will see you later at dinner.' And she inclined her head very slightly towards the Sheikh.

Latifah led the way through a maze of dark, cool corridors, and when they reached her room she asked Lara in shy, faltering English whether she would like a bath drawn.

But Lara, still reeling slightly from the impact of the lavish suite which she had been shown into, shook her head and smiled.

'I can manage,' she said. 'Honestly, I'm used to doing that kind of thing for myself,' she added gently, as the girl began to protest.

Once she was alone she looked around her—at the arched high ceiling, inlaid with gold, and the leather-bound books which completely lined one wall, beneath which stood an antique and very beautiful writing desk.

It was incredible—like being on the film-set of some lavish epic. The suite was all heavily embroidered drapes and hangings in the richest and most royal of colours. Gold and scarlet, cobalt and jade. The room was thick with the scent of roses which drifted from a copper bowl—all creamy-white and edged with apricot—and Lara touched one of the velvety petals, a shiver running up her spine as she did so.

What was it about this place that seemed to make the senses come to life in a way they never quite did back in England? The room looked so stunningly opulent, and the roses seemed more fragrant than any she had ever smelt before. Through the half-open shutters a warm breeze ruffled her hair like the fingers of a lover, and she closed her eyes, trying to put it all into perspective.

Was it just that Maraban was a world away from her normal life? A world free from pollution and care and worries? At least, it certainly was here—in this isolated and splendid palace.

But there were worries waiting to rear their heads, and the main one was Darian, who had scarcely spoken a word to her since they had left London. All she had been aware of whenever she looked at him was a sensual, smouldering intent that excited her even as it terrified her.

But she ran herself a bath, determined not to fall into

the trap of thinking that just because they were here—and just because of the discovery of his royal blood—he was in some way her superior. He was not. He was her equal, no matter what.

Actually, the bath was more like a mini-swimming pool, she realised with a small sigh of pleasure as she lowered her body into the warm, sudsy water and sniffed at the steamy fragrance of patchouli and sandalwood which filled the air.

Aware that she was indeed very tired, she did not dare soak for too long for fear that she might fall asleep, but she washed her hair, noting that all the luxury beauty products were exclusively French and that it felt like sheer indulgence to use them. It was like being in the most gorgeous hotel, only better.

She had just wrapped herself in a thick towelling robe, and was rubbing at the damp tendrils of her curls, when she heard the sound of a door opening and then closing again. She frowned, standing dead still and thinking that she must have imagined it.

But she had not imagined it. She felt the unmistakable sense of a presence in the adjoining room, and her heart began to pound strong and loud and fast.

She would not run away. She would confront her fear—except that it was not strictly accurate to define it as fear. Not when she knew almost certainly the identity of the person who was moving around. And there was no way she was ever going to be frightened of *him*.

She walked into the bedroom and there, leaning against the shuttered window, his thumbs looped arrogantly in the belt of his trousers, as if he had every right to be there, in *her* room, was Darian.

Lara opened her mouth to speak, and never had speaking seemed such an effort. 'What the hell are you doing in here?'

He gave a smile, the kind of smile which a cobra would probably give if it could, just before it devoured a small animal—whole.

'I'm just waiting for your towel to fall,' he drawled, running his eyes over her with a look of smoky anticipation. 'To see you in all your pink and white nakedness, with little droplets of water still clinging to your soft skin. I would lick them off with my tongue. Every one,' he finished on a murmur, and his tongue snaked out as if to illustrate his words—if any illustration was needed.

Lara tried to look outraged, but the reality was that her body was betraying her sense of shock and debilitating sensual awareness as she imagined him doing just that. Beneath the towel she felt the prickling of her nipples, budding and pointing almost painfully in response to his words. Even worse was the honeyed rush right at the very cradle of her, and she found herself squeezing her thighs together—the way you were taught to in an exercise class. But, oh, what a long way away the gym seemed right at this moment!

'Get out,' she whispered.

He laughed, but it was a cruel, cold laugh.

'You don't want me to go anywhere, you lying little bitch,' he taunted.

She recoiled from his harsh words as if he had struck her. 'Yes, I do.'

'Oh, no.' His voice became a caress of silk and of velvet. 'You want me. You want me to touch you.'

'You're mad!'

He nodded. 'Quite probably,' he mused. 'I must have been mad to have wondered why you were so deliciously compliant on our so-called ''date''. I may have had a moderate degree of success with women, but they usually require a little more wooing than one course at an inexpensive restaurant and a short massage around the shoulderblades.'

It was as insulting as it could possibly be, but that was what he wanted. He wanted her to react. And she wouldn't.

'You were the one who invited *me* out—remember?'

'True.'

He removed one hand from where it had been poised over his belt, like some gun-slinger, and rubbed thoughtfully at the darkening shadow which emphasised the masculine jut of his jaw. As macho gestures went, he really couldn't have bettered it, thought Lara weakly.

'But you played the siren, didn't you, Lara? That supersmart confidence at the casting. The way you spoke to me as if you didn't care.' He nodded, as if he had been shown a glimpse into the workings of a criminal mind. 'Very clever. Did someone once tell you that what powerful men crave more than anything is for someone to speak to them as if they aren't? To treat them just like everyone else?'

Lara gave a low laugh. 'I wish I had a tape recorder,' she vowed fervently. 'Then I could play this back to you in the morning—I think that even you might be appalled at your own arrogance and conceit.'

He raised his eyebrows in a mocking challenge. 'It would make for a very interesting morning,' he agreed laconically. 'But, there again, it's going to be an interesting morning anyway—isn't it?'

It took a moment or two for his meaning to sink in, and when it did Lara underwent an uncomfortable sensation of shock coupled with excitement, which made her want to squirm—except she didn't dare to, for fear that he would misinterpret it. Or—even worse—interpret it correctly.

'I hope you aren't suggesting that you're spending the night here? With me!'

'Of course not.'

Lara frowned, feeling like a mouse being teased by a very clever cat. 'You're…not?'

'I'm not suggesting anything, Lara. Just stating a fact. Of course I'll be here in the morning—we're sharing a room.'

It was like that feeling you got when you'd eaten three chocolate biscuits and knew that you were going to eat a fourth, even though you shouldn't.

Lara didn't *want* Darian Wildman anywhere near her. She didn't.

Okay, she did.

But that was on some stupid fundamental level. That was a Lara who didn't exist, wanting to be with a Darian who didn't exist. If only they could be standing here, a man and a woman who had just met…but that was crazy.

If they had only just met then they most definitely *wouldn't* be standing here—and neither would she be wearing just a towel covering her nakedness. A nakedness she was pretty sure he was responding to, judging from that dark, seductive look in his eyes, as if he were running those long, experienced fingers over every single crevice of her body. And yet the contrast between that hot look of desire and the cold contempt which rang from his voice was almost unbearable.

'Darian,' she breathed. 'We…we can't!'

'Can't what?' he enquired unhelpfully.

'We can't share a room together—you know we can't!'

'Afraid that you won't be able to resist me?' he questioned insultingly.

Yes! 'No! I will not stay here—not with you!'

'But our host has allotted us this room,' he ground out. 'We cannot question the Sheikh or his judgement.'

'Oh, really?' she demanded furiously. 'He just *happened* to put us in here together, did he? Without any pressure from you?'

'No pressure from me, I can assure you.' He gave a slow smile, pleased to see her give an instinctive little wriggle of frustration, knowing that her body craved him even while her mind fought him. 'He simply asked whether or not we were lovers, and I told him that yes, we were. So here we are,' he finished, on a murmur which somehow managed to sound like a sultry threat.

'We are *not* lovers!' she declared.

'Want to do something about that?' he drawled, and began to unbutton his shirt.

'Darian, stop it!'

'Stop what?'

'Un…' The shirt fluttered to the floor and Lara watched it in fascinated horror, lifting her eyes only to be confronted by the infinitely more disturbing vision of Darian's bare chest—the tawny flesh gleaming enticingly. 'Undressing!' she managed to get out.

'But I have to undress,' he said seriously. 'I'm going to take a shower.'

His belt was unclipped and she heard the rasping of a zip. She closed her eyes in horror.

'I refuse to share a room with you!'

'Then go and tell Khalim that yourself!'

The silky challenge made her open her eyes again, and she wished she hadn't—because he was completely naked. And completely at ease with it.

Lara went hot. Then cold.

'Are you trying to torment me?' she gasped.

He frosted her with an icy smile. 'That's about the most honest thing you've said so far,' he clipped out. 'But then, honesty isn't really your forte, is it, Lara?'

She wanted to appeal to his better judgement. But how could she appeal to anything when now he wasn't just naked, but was showing unmistakable signs of…

She turned her back, biting her teeth down into the flesh

of her bottom lip, hearing his low laugh with something approaching despair as he walked towards the bathroom and slammed the door behind him.

Lara had never dressed more quickly in her life. Whipping through the few outfits she had brought for herself, she slithered into a dress she had bought on a modelling assignment in Singapore. It was a long, fitted dress in bright scarlet silk piped with black—high-necked and skimming her body to fall demurely to her ankles. She controlled the most wayward of her curls with tiny jet-covered clips, applied mascara and lipstick with a trembling hand, and then went over to the bookcase which stood in one corner of the large room, determined to have something to occupy her. Anything to keep her mind and her eyes off the impending and disturbing prospect of Darian emerging from the bathroom...

But it was difficult to concentrate on the book—a beautifully photographed history of Maraban—which would normally have fascinated her. She could hear the splash, splash of the shower, and the sound of Darian singing, loudly and rather tunelessly—as if he hadn't a care in the world.

He seemed to have settled in and coped with his momentous news with amazing ease, she thought, her eyes nearly popping out of her head as she studied a photo of Khalim and Rose's wedding—and her *own* unmistakable profile as she bent to adjust Rose's train!

Darian switched off the powerful jet of water and stepped out of the shower, shaking his dark head slightly as he began to rub the droplets of water away. This felt like a dream from which he would in a minute wake—and he wasn't sure he wanted to.

The emotions he had felt when confronted with what seemed like the uncontradictable truth of his heritage had been varied. There had been confusion, yes—and yet a strange sense of calm, as though the answer to a question he had never dared to ask had finally been given.

Didn't this news of his father's identity make a whole lot about himself clearer and more understandable? That sense of being *different*, of being an outsider, had always burned much stronger in him than in any of the other fatherless boys he had grown up with. It hadn't just been the strange and exotic colour of his skin and the unusual gold of his eyes; it had gone far deeper than that.

Even as a child Darian had always been a loner. He had kept his emotions and his affections severely contained and restrained. So had that been something he'd been born with, or something he had learned along the way?

He had not grown up in an environment where you got close to people, and this was a habit he had carried with him into his adult life. In a way it had made his success more achievable—if you didn't carry around the baggage of close relationships then you had a lot less to distract you from your ambition.

He reflected on the bizarre events of the day, thinking that Khalim, too, had been a surprise—in more than one sense. From making the discovery that he was related to the dark, powerful and enigmatic leader it had proved a disturbingly short step to discovering that he might actually like him—maybe even form some kind of tenuous bond with him.

He didn't know what the outcome of this strange and totally unexpected visit to Maraban would be, and for once in his life it didn't bother him. Usually Darian liked everything mapped out, to know where he was going and what he was doing, but suddenly he recognised that sometimes you just had to go with the flow.

In fact, the only shadow on the current landscape took

the form of the woman he could hear moving around in the adjoining room. His mouth twisted with a mixture of contempt and desire.

What could have been a straightforward—if highly unusual—state of affairs had been complicated and made distasteful by the behaviour of Lara Black.

He felt the slow, steady pulsing of his heart, wondering why it should bother him—why he couldn't just dismiss the thought of her. Heaven knew, he usually managed that just fine. But she was like an itch. Something niggling away at him, stinging at his skin and making him feel aware of her in a way he didn't want to be. He needed to get her completely out of his system, he decided grimly, and there was one surefire way to do that.

But this time Lara would fight him all the way, he recognised, and somehow that sharpened his senses even more. He gave a slow smile of anticipation as he wrapped a towel around his narrow hips and sauntered back into the bedroom.

She was lost in the book she had been reading, but at the sound of his footfall she automatically looked up and her mouth dried. 'Oh, I see you've bothered to put something on,' she observed caustically, even though her heart was thudding away like a piston.

His fingers hovered provocatively over the knot of the towel at his hip and he raised his eyebrows mockingly. 'Is that disapproval I hear in your voice, Lara? You'd prefer me to lose it, would you?'

She swallowed down the infuriating desire to say yes. 'I'll just carry on reading my book while you get dressed,' she said, then glanced at her watch. 'Better hurry up,' she added sweetly. 'Khalim is not a man who should be kept waiting.'

She saw him shrug and then stared unseeingly at the words on the page, listening while he pulled on his clothes, not saying a word. The silence seemed to grow until it became huge and unwelcome. And suddenly all Lara's doubts and fears and uncertainties began to nag at her. She was angry at him for all kinds of complex reasons, but deep down she feared that her main motive was self-seeking. Wasn't she angry because he had shown a decided lack of interest in her as a person—because she had started to fall for him in a big way and he clearly hadn't reciprocated her feelings? And wasn't that a rather shameful reason for helping to maintain this sizzling undercurrent of tension between them? What good was that going to do any of them?

Maybe it was up to her to try and make peace.

She waited until he had slipped his shoes on, and then looked up to see him running his fingers through still-damp hair.

'Darian?' she said quietly.

The look he gave her was deliberately impartial—but then he wasn't foolish enough to get himself worked up into a state of sexual desire just before dinner, not when there wasn't enough time to see it through to its ultimate conclusion. 'Yes, Lara?'

She closed the pages of the book and put her fingertips on the soft leather which bound it. 'I'm sorry that I deceived you.'

'Sorry that you deceived me?' he questioned tonelessly. 'Or just sorry that I found out?'

'But it was inevitable that you would find out!' she argued. 'You must understand why I wanted to get to know you before I decided what action to take about the letter— why, you could have been any kind of maniac, for all I knew!'

'As opposed to a red-hot stud, you mean?'

'You flatter yourself, Darian.'

Their eyes met, his gaze boring into her until her cheeks

began to burn. 'Oh, I don't think so,' he said softly. 'You may be an actress, Lara, and a very good one at that—but I know enough about women to realise that you weren't faking it.'

She slapped her palms to her hot cheeks. 'Don't!'

'Don't speak the truth? No, I can see that might bother someone with your morals.'

This was just getting worse instead of better. She drew a deep breath, hoping to appeal to his sense of reason—to something...anything that would make him stop looking at her with that reluctant desire which made her feel so small.

'Surely you can understand why I didn't mention anything to you, Darian? At least not until I'd spoken to Khalim? I've known him and Rose for a long time—I didn't know you at all!'

'But you sure knew me better after dinner, didn't you?' He gave a low and insulting laugh. 'Did you want to make sure that the brother to the Sheikh fulfilled *all* the criteria for being a man?'

Her temper snapped. 'Now you are wilfully twisting everything I say! I had no intention of letting you make love to me that night. It just...it just...happened,' she finished lamely.

'Does it happen a lot for you that way?' he enquired, with the sardonic air of someone asking an unnecessary question.

'Never!' she retorted. 'I told you that at the time!'

'So it *was* just me,' he mused. 'In which case—I *should* be flattered.' He lowered his voice to a sultry promise. 'It was pretty good for me, too, Lara, if you really want to know—which makes me wonder why you're being so unnecessarily prim. After all, if you had sex with me when we barely knew each other, then I should have thought you would be eager to repeat the experience now that we're so much better acquainted.' He smiled as he let his gaze travel to the huge brocade-covered bed. 'It seems a bit of a waste of a good opportunity otherwise, don't you think?'

He couldn't have made it sound more mechanical if he had tried—a man and a woman who were fiercely attracted to one another—simply making use of the facilities on offer! But while Darian might have a heart of stone Lara was simply not made that way.

She opened her mouth to tell him that he was the last person on the planet she would ever get intimate with after what he had said to her, but at that precise moment there was a light rap on the door.

Darian raised his eyebrows. 'Shall we continue this fascinating conversation later?' he drawled. 'I think we're being summoned to dinner.'

CHAPTER ELEVEN

THE table was set in a small banqueting room—a surprisingly intimate table, even though it was laid with plates of solid gold which gleamed beneath the light from the dazzling chandelier overhead. Heavy crystal glasses threw off rainbow lights, and overblown crimson roses were crammed into low golden bowls.

'Isn't it beautiful?' Lara breathed automatically.

Darian turned to look at her, at the elegant little curve of her nose and the way her soft lips had parted. She had clipped some of her hair back—he had never seen it like that before. The rampant curls had been subdued, emphasising her long, elegant neck, and the overall impression was to make her look rather pure and innocent. But then, she was an actress, he reminded himself. A chameleon. She wore so many different masks.

'Exquisite,' he said curtly, his head turning as Khalim walked into the room accompanied by a retinue of servants, most of whom he dismissed immediately.

He had changed from his Western suit into one of the garments tradionally worn by the Marabanesh—only his was fashioned from the finest silk, denoting his royal status. It was a fluid and flowing robe in a silvery colour which made Lara think of a river. He indicated for them to take their seats and ran a finger reflectively over a rose in one of the bowls, rather in the way that Lara had done in her room, earlier.

'You know, it is a strict rule at the palace to have only roses placed on the table at royal functions,' he said gravely as he took his seat, though his black eyes were glinting with mischief. 'In honour of my darling Rose.'

Lara frowned as she unfolded the heavy linen napkin. 'Won't Rose think it strange you haven't told her I'm here, Khalim? Won't she be upset?'

'Why would she be?' Khalim looked at her steadily. 'Rose loves me and trusts me,' he said simply. 'And she trusts my judgement,' he added softly. 'She will know soon enough, when the time is right, but she must not be troubled by events over which she has no control. Especially not now, when she carries my child within her.'

He spoke in a way in which few men did—his words were poetic and romantic and they came straight from the heart. Lara had not spent her life looking for love—women who did that were doomed, in her opinion—but as she listened she experienced a great ache of longing. She tried to imagine what it must be like to have a man profess his love for you in such a profound and moving way as that. Didn't Rose have what most women dreamed of? Oh, not the prince or the palaces or the untold riches—but the steadfast and passionate love of the man she adored.

And what a man Khalim was. She recognised then that somewhere in the back of her mind she had thought that no man could ever match someone like Khalim—his strength and his passion and his sheer, overriding masculinity. Only now she had met another such man.

Covertly, she studied Darian from beneath her lashes. His half-brother had those same qualities—qualities which had been born in him, not fashioned by his upbringing in a place of riches and privilege. Darian would be a man whose love would be worth more than a king's ransom.

And she had blown it.

'You will drink some wine, Darian?' Khalim was saying.

'No, thanks.' Darian pointed to a decanter filled with a rich gold liquid. 'I'll have some of what you're having.'

Khalim nodded, looking pleased. 'It is a special Maraban concoction—made from honey and water taken from the crystal streams of mountain rivers and scented with rose and cinnamon.'

Darian took the goblet and sipped some. 'Here,' he murmured, and passed the goblet to Lara.

The gesture seemed somehow symbolic of sharing, and yet at the same time a mockery. Part of her wanted to refuse—but how could she in front of Khalim, and risk appearing churlish or rude? The goblet was so heavy and her fingers were so unsteady that she had to hold onto it with two hands. 'Th—thanks,' she stumbled.

The glittering look he sent her was impenetrable, and Lara found herself wondering how she was going to be able to fight him off later, when they were alone in their sumptuous room. Especially when there was a part of her which didn't want to fight him at all...

A feast was brought before them—dish after tiny dish of subtly flavoured delicacies, some of which Lara had tasted before and some of which were new to her. She looked at the mound of glistening saffron-scented rice, studded with pistachios and cardamom seeds, and tried to summon up an appetite for it.

But during the meal she found herself cast in the role of spectator, listening while Darian continued to ask questions about Maraban's history and about Khalim's ongoing task of making sure that the country embraced new technology while losing nothing of its tradition and traditional values. She could have listened all night to the Prince describing dark conquests, the battles of his ancestors as they strove to liberate Maraban from marauding neighbouring countries.

'Tomorrow we shall ride,' announced Khalim as tiny little cups of thick, dark coffee were placed before them.

Darian dropped a single sugar cube into his cup and absently stirred at it. 'I've never ridden before.'

'It alarms you?'

Darian's eyes narrowed into golden shards. 'On the contrary. I have always enjoyed rising to a challenge.'

'Of course. But I shall give you our quietest mount.'

'Oh, no, you won't.' Darian's voice was low, but it carried with it a steely determination, and Lara couldn't miss the unmistakable look of horror which crossed the face of one of the servants. You wouldn't need to speak English to be aware that this guest was arguing with the Prince!

'I will take a mount that you favour,' Darian emphasised.

This time Khalim frowned. 'But it would be sheer folly to put a novice on a spirited horse!'

'And would you not do the same in my situation?' challenged Darian softly.

The eyes of the two men clashed a silent duel over the ornate table, until at last Khalim nodded his head.

'Indeed I would.'

There was silence for a moment, as if another unspoken test had been set and passed.

'And can I come and watch?' asked Lara.

They turned to look at her, as if they had forgotten she was there.

'Of course you can,' said Khalim indulgently. 'You don't mind, Darian?'

'Why should I mind?' But of course Darian did mind. He minded a lot. He had never ridden before, and as Khalim had pointed out he *was* a novice. Did he really want Lara to witness him at the very bottom of a learning curve—he who liked to be seen to be accomplished in all things?

'Good. That is settled.' Khalim rose to his feet. 'You will forgive me if I leave you now? I have affairs of state to attend to, and I must telephone Rose before she retires. You may linger here, over coffee—or one of the servants will show you where a television can be found, should you wish it. Or...' His voice softened. 'You can take Lara for a walk through the rose gardens—they are smaller than those at the Golden Palace, but they are beautiful indeed, and the perfect place for lovers on such a starlit evening.'

Lara opened her mouth to protest, to end this ridiculous charade here and now, but before she could speak Darian had answered for her.

'Thanks, but I think we'll go straight to bed. Lara's very tired—aren't you, darling?'

The mock concern in his voice made her want to rail against him. But what could she possibly say that would not embarrass her host? She nodded, and even managed to curve her lips into a smile. 'Very tired,' she agreed demurely.

She saw Khalim narrow his eyes fractionally. 'Then I will bid you both goodnight and sweet dreams.'

They listened to the sound of his retreating footsteps as they echoed down the marble corridor, and then Darian bent his head to speak softly in her ear.

'Why, Lara—you smiled like you almost meant it then,' he murmured. 'How useful it must be to have a talent for acting—you can use it in any given situation!'

The subtle masculine scent of him was playing havoc with her senses. She wanted to sway against him, to have him hold her close to him, to kiss her and blot out all this pain and uncertainty. But she fought it, turning on him instead. 'How dare you imply that we can't wait to get back to our room for a night of hot, no-holds-barred sex?'

Well, it was pretty easy to read what was uppermost in *her* mind. 'Is that what I was doing?' he questioned innocently, but the ache in his body felt far from innocent. 'Then we'd better make our way back, hadn't we—and quickly? I should hate to keep you waiting for your hot, no-holds-barred sex, Lara!'

Her eyes flashed blue fury at him, but she kept a tight rein on it. She would hang onto her dignity. She wasn't going to answer him back there and then. Not with a silent servant guiding them back to their quarters. Still, he was labouring under a very big misapprehension indeed if he thought that she was about to leap into bed with him.

The servant opened their door and Lara went straight into the bathroom without a word. She locked the door behind her, not emerging until her face was scrubbed clean and her teeth brushed. She was wearing a pair of pyjamas which, though light and silky for the sultry temperature, could by no stretch of the imagination ever be described as sexy.

Darian looked up from where he had been flicking through the book she had been reading earlier. He had removed his cuff-links, she noted, but that was all.

'Finished in the bathroom, *darling*?' he questioned sardonically.

'It's all yours.' Lara hesitated, then pointedly looked at the long, low divan which stood underneath the shuttered windows. 'That divan looks very comfortable, doesn't it?'

'Indeed it does,' he agreed gravely. 'I imagine it's probably just as comfortable as the bed. One would be certain to get a good night's sleep on it, anyway.'

'Absolutely,' said Lara, relieved, and yet annoyingly just a bit infuriated, too. She hadn't expected him to agree quite so gracefully! And didn't you want him to try and make you put up a bit of a fight? taunted a rogue voice inside her head. Weren't you looking forward to at least one impassioned kiss before you finally pushed him away?

Darian saw her face and gave a small smile as he walked

towards the bathroom. For someone who made her living from acting she could be remarkably transparent at times!

He undressed and showered, glad of the heavy beat of the cool water to subdue unwanted appetites and bring him back to some degree of normality. For it would be all too easy to get carried away—to be seduced by life out here in this strange, magical land, where men really did seem to live as they were born to.

He thought of the traffic crushes and the noise and pollution of the city, and his mouth twisted as he turned off the shower jets. Did places like this always inject you with a kind of wistfulness? he wondered. He couldn't even blame the wine at dinner, since he hadn't had any! He shook his head slightly, dispersing droplets of water and reflecting that he was badly in need of a reality check.

When he returned to the bedroom Lara was lying in bed, the covers right up to her neck, her eyes tightly closed.

'Asleep already?' he mocked softly.

She didn't reply, taking care to make her breathing as slow and as steady and as deep as if she really *was* asleep.

It was torture, just lying there, hearing the unhurried removal of his clothes. She wanted to tell him to turn the wretched light off, but if she did that then he would know she wasn't asleep, and would probably start to engage her in conversation.

Or worse…

She wanted to squirm, too. Her pyjamas felt hot and constricting, burning against her skin where the material touched. And her pulse was hammering so loudly that she was amazed he hadn't heard it and made some hateful remark about it. Her breasts were all tingling and tight, and…

He heard the almost inaudible change in the pace of her breathing. Now it sounded shallow, and rapid. Darian smiled as he snapped the light off and climbed into bed.

As the bed dipped beneath his weight Lara sat up as if she'd been electrocuted—and with the nearness and warmth of his naked body she might as well have been. 'What the hell do you think you're doing?'

He yawned. 'Going to sleep. Why—did you have something else in mind?'

She snapped the light on with shaking fingers, still shocked and yet excited beyond belief to see him arrogantly sprawled out next to her, not even having bothered to cover up the bare tawny chest.

'You're not sleeping here!'

'Yes, I am.'

'But…but you said…you said you'd sleep on the divan!' she spluttered.

Darian shook his head. 'No, I didn't, Lara. You commented on how comfortable it looked. I agreed, and you mistakenly took that to mean that I would be sleeping on it. Well, you were wrong. This bed is big enough for both of us, and I am not, repeat *not* sleeping on the divan!'

'You don't think that as a *gentleman*, you might offer to take it?'

'But I never claimed to be a gentleman.' The golden eyes glittered. 'Just as you never claimed to be a lady.'

'I'm not going to react to that.'

'Suits me.'

Now he was punching the pillow around with his fist, rearranging it, and Lara stared at him in disbelief. 'And that's your last word on the subject?'

'I think we've said just about everything there is to say on the subject of beds and divans, don't you?' he questioned, his voice bored.

'Well, if you won't sleep there—I will!'

'Fine.'

He turned over and shut his eyes, and Lara stared at him

with mounting frustration and indignation. He meant it! He actually meant it!

Well, so did she! She grabbed her pillow and one of the covers, hastily turning her head rather than be confronted by the sight of the remaining covers clinging so lovingly to his long, lean frame.

And she had been wrong—the divan was not comfortable at all. It had probably been designed for a woman to lie on alluringly, showing off her body for her sheikh, not for a tall, tired woman to try and get eight hours' sleep on.

Lara tossed and turned, her frustration mounting as she heard Darian's immediate steady breathing. As the night wore on tiredness gave way to anger and hot tears began to scald at the corners of her eyes. She felt alone and afraid and abandoned.

That's only because it's the middle of the night, she told herself. The lowest ebb of all is the hour just before dawn, when you seem to be the only person in the world.

Darian woke to a sound. A little sniff. In the darkness, he frowned, wanting to ignore it, but there it was again, another tiny little sound, and he sighed. 'Why are you crying, Lara?' he asked softly.

'I'm not.'

'I know this must be a difficult concept for you to embrace, but couldn't you just try telling the truth for once?' he drawled sardonically.

She contemplated ignoring him, but just the sound of his voice reached out and comforted her, like a warm fire. A human voice in the dead of night. 'Why do you think? It's bloody uncomfortable on this thing!'

'Well, you do have a choice,' he remarked sagely.

Yes, she did. She could lie here like a martyr, or she could take a little decisive action. Picking up her pillow, she walked back over to the vast bed and slid in beside him, taking care to lie on the very edge.

'Be careful you don't slip off.'

His voice sounded amused, and it was the amusement which finally made the anger and frustration inside her snap. She flicked the light on, sat up and glared at him, spirals of hair tumbling all over her face. She impatiently pushed them away with the back of her hand.

'Just why did you bring me here, Darian?'

'It seemed like a good idea at the time.'

'I'm serious!' she hissed.

He could see that. The woman who had so entranced him with her feistiness at the casting was back. And how. Her cheeks flamed like roses and her eyes sparked a bright sapphire fire. His eyes drifted to her breasts and he felt his body jerk in reaction.

'Why do you think I asked you?' he asked tightly. 'Because I was angry with you.'

'Surely if you were angry with me then the most sensible solution would have been to wish me as far away as possible?'

'But sense doesn't come into it when sex is involved,' he said bluntly. 'Does it?'

His voice was curt, almost cruel. 'No,' she said flatly. 'It doesn't.'

He had planned to have his fill of her. To make love to her over and over again, in every way and in every position. To learn every inch of her body like a man conquering a brand-new country. And only when he had done that would he move on and forget her.

But the time had not been right. Not before dinner, and strangely enough not now, even though they were in bed together and he was naked beside her.

If it had been any other woman he would have started to kiss her. He was experienced enough to kiss away her doubts and have her sighing with pleasure, a consummate enough lover to know how to make her beg for him. But he saw the dried track of a tear, the sudden tremble of her mouth, and something stopped him and he knew that he could not. Not when she looked so cold and so lost and so damned vulnerable.

She's just *acting* again, he told himself furiously, but that didn't seem to make any difference. And deep down he didn't think she was acting at all—she wouldn't bother pretending not to have been crying quietly in the dark if she was, would she? He got out of bed and slid on a pair of boxer shorts before climbing back in.

'What are you doing now?' she asked, a slight tinge of hysteria to her voice.

'Allaying your fears that I might try it on in the middle of the night,' he said gravely. 'See? I'm quite decent now, Lara.'

Decent? If he had swathed himself from head to toe in voluminous sackcloth, then 'decent' would still be the last word she would have used. And now she was confused— from being fearful that he *would* try it on, that she would have trouble resisting him, her self-esteem had taken a great plummet. Didn't he want her any more?

'Come here,' he said, almost gently, and pulled her against him.

'No.' She tried to resist the impact of that warm, living flesh. 'Go away,' she mumbled, but she didn't move.

He smoothed the silken tumble of her curls, thinking how soft they felt, the scent of her shampoo drifting towards his nostrils with its wholesome fragrance. For the first time in his life he felt disarmed by a sense of protectiveness—he didn't know how and he didn't know why. He just knew that it couldn't have come at a more unwelcome time. 'Just go to sleep, Lara,' he sighed.

With one final sniff she snuggled against him, and it felt

like coming home. Like walking into a room with a fire when you had been outside in the cold. But that was all an illusion, she reminded herself. A wish and a dream and a desire—all mixed up in her head and a million miles away from reality simply because she *was* a million miles from reality.

Yet the warmth of his embrace was irresistible, as was the rhythmic movement of his hand stroking her hair as he lulled her into a state of utter defencelessness. She couldn't have moved if she'd wanted to, and she didn't want to.

Her last thought before drifting off into a fitful and dreamless sleep was that this was the kind of thing you should do with a man before you had sex with him. Being intimate without being too intimate. Building something slowly instead of grabbing at it. She felt like a child who had gobbled all the icing off the top of the cake. And how she wished she hadn't.

When Lara's eyelids fluttered open, it was to find Darian's space beside her empty. In fact, the room was empty. She blinked her eyes and rubbed them just as the door opened and in he walked, carrying a pile of clothes. Her heart flipped over when she saw him.

It's just because he's wearing jodhpurs, she thought—all men looked good in jodhpurs.

The cream trousers defined every sinew of his muscular thighs, clinging to the narrow jut of his hips and the high, hard curve of his buttocks. His shirt was loose and cool, though the fine, filmy material did nothing to disguise the rocky torso and the broad span of his shoulders. Long, soft black leather riding boots completed the ensemble, and for the first time in her life Lara understood why leather was considered synonymous with sex.

But sex was not what she wanted from Darian, she realised, her heart sinking. Or rather, not sex on its own. She wanted more. She wanted affection and respect and tenderness and regard. There was a word for what she desired, and that word was love.

And, judging by the cool, non-committal look on his face, she wanted far more than she could ever have.

'Good morning,' she said, feeling almost more shy than if they *had* had sex.

'You slept.' It was a statement. He knew it for fact simply because he had not. The moment she had got into bed with him had been the moment when sleep became, for him, a distant memory.

He must have been out of his head. Playing the protector and the carer when all he'd really wanted to do was drive himself into her sweet and yielding flesh, over and over again. Punishing his body with the nearness of hers and the sweet, feminine scent of her which had invaded his senses until the sun had risen, and unable to do a damned thing about it. He had never known such an acute and excruciating sense of frustration in his life.

'Yes. Yes, I did get to sleep,' she agreed. 'Eventually.' This was awful—she felt as if he was someone she had just met in the doctor's waiting room. She looked instead at the pile of clothes he was carrying. 'What's that?'

He dropped it onto the foot of the bed. 'Riding clothes,' he said shortly. 'Khalim sent them for you. They belong to Rose and he says you're pretty much the same size. I've eaten breakfast and I'm just off to the stables—so do join us when you're ready. If you're still inclined to.'

The dark, unfriendly note in his voice told her that he would rather she didn't, and with something which she supposed was a smile he was gone, leaving Lara staring after him, wondering what she had done to make him look as if he had been eating something with a distinctly sour taste. Was it sexual frustration he felt? Or frustration that he *had* actually ended up playing the gentleman?

Wasn't it crazy that just lying innocently in his arms, with him stroking her hair like that, should have made her feel so…so…dreamy? But tenderness could mean so much more than even the most spectacular orgasm in the world. Even if it *was* only pretend tenderness.

She showered and put the riding clothes on. Khalim was right—the two women were pretty similar in size, though Lara was taller and, judging by the shirt, her breasts were now smaller than Rose's. But Rose had had one child already, and everyone knew that pregnancy changed your shape.

Lara stared in the mirror, at her slim hips and breasts untouched by childbirth, and a sudden yearning stabbed at her. Babies were something she had never even considered before, yet now she saw a sharp, snapshot image of a baby at her breast, a beautiful baby with golden eyes and dark ruffled hair.

Stop it, she thought impatiently. Just stop it. He's gorgeous and he's a challenge. He's good in bed, and occasionally he can be tender—but that's all. You aren't in love with him, and he certainly isn't in love with *you*.

And she tied her hair back so tightly that it made her wince, then set off for the stables.

CHAPTER TWELVE

LARA burst into a peal of laughter and was met with a furious gold stare.

'It isn't funny,' he growled.

'Oh, I'm sorry, Darian, but it is. Very.' She held her hand out to him. 'Here.'

He eyed it suspiciously for a moment before grasping it, and then swung himself up from the dust onto which he had just tumbled, bringing himself right up close to Lara, enjoying the immediate darkening of her eyes.

'Do you like watching me fall, Lara?'

Actually, it was strange watching him not being perfectly proficient at something, to see him cast in the role of novice. Strange and almost *endearing*. If it had been anyone else she might have said *cute*, except that four-letter words like *nice* and *cute* didn't really sit well on Darian.

'A fallen man?' she mused. 'Yes, I *do* think I like it!' She could smell the sweat on him, and it gleamed on his skin as brilliantly as on the highly polished flanks of the Akhal-Teke horse from which he had just plummeted.

He let go of her hand and placed both his own on the horse again.

'You're getting back up?' she asked, in surprise.

'Isn't that the first rule of riding?' he questioned. 'That you get straight back on?'

She nodded as he swung himself up. He was persistent; she would say that for him. From having been shown the rudiments of riding by Khalim himself, he had persevered with learning the new skill every spare minute, like a man driven to conquer.

He was up by first light, out helping the grooms to muck the horses out. He told her that he was determined to learn as much as possible about this creature who seemed so reluctant to have him on its back. Lara was quickly learning that there were no half-measures where Darian Wildman was concerned.

Khalim had found him the most beautiful palomino— the usual metallic sheen even more pronounced in this case. The horse's coat gleamed as golden as the eyes of the man who rode him. And when he did manage to stay astride Darian made the most magnificent vision, Lara was forced to admit. Though that shouldn't have surprised her. Nothing really surprised her where he was concerned.

The night when he had held her in his arms had completed her captivation. He had disarmed her with his gentleness, leaving her happily open to the suggestion that they become lovers once more. Except that no such suggestion had been made, and neither had that comforting and innocent night been repeated—because Darian had taken to sleeping on the uncomfortable divan beneath the window.

She was the one all alone in the big, comfortable bed now, and *she* was the one who was lying awake until the small hours, while he slept as deeply as a child.

'How's that?' he called.

She watched him trot around the dusty paddock and nodded. 'Better,' she called back. 'But not so tight on the reins!'

He relaxed his grip by a fraction, enjoying the feel of the powerful animal between his thighs. He was getting the hang of this riding thing now, and about time, too. It had been galling to accept that not only was Khalim a superb rider but that Lara was, too. All those years of wholesome upbringing in the English countryside had made her into a confident horsewoman. She looked good on a horse—but then she looked good doing just about anything.

They had been here for just over a week, and this morning Khalim had had to go off to meet with a visiting dignitary and had left Lara in charge of Darian's riding lessons.

'You will take my place and teach him?' he'd asked her softly.

Lara enjoyed the flash of irritation which sparked from the golden eyes. 'Of course. I'll enjoy cracking the whip!' she joked.

'You can try,' Darian whispered softly.

Lara looked down at the dusty ground, afraid that Khalim would see the naked look of desire in her eyes, and afraid that Darian would see it, too. Horseriding was supposed to be an innocent pursuit, yet somehow he had managed to make the atmosphere heavy with tension and expectation—shimmering like the heat from the sun above them.

'You won't mind taking orders from a woman?' she questioned, once Khalim had gone.

His tone was dry. 'It will be another new experience.'

'And do you enjoy new experiences?' she asked, her eyes slanting at him.

Darian smiled. 'Oh, yes,' he murmured.

She was flirting with him again, he noted now. Indeed, she had been doing that ever since the night when he had held her so chastely in his arms. Women could be so contrary. Put something out of reach and they immediately wanted it! But the trouble was that now the boot was on the other foot he wasn't sure that *he* wanted it. Not any more.

Because sex with Lara would be complicated this time

around. He recognised that with a grim kind of certainty. And wasn't his life complicated enough already? So much had happened—and not just between the two of them. He was only just getting used to the fact that he had a brother, a brother who he was getting to know little by little—not easy when both were men who rarely let their guard down, Darian through instinct and Khalim through necessity.

The two of them would sit up late at night, talking—sometimes into the early hours. They had described their childhoods to each other, and Darian had done his best not to feel envy at the privilege of Khalim's early years. But the Prince had sensed it with an intuitive sensitivity.

'Yes, I had the riches, Darian,' he had said softly. 'But you were given the gift of freedom. Riches can be earned, but complete freedom cannot—not when you carry the responsibilities which come with having royal blood.'

It was a different way of looking at things—but then, didn't this place make you look at things differently anyway? And, yes, Khalim had all the burdens and responsibilities which came with governing his country—but his life was clearly defined in ways that Darian was growing to envy.

Because for all the paraphernalia and trappings which came with his royal status—the palaces and the servants—Khalim enjoyed such simple pleasures. Perhaps it was because his riches had always been taken for granted that he was able to look beyond material things. It was another lesson to be learnt.

Khalim had taken Darian walking beneath the star-filled skies, pointing out constellations which were not visible even from his penthouse apartment in London. There were no cars out here in the isolated splendour of the countryside which surrounded the palace. Nor noise, nor crowds.

In fact, the only blot on this surreal landscape remained Lara herself. With his self-imposed sexual limits, he had begun to get to know her. And to like her. Even though liking her was something he had tried to put up barriers against, telling himself that she was an actress, that she had deceived him, and if she could do it once she could do it again.

Which was why he had taken up riding with such fervour. Apart from wanting to excel at it—which was inherent in his nature—he also used it as a form of diversion, driving himself at it, hour after hour, so that by the time he fell onto that damned concrete block of a divan he was so bushed that he slept the night through.

And he would be lying if he did not admit to taking a certain amount of pleasure at the sight of Lara's dark-rimmed eyes which met his each morning.

A servant arrived, bearing a tray of iced orange water, and he watched while he set it down in the shade and Lara sat down prettily in her jodhpurs and beckoned him over.

His throat felt dry as he dismounted, but it was a dryness caused by more than mere thirst. Khalim had gone, and for the first time it was just the two of them. As he approached he could see the shape of her breasts peaking beneath the fine silk shirt, and he felt the debilitating jerk of desire as he imagined slowly peeling the shirt from her body.

Forget it, he told himself. Lara's trouble. She's been trouble since the moment you first set eyes on her, and if you get involved with her then there's plenty more where that came from.

But that didn't stop him from issuing a curt command to the groom, who bowed his head in response.

Lara had been watching the little interchange and looked up at him in surprise as he approached. 'Wasn't that Marabanese you were speaking to the groom?'

'It was.'

'Who taught you?'

The golden eyes glittered. 'Khalim has been instructing me in the basics of the language.'

He sat down beside her, took the glass from her and drank deeply, putting the empty glass down and wiping his lips with the back of his hand.

'You're acting more and more like a sheikh every day!' she teased.

'Yeah.' He stared moodily into the middle distance.

'And sounding like one, too!' She wished she knew what was going on in that head of his. She'd thought they were supposed to have abandoned hostilities and declared an unspoken truce of sorts. Were they or were they not able to exist in relative harmony? In theory, yes, of course they were—except that there was this terrible hunger bubbling away inside her. An overwhelming longing to feel his lips on hers once more.

Maybe it was one-sided. Maybe he just didn't feel it any more and the way she had deceived him had killed his desire for her stone-dead. They were sharing a bedroom, but that was the one place she barely saw him. He crept into the bedroom in the early hours, completely ignoring her and the large, empty space in the bed beside her, and was gone when she woke in the morning.

She watched while the groom led the horse away. 'Exotically beautiful, isn't he?' she remarked.

'Mmm,' he said, non-committally.

'They're a unique breed, you know.'

'Are they?'

Lara drew a breath. 'Yep. Arguably the oldest surviving cultured equine breed.'

'You don't say?'

Well, she had to say *something*, or else she was going to come out with something like, *Don't you find me attractive any more, Darian?*

'They're known for their speed, stamina and intelligence,' she continued, the words coming out in a flurry.

He turned his head to look at her, drowning in the blue of her eyes, then looked away again. 'A little like me, then?'

Her heart pounded. 'A little, I guess.'

There was a split-second pause, and when he spoke his voice was lazy. 'What else about them, Lara?'

'They're hot-bloods, definitely not warm-bloods.'

He didn't say anything.

'And unusually sensitive to the way they are treated,' she rushed on. 'They're responsive to gentle training, and can be stubborn or resentful if treated rudely.' She paused and held her breath as he turned to her again, only this time he didn't look away. 'A little like me, in fact.'

He saw the pulse at her temple begin a frantic little beat, and suddenly all his defences left him. He brushed a line over the fine skin there and felt its throbbing beneath his fingertip. 'Is that so?' he murmured.

'Y-yes.' She held her breath as his fingertip traced its way down her cheek, lingering on the line of her jaw, then down to the hollow of her neck. She could feel the flutter of her heart and the honey-rush of sweet desire, but she didn't dare move. It was like being in the middle of a spell—one wrong word or gesture and it would be broken, and she would be back to frustrated longing once again.

'What else?' he murmured, only now his fingertip was teasing the tip of her breast.

Lara swallowed. 'Their eyes are…'

'Are what, Lara?' He felt the nipple bud and harden and he sucked in a breath.

'Are l-large and expressive. And sometimes almond-shaped.'

The golden blaze almost blinded her. 'Like your eyes,' he observed softly. 'What else?'

Now his hand was drifting down over her torso and she could scarcely breathe.

'Tell me, Lara,' he urged. 'I want to know.'

'Their…their bodies are long and lean.' She swallowed again. 'The muscling well-defined, s-smoothly hugging the bone.'

'That's me,' he whispered. 'Isn't it?'

By now his fingertip had edged down to the fork in her legs, drifting forward and back, forward and back, so that Lara closed her eyes and gasped.

'Isn't it, Lara?'

'Well, yes. You know it is.'

'Don't you want to feel for yourself how it feels?' he purred. 'Feel the muscle which hugs the bone…?'

She didn't need to be asked twice. Her hands flew to his chest, feeling the masculine heat of him through the damp shirt, and all the while his finger continued its erotic little dance, the material of the jodhpurs both restricting and heightening her pleasure.

'Darian!' she gasped.

'Mmm?'

'We can't do this here!'

'Do what?' he questioned innocently, enjoying the way her thighs were now parting, revelling in the urgent little grind of her hips. 'We're not doing anything, are we? Not really. I'm just playing with you a little. Touching you there.' He felt her squirm. 'And *there*.' He increased the pressure of his finger and her head fell back.

'Someone might come!' she protested, in a thick, slurred voice which didn't sound like her own.

'I think someone might,' he agreed unsteadily. 'But all the grooms have gone, if that's what you're worried about.'

Too late, she realised just where he was taking her. 'Kiss me, Darian,' she pleaded on a moan. 'Please. Just kiss me.'

'No.'

The single word should have terminated her pleasure with all the finality of a bucket of cold water being thrown over her, but it did no such thing. If anything, the cold, harsh word only increased her ascent into that tantalising, nebulous place which made such mockery of almost everything else which existed. Maybe she wasn't so like the Akhal-Teke at all, she thought desperately, for there was no resentment on her part about the way he was treating her—and shouldn't there have been? *Shouldn't there have been?*

But then it happened, great wave upon wave of engulfing pleasure, and she opened her mouth, the pleasure so intense that she wanted to scream. And that was when he kissed her at last, swallowing up her cries with the fierce, hard pressure of his mouth, clamping his hand possessively over her jodhpurs while she still pulsed with sweet, dying spasms and her head fell uselessly to his shoulder.

'Oh,' she moaned. It was a helpless little cry, and it was edged with sorrow as well as fulfillment—for hadn't the kiss been merely a silencing technique instead of a demonstration of affection?

'Touch me,' he urged. 'Please.'

Her hand moved down and her eyes snapped open. 'Oh!' she breathed. He was hard, so very, very hard.

'Yes—oh,' he murmured wryly.

'Wh-what do you want to do now?'

'I want you,' he shuddered. 'That's what I want. And I want you to undress me. Now.'

She felt the flush move from her neck to her cheeks, so that they burned like fire. It was a stark and unequivocal sexual command, dark with promise but devoid of all tenderness. 'Wouldn't you rather go back to our room?'

He was sliding her jodhpurs down now, with difficulty.

'Practically?' He groaned. 'Lara, I don't think I can. Take your boots off.'

With trembling hands she obeyed him, sliding the soft leather down over her calves and kicking them off into the dust.

'Now, come here,' he said softly. 'Come here, Lara.' And he lifted her up, slithering her jodhpurs and her panties away with one brief, economical movement, then lowering her down on top of him, closing his eyes and groaning again as he felt himself encased in her tight, molten heat. 'Oh, yes,' he bit out. 'Oh, yes!'

She held onto his shoulders and began to move.

He opened his eyes and watched her through his lashes. 'Ride me, Lara,' he urged thickly. 'Ride me.'

She abandoned all restraint and misgivings, and all inhibitions, too, forgetting everything except just how delicious it felt, with the hot sun beating down on her and the hot feel of him inside her. She closed her eyes and let her hips slide towards him so that he filled her completely, and she gave a soft, low moan of pleasure as they began to move in rhythm.

Darian was lost in a place more magical than Maraban, his hands holding onto her slender hips as she moved on him and around him, feeling the warmth rise and rise until he heard her shattered and disbelieving little cries once more. And then it was impossible to contain his own pleasure for a second longer as his world split into a thousand shards of sharp-edged ecstasy.

There was silence, bar the distant sound of the mountain wind the Marabanesh called the *rabi*, which seemed to echo the sounds of their small, gasping breaths.

Lara wiped the palm of her hand over her damp, flushed cheeks and looked down at him, just as the thick black lashes parted and the golden eyes gleamed up at her.

She wanted to bend her head to kiss him, but this did

not seem to be the kind of situation which demanded soft and tender kisses. What had just happened had been fulfilling, yes, but in a purely physical way, she recognised with a heavy heart. She wanted more than just physical perfection—but he was not the man to give her more than that.

'I'd better move—' she began, but he halted her with a touch to her belly, making her shiver.

'No, don't. Not yet. Stay there—just for a minute.'

'But the grooms—'

'They won't return. I told them not to.'

Lara raised her eyebrows in surprise. 'I didn't know your Marabanese was *that* good.'

He smiled. 'It isn't. But, like I said, Khalim taught me a few...*key*...phrases.'

Lara's heart began to pound. 'Like what?'

He felt her move away from him, and he missed her warm, sticky heat. 'Oh, just the kind of command to ensure a certain degree of...privacy. You know.'

Yes, she knew...or rather she was beginning to get the idea. Royal men took lovers, and for that they would not want a retinue of servants hanging around in the wings. But it was more than just privacy, she realised. For hadn't Darian just demonstrated in the most efficient way possible just how much he had been accepted into the royal fold?

What else had he discussed with Khalim, apart from how to ensure you could make love to a woman undisturbed? And that was the difference between the two men—Khalim would confide in Rose, but Darian would not do the same with her. Why would he? They were barely more than lovers, and even that was a tenuous link—one which would be broken once they had left Maraban.

Lara reached out for her jodhpurs, and the pair of panties

which were still rumpled up inside them, biting her lip as she thought how compliant she always was around him.

'Stop frowning, Lara,' he urged gently. 'Get dressed and we'll go back to our room.'

Her senses leapt in response to what he obviously had in mind, but she was troubled, too.

She had fallen for Darian big-time, but she had no idea where it was leading.

Or maybe she did. Maybe it was *that* which troubled her. For this thing between them—whatever it was— wasn't leading anywhere other than to the inevitable road to heartbreak.

CHAPTER THIRTEEN

BACK in their room, Darian turned to her and smiled. 'I feel pretty hot and dusty,' he murmured. 'And that bath is big enough for both of us. Shall we take a bath together, Lara?'

She must snap out of it. They were lovers again, and hadn't she been wanting that to happen? What did she expect—that because they had just shared a delicious and erotic encounter in the stables that he would start offering her the moon and the stars?

She stretched, and yawned. 'Go and run it, then.'

'Or shall I have one of the servants do it?' he teased.

'Careful, Darian,' she said steadily. 'Much more of this and you'll come back down to earth with a bump when you get back to England!'

He didn't answer, just went into the bathroom and filled the tub with hot, soapy bubbles, and when he called her to tell her that it was ready she was already naked, and when he saw her his heart missed a beat. Their short and tumultuous history had not embraced any of the *normal* stuff, he realised. This was the first time he had seen her completely naked.

'You are very beautiful,' he said evenly.

But as his golden eyes slid over her Lara felt a little like one of the Akhal-Teke horses, being appraised for her physical attributes alone. 'Thank you.'

He pulled her into his arms, feeling her tension dissolve as he ran his fingertips up and down the smooth, satin flesh. 'Get into the bath,' he said huskily. 'You're shivering.'

148

The warm, silken water lapped over her skin, and she sank deep into it, watching while he stripped off his shirt and his jodhpurs until he was as naked as a gleaming, golden statue.

'Move over,' he instructed, and then his eyes became smoky and he smiled, his voice softening to a whisper. 'Actually, don't. Stay just where you are.'

Lara had never made love in a bath before and it was another out-of-world experience—the water providing weightlessness and making their kisses slippery wet, their limbs sliding and entwining and mingling until the obliteration of orgasm left her reeling and empty.

The water was cool by the time she opened her eyes, to find him looking at her.

'We'd better get out,' he said.

She nodded, but drew a deep breath, knowing that unless the subject were broached it would always be like an unspoken barrier between them. 'Darian, have you…have you forgiven me?'

'For?'

'For keeping secrets. And one in particular.'

His eyes narrowed. Why bring that up again, and especially now? 'It's forgotten.'

'Seriously?'

He shrugged his broad, gleaming shoulders, and tiny droplets of water ran down the tawny skin. 'I understand why you did it, okay?'

'That isn't the same as forgiveness.'

'Hell, Lara—can't you just leave it alone?'

'No, I can't!' With an effort she disentangled herself and climbed out of the bath—because somehow this needed to be said when she wasn't touching him, because touching distracted them both and detracted from the importance of what she was saying. 'I need you to know that when I said sorry I really meant it.'

He sighed as he followed her out and let the water go, hearing it gurgling and sucking away. Her words had the unmistakable ring of truth and regret, and they chipped away at his resolve. It was easier to think of her as foxy and deceptive, rather than soft and giving and warm and regretful. Qualities like that made him forget that this was something not dissimilar to a holiday romance. Two attractive people thrown together in a beautiful place, giving in to the pleasures of the senses without any of the hassle of normal day-to-day living.

'Forgiven and forgotten,' he said, and took her into his arms. 'Now, smile for me.' He dropped a kiss onto her trembling lips. 'That's better. Mmm. That's much better. Let's go to bed.'

'Now?'

'Sure—why not? Dinner isn't for hours.'

His body was close. Close and warm and overwhelming. 'That wasn't what I meant,' she said weakly.

He pushed himself even closer. 'I know it wasn't. But, in answer to your unspoken and rather sweet question, the answer is yes, I want to go to bed and make love to you. Again. But if you're tired…? He tilted her chin upwards, dazzled by the lost, dazed look in her blue eyes.

Tired? She had never felt more awake nor more on fire in her life. She stared into his face. The tawny hue of his skin was shadowed by the sculpted cheekbones and the faint darkening around his jaw. His lips parted a fraction and she touched her fingertip to them, tracing a line around them, biting back a wistful sigh. She wished that the doors of the palace could be boarded up and the two of them locked in here for ever, because she recognised that she had fallen in love with him, without rhyme or reason, nor even the comfort of having known him first as a friend.

She lowered her lashes, afraid that he might be able to read the emotion in her eyes, terrified that it would send him running—as surely it would. 'No, I'm not tired,' she murmured.

He gave a low laugh of delight, loving the way she gave him that demure little look even while the tension which was shivering over her body told him that she was feeling anything but demure.

He reached out and untied the knot of the belt at her waist, so that the robe fell open. He slid his hand inside, to cup her breast, its sinful weight resting in the palm of his hand, and felt the swift spasm of desire so strong and so intense that it was close to pain.

He was almost beyond words. Again. He shook his head, as if doing that would make clear some of the confusion making it spin. One touch and he was lost—or was that simply because he had been fighting her since they had arrived in Maraban? Surely it was just his appetite made keener by deprivation, rather than some dark, erotic power exerted by Lara, who could switch from wanton to demure and then back again?

'Come on,' he said huskily. 'Let's lie down before I fall down.'

'Not again! You really *are* a fallen man, aren't you?' she teased, because somehow it was easier to keep it light than to struggle with the enormity of how her feelings for him had just crept up and changed irrevocably. She wound her arms around his neck and looked up at him.

'I'll show you just how much, shall I?' he questioned softly, and picked her up and carried her through to the bed.

They slid between the Egyptian cotton sheets and he ran his fingertips lightly over her.

'Do you realise we're in bed properly together, at last? No sofas, no stables and no baths.' He gave her a look of mocking query. 'Isn't this how *most* people tend to do it, Lara?'

She doubted it. That was her last sane thought as he moved his hand between her legs. Surely it couldn't feel this good for other people? Surely they had just invented something new—just him and her? And could it just get better and better, like this? she asked herself afterwards in disbelief, as wave after wave of pleasure racked through her body once more.

Don't analyse; enjoy. Pretend it's a dream from which you'll never waken.

From that day on it felt like a honeymoon—without the declared love and the wedding, of course, but the days had about them a dreamy and blissful quality which was how she had always imagined a honeymoon to be. No worries and no reality. Lazy mornings and long, beautiful nights. And if Lara was acutely aware that it couldn't last for ever, that the sands of time were running out for what was only ever intended to be a short stay, she didn't confront it. Sometimes it was easier to hide from reality than have to face it.

Darian was no longer up at the crack of dawn to go to the stables, but Khalim still took them both out riding straight after breakfast each morning. Darian improved day by day—he was like a sponge, soaking up every single thing that Khalim told him and then fearlessly putting it into action.

'He will beat me yet,' Khalim sighed to Lara the first time Darian galloped, giving an exultant little whoop as he did so, and looking more carefree than she had ever seen him.

She nodded. 'Probably.' But he has me beaten already, she thought. Certainly my resolve not to fall in love with him.

'You are in love with him?' probed Khalim quietly, uncannily seeming to echo her thoughts. But then, he was a very perceptive man. He watched and he observed and he allowed instinct to guide him.

'Khalim!' She turned to him, knowing that her cheeks had grown pink. 'You can't possibly ask me a question like that.'

'I can ask anything I like—for I am the Sheikh!' he teased, but then his eyes unexpectedly softened. 'I think that you are, Lara. It is there for all to read when you are watching him and he cannot see you.'

'And Darian?' she questioned, her heart pounding, afraid of what she might hear. 'What do you see when he watches me?'

'I see a wary man,' said Khalim truthfully. 'He looks at you as I would a spirited horse who was perplexing me!'

Which was an ironic comparison when she stopped to think about it. 'Did he...did he say anything to you of what went on between us...before we arrived here?'

Khalim shook his head. 'He is a man who keeps his own counsel. He told me nothing, though some of it I have guessed.' He smiled. 'Do not worry yourself, Lara—these things have a habit of working out in the way that fate intends them to. Give it time.'

But it was borrowed time, and she did not know how long it would last. How long before this suspended state would be broken into by the demands of real living?

And then her question was answered. She saw the end in sight and a slow, waking dread came to life inside her.

They were waiting in the dining room when Khalim swept in. Only for once he did not dismiss the retinue which always accompanied him. His face was unusually stern, and Lara saw Darian's eyes narrow, as if he sensed that something was wrong.

'I must go to Dar-gar,' Khalim said immediately.

'Is it Rose?' questioned Lara at once. 'Is the baby all right?'

Khalim shook his head. 'Rose is fine and so is the baby,' he said gently. 'Though I have been away from her too long. No, my police have brought me news of a divisive element which is growing within the city walls, and my place is there.' He turned to Darian. 'You will accompany me?'

'Of course.'

Darian had agreed without hesitation, without even thinking about it for a moment, thought Lara sadly. But her sadness was for what might have been—for shouldn't she be joyful that Darian had a place here, that Khalim needed him, wanted him beside him to face the adversities as well as enjoy the pleasures of being ruler?

Darian had changed, even in the short time they had been here. It was perfectly plain to see if you looked properly—though maybe up until this moment she hadn't wanted to, or dared to.

Here in Maraban his presence seemed even more dominating than it had the first time she had seen him. He exuded an indefinable air that was much more than the power he had attained through his own successful career as a businessman. It was something which went deeper than that, and it was all to do with his royal blood. She had thought it when she had met him, and it was even more evident now. Maraban had released something in him, and in so doing it had bound him to the place for ever.

Darian belonged here, Lara recognised with a sinking heart. He did not need to wear the flowing robes of Khalim for anyone to be able to tell that at heart he was a true sheikh.

She had seen him discover a part of himself here which had been missing before. The golden eyes had become even more alive. She had watched the way they looked up at the clear Maraban sky every morning, watched him suck in a breath of pure, clean air and smile the smile of a contented man.

She had listened to the way he devoured facts about the country from Khalim, asking him this and asking him that, nodding his head as he absorbed as much of its history as was possible. Even the food they were served and the different drinks—he tried each and every one, and savoured them with the air of someone who had never really tasted before.

Last night, in bed, she had dared broach the subject of what might have been.

'Does it hurt?' she'd said softly. 'Or make you angry to think your mother had to struggle to survive when all this wealth was here for the taking?'

There was silence, so that for a moment she wondered whether or not he had heard her. Or overstepped the mark, perhaps, by trying to delve into his innermost thoughts.

Darian stared at the ceiling. He had been thinking about it a great deal, knowing that he had to come to terms with certain things or he would be unable to move on. If circumstances had decreed it, then he would have led a very different life.

'The question is whether or not Makim knew that she was pregnant,' he said slowly. 'Whether he refused to stand by her—*that* would make a difference to the way I felt.'

She stroked at his temple. 'And is there no way of finding out?'

'Oh, yes. He kept diaries. Khalim told me.'

'So read them! Find out.'

'There's a fifty-year rule about opening them,' he said slowly. 'Or at least it's fifty years before they can be brought into the public domain.'

So he would never know, or at least not until he was an old man, when the knowledge would no longer matter as much as it mattered now. 'Oh, Darian,' she said softly, and kissed his cheek.

Sometimes she was so damned soft and tender that he felt as weak as water, and Darian liked to feel strong. He turned over onto his elbow and concentrated on her pink and white naked body instead. 'Oh, Darian—what?' he questioned sulkily.

She remembered thinking fleetingly that he always put barriers up—that he went only so far before the shutters came down. But then he had made love to her in a way which made her misgivings melt away with the sureness of his touch, and afterwards she had cried softly, and she wasn't quite sure why.

She stood watching now as he talked to Khalim, their heads bent and deep in low conversation, excluding her completely.

'Lara, I will have the jet prepared for you,' said Khalim, straightening up.

She looked directly into the golden eyes which were trained on her watchfully. Make it easy for him, thought Lara. No bitterness, nor regrets, no tears or recriminations. Let it be a fond memory, something to warm him during the long, cold Maraban nights, until he finds another woman to replace me.

She nodded. 'I shall leave as soon as possible,' she said.

'How soon is soon?' demanded Darian.

Khalim glanced at his watch. 'You can be airborne within the hour.'

That quickly? Her head swam. But wasn't anything possible for the Sheikh of Maraban? That didn't even leave them time for one last, loving goodbye.

'I'll go and pack,' she said, noticing that Darian didn't attempt to change her mind for her.

She went back to their room, looking sadly at the rumpled sheets, which would normally have been changed while they were at dinner so that they would return to a neat and pristine bed for another night of long lovemaking.

It wasn't enough, she thought sadly. It had been too brief and all too beautiful, and then snatched away by chance and circumstance.

The door opened and her expression of regret quickly changed to one of acceptance. She would not burden him with her sadness, nor leave him remembering her face all crestfallen. And maybe in a way this was for the best. Ending naturally at its height rather than leaving her with a sour taste when it faded away, or he tired of her.

But inside her heart was breaking into a million pieces. She clipped the suitcase closed and smiled. 'There!'

Darian looked at the tumble of dark, silken curls, the brittle way she was smiling at him. Something had changed. He knew it and she knew it, too. Yet wasn't it human nature to want things to stay exactly as they were?

'I don't want you to go, Lara.'

But Lara recognised that his words were inadequate, spoken only because it was the 'right' thing to say at a time like this. She shook her head. 'You need me to go, Darian. There is stuff here for you to do, and my presence isn't helping.'

'Yes.' There was silence for a moment, and when he spoke his voice was heavy. 'You know, I can't promise you anything, Lara. Not even whether or not I'll see you again.'

'I know that.' Her eyes were very bright, but her voice was steady. 'And neither should you. This has all been a very strange experience—perhaps it's best that we put it down to just that…an experience.'

She was moving away from him, and unexpectedly he felt a wrench. He reached out his arms to her, but she shook her head and turned away. If he touched her she would dissolve with the tears which were threatening to fill her eyes—and why leave him with *that* as an enduring vision?

'I'd better get going,' she said brightly. 'Can't keep Khalim waiting, can we?'

But he kissed her on the airfield, in full view of Khalim and servants and flight attendants and all. He brought his lips down on hers in a hard, almost punishing kiss, as if he wanted to physically imprint himself on her and leave her with a memory of him which no one else would ever be able to match.

But he hadn't needed to kiss her to do that.

CHAPTER FOURTEEN

THE first thing Lara saw on her return to England was her face—only for a moment she didn't quite recognise it, for it was magnified to sixty-eight times its normal size, the blue eyes staring moodily down at her from a giant hoarding as her taxi drove out of Heathrow.

For a minute she blinked, disconcerted.

She had forgotten all about the job—the means she had used to get to Darian in the first place, which had ended up, ironically, with her winning the contract.

It was strange to see your features so enlarged. She looked all eyes—their sapphire-blue colour blinding—but there was a haunted, almost distracted quality to her smile, and she knew why.

It was the very first shot, and it had been taken just after he had put the shawl around her shoulders, when she had been disarmed by the soft and solicitous gesture. She was wearing the chiffon dress and holding the phone to her ear, and there was a dazed, almost dreamy expression on her face. It looked like the expression of a woman in love, but that was crazy. You couldn't fall in love that quickly could you?

She supposed that depended on what your definition of love was. Maybe she should settle for having been blown away by the man—a feeling which had subsequently grown. Now she was back in England and he was over in Maraban she was missing him already.

'That ain't you, is it?' asked the taxi driver, cocking his

head at the poster and then turning slightly to snatch a glance at her.

'Yes, it is.'

'Cor! Nice work if you can get it!' he enthused, and he screwed his nose up. 'Pay much, does it?'

It paid well, though not half as well as most people imagined. But in the end she had been the one who paid, and she had paid with her heart.

There was a light on in the apartment when she arrived home, and she didn't even have the energy or the inclination to fish around in her bag for her keys, just jammed her thumb on the bell and kept it there.

'What the bloody hell....?' An irate Jake flung the door open, his face immediately dissolving into an expression of concern when he saw her. 'Lara!' he exclaimed softly. 'Darling, are you all right? What in heaven's name has happened to you?'

'Oh, Jake!' And she dropped her bag onto the floor and collapsed, sobbing, into his arms.

It wasn't until she was settled on the sofa, a fire lit and a huge mug of steaming tea beside her, along with the remains of a box of tissues, that she felt ready to face his anxious questions. But the whole set-up sounded mad—in fact, it *was* mad—and nobody had told her what to say. Or what not to say. It was Darian's secret to tell. His story, not hers. And Jake was a darling, but what if he happened to let it slip to someone? She knew what the outcome of *that* would be. The press would have an absolute field-day, and Darian and Khalim's lives would be made hell.

'It's a broken heart, Jake,' she said. 'It's that simple.'

Jake was shaking his head. 'And it's that Darian Wildman who broke it? The one who, I hasten to add, was so foul-tempered to me! Want me to punch him for you, darling?'

Lara almost choked on her tea and laughed; it was a

relief to find that she still could. *'You?'* she questioned, with more emphasis than she had intended. 'Punch Darian? I don't think so, but thank you all the same!'

'I'll have you know that I came top in boxing in my year at drama school!' The famous blue eyes crinkled at the corners. 'But it's good to see you smiling. Now, sit there and put your feet up. I'm going to make us some supper.'

'Jake, you'd make someone a wonderful wife,' she sighed.

He turned round and raised his brows and for a moment looked so...so *imperious* that Lara suddenly got a good idea why he always featured in the 'Top Ten Most Wanted Men' lists which were periodically featured in newspapers and magazines.

'Don't push it, Lara!' he warned.

It felt weird to be back in England.

She tried rationalising it—telling herself that she had been in Maraban hardly any time at all, and certainly not as long as the time she had gone on a safari in Africa and ended up staying three months.

But comparisons didn't work. Maraban *wasn't* like anywhere else—its magic and its differences touched a part of her in a way that no other place did. And anyway, it wasn't the country she was yearning for. It was the man she had left behind there.

She forced herself to take a shower, even though she was reluctant to wash away the scent of him which still clung to her skin. That night her bed felt cold and empty, but not nearly so much as her body did. Strange how you could become used to someone. How quickly she had accommodated Darian's physical presence—and how badly she missed the warmth of him, holding her in the night.

The night wore on, the clock ticking away with a vengeance, as if calling time on her affair, and she told herself for the last time she would allow herself to cry, the tears sliding wet and warm down her cheeks and falling on the pillow.

In a way, it might have been better if it *had* been finished when she had left—at least then she might be able to mourn it properly and put a sense of closure on it. But it had been left unsatisfactorily open.

What had he said? *I can't promise you anything, Lara.*

It was hard not to try to read stuff into that—but if a girlfriend had told *her* a man had said that to her then how would Lara interpret it? As a courteous way of telling her there was no future in it?

Not even whether or not I'll see you again.

Definitely no future.

At least it didn't look as if there was going to be time to mope around the place, because the success of the poster campaign meant that work offers came flooding in. It was the highest public profile she had ever had, and suddenly it seemed that the world wanted to hire the tumble-haired brunette with the wide blue eyes.

Her professional life, it seemed, was on an all-time high, and she was impatient with herself for feeling that it was a very superficial kind of achievement. You worked all your life for something, and then when it came you couldn't appreciate it because you couldn't stop thinking about a wretched man!

She filmed a television commercial for a new brand of deodorant, and there were two magazine shoots lined up, as well as a whole diary full of 'go-sees'. And if she suddenly found the work curiously hollow, then surely that was to do with the constant aching in her heart.

Time was a great healer, that was what all the relationship experts said, and it had to be true or they wouldn't say it. If she never heard from Darian again then at least she could tell herself that what she had known with him in Maraban had been perfect. Too perfect, really, but there was no point dwelling on that. If she allowed herself to remember the way he had made her feel then it didn't exactly make the future seem a very rosy prospect, for she couldn't imagine ever recapturing that with anyone else. But at least she had felt it—no matter how fleetingly. Many people lived their lives without even coming close to it.

She walked into the apartment one night to find Jake lying on the sofa. She hadn't seen him for days because he'd been in Scotland, filming a new romantic comedy which was a follow-up to his last record-breaking success, and her mouth broke into a smile of welcome.

'Jake! Oh, how lovely to see you!'

'Hello, darling!' He looked her up and down. 'What's with the weight-loss?'

'Have I?'

'*Have I?*' he mimicked. 'Lara, you've dropped at least one dress size.' He frowned. 'From which I must deduce that you haven't heard from the Wild-Man?'

'I don't know why you call him that!' she said lightly.

'Because it's his name—only with maybe a slightly more sinister emphasis!' He narrowed his eyes. 'So have you?'

'No.'

'And how long's it been?'

Superstitiously, she didn't want to say it—because if she acknowledged just how long it had been then it might force her to confront the fact that it really was over. 'Six weeks,' she admitted reluctantly.

'So that's it, then? It's over?'

'Yes, Jake—that's it! I don't think you need to be a relationship counsellor to work that out! Now, I'm just going to send my sister an e-mail, and then I'll...I'll cook you supper—how about that?'

He smiled. 'That's my girl—welcome back to reality, Lara!'

He could keep it, she thought moodily as she sat down at the desk.

At least the computer provided a kind of refuge; she could see the appeal of a life spent surfing in cyberspace. If you were staring at, and communicating with a screen, it meant that you could escape from the real world and all the cares and worries it generated.

She switched on, gazing out of the window while the computer chugged into life, at the bare branches of the trees which were sketched across the ice-blue beauty of the winter sky. Would it ever be spring again? She gave a wan smile as she clicked the mouse onto her inbox. It was time to stop dreaming and get real indeed.

Twelve messages. One from each of her sisters. One from her agent and one from a schoolfriend with whom she corresponded sporadically. The rest were junk—which seemed to arrive daily, no matter what. She scrolled down, ticking each little box to delete them, then she stopped. Her head spun and her mouth dried.

Golden Palace?

Her heart seemed to miss a beat, even though she told herself that it was probably a Chinese restaurant touting for new business. But a Chinese restaurant would hardly title its subject matter: *Akhal-Teke and other things.*

Would it?

She clicked onto it, and now her heart was pounding with excitement. A sense of relief and delight washed over her as she realised that it was from him. Darian had e-mailed her!

The message read:

Khalim and I have just arrived back from several weeks in the Dahab desert.

So that was why she hadn't heard from him!

Where he foisted upon me the most spirited Akhal-Teke you could imagine and told me to break her in! I did—after much bruising—and inevitably my new nickname as 'Fallen Man' has been confirmed. How's life in London? Darian.

She read it over. And over. And over again. Her heart was bubbling with a kind of happiness that she was sure was inappropriate. It was only an e-mail, after all. But deep down she knew it was more than that. He had re-established contact. He was still in her life. She wasn't sure in just what capacity, but at least he was there.

Should she wait to reply?

Hell, no! She had waited six weeks to hear from him—why punish herself by doing something just to appear 'cool' when she didn't feel in the least bit like that? In fact, her cheeks were flushed with a crazy excitement.

Her fingers were trembling. Keep it short, she told herself. And sweet.

London seems crazy and crowded—

And lonely of course...

But maybe that's because I'm comparing it with Maraban, which seems a very long way away.

And then, because she couldn't possibly write what she really wanted, which was When are you coming home?—

he might have decided that Maraban was his home now—
or, Darian, I love you and I really miss you—because that
would be wholly inappropriate and he probably didn't feel
the same way, she signed it, simply. *Lara.*

'What's up?' asked Jake, when she walked back into the
sitting room.

'He's written! E-mailed me!'

'Wild-Man, I take it?' he questioned wryly.

'Will you stop calling him that?'

'That's his name, isn't it?'

'Oh, Jake,' she sighed. 'I didn't know they had e-mail
in Maraban.'

'But they've got an army and a navy and an airforce,'
he answered seriously. 'Why wouldn't they? What did he
say?'

'Oh, just that he's spent several weeks in the desert with
Khalim, that's all.'

'As you do!' joked Jake.

But Lara felt happy for the first time since she'd arrived
back, and she hummed a little tune underneath her breath
as she began to prepare a stir-fry for herself and Jake.

She developed a sudden and passionate interest in her
e-mail inbox, forcing herself to only check it twice a day—
once in the morning and once in the evening—though the
temptation to sit there online all day, staring hopefully at
the screen in case his name should float up, was almost
overwhelming.

She knew that people said an e-mail didn't carry the
same kind of clout as a letter. A letter you had to sit down
and think about while an e-mail was fast and instant.
Though this was not quite true in her case, because she
would sit there dreamily gazing into space while thinking
up replies, searching for just the right note to strike, read-

ing and re-reading every one in case the wrong interpretation could be made of an innocent sentence.

She kept it light, told him about her jobs and her life, and sent some amusing anecdotes about a bunch of female fans who had discovered where Jake lived and were laying seige to the house.

A rather stern reply bounced back.

Are they bothering you?
Get the police to move them on if they show any sign of trouble.

And on one rare and wonderful occasion they managed to be online at the same time and he told her that he had met Rose. She wrote:

Was she angry that I'd been there without getting in touch?

He replied:

She seemed to understand, just as Khalim said she would. I like her very much.
She says to send you her love.

She typed, *Send mine back,* and waited, but that was it.

E-mailing could be a frustrating form of communication, she was coming to realise. One of you had to break it off first, and she could have sat writing to him all day. It wasn't as good as seeing him in the flesh, but it was a damned sight better than nothing.

And, in a way, it was another way of getting to know him—by the written word. It was rewarding and it was sweet to discover that she could make him laugh with some of the things she wrote—as he did her.

Christmas came and went and there was no present or card—but then they didn't celebrate Christmas in Maraban, and she didn't want a token anything from him. There was only one thing she really wanted, and that was the man himself.

But he sent her a sweet e-mail on Christmas Eve, reminding her to leave a mince pie for Santa and a carrot for the reindeer, and Lara went off happily to her parents' farmhouse, sighing as she hung up her stocking, knowing exactly what—or who—she would love to find inside on the following morning, pleased to lose herself in the messy, noisy chaos of a family Christmas.

But as a frozen January slipped into an even icier February, the e-mails became less frequent and when they did come they usually began with an apology.

Sorry I haven't written for so long, but Khalim has been inducting me into the way of State Ceremonies.

Lara strove to reassure him.

It doesn't matter. Honestly. It's just lovely to hear when you do have time.

And then, one evening, Jake took her to task.

She had just trailed into the sitting room when he looked up from his film script and pulled a face.

'War just started, has it?' he questioned acidly. 'No, let me guess—you haven't heard from Lover-Boy!'

'Leave it, Jake.'

'No, Lara—I will not leave it. How long are you going to continue living in a half-world? Happy when he writes—which is hardly ever—and miserable as sin when he doesn't?'

'He's been busy with Khalim,' she said miserably.

'Busy being an international playboy, probably,' said Jake darkly. 'It beats me why Khalim seems to have taken such a shine to him.'

And she couldn't tell him. She couldn't. She shrugged instead. 'I love him, Jake,' she said simply.

'Well, it doesn't look like he loves you back,' said Jake brutally. 'Better get used to it.'

Lara turned away, biting her lip and willing away the tears which were making her eyes swim. But deep down she knew he was right. She wasn't living, not really, or if she was it was in a fantasy world, just waiting for him to e-mail or recalling things he had said, things he had done—reading far too much into a remembered gesture or word.

Nothing had changed. He hadn't promised her anything then and he still hadn't, only now distance seemed to be asserting its natural power. The e-mails were fading away, and so, probably, were his memories of her.

Better join the real world again, Lara, she told herself.

That was what she did. She went to parties with Jake and fixed a bright smile of determined enjoyment on her face.

'That's my girl,' he murmured fondly. 'Pretend you're happy and one of these days you'll turn around and find that you actually are.'

She had to trust him on that one.

She needed a break, and a heavensent opportunity came in the shape of a weekend visit to her parents' farmhouse. It was their wedding anniversary and they were having a family party to celebrate. Lara hadn't been down since Christmas, and she was looking forward to seeing all her nephews and nieces. At least they wouldn't ask questions she would rather not answer about Darian—simply because she hadn't told them anything about him.

It was easier that way.

It began to snow as she left London, and the weather deteriorated still further on the way down, with great flurries of white flakes falling down endlessly from a gunmetal-grey sky. By the time she arrived she was frozen.

Her mother opened the door to her, looking anxious. 'Thank heavens you're here!' she exclaimed as an icy wind blew swirling snowflakes all around the hall. 'Come in and sit by the fire!' Then she frowned. 'And then, my girl, you are going to get some food inside you!'

Why did people keep trying to feed her up? Didn't they realise that food wouldn't fill the aching emptiness inside? 'Lovely,' she said obediently.

They had just finished a blow-out roast lunch and the noise levels had reached crescendo point. The table was a mass of crumpled napkins and half-eaten pudding, and one of her brothers-in-law was passing around some port which nobody really needed. Lara had her nephew sitting chubbily on her lap, attempting to build a little plastic aeroplane, when Lara's father frowned at his wife.

'Did you hear something outside?'

She smiled, fingering the gold necklace he had bought her like a newlywed. 'No, dear!'

'Maybe it's the lorry the necklace probably fell off the back of!' hiccuped the brother-in-law who had drunk the most port.

'Will you please shut-*up*, Jeremy?' demanded his wife.

The front doorbell chimed loudly and Lara's father frowned again.

'Not expecting anyone, are you, darling?'

Lara's mother shook her head. 'Today? And in *this* weather? Of course not.'

There was a pause, and Lara was filled with the strangest, giddiest sense of expectation.

'Better go and answer it, hadn't you?' she said, her heart beating so fast that her words sounded strangled.

Both her sisters turned and looked at her, both sets of eyebrows raised in identical sisterly question.

Even the children were silent.

They heard the door open and the sound of Lara's father speaking to someone, then a low, murmured reply. Ten expectant faces were turned towards the door of the dining room, listening as two pairs of footsteps approached.

'Wassamatter, Arnie La-La?' demanded her nephew, and Lara realised that she was gripping onto him very tightly indeed, instinct and a deep sense of hope and longing telling her who the caller might be.

She wanted it to be…but surely it couldn't…it just couldn't…

The world stood still and her heart clenched tightly in her chest as she stared straight up into a pair of rueful golden eyes, vaguely aware of her sisters both sitting bolt upright, making twin sounds of disbelief.

Well, she felt a bit like that herself—he looked so gorgeous. Strong and tall and lean as he stood there, just looking at her. She could scarcely think straight and her hands felt clammy.

'Darian,' she breathed.

'Hello, Lara,' said Darian softly.

CHAPTER FIFTEEN

THERE was another pin-drop silence, and Lara wasn't surprised—because the sight of Darian standing in her parents' beautiful old farmhouse was slightly surreal—as if
they had all been taking part in a black and white film and
somebody had just stepped in in full Technicolor.

He wore jeans, and beneath a battered leather jacket was
a warm, soft sweater, just like the one he had been wearing
the first time she'd seen him. His hair was all ruffled, and
sprinkled with snowflakes, and his skin looked even more
vibrant and glowing than usual, his eyes shining with
health and vitality.

Lara's mother coughed. 'Er, aren't you going to introduce us, Lara?'

'Yes, do, Lara,' said Heather, her oldest sister, in a voice
which couldn't disguise her restrained excitement.

'This is Darian Wildman,' said Lara breathlessly. 'He's
a…he's a friend of mine.'

The golden eyes gleamed in silent challenge.

'Won't you sit down, Darian?' said Lara's mother
mildly, as if men who looked like Hollywood film stars
suddenly appeared in her dining room every day of the
week. 'And have some tea? Or I could probably rustle you
up some lunch if you haven't already eaten.'

He smiled at her, and Lara watched her mother melt.
'I'd like that very much, Mrs. Black, but I wonder if first
I could have a few words with Lara? In private?'

'Of course.' She looked at her daughter. 'Lara?'

Lara rose to her feet on legs which felt as if they had

172

suddenly been transformed into jelly. 'Let's go into the sitting room,' she said unsteadily.

The fire was blazing and there was a photo album lying open on one of the sofas. An empty champagne bottle was upended in the bin and there was crumpled wrapping paper from the anniversary presents lying waiting to be hurled on the fire. It looked messy and warm and homely.

Outside the window, the scene was startlingly white and beautiful, and Darian released a slow sigh as he turned to look at Lara properly, dressed in palest cream, her hair all loose around her shoulders, looking like a winter wonder herself. 'Lara,' he said softly.

Her heart was beating very fast. 'How the hell did you find me?'

'Jake told me where you were.'

'He *did*?'

'Eventually.' It had been like trying to extract blood from a stone, Darian remembered with a kind of grim admiration. 'He didn't want to. Gave me a great long lecture on how wonderful you were and how he wasn't going to stand by and see you hurt—but in the end I asked him whether you would be happier to see me than not, and then he told me where you were.' His eyes were very clear—clear and golden. 'So are you, Lara? Happy to see me?'

'I'm not sure how I feel,' she answered truthfully, because she didn't yet know why it was he had come.

He looked at the way her dark lashes were half lowered. 'You look very beautiful,' he observed softly.

'Thank you.' She let the lashes flutter up, cautious and wary. She felt as if she was skating on ice, without knowing how thin it was.

'But you've lost weight!' he accused softly.

She ran her eyes over the shadows and angles of his gorgeous face. 'Well, so have you!'

'I've been in the saddle every morning, riding through inaccessible parts of Maraban—what's your excuse?'

She didn't answer that. She didn't have to. She wasn't going to tell him that she had missed him and been pining for him, because that way she risked too much. Too much hurt if he told her, as she suspected he was about to, that he was going to stay in Maraban. That his life was there.

But if that was the case...

'Why are you here, Darian?'

'Can't you guess?'

Oh, but guessing was a dangerous game. She knew what she hoped, but she dared not risk saying it. What if her dreams were way off mark? Would that not just put him in the awful position—for him and for her—of having to reject her? But he's here, a little voice reminded her. He is *here*. 'I'm not a mind-reader.'

'Aren't you?' The last time he had made love to her he had thought she could see into his very soul. And he hers. God, it seemed like a lifetime ago now, and in a way maybe it was. 'Come over here, Lara,' he said, in a low, soft voice. 'You're a long way away from me.'

It was only a few steps, but it felt like a million, and Lara's feet took her slowly towards him like a child learning to walk for the first time. That was exactly how she felt. Unsure and uncertain and a tiny bit afraid.

He put his hand up and touched her cheek, saw her eyelashes briefly flutter down to shield her eyes, and when she opened again they were bright. And wary.

'Why have you come here?' she whispered again.

'Because...' He searched for the right words, and wondered why they were so hard to find. Maybe because he wasn't used to saying what was really on his mind. And in his heart. 'I've...missed you.'

'Have you?' Her heart leapt in her chest. It wasn't the biggest declaration in the world, but maybe because of that it felt more real, more solid. For Darian was not a man to use words he did not mean.

He nodded. *Tell her how much.* 'Very much.'

It had been an entirely new sensation, one that he had tried at first to deny and then to rationalise his way out of—until he had realised that there *was* no way out, that for the first time in his adult life there was no template to follow. This was all very new to him, and exciting, and kind of scary.

His eyes gleamed very gold. 'Actually—very, very much.'

She could tell that he was choosing his words carefully, and the flicker of hope became a little steadier. 'Well, I've missed you, too.'

'Have you, now?' He smiled, but he saw how huge her eyes seemed in her face. She looked all wary, on edge. Fragile, as if she might just crumple up or dissolve. He felt a fierce rush of protectiveness and it took him by surprise—but why should it have done, when he stopped to think about it? Hadn't he been exactly that during that chaste first night together in Maraban? 'Don't you think we ought to sit down?'

She was pleased to, because her legs were feeling as wobbly as her emotions. They sat, side by side on the sofa, to the left of the roaring blaze, and while part of her longed for him to take her into his arms and kiss her the other part of her was enjoying his almost Victorian restraint. Passion was easy, but emotion wasn't. Not for Darian. Passion could be something to hide behind, and he wasn't attempting to.

She turned to him. His eyes looked different, she thought, as though he had seen something new—and maybe he had. 'So tell me about Maraban,' she said softly. 'What was it like in the desert?'

Darian's eyes narrowed. He realised that her focus was

absolutely right, though maybe that shouldn't have surprised him. Another woman might have wanted to talk about herself, about them, but Lara didn't. Had she sensed that his whole life and his whole perspective had changed? That change had somehow arisen out of the amazing experiences he had lived through, in the desert especially?

'It was just the two of us,' he began, his eyes narrowing with memory, taking him right back to the way it had been. 'Oh, there were guards stationed further down the mountain, of course, but in effect it was just me and Khalim. We rode, and we walked, and we talked. We did a lot of talking. We lit fires—it was *bloody* cold. The snows had set in, so we had to take food with us.'

'Not too much of it, judging by the look of you,' she said wryly.

'No.' He smiled. 'I guess it must almost have qualified as fasting.'

'And fasting is cleansing,' she observed, remembering the yoga course she had signed up for, until she had found sitting around saying 'Om' a bit boring and dropped out. 'Isn't it?'

'Very.' It had been the first time that he had ever really stopped, slowed down, really given himself time to think and to smell the roses. To look at his life and put it into some kind of perspective. 'Khalim offered me a place there,' he said slowly.

She had guessed that this might happen, had been mentally prepared for it, but even so it was still a shock. 'What kind of place?'

'To rule the western region of Maraban. To publicly acknowledge me as his brother—to legitimately make me...' He laughed. It sounded so bizarre—hell, it *was* bizarre—but that didn't mean it wasn't happening. 'Prince Darian of Maraban.'

Lara nodded. Heady stuff, being offered your own kingdom. Darian had influence and relative power in England, but nothing could compare to that. 'What did you say?'

He nodded slightly. She was perceptive indeed. She had not made any assumption about what his answer had been. 'I told him no.'

'My God,' she breathed. 'Was he angry?'

He shook his head. 'I think he was relieved, in a way. He made the offer out of filial loyalty, because he felt that it was right, and that only confirms what a remarkable man he is.'

'But why did you refuse it?'

For the first time he touched her. Picked up her hand and examined it, stroking the tip of his finger reflectively over the palm. It was both tender and yet curiously erotic, and Lara trembled. Was it still pretend tenderness, or was it real this time?

He felt her tremble and stopped stroking. Not yet, he thought. Not yet.

'I refused it because we are both strong men, and you cannot have two strong men governing side by side—it might work well as an ideal, but the reality of two such mighty egos clashing would be explosive!'

Yes, she could see that. 'But weren't you tempted?'

'By power?' he questioned slowly, and she nodded. 'For about a nano-second.' He looked very reflective for a moment, then gave a wry smile. 'But I could envisage the repercussions, should I accept such an offer. Maraban is Khalim's by birth as well as by blood. He knows his country more intimately than anyone. To bring in a man who is only half Marabanese would be to weaken the throne, supply subversive factions with a legitimate cause to revolt.'

'That's remarkably far-sighted of you,' she observed. 'Lesser men would have grasped at the chance of such power, no matter what the consequences, but not you.'

'No,' he agreed. 'Not me. Because lately I have learned too much to ever disregard what the consequences might be.'

There was a pause, and this time the silence had about it a quality which made Lara still, some instinct telling her that what he was about to say would be profound.

'And Khalim and I read his...*our*,' he amended, with a wry smile, 'father's diaries.'

Lara looked at him in astonishment. 'I thought you said there was a fifty-year rule preventing that?'

'So there is, but as Khalim rather arrogantly announced—why make the laws if you can't break them occasionally, too! Though they will still not be made public until the allotted time.' There was a pause. 'Makim knew nothing about my mother's pregnancy,' he told her quietly. 'That much was clear. He mentions her with great affection, but nothing more than that. It appears to have been a very passionate affair which had consequences of which he knew nothing.'

'And that makes a difference, doesn't it?' she questioned slowly. 'To you?'

He traced the line of her lips with the tip of her finger. 'Yes, it does. Of course it does.' He smiled. 'It means that I was not rejected nor forgotten by the Sheikh, nor denied a heritage that was truly mine. He simply didn't know anything about me.'

He tilted her face so that their eyes collided, blue with gold. 'But that's enough about Maraban.' His voice was soft now. 'I came here to talk about something quite different—something more important still.'

Her heart had begun to race. 'Oh?'

Once more he picked his words with care, recognising their significance and knowing how important it was that she believed them.

'I want to tell you why I came back,' he said simply.

'Oh?'

This was hard, to just come right out and say it, but he knew that he had to. For both their sakes. 'I never felt complete before, Lara.' He hesitated, trying to make sense of it. For her. And for him, too. 'Maybe that's the way it always is when you don't know what your true parentage is. And knowing is one thing, but seeing is something else. Seeing really *is* belicving. When I tasted some of the life in Maraban, saw my father's home and land and the way he must have lived his life, I felt in a way as if I had come home.'

He paused, remembering how Khalim had told him that to feel deeply made you more of a man, not less. But it went against the grain with Darian. Old habits died hard. He had grown up believing that it was a sign of weakness to express your feelings. Yet now he recognised the importance of saying what he really meant, not hiding behind the tough, macho exterior which had been his childhood protection.

'When you discover your identity—you come home. You're at peace with yourself—at least in theory.'

She raised her face to his. 'I…I don't understand.'

It had taken him a little while, too. 'I found the peace which comes with knowing what my roots are, but I had lost something, too—the something that makes everything in life worthwhile. The something that makes living wonderful and the world an empty place if it isn't there.' He felt the thaw around a heart which had always been hard and tough and cold. It was like taking a leap into the unknown, he thought. Unexplored, uncharted territory—which took more courage to confront than any barren and inhospitable Maraban desert.

'Love, Lara,' he said simply. 'I found you, and I found love, and when you went away something was missing.

You'd struck a hammer-blow to my heart and it made me realise how much I wanted you in my life.'

'Oh, Darian,' she whispered, her voice faint, her blood pounding a symphony inside her head, weakened with pleasure and a sense of wonder. 'Darian.'

He smiled. 'But it wasn't the first time I'd felt that way.' His voice softened. 'I experienced it the first time I lay in your arms, but it scared the hell out of me. I put it down to the fact that we'd just had amazing sex. It made me feel vulnerable, you see, in a way I wasn't used to feeling. It's what made me not ring you.' He sucked in a deep breath. 'But I was blinding myself to the truth—then and later.'

'Oh?' The word was barely audible.

'That you were the missing part of the equation, Lara. That once you'd left Maraban it no longer felt like home. Home is where the heart is, and you have my heart. You were the factor which somehow made it all complete. Made *me* complete,' he finished, and it was a declaration so raw and intense that Lara felt rocked, shocked into a disbelieving silence.

'I love you, Lara,' he said simply. 'And I want you in my life. Permanently. Yours is the face I want to see first thing in the morning and last thing at night.'

Part of her was still scared that he was just saying it because he was in a heightened state of emotion, because all his past had coming flooding back in such a dramatic way. But when she looked into his eyes she saw the shining truth written there, and she knew she owed him nothing less in return.

'And I love you,' she said shakily. 'So very, very much.'

He touched her hair with a sense of wonder. 'When did it happen?' he mused. 'And how does it happen? In a moment? In a look, or in a kiss? In an emptiness when someone isn't there any more and you wish they were?'

'All of those things,' she agreed. 'And a few more besides.'

'Yes,' he said thoughtfully.

'Please, Darian,' she begged, 'will you just kiss me now?'

'Oh, God, Lara,' he said unsteadily. 'Try stopping me.'

He kissed her until he had to force himself to stop, drawing his lips away from her dazed and reluctant face.

'Oh!' She pouted. 'Why did you do that?'

He moved away with difficulty. 'I hardly think it will make a good impression on your father if he comes looking for us and finds the door to his sitting room locked! Come on,' he said tenderly. 'Let's go and find your family.'

Nothing more was said, not then, but nothing needed to be and nobody asked. Maybe it was plain for everyone to see, thought Lara. They went back into the dining room, where her mother had cleared the table and made tea, and Darian sat down and was welcomed and introduced properly.

She feasted her eyes on him as he solemnly began to assist her niece in dressing her new dolly while her smallest nephew tugged insistently at the leg of his trouser, and he looked up at her and smiled, and it was all there, written in that silent and loving curve of his lips.

It seemed nothing short of a miracle that the two of them had been brought together, to this sweet, satisfying conclusion. Fate, Khalim would have said. Predestination.

And she believed in it, too.

She didn't know what their future would bring—but then, who did? Life was a journey and so were relationships, and theirs had begun properly today.

I love you, Darian Wildman, her eyes told him, and silently his eyes told her he loved her back.

EPILOGUE

EVERYONE in the village said there had never been an event like it, and they were quite right. The wedding of the youngest Black girl took place in a tiny village church in the middle of the English countryside and was attended by the leading members of the Maraban royal family!

'Won't people ask questions?' Lara had asked Darian anxiously one morning, when she was trying to get out of bed.

He pulled her back into his arms. 'Ask what?' he said, his voice muffled, but then it was very difficult to talk at the same time as you were kissing somebody's neck.

'About...' Lara closed her eyes. This was hopeless. She couldn't think straight—but then, in his arms she always felt like that. 'About why Khalim and Rose and the children will be there.'

'Rose is your friend,' he said simply. 'That's all anyone needs to know.'

For, after much thought and discussion with Rose and Khalim, they had decided to keep Darian's ancestry a secret. Nothing would be gained by him acknowledging a title which he had no intention of claiming, and neither of them wanted the intrusion that media interest would bring, nor the risk of Maraban dissidents knowing where they lived.

But Darian had fallen more than a little bit in love with the country, and his latest career direction had taken that fact into account. He was now establishing new trade links between Maraban and the West, becoming a sympathetic and enthusiastic advisor to Khalim, his brother.

Lara's family had welcomed him with open arms—he had won them over that first day, each and every one of them—and Lara's mother had taken her aside just before they'd left to go back to London.

'You're a lucky girl,' she had said wistfully. 'He loves you very much.'

She didn't need to be told that. Sometimes Lara felt that she had to pinch herself, to see whether it really could be true—but it was. And with love had come other changes. She had taken a new career path, discovering that she no longer wanted to chase bit parts in stupid commercials or play a minor character in a show which seemed to close almost as soon as it had opened. Nor put herself up for rejection every time she went on a 'go-see'. She felt she had been given so much that now she wanted to put something back.

Soon after she moved into Darian's apartment she had enrolled on a course to learn how to teach drama, and that was how she saw her working future. At least until the babies came. Lots and lots of them. She wanted that, and so did Darian. He would find them a house somewhere and they would build a home together, fill it with noise and warmth and, she hoped, children.

She wanted to give him what he had never had. What she had seen on his face that snowy winter day as he had embraced her little nephews and nieces—the joy of being part of a whole big family. He had found part of his family in Khalim and now it would just grow and grow.

Even Jake had come round to accepting him. The two men had gone out for a 'quick' drink one evening, and had rolled in at midnight, both rather tight. Lara had scolded them for not letting her know, bursting into laughter when she returned with a tray of strong coffee to find them both slumped together in companionable sleep.

In front of a video of one of *her* old plays!

It had taken a year before he had asked her to marry him. He had wanted to ask her that day at her parents', but had held off, recognising that they needed something of which they had had precious little.

Time.

But time was a funny thing. It only echoed what you were feeling inside. When you were waiting for a train an hour could seem like an eternity, and when you were sitting an exam that same hour could seem like a minute.

And so it had been with him and Lara. The first time he'd seen her something had touched him, only he had been too stubborn and pig-headed to acknowledge it. Theirs had not been a smooth and easy journey to get to where they were today, but maybe that was what made it so very good. You had to experience pain to appreciate pleasure, and the pleasure she gave him was immeasurable.

Darian turned his head as the organist began to play and Lara began to walk towards him, a vision in a sheath of slippery white satin, her arms full of snowdrops and lily-of-the-valley.

His eyes were on her the whole time, and when she reached him she gave him a loving smile. He smiled back, and the warmth inside his heart increased so that it felt as if he had a small furnace burning away inside him.

After a lifetime of resistance Darian was learning to articulate his feelings, but with Lara that was easy.

He had never known it could be so easy.

The Sheikh & the Princess in Waiting

SUSAN MALLERY

Chapter One

After a long day of working in the delivery room, Emma Kennedy was ready to spend her evening with her feet propped up, the TV on and a bowl of ice cream in her hand. Okay, yes, she would probably eat something decent for dinner first but the ice cream was a must. It had been *that* kind of day.

Nothing had happened all morning, then right at noon, four women had decided to deliver. One had been a terrified teenager, and Emma had stayed with her as much as possible. At twenty-four, Emma had been closest in age of all the nurses, although a lifetime of experiences away from the street-wise, body pierced and tattooed patient.

Emma opened her mailbox, pulled out the cable bill

and a flyer for a sale at Dillard's, then walked toward her apartment.

She was tired, but content. It had been a good day. A happy day. One of the things she loved about her job was the joy new mothers experienced when their babies were born. Being part of the process, even on the periphery, was all the thanks she needed. When she thought about all the—

Emma suddenly stopped in the hallway. Two men in dark suits stood by her front door. They looked respectable enough—clean, short haircuts, polished shoes—but they were definitely *lurking*.

She'd taken several self-defense courses over the years, but she wasn't sure how helpful the information she'd learned would be against two large men.

Glancing first left, then right, she calculated the distance to her nearest neighbor. How long would it take her to run to her car, and what kind of reaction she would get if she screamed?

One of the men looked up and saw her. "Ms. Kennedy? I'm Alex Dunnard from the State Department. This is my associate, Jack Sanders. May we have a moment of your time?"

As the man spoke, he pulled out an ID card complete with picture. His companion did the same. Emma abandoned the idea of bolting and approached her front door.

The pictures matched the men and the cards *looked* official enough, but it wasn't as if she'd seen a State Department ID before and would know the difference.

Alex Dunnard slipped the ID back into his jacket pocket and smiled. "We have some official business to discuss with you. May we come inside, or would you be more comfortable if we met at the coffee shop on the corner?''

Emma noticed that neither option allowed her to get out of talking with them. Which was crazy. What would the State Department want with her?

She gave them the once-over and decided to let them in. Her Dallas suburb was safe, quiet and ordinary. No doubt these men had the wrong person. Once they straightened that out, they would be on their way.

"Come on in," she said, inserting her key in the lock.

They followed her into the smallish living room. It was already dusk, so she turned on both floor lamps and the light in the hall, then motioned to her sofa.

"Have a seat," she said as she plopped down in the club chair opposite.

As she set her purse on the floor, she noticed several stains on the front of her brightly patterned scrub shirt. The pale green pants were also dotted and streaked. Occupational hazard, she reminded herself.

Alex perched on the edge of her sofa, while the other gentleman stood by the sliding glass door.

"Ms. Kennedy, we're here at the behest of the king of Bahania."

Alex kept on talking, but Emma was too caught up in the word *behest*. She wasn't sure she'd ever heard someone say it in normal speech. It was more of a book word. Then the rest of the sentence sunk in.

"Wait a minute," she said, holding up her hand. "Did you say the *king* of Bahania?"

"Yes, ma'am. He contacted the State Department and asked that we locate you and then offer you an official invitation to visit his country."

Emma laughed. Oh, sure. Because that sort of thing happened all the time. "Are you guys selling something? Because if you are, you're wasting your time."

"No, ma'am. We're from the State Department, and we're here—"

She cut him off with a wave. "I know. At the behest. I got that part. You have the wrong person. I'm sure there's another Emma Kennedy floating around who has lots of personal contact with His Royal Highness, but it's not me."

She looked at her modest apartment. If only, she thought humorously. Maybe a small money grant or two could have taken care of her student loans. And she desperately needed new tires for her ten-year-old import. Oh, well. In her next life she would be rich. In this one she was just a single woman struggling to pay the bills.

Alex pulled a piece of paper out of his outer jacket pocket. "Emma Kennedy," he read, then went on to list her birth date, place of birth, her parents' names and the number on her passport. A passport she'd had since she was eighteen, young, innocent and foolish and had thought... Well, she'd thought a lot of things.

"Just a second," she said, and rose to walk into her bedroom.

Her passport was tucked in the back of her sock drawer. She pulled it out and returned to the living room where she had Alex read the number again. It matched.

"This is creepy," she said. "Look, I don't know the king of Bahania. I'm not sure I could find Bahania on the map. There really has to be some kind of mistake. What would he want with me?"

"You are to be his guest for the next two weeks." Alex stood and smiled. "There's a private jet standing by to take you to his country. Ms. Kennedy, Bahania is a valuable ally in the Middle East. Like their neighbor, El Bahar, they are considered the Switzerland of that region. These progressive countries offer a haven of peace and economic stability in a troubled part of the world. They also provide a significant percentage of our country's oil."

Emma might have only taken one political science class at college, but she wasn't stupid. She got the message. When the king of Bahania invited a young Texas nurse to vacation in his country for a couple of weeks, the United States government expected her to go.

Was she being kidnapped?

The idea was both insane and terrifying.

"You can't make me go," she said, more to hear the words than because she believed them. She had a feeling that Alex and his friend could make her do just about anything.

"You're correct. We would not force you to accept the king's invitation. However, your country would be most grateful if you would consider granting him this request." He smiled. "You'll be perfectly safe, Ms. Kennedy. The king is an honorable man. You're not being sold into a harem."

"The thought never crossed my mind," she told him hotly, even though it had. Sort of.

A harem? Her? Not on this planet. Men didn't find her especially appealing, and she... Well, she avoided matters of the heart. She'd fallen in love once and it had been a complete disaster.

"This is a great honor," Alex said. "As a personal guest of the king, you'll be staying at the famed pink palace. It is quite extraordinary."

Emma walked back to her chair and sank down. "Can we stop for a second and reflect on the reality missing from this situation? I'm a nurse. I deliver babies for a living. Unless the king has a pregnant wife or something, why on earth would he be interested in me? I'm assuming if you know my passport number, you also know I've only been out of the country once and that was six years ago. I live a quiet life. I'm boring. You have the wrong person."

Alex's good cheer didn't waiver. "Two weeks, Ms. Kennedy. Is that so much to ask? Those volunteering for military service give much more."

Oh, darn the man. He was going for guilt. She really didn't like that. Her parents had been experts at it and she hated the sense of having disappointed anyone.

"I'll accompany you to Bahania," Alex continued. "To assure your safe arrival. Once you're settled, I'll return to Washington." He paused. "You're being given a wonderful opportunity, Ms. Kennedy. I hope you'll consider it. If we can leave for the airport in the next hour, we will be in Bahania by sunset tomorrow."

Her mind swirled. "You want me to go with you right now?"

"Please."

Emma glanced from Alex to his friend by the sliding glass door. She had a bad feeling that if she refused, she would be taken against her will. Not exactly thoughts to warm her heart. It looked as if she were going on a trip.

Two and a half hours later, Emma found herself sitting on a luxurious private jet as the lights of Dallas disappeared below. She had a large suitcase in the cargo bay, a small overnight case next to her feet and, as promised, Alex Dunnard in the seat across from hers.

She still wasn't sure how it had all happened. Somehow Alex had gently ushered her through the process of calling the hospital for time off, packing and leaving a message for her parents that she'd gone away with a friend. The white lie had been his suggestion, made so that her parents wouldn't worry.

Then she'd showered, changed and found herself in a limo the size of a football field. Now she was on a plane and sitting in leather seats so soft and comfy, she wouldn't mind having the material made into a jacket.

On the bright side, if she *was* being kidnapped, it was by someone with money and style. The downside was that she'd managed to put her entire life on hold for two weeks with exactly two phone calls and a request that her neighbor pick up her mail. What did that say about her world?

Before she could decide, a uniformed young woman approached. ''Ms. Kennedy, I'm Aneesa and it will be my pleasure to serve you on our flight to Bahania.''

Aneesa rattled off the expected flying time, mentioned a stop for gas in Spain and offered selections for dinner.

''When you're ready to retire for the evening,'' she continued, ''there is a sleeping compartment for your use.'' She smiled. ''Along with a bathroom, complete with shower.''

''That's great,'' Emma told her, trying to sound calm. As if this sort of thing happened to her all the time.

''Shall I serve dinner?'' Aneesa asked.

''Uh, sure. Why not?''

When the attendant had disappeared to what must be the plane's galley, Emma turned to Alex.

''Are you going to tell me what's really going on here?'' she asked.

''I've told you all I know.''

''That the king wants me as his guest for two weeks,'' she summarized.

''Yes.''

''And you don't know why?''

''No.''

Not exactly helpful.

She returned her attention to the countryside below and wondered if she would ever see Texas again. Then, determined not to wallow in unpleasant and scary thoughts, she pulled out the entertainment guide and pretended interest in the various DVDs available for her viewing pleasure.

A half hour later, the meal was served. The food was beautifully prepared and delicious, if Alex's speed of consumption was anything to go by. Emma picked at the baked chicken dish and refused wine. She studied her travel companion—a well-dressed man in his mid to late forties. Nice looking, married— if the wedding ring was anything to go by. Did Mrs. Dunnard mind her husband flying off at a moment's notice? Had it been a moment's notice for him or had he known about the trip in advance? And why on earth did the king of Bahania want to meet with *her?*

More questions she was unlikely to get answered. When she tried pumping Alex for information, he remained pleasant but uncommunicative.

One restless night in a luxury cabin, several time zones and a pit stop for gas later, Emma didn't know any more than she had when she'd stepped onto the plane in Dallas. The difference was they were coming in for landing at an airport on the edge of the desert.

She stared out the window and tried to keep her mouth from falling open. The sights beneath were so beautiful they nearly took her breath away.

Turquoise-blue water lapped up against a pure white beach. There were miles of buildings, lush foliage and sprawling suburbs that gradually gave way to the endless beige and browns of the desert. Emma could see pockets of industry, large buildings that appeared ancient and what looked like dozens of parks throughout the city before the plane banked and headed for the airport.

They landed with a light bump, then taxied to a low one-story building. As Alex picked up his small overnight case, Emma fumbled for her purse.

She was escorted onto the tarmac where the late afternoon was warm, sunny and dry. And bright. After the confines of the plane, she found the sunlight nearly blinding. Three steps later, she entered a pleasant room where a man in uniform actually bowed when she presented herself and her open passport.

"Ms. Kennedy," he said, flashing a smile, "welcome to Bahania. May your journey be pleasant and blessed."

"Thank you," she murmured, wondering if everyone was always so polite. Not that she was going to complain. She could get used to this level of service.

The surprises weren't over. Minutes later Alex escorted her to another large limo. Inside she found a bottle of champagne sitting on ice and a small bouquet of flowers.

"For me?" she asked as Alex sat next to her.

"I doubt the king meant them for me," he told her.

Good point. Emma sniffed the roses. When Alex pointed to the bottle of champagne, she shook her head.

"I didn't sleep," she admitted. "Between being exhausted, the strange circumstances and the time change, the last thing I need is liquor."

She already felt woozy enough.

As they pulled out of the airport, Alex began to talk to her about the city. He pointed out the financial district, the old shopping bazaar, the entrance to the famous Bahanian beaches. Emma did her best to pay attention, but the longer they were on the road, the more she regretted her decision to come. Sure, Bahania was beautiful and all, but she'd just traveled halfway around the world with a man she didn't know to meet a king she'd barely heard of, and aside from her traveling companion and the king, no one on the planet knew where she was.

It was not a situation designed to make one relax.

Forty minutes later, the limo drove through an open gate, past several guards and what felt like miles of manicured grounds. She stared out the window until she saw the first hints of the fabled pink palace.

"This is so not happening," she murmured, still unable to believe this was real.

The limo pulled up in front of the entrance. At least she assumed that's what the arched doorway and alcove big enough for a marching band was for.

"We're here," Alex said, confirming her suspicions.

She glanced at him. "What happens now?"

"You meet the king."

Great. If there was a survey at the end of this, she was going to mention Alex's lack of information as one of her complaints.

The limo door opened. Alex climbed out, then stepped aside so she could exit. Emma smoothed down the skirt she'd changed into on the plane and sucked in a breath for courage. It wasn't close to enough, so she wasn't surprised to find herself shaking as she stepped out in the warm afternoon.

Several people stood by the palace: Alex, the limo driver, a few uniformed men who could have been servants, but no one who looked like a king. So did royalty wait indoors for their visitors? Shouldn't Alex have briefed her on that sort of thing?

Before she could ask him, there was a movement to her left. Emma turned and saw a man step out of the shadows. He was tall, darkly handsome and almost familiar. Then the sun hit him full in the face and she gasped in stunned amazement. It couldn't be. Not after all this time. She'd thought… He would never…

The combination of shock, lack of sleep and food, and jet lag, conspired to increase her heart rate from nervous to hummingbird speed. The blood rushed from her head to her feet in two seconds flat. The world spun, blurred, then faded completely as she collapsed to the ground.

Prince Reyhan glanced at his father, the king of Bahania, and shook his head.

"That went well."

Chapter Two

Several servants rushed toward the fallen woman. Reyhan brushed them aside and crouched beside Emma. He took her wrist in his hand and felt her pulse.

Rapid, but steady.

"Call a doctor," he said firmly.

Someone went scuttling to do his bidding.

"She didn't hit her head," a young woman told him as she gently touched Emma's forehead. "I was watching as she fainted, Your Highness."

"Thank you. Are her rooms prepared?"

The woman nodded.

Reyhan gathered Emma into his arms. She lay limp, one hand pressing against his chest, the other dangling by her side. Her skin had paled and her breathing slowed.

He took a moment to study her long lashes and the fullness of her mouth. The thick, red hair he remembered hung in loose waves around her face. So much was the same, he thought. No doubt if he counted, he would find that there were still eleven freckles on her nose and cheeks.

How much had changed? Even as he silently asked the question, he found he didn't want to know. He rose and walked into the palace.

The king fell into step with him.

"At least she remembered you," his father said.

"Obviously with great joy."

"Perhaps she fainted with relief that you were to be together."

Reyhan didn't bother answering. Emma hadn't seen him in six years, and from what he'd been able to find out, she'd never made any attempt to get in touch with him. He had no idea what she recalled of their brief…relationship, but he doubted her fainting had anything to do with relief.

The guest quarters were on the second floor. Reyhan went directly there, wondering if his father would mention that other arrangements could have been made. Fortunately, the king remained silent.

Reyhan swept inside the suite of rooms he'd had prepared for Emma and set her on the sofa. A maid hovered in the corner.

"Find out when the doctor will arrive," he said.

The woman nodded and picked up a phone from the small table in the corner.

Reyhan returned his attention to Emma. She lay perfectly still. She hadn't moved at all while he'd carried her.

He sat next to her on the sofa and took her hand in his. Her fingers were cold. He brought them to his mouth and breathed on them.

"Emma," he murmured. "You must awaken."

She moved her head slightly and moaned.

"The doctor will be here in fifteen minutes," the maid told him.

"Thank you. A glass of water, please."

"Yes, Your Highness."

"Someone else could have carried her," the king said from the seat he'd taken across from the sofa. "Someone else can care for her now."

Reyhan narrowed his gaze. "No one touches my wife."

His father rose and crossed to the door. "It has been six years, Reyhan. Are you sure you still wish to claim the title of husband?"

Wish it or not, it was his. As was she.

Emma felt as if she were swimming against a very strong tide. But instead of water, she was trapped by air she had to push through to reach the surface. Thoughts formed and separated, her body felt heavy. Something had happened. She remembered that much. But what?

A cool, smooth surface pressed against her mouth as a strong, male voice demanded, "Drink this."

She parted her lips without considering refusing the request.

Water slipped into her mouth. She drank gratefully, then sighed when the glass was removed. Better, she thought, and opened her eyes.

Oh, my—it was him! Her eyes hadn't been playing tricks on her. She could feel the heat and strength of him as he sat next to her on the sofa. His hip pressed against her thigh. One of his hands held her own, while his dark gaze trapped her as neatly as a cage held a small bird.

Reyhan.

She wasn't sure if she said the name or merely thought it. Was it possible? After all these years?

She blinked and wondered if this was nothing more than a vivid dream. Only, her luck wasn't that good. No, the truth was he was real and she was in his presence, which didn't seem possible. It had been six years, she reminded herself again. Six years since he'd used her and tossed her aside. Six years since she'd hidden at her parents' house, crying for what could have been, secretly waiting for him to come and claim her, only to find out she'd waited in vain. He'd never come, and eventually she'd returned to her life—older, wiser and emotionally battered.

"So you return to us," he said, his low voice rumbling like distant thunder. "I don't remember you fainting before."

She bristled at the assumption that he *knew* things about her.

"I don't faint," she told him.

"Recent events suggest that you do. It was a long trip. Were you able to sleep at all?"

He spoke so casually, she thought in amazement.

As if nothing out of the ordinary had happened. As if it had been a few days rather than years since they were last together.

Outrage blossomed into fury. She wanted to yell at him, to scream or maybe even throw something. But years of being told that a lady didn't show her anger made it difficult for her to do more than glare.

Reyhan lightly touched her cheek. "I see by the shadows under your eyes you did not sleep on the plane. At least not for long. Hardly a surprise, I suppose. You were not told why you were brought here. As I recall, you were always impatient and eager to find out things."

Her attention split neatly between his words, which annoyed her, and the light stroking of his fingers against her skin. When his thumb grazed her lower lip, she was stunned by a jolt of awareness. The sensation cut through her like lightning, heating and melting everywhere it touched.

No! She would not react, she told herself. She wouldn't feel anything. She refused to. If this man really was Reyhan, then he filled her with nothing but contempt. He was beneath her notice.

One corner of his firm mouth turned up slightly. "I see you want to spit at me like an ill-tempered kitten," he murmured. "There is anger in your eyes." He glanced at her fingers. "No claws. I doubt you can do much damage."

Then he stunned her by kissing her knuckles.

She felt the warm brush of his mouth clear down to her toes. The hot, melting sensation grew until she wanted to purr like the kitten he'd mentioned. She thought about—

"Stop that right now," she said, snatching her hand back and folding her arms across her chest. The instruction was meant for both of them. In the past twenty-four hours, her world had taken a turn for the confusing, but she was determined to figure out what was going on. Which meant staying focused on the task at hand and not getting caught up in being in the same room as Reyhan.

She shifted away from him and pushed herself up into a sitting position. When he took hold of her arm to help her, she shook off his hand.

"I'm fine," she told him, her tone as icy as she could make it. "What I need from you is information. What is going on? What am I doing here? And while we're on the subject, what are *you* doing here?"

Before he could speak, there was a blur of movement, then a long-haired cream-colored cat with nearly violet eyes jumped up on her lap. She stared at it in amazement. Cats in the palace?

Reyhan grabbed the animal and set it back on the floor. The cat glared at him, gave a sniff of disgust and stalked off.

"Are you allergic to cats?" he asked.

"What? No."

"Good. The palace is filled with them. They are my father's."

His father? She rubbed her temple and tried to decide if she wanted to ask who his father was. While she would like the information, she was also afraid of it. Because crazy as it sounded, she had a feeling there was a better-than-even chance that Reyhan was somehow related to the king of Bahania.

Don't go there, she told herself as Reyhan held out the glass of water again. As she took it from him she found herself caught in his gaze.

She remembered his eyes most of all, she thought. How dark they were. How well they kept secrets. She'd once thought that if she could learn to read his eyes, she would know the man. But their few weeks together had not given them the time to learn very much about each other.

Sadness threatened. She tried to banish it by recalling what Reyhan had done to her—how he'd left and how she'd been alone and so afraid. Better to be angry. There was energy in anger and she had the feeling she was going to need it.

"I don't know what this game is," she told him, "but I'm not going to play. I wish to return home immediately. Please call Alex and have him take me back to the plane."

"Your escort from the State Department has already left the palace. He will spend the night at one of our most beautiful oceanside hotels, then fly back to your country in the morning." Reyhan dismissed the man with a flick of his wrist. "You will not see him again."

Anger faded as fear took its place. Alex was gone? So she was truly alone in the palace? Alone in this country?

Emma didn't know if she should try to bolt for freedom or bluff her way through. Her head was still spinning and she didn't look forward to trying to stand up, so that left bluffing. Something she'd never been very good at.

"What am I doing here?" she demanded. "Why did the king of Bahania ask me to come here for two weeks? And what are *you* doing here? You can't have anything to do with what's going on with me."

That last bit was more plea than forceful statement.

Reyhan stared at her. His strong, handsome features could have been set in stone—or steel—for all they gave away.

"Haven't you guessed?" he asked with quiet amusement, as if she were a child who had just performed the alphabet song flawlessly for the first time. "The king is my father, and the invitation is as much mine as his."

Her mind went blank. Completely and totally. It was like losing the lights during a thunderstorm.

The man next to her rose and squared his shoulders. Then he stared down at her with a haughty expression possibly honed through a lifetime of royal arrogance.

"I am Prince Reyhan, third oldest son of King Hassan of Bahania."

She blinked. Not possible, she told herself as some semicoherent thought process began in her brain. Not possible, not likely and she refused to believe it.

"A p-prince?" she asked, stumbling over the word.

No. No. No. Emma stared at the man standing in front of her. He couldn't be. A prince? Him? But they'd met at college. They'd dated. He'd taken her away with him and...hurt her dreadfully.

"The king decided it was time for me to marry,"

Reyhan told her. "There was no way I could agree to any match as I was already married. To you."

He kept on talking, but she wasn't listening. She couldn't. A prince? Married?

"But I..." She swallowed and tried again. "That wasn't real. Not any of it."

She remembered the quiet of the Caribbean island, the soft breezes, the lap of the ocean outside their hotel room. Reyhan had asked her to go away with him, and she'd agreed because she could refuse him nothing. At eighteen, she'd been more innocent than he'd realized. She'd been too ashamed to tell him she'd never dated before. He'd been her first, in every sense of the word.

Years later, when she'd looked back on the blur of hot days and long, endless nights, she'd comforted herself with the fact that she'd been too swept up in thinking she was in love to refuse Reyhan anything. She would never have considered asking him to go more slowly, to give her time to adjust. As for their marriage—her parents' lawyer had told her that had been a fake.

For a long time the realization had nearly destroyed her. She'd hated her weakness where he was concerned. Hated that she could still want him, even as he'd used and abandoned her. Time had healed her enough to give her perspective.

Reyhan's dark eyebrows drew together. "What wasn't real?"

"Our marriage. You just did that to get me into bed. Or get a green card."

As soon as she spoke the words, she realized she

might have made a mistake. Reyhan seemed to get bigger and taller as his temper grew. His anger was as tangible as the sofa she sat on, but a lot more frightening. His gaze narrowed and his mouth twisted into a disapproving and scornful line.

"A green card?" he asked, his voice thick with tension. "Why would I need that? I am Prince Reyhan. I am heir to the king of Bahania. I have no need to seek asylum elsewhere. This is my country."

He spoke proudly and with the confidence of who knew how many generations of royalty behind him.

"Yes, well." She cleared her throat. At the time, him wanting a green card had made sense. But now… "So that's not why you married me."

"It was not. I was in your country to continue my education. I earned my master's degree there." His expression turned contemptuous. "I honored you by giving you my name and my protection. As for trying to get you into my bed, the effort was hardly worth the meager reward."

She shrank back into the cushions. Humiliation joined the fear. As much as she tried to block out their nights together, they continued to haunt her. She supposed her part of it could be an illustration of what *not* to do on one's wedding night and the few nights that followed.

Not that it was her fault, she told herself, trying to grab on to a little temper to give her courage. She'd been the virgin. He should have done better, too.

But if Reyhan hadn't married her to get a green card or to sleep with her, why had he?

"Are you sure the marriage was real?" she asked. "My parents' lawyer said that it wasn't."

"Then their lawyer was mistaken." Reyhan glared at her. "You are my wife. That is why you were brought here. Now that you are in my country, in my home, you will treat me with respect and reverence. Is that understood?"

The need to bolt for freedom grew exponentially.

"Reyhan, I—"

But she never got to say whatever she'd been about to blurt out. For just at that moment, a petite, curvy, beautiful young woman walked into the room.

"This isn't good," the woman said. "I heard Emma had arrived and fainted at the sight of you. Is that true?"

Reyhan turned his attention from Emma to the woman. His glare only deepened.

The woman rolled her eyes. "Yeah, yeah, I know. You're insulted. But don't forget, I gave birth to your older brother's firstborn, so you have to be nice to me."

"One wonders what Sadik sees in you."

The woman leaned close and smiled. "I'm a hottie. It's a curse, but there we are."

Emma didn't think things could get more shocking, but she was proved wrong when Reyhan actually smiled at the woman, then kissed her forehead.

"Can you fix this?" he asked the woman.

"I'm not sure if you mean Emma or the situation. If you ask me, the one who needs fixing is you." She held up her hand before he could speak. "I'll do my best. I promise. Now why don't you give us some girl time together? I'll answer Emma's questions and make her feel at home. You can go work on your charm.''

Reyhan raised his eyebrows. "I'm very charming."

"Uh-huh. Just a tip here. The 'I'm Prince Reyhan of Bahania' thing gets old really fast. Trust me. Sadik tried it on me, too."

"You're a troublemaker."

"That's true."

Reyhan nodded at Emma, then at the woman and left. Emma watched him go.

"Is this really happening?" she asked, feeling both weary and more confused than ever.

"It sure is," the other woman told her. "Right down to you sitting in the middle of the Bahanian royal palace." She plopped down next to Emma on the sofa and smiled. "Let's start at the beginning. Hi. I'm Cleo."

"I'm Emma. Emma Kennedy."

Cleo looked her over. "Love the hair. My sister-in-law Sabrina puts red highlights in hers, but the color is nothing like this. Is it real?"

It took Emma a second to process the question and realize Cleo wasn't asking about the hair itself, but the color.

"Yes, it's natural."

"Me, too," Cleo said, tugging on her short, spiky blond hair. "I put in gold highlights once, but was *that* a mistake. I thought I'd look more elegant and classy, which is so not going to happen. I'm stuck being a tacky bottle blonde for the rest of my life. No biggie. I mean I'm a princess, so now I can be royal and tacky, which I like.''

Emma felt as if she'd fallen into an alternate universe. ''I'm sorry. I don't understand.''

Cleo grinned. ''I know. I'm rambling. Plus, do you really care about my hair? So here's the thing. You're in Bahania, and Reyhan really is a prince. There are four of them altogether. Murat is the oldest and heir to the throne. Then Sadik, my husband. He's in charge of finance. Reyhan is next. He runs the whole oil thing, and let me tell you, do they have a bunch of that floating around under the sand. Then Jefri, who is putting together a joint air force with El Bahar. There's also Zara, who was my foster sister and didn't know she was a princess until about a year ago, and Sabrina, the king's daughter. She lives in the desert, but that's a whole other story.''

''Oh.'' Emma wasn't sure what to say. Her level of confusion had just gone off the scale. ''That's a lot of people.'' She swallowed. ''And you're Princess Cleo?''

''In the flesh.'' Cleo leaned close. ''I'm from Spokane, Washington. That's right by Idaho. I know— not exactly the birthplace of a lot of royals. I had a ton to learn—protocol and how to address everyone. I've gotten involved with some charity work, which is pretty cool, and I have a new baby. Calah.'' Cleo's expression softened. ''She's a dream. Just three months old.''

Emma wanted to ask for note cards so she could write all this down and try to keep everyone and everything straight.

Reyhan, a Bahanian prince? Was it possible? And if he was, why had he married her?

"Do you know—" Emma cleared her throat. "There was a wedding a few years back. I thought maybe... My parents hired a lawyer and he thought it wasn't exactly real."

Cleo patted her arm. "Sorry. From what I've heard, it was plenty real. You're well and truly hitched to Reyhan. And he's just like his brother. All stuffy with an 'I'm the prince' attitude. That reverence and respect stuff. Oh, please. Okay, I'll do the respect thing, but reverence? It is *so* not going to happen."

So she was married. To a prince. *Her.*

"None of this makes sense," she whispered. "I don't understand."

Why had Reyhan done any of it? Why had he married her and disappeared from her life? And why, all of a sudden, did he pick now to get in touch with her? Did he want to marry someone else? The thought of it gave her an odd squeeze in her empty stomach, but still she had to know.

"Is he engaged?" she asked.

Cleo shook her head. "It's not like that. After Calah was born, the king decided it was time for Reyhan to tie the knot and give him more grandchildren. That's when he had to fess up about his relationship with you. That there was already a Mrs. Reyhan floating around."

Emma felt the room begin to fold around the edges. She had a feeling that if she'd been standing, she would have fallen again.

Cleo grabbed her hand. "Keep breathing," she instructed humorously. "I'm supposed to be making things better, not worse."

"It's not you," Emma told her. "It's everything. I can't believe what's happening."

"Hardly a surprise. The good news is, the palace is beautiful and Reyhan is pretty easy on the eyes, too. If you can get past all that honor and tradition, he has a wicked sense of humor. Won't that be nice?"

Nice? As in Emma would enjoy spending time with him? Was that the plan?

She shook her head. This wasn't happening, she told herself. None of it.

A tall man carrying a black case entered the room. Cleo waved a greeting.

"Dr. Johnson. You're still making house calls."

The older man smiled. "Yes, Princess Cleo. As I will continue to do."

Cleo leaned close to Emma. "Dr. Johnson is on call for the royal family. He's pretty cool. You'll like him."

Emma stared into the man's warm blue eyes and felt some of her anxiety fade.

He sat on the coffee table in front of her and reached for her hand. "How are you feeling? I heard you fainted."

"I don't know what happened," she admitted. "One second everything was fine, and the next, I was falling."

"Prince Reyhan filled me in on what occurred." He released her wrist. "Your pulse is normal. Have you blacked out since regaining consciousness?"

"No."

He glanced at Cleo. "Is she speaking coherently?"

"Yup. She's a little shell-shocked, but under the circumstances, who can blame her?"

Dr. Johnson made a noncommittal noise, then pulled out a stethoscope.

Fifteen minutes later he pronounced Emma exhausted, a little dehydrated, but otherwise fit. After giving her something to help her sleep, he said he would check on her the next day.

"Everything will be better in the morning," he promised as he left.

Emma watched him go, then nodded as Cleo excused herself to return to her baby. When Emma was finally alone, she stared around at the luxurious suite and the view of the ocean in the distance.

As much as she would like to believe Dr. Johnson, she had a feeling that the passage of night wasn't going to change one thing about her situation.

Reyhan did not want to speak with his father, but the request had been worded such that he'd known he didn't have a choice in the matter. So he'd appeared on time in the king's private rooms and now paced the length of the salon, all the while stepping to avoid the half-dozen or so cats milling around.

"What do you think now that you've seen her?" his father asked.

"That Emma should not have been brought here. A divorce could have been arranged without her presence."

"You defied me by marrying this young woman.

Six years have passed, and you never mentioned her or spent time with her. I want to know why.''

Reyhan had no answers to the questions, nor did he want to make up any. Thinking about Emma, being with her... He reached the window and stared out at the garden below. Seeing her again—it had been worse than he'd imagined.

His father stood and crossed the room to stand next to him. ''You are my son and a prince,'' he said. ''As such, you were not permitted to take a wife without my permission. Now it is done. Before I approve your divorce, I will get to know this young woman. Two weeks, Reyhan. Surely that is not too much to ask.''

Reyhan knew it was not. His father's request was more than reasonable, and yet he would have given much to keep Emma away.

He nodded once and walked to the door. ''Excuse me, Father. My presence is required at a meeting.''

The king nodded, and Reyhan left.

As Reyhan walked toward the business wing of the palace, he wondered how he would endure the next fourteen days. There was much to occupy his time— negotiations for oil purchases, dealing with a small band of renegades, reviewing a list of potential brides. Yet he knew none of that would fill his mind. Instead he would think of a woman—the woman he had married. Emma. Their time apart had done nothing to diminish his need for her. Six years ago she had been his greatest weakness, and so she remained.

He paused at the door to his office. No one would ever be permitted to know, he promised himself. Wanting her, *needing* her, had nearly destroyed him once before. That would not happen again. In two weeks the king would grant their divorce, she would be gone and he, Reyhan, would be allowed to remain strong. That he would live the rest of his life without her was of little consequence. He had survived this long. He would survive the rest of his days. Survive— not live. He reminded himself that most of the time, enduring was more than enough.

Chapter Three

Emma awoke to the not-so-surprising realization that, despite the doctor's promise, little about her situation had changed or improved during the night. Not that she'd expected either, although it would have been nice.

She sat up in the huge bed and pulled her knees to her chest. She remembered the doctor insisting she take something to help her sleep, then she'd changed into her nightgown and nearly collapsed into bed. Then nothing.

The good news was she felt more rested. The bad news…well, where exactly was she going to start? There was so much to consider. That she might really be married to Reyhan and might have been married all this time. That she was in Bahania and he was the son of the king.

She shook her head. Way too many difficult thoughts for first thing in the morning. She should take a few minutes and get her bearings, then deal with the weirdness that was her life.

Emma rose. Her toes curled in the plush carpet that was thick enough to serve as a mattress in a pinch.

The bedroom had been decorated in pale yellows and blues. Ornate, carved dark wood furniture made up the elaborate headboard, footboard and matching nightstands. An armoire stood across the room. When she crossed to it she found a large television inside, along with a DVD player and a wide assortment of movies. There was also a detailed listing of the various channels available via satellite.

"Amazing," she murmured as she touched the carved birds and flowers on the door.

The bedroom itself was about the size of the average three-bedroom house back home in Dallas. She remembered the living room had been equally huge. With two parts anticipation and one part trepidation, she walked into the bathroom.

Huge didn't begin to describe it. Her entire apartment could have fit inside, with room to spare. The long marble vanity was about twice the length of her main kitchen counter. The tub had whirlpool jets and could have served as a playground for an entire water park full of seals. There was a glass-enclosed shower, towels as big as bedsheets and every toiletry known to womankind.

Emma turned in a slow circle and tried to imagine

what it would be like to live somewhere like this permanently. Was it possible to get used to this level of luxury, and would the palace continue to be a delight?

Twenty minutes later she'd showered and washed her face. After dressing, applying mascara and some lip gloss, she returned to the bedroom and put away the rest of her clothes. With that done, there was little to do but explore the rest of the suite and try to figure out what she was going to say when she next saw Reyhan.

In the light of day she knew that there was more to their relationship than her parents had told her six years ago when she'd returned home brokenhearted. But what exactly?

She left the bedroom and walked into the living room of the suite. The shutters were open and pulled back. The view was so amazing—blue ocean, bright sky, the tops of several trees—that she hadn't noticed Reyhan. But when she turned, she saw him seated at the dining room table in the corner. He studied the newspaper in front of him and hadn't seen her, either.

Her first thought was to bolt for the safety of her bedroom, but before she could get her feet to move, she found herself mesmerized by the man himself.

He was so handsome, she thought, remembering how his dark good looks had stunned her the first time they'd met. His hair was cropped short, in a stylish cut. Strong cheekbones emphasized the leanness of his features. His eyebrows were pulled together, giving him a stern expression. He looked intense and dangerous, something she remembered from their past together. Being around him had always left her tongue-tied and feeling more than a little foolish. That sensation returned big-time.

She winced as she recalled accusing him of marrying her to get a green card. He was a member of the Bahanian royal family. No doubt he could come or go at will just about anywhere in the world. As for wanting her in his bed…she had her doubts. The experience had been a disaster and after those first couple of nights, Reyhan had never come looking for her again.

"How long are you going to stand there?" he asked without looking up from his paper. "I have ordered you breakfast, Emma. You didn't eat before or after you arrived at the palace. I don't want you making yourself ill."

He set down the paper and looked at her. His dark gaze seemed to see all the way inside to her quivering heart. He raised one eyebrow.

"Are you so afraid of me? I swear that I have never attacked before ten or eleven in the morning. It is not civilized."

She glanced at the antique grandfather clock by the entryway. "So I'm safe for another ninety minutes?"

"At least."

He rose and pulled out a chair. Not knowing what else to do, she settled in it then watched as he lifted the tops off several serving dishes on the sideboard.

"What would you like?" he asked.

She blinked at him. "You're going to serve me?"

"You are my guest. In the interest of privacy I sent the maid away, so there is just the two of us this morning."

The implication being she was his responsibility? Reyhan had always had the most amazing manners. Apparently that hadn't changed.

She stood and crossed to the sideboard where she studied the assortment of offerings. There were eggs and bacon, fresh fruit, croissants, Danish and a selection of cereals, both hot and cold.

"I can't eat all this," she told him.

"I'll help." He motioned to the plates stacked on the left. "Please begin."

She reached for the plate. As she leaned forward, Reyhan moved and her hand grazed his arm. The instant heat nearly made her stumble. Awareness rippled along her skin like a sudden cool breeze, making her shiver and break out in goose bumps. She found herself wanting to touch him again, wanting to move closer, to have him touch her. Erotic images sprang into her mind, and before she knew what was happening, she realized it was difficult for her to catch her breath.

All of this happened in a matter of seconds. Then she became aware of herself, of Reyhan's expression of polite interest and she quickly stepped back and turned toward the food.

This was not good, she thought frantically. Not good at all. She didn't like how her heart raced whenever he was nearby. That hadn't happened before. If anything, he'd terrified her as much as he'd intrigued her. Not that she was any less terrified, it was just now she was frightened for a different reason.

She scooped fresh fruit onto her plate, along with some eggs. After taking a biscuit and butter, she returned to the table and poured them each coffee. Reyhan waited until she was seated before claiming his chair.

"You slept well?" he asked.

"Yes, thank you."

"Dr. Johnson said that your fainting was not likely to reoccur. He decided it was the combination of lack of food and sleep, along with minor dehydration and the shock of seeing me again." Reyhan's steady gaze never left her face. "Had I known you would react so strongly, I would have given you some warning. Stunning you into fainting wasn't my goal."

"Imagine what you could do if it was," she said lightly.

She noticed his single raised eyebrow again, but Emma refused to be intimidated, despite the instinct to cringe and apologize. She turned her attention to her breakfast instead and plunged her fork into a piece of mango. Sexual awareness swirled through the room like an erotic mist, but she was determined to ignore it.

Maybe she always had reacted so strongly to Reyhan but wasn't aware of it, she thought wryly. Maybe when they'd first met there had been this same powerful physical attraction between them but she'd been too young and innocent to recognize it. All she'd known back then was that she loved him and feared him with equal intensity. It was amazing she'd managed to find the strength to leave him.

Then she reminded herself that she hadn't left him. He'd left her and she'd hid out at her parents' home. Any additional contact had been through them. She hadn't even had the courage to tell him she didn't want to see him again. Not that he'd tried very hard.

"Why the heavy sigh?" he asked.

She looked up. "Did I sigh? I didn't mean to."

"You were thinking of the past."

"It's a logical place to go."

He nodded. "We will speak of it."

A statement or a command? "And if I don't want to?"

The words were out before she could stop them.

His mouth curved up in amusement. "You defy me?"

"Will that get me fifty lashes or time in the tower?"

"Nothing so boring." He sipped his coffee. "Why do you not wish to talk about our situation?"

"I do." She shrugged. "Knee-jerk reaction, I guess. My parents were always so protective. They meant well—they still do. My independence is hard-won and I get my back up when someone gives me orders."

"I see."

She had no idea what the silken words meant, nor did she want to ask for an explanation. She doubted whatever contact Reyhan had had with her parents had been especially pleasant.

"You're right," she said. "We need to talk about what happened and what's going to happen."

He nodded slightly. "If you wish."

"You're mocking me."

"I am terrified by your steely will."

Emma doubted anything terrified Reyhan. Which

meant he was teasing her. Interesting. She wouldn't have thought royal princes had senses of humor.

"Do you believe our marriage was real?" he asked.

"I don't want to, but, yes. You have no reason to lie, and my presence here is more than enough proof." She shifted in her seat. She'd been married for six years and hadn't known. Talk about being a fool.

"Why did you marry me?" she asked him, knowing it hadn't been for any of the usual reasons. At the time she'd thought Reyhan had loved her, but his behavior proved otherwise.

He chewed and swallowed. "You were a virgin," he said calmly. "I would not have defiled you."

Ten simple words that made her drop her fork, push back her chair and spring to her feet.

"What?" she demanded. "You married me to sleep with me? The whole thing was about sex?"

If love was out of the question, shouldn't he have at least liked her? Shouldn't he have pretended to care?

"Sit down, Emma. You're overreacting."

She took her seat before she remembered she wasn't going to let anyone run her life ever again. Once seated, it seemed silly to stand up and make a fuss. She settled on glaring at him.

Reyhan looked at her. "Why are you so outraged? Do you think there are any men who marry without the thought of their wives being a sexual partner?"

"Most men think about more than just doing it."

That made him get stiff and stern. His gaze narrowed. "I am Prince Reyhan of Bahania. When I married you, I not only gave you my name and protection, but honored you by making you a princess of my country. Had you been willing to continue our relationship, I would have brought you here where you would have lived in this palace. Neither you nor our children would have wanted for anything. I would have been faithful to you until I breathed my last breath. Who and what you are would have been passed along to our children, and through that, you would have joined in the history of my people. I believe that would be defined as more than just doing it."

"But you never told me any of this," she reminded him, feeling more than a little embarrassed. "Nor did you ask me if this is what I wanted with my life. What about my plans? My dreams? Marrying you could have changed my world forever."

"Is that such a bad thing?"

She thought of her small apartment and her quiet life. She remembered her conversation with Cleo the previous night and what she'd said about the palace and the princes.

"You didn't give me a choice," she said. "Not about staying or going. You married me without telling me the truth, then you disappeared without a word."

Reyhan leaned back in his chair. "Our recollection of the events that happened are very different, but that is of no consequence. What matters is our present circumstances. We are married—something neither of us wishes to continue. The king's permission is required for a prince to divorce, and he has insisted you spend two weeks here until he will grant the decree.''

Countless years of having her life run by her parents had made Emma hypersensitive to being told what to do. Her first instinct was to tell Reyhan that maybe she didn't want a divorce, thank you very much. Maybe she wanted to stay married.

She stopped herself before she could blurt out the irrational statement. She didn't know the man. She didn't want anything to do with him. Of course she wanted to go get a divorce and go back to her life.

''You didn't need his permission to get married, but you need it for a divorce,'' she said. ''That doesn't make sense.''

''I did need his permission to marry. I defied him.''

Simple words, she thought, but stunning. He'd defied the king? To marry her? Which brought her back to her original question—why?

For sex? He was a handsome, wealthy, royal guy. Couldn't he get any woman he wanted? So why her?

She had a feeling that the earth would stop turning before she found out the answer to that one, so she chose another topic of conversation.

''So after the divorce you'll marry someone else.'' A thought occurred to her. ''Have you already chosen your new bride?'' Cleo had said he wasn't engaged, but was he already in love?

Reyhan shook his head. ''My marriage will be arranged.''

Emma blinked at him. ''You mean she'll be picked by someone else? What if you don't like her?''

He shrugged. ''That is of little consequence.''

It felt like a really big consequence to her.

"But she could make you crazy."

"Then we will have little contact. My duty is to produce heirs for the kingdom. I will not turn my back on my responsibility."

He had a duty? But where had all that duty been when he'd married her? And why would he agree to a wife he might not even like?

"Do you get to spend time with the potential brides in advance? Like *The Bachelor* for royalty?"

"No."

"But—"

He rose, cutting her off. "I have a meeting," he said politely. "Please think of your time here in Bahania as a vacation. In two weeks you can return to Texas as if nothing ever happened. In the meantime, if you need anything, please ask one of the servants. You are an honored guest of the king."

With that he nodded and left.

Emma stared after him. She might be going home, but she doubted she would ever forget what had happened here. In a matter of hours, her world had turned upside down.

She rose and crossed to the French doors that led to a beautiful balcony. When she stepped outside, she saw the balcony stretched the length of the palace, perhaps even circling around it. A nice place to take a walk, she thought as she moved to the carved railing and leaned down to inspect the wonderful gardens below.

Stone paths meandered through what looked like a

formal English garden. A fountain gurgled, while birds sang from nearby trees.

Hardly what she'd expected for a desert nation, she thought, then remembered the desalinization plant Alex had pointed out on their drive from the airport. Bahania created much of the fresh water her people used. Interesting, but hardly what was on her mind.

She turned her attention from the garden to her left hand. Reyhan had placed a simple gold band there after the ceremony. He'd kissed her and promised to replace it with any ring she would like. At the time she'd thought he'd been caught up in the romance of the moment, making promises he could never keep. Now she knew he'd been telling the truth.

But why hadn't he told her the rest of it? About him being the prince and that he'd always planned to return there? And why hadn't her parents been able to find out that she was really married? Who had told them the ceremony had been a sham and why hadn't they questioned the information?

Would it have made a difference? After the fact, she could say yes. But at the time? She'd been hurt and afraid and not that interested in being Reyhan's wife. Their few days together as husband and wife had been spent in bed. He had wanted her with a passion that had terrified and confused her. While she hadn't minded him touching her, she hadn't much liked it, either. He'd been too intense, too hungry, too everything.

Now the thought of those dark eyes gazing at her with unmistakable desire made her breathing quicken. Which so did not make sense. She had no reason to be attracted to Reyhan. She barely knew him. She wasn't even sure she liked him. So why was she anticipating the next time she saw him?

Reyhan walked from the residential wing of the palace toward the business wing, moving quickly but with his thoughts still outpacing his steps.

There wasn't a part of him that was not on fire with desire for Emma. He needed her as he needed the wide spaces of the desert. She was as much a part of him, and yet as out of reach as the stars.

If only he'd been able to keep her from coming to Bahania. But his father had insisted on meeting the woman Reyhan had married and then left behind. Royal pronouncements could only be avoided for so long, and in the end he had run out of excuses. So Emma was here—haunting him. He wanted her with a grim desperation that threatened his world, and he could not have her. Not before and not now. She was, he acknowledged, the one woman on earth who could bring him to his knees. Him—a prince. A man of power and action. If she knew how he really felt...

He reminded himself she did not know, nor would she be affected if she did. She'd made her feelings clear six years ago and there was no reason to think they would have changed.

Only twelve more days, he told himself. He could survive that, especially if he avoided her.

He reached the business wing and asked his assistant to come into his office. When the young man was seated, Reyhan pulled out his schedule. He was about to find himself very, very busy.

* * *

Emma restlessly wandered around the suite. She might be an honored guest of the king, but she wasn't sure what that meant in terms of what she could and could not do. Were there self-guided tours of the palace? The maid had disappeared and she didn't know who else to ask. The last thing she wanted was to wander into some forbidden room and find herself at the wrong end of a pointy sword.

She stared at the phone and wondered what would happen if she picked it up. Did the palace have an operator? In movies, the White House always did, and the palace was at least twice as big. Wasn't an operator required?

A knock on the suite's main door saved her from finding out. For a split second, her heart fluttered in anticipation. Reyhan? Had his meeting ended early and had he decided to return to speak with her? Had…

She pulled open the door and tried not to look disappointed when she saw Cleo standing there. The petite blonde had a baby in her arms.

"Remember me?" Cleo asked. "We met last night."

"Of course," Emma said with a smile. "You came to rescue me."

Cleo grinned. "Someone had to. These princes," she said, shaking her head. "They have no idea how intimidating they can be, and between you and me, we can't ever let them know."

She walked into the suite and held out her daughter. "This is Calah. I'm going to say 'Isn't she beautiful?'"

and I really need you to agree with me. I know, I know. Every mother thinks her baby is beautiful. I hate being a cliché, but there it is.''

Emma glanced at the sleeping baby. "She *is* beautiful. You and your husband are going to have to beat boys off with a stick.''

"I suspect Sadik will just glare menacingly and that will be enough.'' Cleo plopped down on the sofa and held out the baby. "Are you a cuddler or do infants make you uneasy?''

Emma sat next to her and took Calah in her arms. "I love holding babies. I'm a delivery room nurse so I'm around newborns all the time. It's a great specialty and I love it, but every now and then I get the urge to move to pediatrics.''

Cleo's eyebrows arched. "Ah, so you love children. Does Reyhan know?''

"I don't think so.'' The information would hardly matter. He might want heirs but not with her.

"Interesting. So tell me everything about your life.''

Emma gently rocked the baby and breathed in the sweet scent of her. "There's not much to tell. I'm a nurse, I live in Dallas and now I'm here. But what about you? How did you come to be here, and married to a prince?''

Cleo drew her feet up and leaned back against the sofa. "Well, I already told you I'm from Spokane. I grew up dirt-poor and without much family. Eventually I went into the foster care system, which turned out to be a good thing because I got to meet Zara. She was the daughter of the woman who took me in.

Anyway, we became good friends, then practically sisters. Years after her mother had died, Zara went through her things and found these letters to her mother from the king of Bahania.''

Emma stared at her. "You're kidding."

"Nope. He'd met her when she'd been a dancer and he'd fallen for her big-time. Apparently theirs was a great love, but Zara's mom knew it would never last so she bailed without telling him."

"How sad," Emma said.

"I agree. I mean she could have *tried* to make it work. Anyway, Zara found the letters and the two of us headed over here to see if the king really was her father. And he was."

"That must have been a shock for both of them."

"It was. I mean violà, instant princess. She also met Rafe, who is American but also a sheik, and she married him—but that is a more complicated story."

Emma laughed. "Oh, right. Because this one isn't. So you stayed with Zara and then married Prince Sadik?"

"Not exactly. He and I—well, it was sort of spontaneous combustion. But he was a prince and I worked at a copy store. I mean until I'd come to Bahania I'd never been anywhere. I knew I wasn't princess material. So I went home. But I had to come back for Zara's wedding to Rafe, and I was pregnant and I didn't want anyone to know. The king found out, then Sadik, then we got married, but he wouldn't admit he loved me and it was horrible, but he came to his senses and now we're blissfully happy."

Emma didn't know what to say. "That's an amazing story."

Cleo grinned. "I know. I can't wait until Calah is old enough to hear the romantic bits. I won't tell her about getting pregnant or anything." Her eyes widened. "Oh, I should warn you. Both Zara and Sabrina are pregnant. I think there's something in the water, so don't drink anything but bottled." She glanced at her daughter. "Unless you want one of your own."

Emma was dealing with enough changes right now, although a child... She shook off the thought. No point in going there. Not now.

"I don't think this is a good time for me," she said. "Plus there's the whole needing-a-man thing."

"Is this where I point out that you have a husband?"

One who had made it plain he'd found her anything but interesting in bed? "No, thanks."

Cleo nodded. "I understand. But that doesn't mean I won't think it. So how did you and Reyhan meet?"

"It was at college. My first semester." Those days felt like a lifetime ago. "I was a brand-new freshman—technically an adult, but not emotionally. Not even close." She shrugged. "I'm the only child of older parents. They'd given up on ever having children when I came along. I was a surprise, but a happy one. My parents were so thrilled, they were determined to keep me safe no matter what. Which meant keeping me sheltered. It took my entire senior year of high school to convince them to let me go to a college that required me living a couple hundred miles away."

"Reyhan's older, right?" Cleo asked. "You couldn't have had a class together."

"We didn't. I was socially backward, and I would never have had the courage to talk to an actual man. I was walking home from the library when a couple of drunk guys started hassling me. I'm sure it was harmless, but I was too inexperienced to know what to do. I panicked and started pleading with them, which they found pretty funny. I was terrified and took off running. I ran smack into Reyhan. My books went flying, I'm sure I screamed and it was a mess. By the time it was sorted out, the guys were long gone and I was convinced Reyhan had rescued me from certain death."

Cleo sighed. "That sounds romantic."

Emma hadn't thought of it in that way. "I thought he was handsome and mysterious. Very attractive, of course. I was stunned when he asked me out." She shifted the baby, taking more of her weight on her lap.

"But you said yes."

"Would you have said anything else?"

"Probably not. The rescue would be really tough to ignore. It's very princely." She laughed. "I say that so calmly, but I'm used to Sadik being royal now. At the beginning it was a big deal to me."

"Do you miss your old life?"

"Not even for a minute. Not just because this is so much nicer—which it is. But because of Sadik. I love him." Her dark blue eyes glowed with affection. "He makes me insane, but that's okay. I drive him crazy, too. Besides, being different keeps things interesting.

And he loves me.'' She glanced at Emma. ''Handsome, arrogant prince types may be hard to tame, but when they love, it's with every part of themselves.''

Emma fought against a surge of envy. She had always wanted to be loved like that by a man. It wasn't that her parents hadn't cared for her, they had. But their love had been about protecting her from a difficult and frightening world. She'd always wanted just to be loved for herself.

Cleo shrugged. ''Okay, I get carried away. That's part of my charm. So enough about me and my past. Are you excited about living in the palace?''

''It should be an interesting vacation. At least that's how I'm trying to look at it.''

''Your one chance to be a princess?''

''Something like that.''

Cleo grinned. ''What if you find you like it so much, you want to stay?''

''Not an option. As soon as my two weeks are up, I'm heading back to Dallas.'' And her regularly scheduled life. There was nothing for her here in Bahania. She ignored the little voice inside that whispered there wasn't much for her back in Dallas, either.

Chapter Four

Reyhan had hoped the large palace would provide enough room for him to avoid Emma, but he had not taken his father's need to meddle into account. Now that the king had passed control of much of the day-to-day details of the country on to his sons, he had far too much free time to plan ways to torment them. His newest strategy began with an invitation for both Reyhan and Emma to join him for dinner.

Reyhan studied the casually worded e-mail and knew the phrase "if it's convenient" was there for show. Should Reyhan protest it was not convenient, his father would change the request to an order. Defying one's father was easily accomplished. Refusing the king was another matter, especially when Reyhan needed the monarch's agreement to the divorce.

Which was why he found himself walking toward his father's private quarters that evening, trying not to think about how he would survive several hours in Emma's company.

Before she had arrived, he had nearly convinced himself that everything was different. That he no longer had feelings for her, and even if he did, that she was not the same woman. But a few minutes with her had told him that not only did she still have that ultimate power over him, she had somehow retained the gentle sweetness that had first drawn him to her.

When he reached his father's suite, he squared his shoulders. He was Prince Reyhan of Bahania. Royal, powerful and without weakness. He would survive this meeting and any others. He would endure and in the end, Emma would be out of his life forever.

"My son," his father said happily as Reyhan walked into the main salon. "How good to see you."

"And you, my father."

The king's cheer warned Reyhan that his father might have a trick or two coming during the dinner and that he would be wise to stay alert.

He crossed to the wet bar and poured himself a Scotch, then walked to the large sofa facing the French doors leading to the balcony. Only one cat lay on a center cushion. Reyhan avoided it as he sat down.

"Emma should be here shortly," his father said, stroking the large Persian draped across his lap.

Reyhan had offered to escort her himself, but the king had said he preferred to speak with his son privately first. Now Reyhan waited patiently.

"Your wife is a very pretty young woman," his father said.

Reyhan nodded. He never thought of Emma as "his wife." If he had, he would have claimed her, despite her wishes to be as far away from him as possible. He would have wanted to have her, take her, *be* with her. It had been safer for them both to be on opposite sides of the planet. Literally. He'd forced himself to think of her only on rare occasions, usually at night, when he couldn't sleep and the sounds of the Arabian Sea had echoed with her soft voice.

"I arranged tonight's dinner so I could get to know her," his father said.

Reyhan didn't like the sound of that. "She will be leaving in a few days."

"Until then, she is my daughter-in-law. A relationship of some importance."

Reyhan wasn't sure if his father meant that or was trying to make trouble. On the king's side was his close ties with Cleo, Sadik's wife. She was a favorite and spent much time in the king's company. If that happened with Emma, as well, his father might not want to agree to the divorce. Reyhan knew he could not stay married. Not to her. Not with his need burning so hotly inside.

Before he could come up with a reason to keep them apart, there was a knock at the main door. He rose, bracing himself for the impact of seeing her again.

"Come in," the king called.

A young woman pushed opened the door, entered

and bowed her head. Emma followed her, pausing uncertainly just past her escort.

Reyhan set down his drink, then crossed to her. As he approached, he took in the emerald-green sheath that clung to her sensual curves, the elegant upswept way she'd styled her dark red hair and the makeup emphasizing her eyes and mouth. She needed no artifice to make her more beautiful, yet he appreciated the effort…and the results.

Wanting flared, as did heat. He ignored both, concentrating instead on the excitement and apprehension battling in Emma's green eyes. A tentative smile tugged on the corners of her mouth, as if she wasn't sure which emotion would win.

When he stopped beside her, he reached for her hand. The second his fingers closed around hers, the ache inside of him increased to unbearable. Still, he dismissed the painful need and settled her small hand in the crook of his arm. He urged her toward his father, who had put down the cat and risen.

"Father, this is Princess Emma, my wife. Emma, this is King Hassan of Bahania."

He felt her stiffen at "Princess" and wondered if she'd considered her position here. As long as they were married, she was a member of the royal family. Bahania was a long way from her life in Texas.

"Enchanted," the older man said as he took her free hand and lightly kissed the back of it. "Would you like something to drink? Champagne? We should toast the moment."

"No. I—I'm fine."

The king drew her from Reyhan and settled her on

the sofa, next to the sleeping Siamese. He took the opposite side of the couch, leaving Reyhan the chair.

Not difficult duty, Reyhan thought as he sat. Emma was in his direct line of vision. He could visually trace her profile, the line of her neck, the length of her bare arms. And while looking at her, he could remember their few nights together. How she'd felt when he'd touched her. How she'd tasted when he'd kissed her. The tight dampness of her virgin body when he'd first claimed her as his own.

The images had an expected result, and he was forced to shift slightly in his chair. Stop, he ordered himself. Thinking about what had been once and never would be again offered torment but little else.

"Tell me about yourself," the king said. "You are from Texas?"

Emma nodded. "The Dallas area. I've lived there nearly all my life. Except when I was at college."

"Do you have brothers and sisters?"

"No. My parents had actually given up on ever having children when I came along." She smiled. "I was a surprise."

The sweet pull of her lips hit Reyhan like a punch in the gut. He consciously relaxed his muscles and sucked in a breath. Soon she would be gone and then he could forget she had ever lived, he told himself.

"A happy one," his father said.

Emma laughed. "You're right. My parents have made it very clear how much they adore me." Her humor faded slightly. "They are extremely protective."

"As they should be. A daughter such as yourself is a rare treasure."

"Thank you," she murmured as she bowed her head.

Reyhan caught the light flush on her cheek. So she still blushed. When he had first met her it seemed that everything he did caused her to blush. A compliment, a kiss, a whisper of desire. She had been the most innocent woman he'd ever met.

"Treasure or not, they made it difficult to have a life," she said. "Not that I don't love them dearly. But there were things I wanted to do." Her voice had turned wistful. "They were very strict about things like school dances and dating."

His father raised his eyebrows. Reyhan stepped into the conversation.

"Many Western high schools offer chaperoned dances for the students," he said.

"A dangerous practice," the king said. "Now you know why I sent you to England for much of your education."

"An all-boys school," Reyhan said dryly. "It was thrilling."

Emma glanced at him and smiled. For that second, there was a connection between them. He could nearly see the sparks arcing across the room and feel the temperature increasing.

"Where did you meet my son?" the king asked, breaking the spell.

Emma returned her attention to the monarch. "At college. It was my first year there. I'd had to beg my parents to let me go. I was very excited, but scared, too."

"And did he sweep you off your feet?"

She swallowed, blushed, then nodded. "Yes. He was very charming. Very...worldly."

Reyhan thought of the young man he'd been at twenty-four. Hardly worldly, except in Emma's inexperienced view. He'd wanted her and he'd pursued her with a single-minded focus that had left her nowhere to escape. He'd been determined to have her, and, upon discovering she was a virgin, he'd married her.

"Yours was a brief courtship," the king said.

Emma glanced at Reyhan. "I...we..."

"She knew nothing of who I was," Reyhan said, interrupting her hesitation. "I alone defied you, Father. The blame, the responsibility, is mine."

Emma's eyes widened slightly, but she didn't say anything. The king nodded.

"You stayed together only a short time." The king's words were more statement than question.

"You know this," Reyhan said as he stepped in again. "I was called home because of Sheza's death." He glanced at Emma. "My aunt."

"But you did not return to your wife."

He had tried, Reyhan thought bitterly. He had called and attempted to see her, but she refused to have anything to do with him. Eventually her father had ordered him to stay away. No explanation save that Emma regretted the marriage and never wanted to see him again.

He'd told himself the sting he'd felt was little more

than wounded pride. That he hadn't actually cared about her. Loved her.

He shrugged with a casualness he didn't feel. "The past is finished. What value is there in discussing it now?"

"I wish to know," his father said. He looked at Emma. "So after things did not work out with Reyhan, you returned to your parents?"

Reyhan didn't save her from that probing question mostly because he wanted to hear her answer.

"I, ah, stayed with them until the new semester started, then I returned to college. By then, Reyhan was gone."

True enough. Once he'd realized he'd lost her, he'd finished the requirements for his master's and had gone back to Bahania. He'd never tried to see Emma again.

"And what do you do now?" the king asked. "How do you spend your days?"

Emma looked confused, as if she expected them to already know this. "I'm a delivery room nurse. I received my RN and went to work in a Dallas hospital." She shifted in her seat and smiled. "It wasn't easy, let me tell you. My parents really hated the idea of me living on my own, but I knew it was time. I have a good job. I can support myself."

Reyhan stiffened. "You what?"

His father glared at him. "You abandoned your responsibility?"

"I did not." He turned to Emma. He wasn't surprised that she worked. Many women preferred to fill their day with a job, especially when there weren't small children to tend to. But that she acted as if she *needed* the money. "You do not need to work to support yourself."

She stared at him. "Excuse me? How would you know what I need and don't need?"

"I left you financially provided for."

Emma leaned back in the sofa, trying to put a little distance between herself and an obviously furious Reyhan. She wouldn't mind his temper so much if she knew what he was so mad about. Nothing made sense. He hadn't left her a dime.

"You didn't do anything when you left," she said, then winced when he seemed to puff up and get even madder.

"After we were married, I opened a checking account for your personal use. Two hundred and fifty thousand dollars were put in a checking account. When the balance reached below a hundred thousand, the account was to be replenished."

Two hundred and fifty *thousand* dollars? He'd left her money?

"I don't understand," she whispered.

"What is complicated about the information?"

Good point, she thought. But her head was spinning and nothing made sense. "Why would you take care of me?"

Wrong question, she thought as he stiffened even more.

"I am Prince Reyhan of Bahania and you are my wife. You are my responsibility. When you did not use the money, I assumed it was out of pride and anger. I sent a letter requesting you reconsider, and then funds were withdrawn, as they have been ever since.''

Now it was her turn to get all huffy. ''Wait a minute. I didn't know about any money and I sure didn't spend it.''

''You knew. When you refused to see me, I spoke with your father. I gave him the account information.''

Her father? ''You came to see me?''

''Of course.''

No. That's not how it happened. Emma distinctly remembered being curled up on her bed back in her parents' house, praying for Reyhan to contact her. But he never had. Not a note, not a phone call and certainly not a visit.

Unless he'd shown up while she'd been...ill.

''I was sick for a while,'' she said, telling herself it wasn't exactly a lie. There'd been a sickness of spirit.

''I came by several times, in fact.''

Had he? Was it possible her parents had kept the information from her?

She thought they might not have wanted to tell her that Reyhan had been by to see her, but they never would have kept information about that kind of money from her. They loved her. They were devoted to her.

''I don't believe you,'' she said. ''Not about the money. If I don't know about it, who withdrew funds? Not my parents. They would never do that. This doesn't make sense. You disappeared from my life for six years, only to drag me over here and tell me you want a divorce. Why should I believe anything you say?''

''Because I do not lie.''

She glanced at the king, but he seemed more amused than upset by the argument. Which was fine. She was upset enough for two people. She turned back to Reyhan. ''Liar or not, you've insulted my parents and for no good reason. I don't know what this game is, but I'm done playing it.''

She stood and walked out of the room.

After fifty feet down the hall she had the unsettling thought that it was probably considered a very bad thing to walk out on the king of Bahania. She paused, not sure if she should go back and apologize, or keep going. Before she could decide, she heard footsteps, then Reyhan rounded the corner and stopped in front of her.

He was obviously furious—tight-lipped and hard-eyed. Without speaking, he took her by the arm and led her away. She didn't recognize the twists and turns they took, even when they ended up in front of her suite. Reyhan opened the door and hustled her inside.

When he released her, she had the strangest urge not to move away. For a split second she thought about throwing herself into his arms and begging him to hold her. As if his embrace would make things right.

Not in this universe, she thought, taking a step back and bracing herself for whatever he had to say.

His gaze narrowed. ''Why do you question what I tell you?''

"Why shouldn't I?"

"Because there is proof of everything. For weeks I kept vigil outside of your parents' home. I called or came by every day. I returned to claim you as my wife only to be told you refused to see me. I left when I received your letter."

Emma didn't understand any of this. "What letter?"

"The one you wrote telling me you regretted meeting me and everything about our marriage and that you only wanted me to disappear."

He spoke stiffly, as if the words were difficult to say.

"That's crazy," she told him. "I never wrote that."

She hadn't thought it, either. Not at the time. She'd longed to see Reyhan, but he'd abandoned her.

"You used me," she continued. "I don't know why, but you got it in your head you wanted to sleep with me, so you pretended to care about me." She couldn't say the word *love,* not even now. "You took advantage of me for a long weekend, then took off. No explanation, nothing."

It took a lot to get her angry, but once she was on a roll, she liked to keep going. She remembered the pain and humiliation of being tossed aside like a broken toy.

"You promised me things," she said, her voice rising. "You talked about our life together and I believed you. I trusted you and you just took what you wanted and walked away."

"I left because a beloved aunt died."

"Did the funeral take six weeks to prepare? Did you ever once call me? Did you think to tell me what was going on?"

He frowned. "Of course. I phoned nearly every day."

She rolled her eyes. "Oh, right. And I just happened to be out."

"That is what I was told."

She turned her back on him and walked to the floor-to-ceiling glass wall. None of this mattered, she told herself, trying to cool her temper. Soon it would be behind her. She had to remember the big picture.

Reyhan spoke into the silence. "If you think so little of men, you must be pleased to be rid of me. Just a few more days and the marriage will be over. As if it had never existed."

Fury surged. "Right. Because you can dismiss what happened. Because it didn't matter." She spun back to face it. "It mattered to me. Do you have any idea how innocent I was? I'd barely kissed one boy in high school. And then there was you. You didn't just seduce me, Reyhan, you took what you wanted, without regard for my feelings. I'll never forgive that."

His expression turned menacing. "You were more than willing."

"I was terrified. Now I'd know better. Now I'd tell you no."

"Are you saying I had you against your will?"

He hadn't, not exactly, but she was mad. "Yes."

"You were a child, only interested in chaste kisses

and expensive presents. A child who couldn't please a man.''

That hurt. She tried not to remember how embarrassed she'd been, how awkward and unsure.

"You were a man who couldn't be bothered with seducing his bride. Instead you just took.''

They were both enraged, breathing hard and glaring at each other. A part of her was terrified, but she refused to back down. Not even when he moved closer still. Not even when he reached behind her and grabbed her by the hair and pulled her up against him.

"If that is who I am,'' he said with frighteningly soft menace, "a liar and a defiler of women, then there is no point in holding back now.''

He kissed her. Not the soft kiss of seduction or coaxing, but a kiss of power. He was a man with something to prove. His firm lips pressed hard against her own, claiming her with passion.

She wanted to protest, to scream, to pull back, but she could not. They touched everywhere. Her body pressed against his, their legs tangled. She put up her hands to push him away, but when her palms brushed against the hard planes of his suit-covered chest, she found herself unable to protest...or even breathe.

Fire consumed her. Hot and hungry, it swept through her, melting her resolve, her reason. Against her will, she found herself moving her hands from his chest to his shoulders. She clung to him because letting go would mean collapsing at his feet. Worse, she kissed him back.

She couldn't explain it, and given the choice, she would probably deny it, but there it was. A need that

grew. Wanting was alive inside of her. In that moment, with his mouth against hers and his hands moving from the back of her head to her shoulders, then
to her hips, she couldn't get close enough.

Emma wanted to surrender, to crawl inside of him.
When his kiss gentled and he stroked her lower lip
with his tongue, she parted for him and anticipated
his more intimate kiss.

At the first stroke of his tongue against her own it
was all she could do not to scream. At the second,
she ceased to have a will of her own. And with the
third, she clamped her lips around him, greedily holding him in place, wanting him to kiss her forever.

She ached. Her breasts, between her legs, all over.
Her skin felt hot and too tight. She wanted to strip
her dress off and have him touch her everywhere. She
wanted to be naked, vulnerable, offering herself to
him.

She rubbed one hand against the back of his neck.
He held on to her hips and then dropped his hands to
her rear where he squeezed the curves. She surged
against him, wanting to rub like a lonely cat. But
before she could put her plan into action he broke the
kiss and stepped away.

They stared at each other. Loud breathing filled the
silence. Emma was pleased to note that Reyhan
looked as swept away by passion as she felt.

Perhaps they should call a truce, she thought. Start
over as friends. Friends who could bring about the
end of the world with just a kiss.

"You have learned much in my absence," Reyhan
said, his cold voice contrasting with the fire in his

eyes. "Before you accuse me of more sins, you should look at yourself. A wife who takes lovers. Isn't there a name for that?"

Her mouth dropped open, but before she could snap back at him, he was gone.

Emma glared at the shut door and yelped in anger and frustration.

"That is not fair!" she yelled into the empty room. "I didn't know we were married and you know it."

Besides, there hadn't been any other men. Not seriously. And she'd never allowed any of them into her bed. If she kissed better now, it was because she was older, and because kissing Reyhan had made her feel things she'd never felt before. Not even *with* him.

Emma slowed her breathing and tried to calm down. She was shaking and not just because she was mad. She was shaking in reaction to what had happened when Reyhan had kissed her. She'd wanted him. Funny how she'd started to worry that there was something wrong with her because none of the guys she went out with had made her want to get naked and do the wild thing. Just her luck that the first one to push all her buttons was an arrogant prince who just happened to be a man trying to get her out of his life as quickly as possible.

"I don't think I can handle any more," she said quietly as she stepped out onto the balcony. "By the time I get home, I'm going to need a serious vacation."

She crossed to the railing and glanced down into the beautiful gardens. The peaceful setting began to ease her tension and she felt herself relaxing. After a time, she heard voices and searched until she found a couple walking into the gardens.

Even from two stories above, she recognized Cleo. The tall, handsome man at her side must be her husband. Emma couldn't make out the words, but she heard the affection in their voices. Sadik turned to his wife and held out his arms. Cleo willingly stepped into his embrace and they kissed.

Not wanting to intrude on an obviously private moment, Emma stepped back and returned to her suite. Alone in the silence, she paced the length of the living room as she tried to figure out what happened next.

Should she say anything to Reyhan? To the king? Could she just leave?

The musical chimes of a grandfather clock caught her attention. She stared at the face and calculated the time difference with Texas, then crossed to the telephone and pressed zero, hoping to get an operator. Less than a minute later, she heard her mother's voice on the phone.

"Emma! How lovely to hear from you. Where are you, darling? George, it's Emma. Pick up the other phone."

Emma waited until she heard her father's familiar "Hello, kitten," before sighing in relief. The tension fled her body and for the first time in three days she knew everything was going to be all right.

"Are you enjoying your vacation?" her mother asked. "I've heard spring in San Francisco is very beautiful. Are you getting a lot of fog?"

Emma winced as she remembered the lie she'd told her parents. Alex from the State Department had made the suggestion and she'd gone along. Now she wondered if the original idea had been Reyhan's.

"I'm not in San Francisco," she told them.

"What?" Her father's voice turned worried. "Was there a problem with the plane? Do you need us to come and get you?"

"No. I'm fine. I'm in Bahania."

"The Bahamas?" her mother asked.

"No. Bahania. It's next to El Bahar. In the Middle East. I'm here because of Reyhan."

Her mother gasped. "I knew that horrible man wouldn't stay gone. Oh, George, he kidnapped her. We have to call the police. They'll know what to do."

"Now, Janice. Don't jump to conclusions. Kitten, are you all right? Did he hurt you?"

"No, Daddy. Reyhan has been very polite." She had no intention of mentioning the kiss they'd just shared. "Why did you say you didn't think he wouldn't stay away, Mom? You told me he never bothered to come see me."

There was a long silence. Finally her father spoke. "He might have stopped by a time or two."

Deep in her heart Emma wasn't surprised. Her parents loved her and wanted to protect her from everything. That would include what they saw as a dangerous man intent on using their daughter. The problem with them admitting guilt in one area was that now she had to doubt them about everything, involving her pseudomarriage and the time following it.

"Just come home," her mother pleaded. "Emma, you don't belong there with those people. We'll come get you if you like. Wouldn't that be nice? Then we could all go to Galveston together. I'll bet that nice house we used to rent is available. It's not too close to summer. I could call and check and we could—"

"Mom, no. I'm not coming home just yet and I don't want you to come get me. I'm fine. I'm just…" How to explain what she was doing?

"That man is going to bewitch you," her mother said. "Just like he did before. It's not right. He should be in jail."

"For what?" Emma asked. "He married me and provided for me." Sadness overwhelmed her. Sadness for what had happened and what she'd believed. Sadness that her parents couldn't have believed in her enough to tell the truth.

"He abandoned you," her father pointed out. "What kind of man does that? He tried to turn your head, the way he's doing now."

"Emma, you've never been strong enough to take care of yourself," her mother said, her voice pleading. "You can see that, can't you? Oh, darling, come home. You belong here, with us."

Emma ignored the pleas and the claims. She'd been plenty strong—she should know. Her independence had been hard-won.

"He didn't abandon me, Daddy," she said. "He came to see me every day. He called when he was in Bahania for his aunt's funeral, and as soon as he got back to Texas, he practically camped out in front of the house, didn't he?"

"Is that what he told you?"

"Yes. Is he lying?"

Her father was silent for a long time. "He came by a few times."

She clutched the phone tighter. Reyhan had told the truth about everything. "You told him I didn't want to see him. You decided *for* me."

"Kitten, you were in no shape to deal with him. Have you forgotten what you went through?"

No. She would never forget. The pain would be with her always.

"Mom, did you write the letter telling him I never wanted to see him again?"

"I... Oh, Emma. It was for the best."

She closed her eyes and wondered how her life would have been different if she'd known. She'd loved Reyhan as much as her childish heart had allowed, and she would have gone with him in a second. Had her parents realized that? Had they not wanted to see their only child living half a world away in a foreign land?

If she had only known...

"What about the money?" she asked, more resigned than angry. "Why didn't you tell me about that?"

"We thought it was best for you not to worry about that," her mother said primly.

Not to worry? "I have student loans and a ten-year-old car," she said. "You had no right to keep that information to yourself. Spending it or giving it back was my decision to make."

"You were so young, kitten," her father said. "Too young."

For all of this, she thought.

"Reyhan said he sent a letter telling me not to let pride get in the way of the money. After that, some has been withdrawn regularly. What did you do with it?"

"We didn't spend it," her mother said, sounding outraged. "We simply moved it into a money-market account. It's all there, darling. I'll show you the bank statements when you get home."

She felt drained and weary. It had been an evening of too many emotions.

"Were you ever going to tell me the truth?" she asked.

"Of course," her mother said.

"We love you," her father added.

"When? Oh, let me guess. When you thought I was old enough."

"Exactly."

She was twenty-four and living on her own. She had a job, an apartment and something closely resembling a life. What rite of passage had her parents been waiting for?

She was sure in their hearts they had planned to tell her what had happened, but they would have put it off as long as possible. Partly because they wouldn't want to make her angry and partly because they wouldn't want her returning to Reyhan. She was beginning to suspect they would have done anything to keep her close. Even lie about her marriage.

"Why did you tell me the marriage wasn't real?" she asked.

"We weren't sure," her mother said. "That lawyer

we hired couldn't verify it one way or the other. Best to be safe."

"By telling me I wasn't married when I was? What if I'd fallen in love and had gotten married again? I would have been a bigamist."

"If you'd gotten serious about someone, we would have said something," her father told her. "Emma, you have to understand our position in all this. We only want what's best for you."

Words she'd heard her entire life. For a long time she'd believed them, but now she wasn't so sure. Did they want what was best for her or for themselves?

"I need to go," she said. "I'll call when I get home."

"Emma, no!" Her mother sounded frantic. "You can't stay there. It's so far away."

"I'll be back in two weeks. Don't worry. Everything is fine."

"But, Emma—"

She cut them off with a quick "I love you" then hung up.

Alone, confused and weary to her bones, she curled up in a corner of her sofa and wondered when exactly her life had become so messy and what she was going to do to get things in order.

Chapter Five

The next morning Emma awoke with a brain full of questions and an achy feeling low in her belly. She knew the latter came from a night of erotic dreams with her and Reyhan as the stars. In her sleep he'd taken her over and over again and she'd been a willing participant. She'd pleaded and wanted and touched and surrendered happily.

Uneasy and more than a little apprehensive, Emma decided to ignore whatever not-so-subconscious message might be lurking in her dreams. Right now she had bigger problems—namely, what she'd said to Reyhan and how he'd told the truth about everything.

After showering in her Montana-size bathroom and dressing, she skipped breakfast. She owed Reyhan an apology and the nerves clog dancing in her stomach were unlikely to go away until she'd delivered it.

After getting directions to his office from the young woman cleaning the suite, Emma stepped out into the main corridor and walked toward what she hoped was the business wing of the palace. Ten minutes and three more sets of directions later, she walked into what looked like a very busy, very upscale office facility. She crossed to the middle-aged man sitting at a reception desk.

"I would like to speak with Prince Reyhan," she said.

The man's neutral expression didn't change but she thought she caught him eyeing her inexpensive dress and dismissing her.

"Do you have an appointment?" he asked.

She shook her head.

He reached for the large phone console on his desk. "I will call his assistant and check his schedule. May I ask who you are?"

She'd been about to say "Emma Kennedy" but her pride had been bruised. It wasn't her fault that she couldn't afford nice clothes. Besides, she was clean and tidy and she'd taken extra time with her makeup, and did Reyhan think she was badly dressed, too?

She raised her chin slightly and looked the man in the eye.

"His wife."

The man raised his eyebrows, color fled his cheeks and his jaw dropped.

"Of course, Your Highness." He nodded differentially and quickly pushed several buttons on the phone. When he was connected, he announced her and then hung up.

"This way, Princess Emma," he said, rising, then bowing.

Emma felt kind of small and petty for claiming a relationship that barely existed, but it was too late to call back the words.

She was led into a large open area. There were alcoves leading to private offices. The man apologized for making her wait even a second, then scurried off. Emma entertained herself by studying a color-coded map on the wall. She saw the capital city of Bahania and the ocean. El Bahar was also outlined and there were small markers at random intervals.

She moved closer to get a better look, when she felt a tingling at the back of her neck. Turning, she saw Reyhan striding toward her.

If her heart had not been trapped in her chest, it would have taken flight. He was so tall, she thought foolishly. And handsome. A powerful man who ruled an empire. Emotions flashed in his dark eyes but they were gone before she could catalog any of them. Then Reyhan was standing in front of her, staring, and Emma couldn't think. She could only breathe in the scent of him and silently wish he would kiss her again.

"Emma," he said, his voice low and sensual.

That was all. No more than her name and she found herself swaying toward him.

"Reyhan."

"Now that we have established our respective

identities, perhaps you would like to tell me the reason for your presence in my offices.''

''What? Oh.'' She glanced around at the people working. They were trying not to pay attention while hanging on every word. ''Could we please speak in private?''

''Of course.''

He took her arm and led the way into a massive office. A carved wooden desk dominated the center of the room. An exquisite Oriental rug outlined a conversation area, while bookcases lined one entire wall.

She saw another detailed map opposite the window and three different computer systems.

''What is that for?'' she asked, pointing at the map.

''It details the placement of the oil wells and pumping stations here and in El Bahar.''

''There are a lot of them.''

He smiled slightly. ''Yes.''

She'd heard Bahania was a rich nation—now she could see why.

''Our oil production is my area of expertise,'' he said. ''That is why I was in Texas getting my master's degree.''

She thought of all the oil in her own state. ''I guess we're experts, too.''

''Yes.''

He led her to the sofa grouping and motioned for her to sit down. When she'd done so, he settled across from her and assumed a patient expression.

Funny how he looked so remote and distant, she thought. As if he hadn't kissed her the previous evening. As if he hadn't reacted with desire, breathing hard and wanting her. Or had she imagined his re-action? Had he kissed her to show he still had power over her, while not reacting himself?

She didn't have enough experience to be able to tell which it had been—a disadvantage she didn't en-joy because there was no doubt in her mind that Rey-han had known exactly what was going on inside of *her* body.

"What did you wish to speak to me about?" he asked.

She twisted her fingers together on her lap and shrugged. "I spoke with my parents last night."

She waited to see if he would say anything, but when he didn't, she continued.

"You were right…about everything. The marriage, the money, that you tried to get in touch with me."

She glanced at him. He looked neither surprised nor annoyed.

"I'm sorry I doubted you," she whispered.

"Why would you not?" he said. "You have known your parents your entire life. We had been together only a few weeks. I disappeared after the wedding without giving you any information. Your parents would have been suspicious. No doubt they thought the worst."

"They're good at that," she said, surprised he was being so magnanimous. She would have expected a little gloating on his part—he'd more than earned it.

"I should have questioned them," she said. "I wanted to, but I was afraid."

"That I sought you?"

"That you didn't. That I'd been far too forgettable."

He looked at her. "You are many things, Emma, but not that. I, too, could have put more effort into getting in touch with you. I suspected some subterfuge on the part of your father, but I walked away. I assumed that in time you would learn what had occurred and get in contact with me."

There was more to it than that, she thought. Reyhan was a proud man. He wouldn't beg. Not for her. Probably not for any woman.

"I should have been more curious," she told him. "Instead I took the easy way out and I believed them."

She studied the strong lines of his face. Who was this man who had married her and then walked away? If only she hadn't been so young and inexperienced. If only they'd met more as equals. Six years ago she might have intrigued him initially, but in time he would have tired of her childish ways. And now?

She didn't have an answer to that, although she was more than willing to try the kissing again. Not that Reyhan seemed to be offering.

"So all this time after the fact, we make peace with the past," she said. "And in a few days the king will authorize a divorce."

"Yes."

Ouch. His agreement stung a little. Foolish, she told herself. She couldn't possibly have any interest in him. Better to get this all behind her and start over. She would find someone else—someone more like her—and settle down. Have kids. That was her destiny—not a handsome prince from a foreign land.

She stood, and he rose, as well.

There was so much so say, and yet nothing. What could have been would stay a mystery.

"I was wondering about palace tours," she said.

He frowned. "What do you mean?"

"I'm unlikely to get back to Bahania anytime soon. I would like to take advantage of my remaining time here to see something of the palace and the city."

"You may go anywhere you like in the palace."

She laughed. "Gee, thanks, but wandering around lost isn't my idea of a good time. I'm interested in hearing about the palace itself. Maybe some of the history. Is there a regular tour offered? I could join that."

"I will take you anywhere you would like to go."

"That's really nice of you, but unnecessary. I know you're busy."

Not that she would mind spending time with Reyhan. Being around him made her insides flutter—a new and thrilling experience. But he had responsibilities that didn't include her.

"Until the divorce, you are my wife. I will show you the palace and the city. We will begin today after lunch."

"That sounds like more of an order than a request."

He smiled. "You were the one to mention the tour. I am accommodating you."

Hmm, if he said so. Emma figured there was no point in arguing. Not only would Reyhan likely win, but having the argument would prove her to be a complete idiot. She wanted to spend time with him, which he was offering. A smart woman would smile and say yes.

"I look forward to it," she said brightly. "What time?"

"Two o'clock. Is that convenient?"

She laughed. "It's not like I have a full social calendar. I'll be ready."

He reached out and took her hand, then drew it toward his mouth. At the last second, he turned her fingers and pressed his lips against the inside of her wrist.

The hot, damp contact sent shivers zipping up her arm. Tension invaded her body and she would swear her knees were within seconds of buckling.

"Until two," he said, and released her.

Emma left quickly while she could because the alternative seemed to be throwing herself at him and begging him to never let her go. A feeling she couldn't deny, nor could she explain.

Reyhan showed up promptly at two. While he still looked hunky and appealing in the suit he'd been wearing earlier, Emma had agonized over her clothing choices. She'd wanted to look sexy and glamorous and enticing. All a challenge based on the contents of her suitcase. Not that her closet back home would have been that much help. She spent her workdays in scrub pants and brightly colored shirts and her evening attire pretty much consisted of khaki pants or long skirts and casual tops. Not exactly the fashion-forward clothing she would need to catch the eye of a prince.

A prince very interested in divorcing her, she reminded herself as she smoothed the front of her skirt and smiled brightly. Reyhan had made it more than clear he was intent on getting her out of his life. Not exactly the actions of a man prepared to be overwhelmed by her modest charms.

"What interests you most?" he asked as she stepped into the hallway and shut the door of her suite behind her. "There is an impressive display of centuries-old jewelry in a few of the public rooms."

"I'm sure it's lovely," she told him, "but I'm more of an antique furniture and tapestry kind of girl."

Reyhan raised one dark eyebrow, but didn't comment on her statement. Maybe he didn't believe her, which wasn't her problem. Sure, she liked sparkling things as much as the next woman, but they weren't her world.

"Very well," he said. "We'll begin in the older section of the palace. The original structure was built in the late 900s. Since then, the pink palace has been updated and enlarged several times. Once, during the reign of Elizabeth the first, the daughter of a wealthy merchant was captured and held for ransom by the bastard son of the king. After a time, instead of returning her, he fell in love with her. They married and lived happily together. For their tenth anniversary, he presented her with a chapel—a miniature representation of a cathedral she'd seen once in France. We'll begin there."

Emma walked next to him, trying not to get caught up in the heat his body generated. "Were many women captured and held against their will?"

Reyhan smiled. "It is a time-honored tradition for sheiks to take that which they admire."

How comforting. "So there's a harem here in the palace, too?"

"Of course."

She wasn't sure if she wanted to see it or not. Imagine a place where women were held simply to offer pleasure to one man. Of course there would be a lot of free time. She could catch up on her reading.

She glanced at her estranged husband and wondered what it would be like to be captured by him. Would he be kind? Demanding? She shivered at the thought of either. The wanting that was always just below the surface when he was around, burst into life. Her body ached to be close to his. She wanted him to pull her against him, kiss her, caress her. Instead she had to be content with the occasional brush of his arm against hers.

"Do men in Bahania have more than one wife?" she asked.

"No. That practice died out long before it was outlawed. Men quickly came to realize that keeping one wife happy was a full-time job."

"I've never understood why the multiple-wife thing was so popular," she said as they stepped out into a beautiful formal garden. She recognized it as the one she could see from her balcony. Where Cleo and her husband had come to be alone.

"It would be easy for a woman to be with more

than one man in an evening, but after men, um, have their way, they're sort of out of it for a while.''

Halfway through her sentence, she realized she'd stepped into some very dangerous territory. Did she *really* want to be having this conversation with Reyhan?

He stared at her, his expression unreadable but not the least bit friendly. ''You know this from personal experience?''

''No. I've just…heard.''

''It is not about pleasure,'' he told her, his voice slightly strained. ''It is about children. A woman is with child for nine months. In that time, a man can continue to impregnate other women, while she can only bear him one son at a time.''

''Oh. That makes sense.'' She spoke brightly, as if this conversation was no big deal. ''Good point. What's that?''

She pointed at a large statue of a horse rearing. It was life-size and pure white.

''A gift from the king of El Bahar some years ago. We have always had close ties with our neighbor.''

''I remember hearing that.''

Reyhan led the way down a narrow path. Lush plants grew on both sides and tall trees offered shade. It was early April and still pleasant but she was sure by mid-July the temperature, even in morning, would be unbearable.

''Here we are,'' he said, pointing to a small but exquisitely built chapel.

Spires reached toward the heavens. All of the windows were stained glass and looked ancient. Stone steps led into a darkened and cool interior.

Emma walked inside and instantly felt at peace. Half a dozen pews flanked a wide center aisle. In front, more stained-glass windows stretched up to the arched ceiling.

"Master craftsmen were brought in from France," Reyhan told her. "They worked for three years on the chapel, all in secret. While they were here, they trained many local masons who incorporated the designs in their own work."

Emma touched the carved wood pews. The finish was thick and glossy, obviously well cared for. What a private treasure, she thought.

"Are services ever held here?" she asked.

"On special holidays."

She fought a sudden longing to attend one, knowing she would be gone and forgotten before the next occasion.

Reyhan led her back into the palace. They walked down several flights of stone stairs, until she was sure they were underground.

"Long-lost treasures were recently returned to us," he said, pushing opening a massive wooden door. "Tapestries and statues, along with jewels and pieces of furniture. Local experts are restoring our history to us."

He showed her a wall-size tapestry in a frame. Two women matched threads and carefully repaired a large tear. It took Emma a second to see the scene—four men galloping across the desert. Their expressions were intent and fierce, their faces slightly familiar.

She glanced at Reyhan, noting the similarity in the shape of the eyes and build of the bodies.

"Relatives?" she asked.

"Ancestors. This dates back to the 1200s."

She wanted to touch the cloth, but knew too much handling could damage the delicate treasure.

He showed her shelves of statues and stacks of carved furniture. "Pieces are moved around in the palace," he said. "Some things are on display here in the city museum. Others are sent on tour around the world."

"I can't imagine what it would have been like growing up here," she said as they left the storage area and climbed stairs to the main level.

"As a young child, I had little use for the past. It was simply information I needed to learn to please my tutors."

"I suppose. We never appreciate what we have when we're young. Not unless we lose it."

He glanced at her. "What did you lose?"

She thought of her childhood. Loving, if overly protective. "I'm not sure there was anything. I was speaking in general." She glanced around at the city-size rooms they passed. "I think my entire house could have fit in there. You and your brothers must have had a good time playing hide-and-seek in here."

"We were not permitted to play games in the main rooms of the palace."

"Probably just as well. You could have gotten lost for days."

"Our tutors would have come looking for us."

Tutors. Not exactly a reference she could relate to. "You didn't go to the local schools?"

"No. When I was eleven I was sent to boarding school in Britain."

"It's that whole prince thing, huh?"

He glanced at her. One corner of his mouth curved up. "Prince thing?"

She grinned. "You know. Being royal. It made you different."

"We were given many unique opportunities."

"I suppose you would have to learn things regular kids didn't. Like how to behave in certain situations, and rules about running a country. Of course I'll bet each of you had your own horse. I guess it's a trade-off. There are advantages and disadvantages to most circumstances."

They walked into a huge reception room. The ceilings had to be three stories tall. There were carved poles and an intricately inlaid marble floor. Floor-to-ceiling beveled windows let in light. A raised stage stood at one end of the incredible room.

"My apartment doesn't even have a foyer," she murmured, and wondered again why he'd bothered with her all those years ago. "I was little more than a country mouse."

"What?"

She motioned to the gold light fixtures. "I'm going to guess that color isn't just a really nice paint job. Those are real gold."

"Yes, but it is of little consequence."

"Perhaps to you." She turned in a slow circle. Reyhan's leaving her was for the best, she thought sadly. There was no way she could have fit in here then. No way she fit in now.

"Is there another man?" he asked abruptly.

She stared at him. "What? You mean am I seeing anyone?"

He nodded.

"No. I'm not dating anyone right now. I've never been very good at the whole boy-girl thing, but you would know that better than anyone."

Memories crept in of their three nights together after their wedding. How he had taken her over and over and how she'd been unable to be anything but afraid.

Things would be different now, she thought with regret. She was sure she could respond, even hunger for him. But a man intent on getting a divorce was unlikely to be physically interested in the woman he was leaving behind—passionate kisses aside.

"Once you are no longer married, you can change that," he said.

"As can you."

But she didn't want to think about him being with another woman.

"It's scary to think what could have happened," she said to distract herself. "I really didn't know about the marriage being real. If I'd gotten serious about someone and we'd wanted to get married..." Would her parents have told her the truth? She would like to think so, but she was no longer sure about anything.

"I would have been in touch to let you know we were still married."

"How would you have known?"

He stared at her without speaking, and then realization sank in. "You've kept track of me." It was a statement, not a question. She wasn't sure if she was pleased or creeped out.

"At first, I received monthly reports," he told her. "Now, yearly. You are my wife. It is my duty to watch over you."

As he hadn't known about her job, the last report must have been sometime last summer, after her graduation but before she'd started work at the hospital.

"If I'd known we were still married, I would have contacted you," she said. "I mean, being married all these years and being apart doesn't make any sense." She realized how that sounded. "Not that I'm suggesting we *should* have been together."

"I understand. Divorcing is the most sensible plan."

"Right."

Sure. It wasn't as if she knew anything about Reyhan, save the fact that being within ten feet of him reduced her to a quivering mass.

"I wonder what would have happened if I'd known you'd come back for me," she said. "Would you have brought me here?"

"Of course. As my wife, your place is at my side."

"What about my education? I wouldn't have been able to go to college here."

"Should we argue about what never was?"

"Probably not."

But everything would have been different. They would have had children by now. She'd always wanted children, she thought wistfully. And with Reyhan as their father, they would be stronger than her. More able to stand up for themselves.

Would she have been able to keep him happy? Would their marriage have flourished or would her youth have worn on his affections?

Had he loved her, even a little? More questions she wouldn't be asking.

"Reyhan..."

She spoke his name, then paused, not sure what she wanted to say or ask.

He stared at her, his dark eyes narrowing slightly.

"Stop," he ordered.

"What?"

Her chest tightened as it became difficult to breathe. Awareness flickered through her body, making her tremble. Her mouth went dry, her fingers tingled and wanting swelled until she thought she would burst.

Then she was in his arms with no way to understand how she'd come to be there. He held her tightly, possessively and she reveled in belonging to him even for that single moment.

She had less than a heartbeat to anticipate the kiss before he pressed his mouth against hers and claimed her.

She parted instantly, wanting the intimacy, needing to make him desire her. The melting began, in her chest and between her thighs. At the first brush of his tongue against hers, she closed her eyes. At the second, she held in a sigh of contentment. Passion flooded every part of her body, making her squirm to get closer.

She touched his shoulders, his arms, then ran her hands up and down his muscled back. His fingers tangled in her hair. Their tongues stroked and circled and danced before he pulled back slightly and kissed her jaw.

He nibbled his way to her ear where he drew the lobe into his mouth and sucked gently. Her breath caught. He dropped his hands to her hips, then to her fanny where he cupped her curves before pulling her hard against him. As her stomach nestled against him, she felt a bulge.

Fierce gladness flashed through her. Reyhan was aroused. She excited him as much as he excited her. The thought thrilled her then was lost as he licked the sensitive skin under her ear, and she was unable to think about anything other than the exquisite sensations he created.

Heat was everywhere. His fingers burned, his body warmed. She found herself wanting to strip off clothing and bare herself. The large room and hard marble floors offered neither privacy nor comfort, but she didn't care.

She breathed his name, and when his mouth returned to hers, she was the one to slip her tongue against his lower lip before dipping inside.

He tasted faintly of coffee, with a little sweetness she couldn't explain. He continued to press against her, rubbing his arousal against her belly. She wanted to raise herself up on tiptoe so he could rub her *there* and pleasure them both.

One of his hands moved from her rear to her hip, then traveled higher. Her breasts swelled in anticipation of his touch. She wrapped both arms around his neck and clung to him so that when he reached his destination, she would not collapse at his feet.

Closer and closer and closer until she nearly begged him out loud. At last he cupped her right breast and brushed his thumb against her tight nipple.

Pleasure jolted her like lightning. She gasped, then nipped at his lower lip while he continued to stroke her. She could feel tension building between her thighs, the dampness of her panties and the trembling in her legs.

And then he was gone. He stepped back and stared at her. His breath came in rapid pants. Passion brightened his eyes and tightened the lines of his face. She didn't have the courage to glance lower, to *see* that he wanted her, but she knew.

They stared at each other for what seemed like an eternity. Emma wished she knew what to say, or even how to ask why he'd stopped when they were both so obviously willing. But nothing in her life had prepared her for such a reaction, so she couldn't find the words.

"I must return to my office," Reyhan said at last. "You will find your way back to your rooms."

It was a statement rather than a question, and Emma wasn't sure she could speak, let alone argue. She watched him walk away, then she staggered a few feet to one of the columns and leaned against it until her heartbeat slowed to normal.

She didn't understand what was happening with

Reyhan. She hadn't seen him in years. Why was he getting to her? And why did he have to be the only man who made her *want* with such incredible intensity?

"Too many questions," she whispered when she could finally think and breathe like a normal person. "No answers." Just a man who made her burn and a ticking clock that reminded her it would soon be time to leave.

Reyhan didn't return to his office right away. He detoured through the far end of the palace, walking briskly in an attempt to burn off the passion and need that Emma had created.

Nothing had changed. Emma's pull over him remained absolute. She could bring him to his knees with just a glance. When she touched him—he would capture the moon if she so requested.

He could never let her know the power she had over him, could never let her know his weakness for her. He paused by a window and stared uneasily out at the view. He *would* control this, he told himself. He would *stay* in control.

In a few days she would be gone and there would be relief. But instead of anticipation, he felt only pain at the thought of his world without her. The ache inside of him deepened.

So much time had passed, he'd hoped that he could face her and not care, not need. But he'd been wrong. Worse, she responded to him with the wants and desires of an experienced woman. She was no longer the frightened child he'd married.

Who had taught her to kiss so expertly? he wondered grimly. What man had tutored the woman who belonged to *him?* Passion blended with rage as his hands curled into fists. Were that man here now, Reyhan would rip him apart.

No! Control. He had to get control. Emma might be the color in his world, but she was also dangerous. Better to live in shades of gray than risk everything. Just a few more days. Then she would be gone and he would be free.

Chapter Six

The main marketplace was so filled with light and color, it was like stepping inside of a kaleidoscope. Emma didn't know where to look first. Wooden stalls lined the wide stone street and everywhere she turned there were more wonders to be seen. Bright silks puddling like quivering gems, copper pots of every shape and size, fruits, vegetables and rich, supple leather goods tempted her to step closer and touch.

In addition to the visual display, there were also strange and intriguing scents—sandalwood, coconut, exotic flowers and spices blended with wood smoke and the underlying musk of perfumes. A hundred conversations blended into a unique musical accompaniment with the call of the merchants, the barking of dogs and the laughter of the children racing through the back alleys.

"It's wonderful," she breathed, pausing to stare into the eyes of a camel tied up at a corner. "Like something out of a movie."

She smiled at Reyhan, who nodded.

"There are few sights that compare with an open-air market," he told her. "We have one of the oldest and largest in the world."

She smiled at a young woman holding a baby. The woman ducked her head and slowly backed away. Emma knew it wasn't because of her—no one knew her from a rock. Instead it was the presence of a prince, and the three large and hostile-looking bodyguards that were assigned to accompany them. The well-dressed and well-armed men kept the other shoppers at least an arm's distance away and discouraged casual conversation.

Emma wanted to protest, saying they would be fine on their own, but who was she to judge? Besides, Reyhan had explained that the accompanying men were as much for crowd control as protection.

She'd been surprised when Reyhan had offered to take her to the local market. After their last encounter she'd been sure he would want to avoid her, what with how he'd stalked away without saying anything. Yet two days later he'd shown up at her door with the invitation.

She'd been delighted to accept.

"Local dates," Reyhan said, stopping by one of the stands. "Try some."

The merchant, a tiny wizened man with a huge

smile, held out a tray of plump dates. When he nodded encouragingly at her, she took one and tasted.

"They're good," she said.

The merchant beamed. Reyhan reached into his pocket and pulled out a few coins.

"No, no." The old man backed up and shook his head. "It is my honor. My pleasure."

Reyhan smiled. "Such is the power of a beautiful woman."

Emma was so startled by the offhand compliment, she laughed. "Oh, sure. He's overwhelmed by my beauty, not by the fact that you're a prince and traveling with enough muscle to start your own wrestling federation."

His dark gaze settled on her face. "You don't think you're attractive?"

"I'm okay." Passably pretty, she thought. No one had ever looked at her and then run shrieking in the opposite direction. "But I've never overwhelmed anyone."

He continued to study her, then looked away without saying anything. The merchant pressed a bag in her hands. She could feel the soft fruit inside.

"Thank you," she said. "You're very kind."

As they walked away, Reyhan said something in a language she couldn't understand. One of the bodyguards made a note on a small pad he'd pulled from his jacket pocket.

"What was that about?" she asked when they'd drifted down another aisle in the market.

"Someone from the palace will visit the old man's stall later in the week," Reyhan said in a low voice.

"A large quantity of dates will be purchased at a premium price." He jerked his head back the way they'd come. "The old man offered a gift he can scarcely afford to give. Respect from my people shouldn't come at the price of starving."

"It was just a few dates."

"He has nothing else to sell."

An interesting point, she thought, studying Reyhan from the corner of her eye. She would have said he was firm and intelligent. Remote and stern with a hidden well of passion. But she would never have guessed he had a compassionate heart for those in need. One more item on the long list of things she didn't know about her soon-to-be ex prince-husband.

Two young boys ran past them, laughing and yelling as they went. Emma turned to watch them go.

"Did you come play in the market when you were a child?" she asked. "Were you allowed out and about?"

"Sometimes," Reyhan said. "With my brother Jefri." He shrugged. "Once we were playing with more abandon than usual and knocked a cooking pot off an open fire. In our hasty effort to retrieve it before the large and mean-looking owner noticed, we bumped a burning log into the corner of a stall. It was old, dry wood and went up in seconds."

She covered her mouth with her fingers. "Was anyone hurt?"

He shook his head. "No, but three stalls were completely destroyed before the fire was brought under control. Jefri and I were in trouble for a long time. Our father refused to let us simply pay for the damage out of our pocket money. Instead we had to rebuild the stalls and then work in them for several weekends. In the end, the owners came out ahead as people shopped to see the young princes up close.''

''So it was a fitting punishment?'' she asked, even as she thought it sounded a bit harsh. Not the rebuilding. That made sense, but the working in public where the boys would be stared at like zoo animals.

''My father wanted us to learn,'' Reyhan told her, not really answering the question. ''Jefri and I were more careful on our next trip to the marketplace.''

They stopped in front of a stall displaying silver jewelry. The merchant nodded exuberantly and held out dozens of silver bangles. They were large and beautifully carved.

''Something to remember the day by,'' Reyhan said, selecting several and offering them to her.

She wouldn't need a reminder. Everything about this time with him was burned onto her brain. But the bracelets *were* pretty. She reached for one made of linked hearts and slid it on.

He took the bag of dates from her and passed them to one of the bodyguards, then held her hand out in front of her. When he turned her wrist, the light caught the shiny bangle.

''Very nice,'' he said, and gave the jeweler several folded bills.

''Is it terribly expensive?'' she asked, feeling a little guilty. ''I can pay you back. I have my checkbook in my purse.''

Reyhan didn't speak, nor did he turn away. His dark gaze did the talking for him as she remembered who he was and all the money he'd left in her account. No doubt a silver bracelet wasn't going to be a blip on his financial radar.

"Thank you," she said softly. "It's very beautiful."

"You are a woman who deserves beautiful things."

That compliment nearly made her stumble, but she managed to stay upright. Fake it until you believe it, she told herself. Even if the faking lasted right up until the moment she walked into her apartment back in Dallas.

She wanted to ask what made her deserving of beautiful things and if he meant it when he looked at her with fire in his eyes. Did he feel the sparks between them? Did the heat draw him? Had he relived their kisses, as she had, longing for more, for every intimacy?

Rather than risk a potentially embarrassing line of conversation, she went for something safer.

"Did you attend school locally?" she asked.

"No. Just the tutor, then to a British prep school, then an American university."

He placed his hand on the small of her back and urged her down another crowded aisle. Several people bowed and smiled when they saw him. From what she could tell, Reyhan was very popular with his people. Probably a good thing when one was a prince.

"My father thought it was important for his sons to have a diverse education and contact with the West. Much of our business is conducted with American and European interests. Familiarity with mindsets and customs helps the process.''

She thought of her own small life. Aside from now, and except for their brief honeymoon in the Caribbean, she'd never been out of the state.

''I would imagine both Britain and America were different for you,'' she said.

''I knew some of your ways from watching movies. I'd been raised speaking English as well as Bahanian, so I was comfortable with the language. But there were still lessons to be learned.''

She stopped and touched his arm. ''Like what?''

He glanced at her. ''When I first arrived at my university, I told a few people who I was. Word quickly spread and my time there became...difficult.''

''Everyone wanting to rub shoulders with a real, live prince?'' she asked sympathetically.

''Something like that. Some young women were enthusiastic in their effort to get to know me.''

She could imagine. ''You would have been something of a catch.''

One corner of his mouth curved up. ''So I was told. When I went to Texas, I decided not to tell anyone who I was. A few recognized me from various articles in magazines and reports on television, but for the most part I was able to simply be myself.''

''I had no clue,'' she said, more than a little embarrassed by the fact. ''I guess I should have paid more attention to current events.''

He started walking again and drew her along with him. ''Not at all. Your interest in me was about who I was as a person, not who I was as a prince.''

"The whole royalty thing would have over-whelmed me," she admitted. "Actually, I would have run in the opposite direction."

"And I would have chased after you."

"Really?"

She glanced at him, wondering if he was teasing or telling the truth. Would Reyhan have pursued her? She wanted to believe he had been that interested, but was it really possible? She'd just been a very shy, inexperienced eighteen-year-old. Hardly the sort of woman to catch the interest of a sophisticated man of the world.

He took her hand in his and squeezed lightly. "You wanted to be a nurse. I know you graduated with honors, but I'm not that familiar with your work. Tell me what you do."

It was difficult to concentrate with his fingers rubbing against hers. When his thumb brushed against her palm, she nearly moaned. Wanting burned low in her belly, making her ache and need.

So many physical reactions, she thought. Why was her body coming alive now? With him?

Better not to ask, she told herself and focused on Reyhan's question.

"I'm a delivery room nurse," she said.

His expression tightened with surprise. "You assist with births?"

"Pretty much." She smiled. "It's so wonderful to spend my day helping babies being born. It's a time of joy and happiness for everyone involved."

"I suppose that is more fitting than you dealing with men."

"That's not why I chose my specialty. I went into it because I love children and babies and I thought it would be very gratifying. I was right."

"My sister-in-law recently had a baby. My sisters Zara and Sabrina are also pregnant."

"I'd heard. Cleo told me."

As she spoke, she raised her face toward his. Sunlight turned strands of her hair to the color of copper. Humor brightened her eyes and made her skin glow as if lit from within.

Beautiful, Reyhan thought desperately. She had always been beautiful.

Not that her being ugly would have helped, for if he closed his eyes when he was with her, he still wanted her. The sound of her voice was as musical as the rush of the tide. The scent of her body teased and enticed him. Her gentle spirit called to him, as did her intelligence and humor. Blind, deaf and mute, he would have burned for the lightest brush of her touch.

His need for her grew every second he was in her presence. Soon it would be as uncontrollable as a wild animal, and like that animal, he was in danger of devouring her. He had to get away from her but not just yet. One more day, he told himself. Then he would retreat to nurse his wounds and wait out her remaining time in his company.

"What will you do when you return to Dallas?" he asked.

"What do you mean? I'll go back to work."

Amusement tempered his growing desire. "Because you have bills to pay?"

She laughed. "Yes. All the usual things like rent and utilities, plus my student loans."

She was still so innocent.

"I am Prince Reyhan of Bahania."

She blinked at him. "Actually, I know that."

"You are my wife."

She shook her head. "I suppose technically, although not really."

"Legally you are."

"Okay. I guess. But you want a divorce."

"And after the divorce, do you think you'll leave with nothing?"

Emma's green eyes widened in surprised. "I don't want anything. I'm not your responsibility, and I'm perfectly capable of taking care of myself."

How like her, he thought. Other women of his acquaintance would be trying to squeeze out every dollar they could.

"I will provide for you," he told her. "Arrangements will be made for you to purchase a house, then I will set up a checking account as I did before."

"You really don't have to do this."

"I know."

"But we were only together for a few days."

It should have been for a lifetime.

The thought came unbidden. Reyhan did his best to chase it away, but it stayed in place. Stubborn, real and tempting. So much would have been different if he'd simply insisted on her returning with him. When his aunt had died, he'd left Emma behind, to spare her the trauma of finding out who and what he was. He didn't want to thrust her into royal life without some time to get used to the idea, nor did he want her meeting his family at a funeral. But by leaving her behind, he'd lost her.

How would their lives have been different if he'd brought her home right away? She would be a mother by now. His wife in every sense of the word. How would she have handled the responsibilities, the traditions? Would she have grown into them or chafed at the restrictions?

He would never know—about any of it. She could not be his wife; he had chosen a different path. But perhaps they could pretend for a single day.

"All the women I've ever met love to shop," he said. "Are you different in that, as well?"

She smiled. "I don't mind spending an afternoon or two at the mall. Are you trying to tempt me into accepting your more-than-generous offer of a settlement?"

"Not at all. The money will be provided. You don't have a choice in the matter."

She shook her head. "You're pretty high-handed."

"Yes."

She laughed. "That's it. Just a yes? Aren't you going to protest?"

"I get what I want one way or another."

"Must be nice."

"It is."

Except when he wouldn't allow himself what he wanted.

"This way," he said, taking her arm and leading her through the marketplace. The bodyguards trailed along behind.

Emma knew there was no point in protesting or asking where they were going. Reyhan would tell her when he was ready. Besides, she was enjoying her time with him to the point that it didn't much matter to her what came next.

She glanced down at the bangle on her wrist. Something to remember him by, she thought fondly. Not gold and expensive jewels, which weren't her style. Just a simple, silver bracelet.

They turned a corner onto a main street, then stopped in front of a plain storefront. She glanced at the sign that read Aimee's before Reyhan moved inside.

The cool interior was a contrast to the warmth of the afternoon. Emma took in the cream-on-white decorations, the elegant displays of clothing and shoes and instantly felt frumpy in her outlet-sale clothing.

A tall, painfully thin woman approached. "Yes, may I—" The woman touched her perfectly coiffed hair, then smiled. "Prince Reyhan. A pleasure. How may I serve you?"

"This is Emma," he said. "My wife."

The woman's dark eyes widened as she nodded graciously. "Princess. I am Aimee. Welcome to my shop."

Emma offered a smile even as she wondered what Reyhan was doing. It was one thing to tell people they were married in the palace, but why would he do it in public? No one had known they were married and they were going to be divorced very soon. Why bother with the hassle of explaining?

"She needs a complete wardrobe," he continued.

Emma turned to him. "What?"

"Indulge me."

"But..." Aware of the older woman's obvious interest in what was going on, Emma lowered her voice and leaned in close. "I don't need a new wardrobe. Mine is fine. I'm not saying her clothes aren't lovely, but they've got to be really pricey and they don't fit into my regular world."

"You're not in your regular world now, Emma. You're in mine. You're also a beautiful woman who deserves beautiful things. It pleases me to buy these for you."

Protesting too much seemed both ungracious and stupid. Instead she nodded. "Thank you for your kindness."

How bad could it be? she thought as she followed the well-dressed store owner into the dressing room area. A couple of dresses, maybe a pair of jeans or two and she would be done. Reyhan didn't strike her as the kind of man who would enjoy waiting while a woman tried on clothing.

Or was he?

Two hours later Emma was less sure about everything. Reyhan had been remarkably patient as she'd been dressed in everything from simple sundresses to suits to elegant evening wear. Whenever something looked especially nice on her, Aimee urged her to step out into the main salon for him to see. Much to her chagrin, he'd been the one to make the decisions on what to buy and what not to.

"These are supposed to be *my* clothes," she said

as he shook his head over a dark pants suit she quite liked.

"Too severe," he told her. "The cut is too loose."

"I can't spend my day flashing cleavage at the world."

"No. That you save for me."

Instinctively she pressed a hand against the vee neck of the suit. Was he talking as the powerful husband and prince or as man? Were they different? She stared at him, trying to figure out what he was thinking and what he wanted from her. The strong, handsome lines of his face gave away nothing.

But his words had made her *aware* of him again. While she'd been busy trying on outfit after outfit she'd been able to forget the tension lurking just under the surface. She'd managed to forget how much she liked being close to him and how he'd made her feel when he'd kissed her. Now she remembered everything.

"This will be fabulous," Aimee said when Emma returned to the dressing room. The older woman held out a strapless beaded gown in bronze. "The color will bring out the fire in your hair. Perhaps the prince will buy you a necklace of yellow diamonds to complete the look."

Yeah, right. Like that was going to happen. Emma didn't think that soon-to-be divorced wives rated rare gemstones. Of course she hadn't thought they rated new wardrobes, either.

After stripping off the pants suit, she studied the dress. No way was she going to be able to keep on her bra. Aimee stepped outside to give her privacy, so Emma continued undressing until she stood in just her panties, then she stepped into the elegant gown.

It fit her perfectly, sliding over her hips as if it had been made for her. Aimee returned with a pair of strappy sandals and some combs to hold back Emma's hair.

"Excellent," the woman said approvingly. "You look exactly like the princess you are."

Emma glanced in the mirror, then did a double take. She *did* look royal, or at least elegant in a way she never had before.

"I guess clothes really do make the woman," she murmured as she walked out into the salon.

Reyhan looked up from a newspaper, then rose to his feet and nodded. "Yes. That is exactly right. You are stunning."

"Thank you. The dress is amazing and I know it fits great, but there's no way I'm going to keep it."

"Why not?"

"Reyhan, where will I ever wear it? I really appreciate your interest in my wardrobe, but be serious. This isn't me."

He dropped the paper onto the small table by his chair and walked toward her. When he was less than a foot away, he stopped and looked into her face.

She met his gaze and felt the impact of his intense stare. Heat grew until she felt uncomfortable in the strapless gown. She wanted to tug down the hidden zipper and let the dress pool at her feet. She wanted to be naked before him. Naked and vulnerable and slick with wanting. Need made her ache deep inside. Her thighs trembled.

"It pleases me to buy you these things," he said, his voice hoarse. "Why do you object?"

Why, indeed. At this moment, she could deny him nothing. If only he would say that he wanted her. If only he would touch her. Anywhere. Her arms, her face, her breasts. She felt her tight nipples rub against the soft lining of the gown and wished the contact to be against Reyhan's palms instead.

Take me.

She didn't speak the words, but somehow he heard. Fire erupted in his eyes. His muscles tensed and his breathing quickened.

When his gaze shifted to the entrance to the dressing room, she knew what he was thinking. That they could be alone there. Right now. No waiting, no wondering if it was right. Just a man and woman taking pleasure in each other.

It was insane to even consider such a thing, but she wanted to. Desperately. They could—

The click of heels on the tile floor cut through the erotic silence. Before Emma could object, Aimee came out of the back room and Reyhan turned away. It was as if the moment had never been. Reluctantly she returned to the dressing room and took off the dress.

Later, when their limo was filled with boxes and bags from the boutique, and Reyhan sat so carefully at the opposite end of the long leather seat, she tried to figure out what was going on between them.

Six years ago, after their brief marriage ceremony, they'd retired to a hotel suite and spent three days together. Emma remembered the intimacy of making love with him. There had been little desire on her part. Mostly she'd felt embarrassment, fear and occasionally pain. The more Reyhan had wanted her, the more scared she'd become. When he'd been called back to Bahania, she'd been grateful.

Back then she'd simply endured his desires, whereas now she shared them. What was different? Her? Had she grown up to the place where she could meet Reyhan as an equal? Had he changed? Was it chemistry or timing? Was it a quirk of fate that she would find herself falling for a man who planned on divorcing her then have her disappear from his life forever?

Emma paced the length of her suite. She'd already unpacked her beautiful clothes and admired them while trying not to look at the price tags. Some of her evening gowns cost as much as a good used car. She had no idea where she would wear them, but that was really the least of her problems. Instead there was the pressing matter of Reyhan.

What was going on between them? Was acting on their mutual attraction a good thing or would it make her a nominee for idiot of the year? Should she say something to him? Ask him if he'd changed his mind about the divorce? Ask him if he just wanted her for sex? Ignore the whole thing and count the hours until she headed back for Dallas?

"If you were the least bit brave, you'd talk to him," she murmured to herself. "Put it all out on the table and see what happens."

A sensible plan.

She crossed to the phone, intent on calling him at his office, but before she could there was a knock on her suite door.

Reyhan? Her heart pounded at the thought. She replaced the phone and hurried to the door.

But instead of her handsome husband, a young maid stood in the hallway. The girl handed her a note, nodded and left. Emma closed the door, then unfolded the piece of paper. As she read, her chest tightened and her spirits sank.

Emma,
My thanks for a lovely day. Unfortunately, some minor trouble in the oil fields calls me away. By the time you read this I will have left by helicopter. I'm not sure of the date of my return, but I will make sure it is before you leave Bahania for good.

Disappointment swelled inside of her. He was gone and she might not see him again until it was time for her to go back to Dallas. Not exactly the actions of a man overwhelmed by passion. Had she misread him completely?

She hadn't been very good at understanding Reyhan when they'd first met. Apparently time and distance hadn't changed that fact.

"It's for the best," she whispered, crushing the note in her hands. "I'll go home and this will all be forgotten. I'll get on with my life. Find someone else and get married."

Although she had no idea who that someone else might be. Reyhan was going to be a tough act to follow.

Chapter Seven

"For a woman with a brand-new wardrobe, you're pretty down in the mouth," Cleo said the next morning.

Emma nuzzled baby Calah's sweet-smelling head and sighed. "It's guilt. Reyhan spent too much on me. The clothes are beautiful, but…"

Cleo rolled her eyes. "What? You don't deserve them? Emma, we're talking about the royal family. They've been rich for about a thousand years. Trust me. Your shopping spree didn't even count as pocket change."

Emma wanted to mention that the trip to the boutique hadn't been her idea, but she thought it might sound like she was making too big a deal of things. Cleo didn't think anything was out of the ordinary.

Reyhan hadn't minded. He'd wanted her to buy more than she had. The guilt was hers and she should deal with it by herself. Except…

"I didn't really need them."

Cleo laughed. "That's your mother talking. It's a very parental thing to say. Isn't it fun to buy things you *don't* need and not have to worry about cost? Think of this as the fulfillment of your every-female shopping fantasy. Besides, I know you made Reyhan happy. From what I can tell, all the princes like to take care of women. It can be occasionally annoying but for the most part it's pretty nice."

"So you're saying I went shopping just to keep *him* happy?"

"If it helps with the guilt, sure."

Emma smiled. "I'm going to look pretty silly wearing a beaded gown in the grocery store on Saturday morning."

"Not if you're over in the imported foods section. Tell everyone you're European."

"That might work." Emma thought of the beautiful evening gowns sitting in the suite's large closet. "Are there a lot of formal functions here at the palace?"

"Two or three each month. I've only just started attending them, what with being pregnant and all." She rubbed her baby's arm. "But now that Calah is here and I've had a chance to recover, I have social obligations, not to mention charitable ones."

"What do you mean?"

Cleo blew her daughter a kiss, then turned back to Emma. "I'm in a unique position to help people. In a way, that's a bigger dream fulfillment than the shopping. I've spoken with Sadik and the king, and I'm getting involved with homeless children. There aren't very many in Bahania and El Bahar, but it's a big problem in other countries. I had something of a twisted upbringing for my first few years and I know what it's like to be alone and scared. Sabrina and Zara, the king's other daughters, each have their causes. Sabrina's seriously into finding antiquities and returning them to their rightful countries so people can enjoy their heritage. Zara is a former professor. She's working on a network of scholarships for girls who want to go to college but can't afford it.''

"Sounds exciting," Emma said, hoping she didn't sound as wistful as she felt. Cleo was right. The chance to help people by using nearly unlimited resources would be a wonderful way to spend her life.

What would she have done if she and Reyhan had stayed together? She'd always loved children, especially babies. Maybe something with prenatal care. Not that she was going to get the chance to find out.

"How much longer do you have here?" Cleo asked. "I was hoping we could fit in a field trip so you could meet Sabrina and Zara. They live in a very interesting place."

"Not here in the city?"

"Not exactly."

When Cleo didn't seem willing to say anything else, Emma considered her question. "I was told I would be here two weeks, but I don't have an exact date for my return. I guess that's up to the king."

Not that she was all that anxious to head out, she

thought. Spending time with Reyhan had been exciting and fun and something she wouldn't mind doing more. But with him gone... She sighed. Her simple life had sure had gotten confusing.

"How are things with you and Reyhan?" Cleo asked. "Or is that too personal? I just meant it's been a long time. Is he the same guy you remembered?"

Emma chuckled. "Are we allowed to refer to a Bahanian prince as a guy?"

"Hmm, good point. We might be risking a beheading. Fortunately Calah is too young to turn us in."

Emma bounced the baby on her lap. "She would never betray us, would you, honey? You're one of the girls. We have to stick together." She looked at Cleo. "As for Reyhan being the same or different... Honestly, *everything* is different. When we met, I was a freshman, away from home for the first time in my life. He was a sophisticated older man who swept me off my feet. I spent most of our time together trying not to sound too young or stupid. That took most of my energy. I can't say I *did* ever know him."

"And now?"

Interesting question. "He's terrific. Not just those handsome dark good looks, either."

Cleo sighed. "Agreed. Sadik would be a catch even if he were a brainless fool. I could happily suspend my life simply looking at him. But there's a genuine person buried inside. I'm guessing Reyhan is the same."

"Yeah. He's smart and serious, but funny, too." And sexy. Too sexy, she thought remembering their almost close encounter in the boutique. She would have sworn he'd wanted her as much as she'd wanted him. So why had he just up and disappeared without seeing her to say goodbye?

"So the girl in you was overwhelmed the first time around," Cleo said. "How does the woman feel the second time around?"

"She's impressed," Emma admitted.

"Which doesn't make you sound like a woman who's hot for a divorce."

"Of course I am. Maybe not eager, but it's why I'm here. Reyhan is ready to get on with his life and his plan doesn't include me."

Cleo's blue eyes widened slightly. "You don't have to blindly agree, you know. You could take some time, see where things go."

Emma blinked at her. Could she? Was that an option? "I never thought I had a say in things."

"Arrogant princes prefer the world to do their bidding, but it doesn't always have to happen that way. You're half of the couple. You get a vote." She touched Emma's hand. "Seriously. If you're not sure what you want, tell the king. I'm sure he'd be more than willing to hold off the divorce for a while."

Tempting, Emma thought a half second before she shook her head. "No. There's no point. I don't belong here."

Cleo arched her eyebrows. "Oh, and I did? When I met Sadik I was the night manager of a copy shop. Not exactly princess material." She waved her fingers at the room. "It's not about the trappings, or even tradition. The king wants his sons to fall in love.

Prince Jefri has decided on an arranged match, but he's the only one.''

Cleo was wrong, Emma thought sadly. Reyhan wanted one, as well. He'd told her.

"Maybe if things had worked out differently when we'd first met," Emma said firmly. "But that time is past. We're different people. I have my own life back in Texas."

"Sure," Cleo said. "If you're not falling for Reyhan, there's no reason to stay. So tell me about your work in the hospital. You work in the delivery room, right?"

"Yes, it's wonderful."

Emma talked about a typical day, if there was such a thing, and how she loved what she did. But in the back of her mind, she kept hearing Cleo's words over and over again. *If you're not falling for Reyhan.*

She wasn't, she told herself firmly. She hadn't and she wouldn't. Falling for him after all these years apart would be just plain stupid. The fact that she enjoyed spending time with him was interesting but not significant. She wouldn't let it matter. She couldn't. Because Reyhan had made it clear he was only interested in moving on.

"They're making threats again," Will O'Rourke said quietly.

"The usual?" Reyhan asked from his place by the fire.

"Death and destruction. Interruption of oil production. The usual."

Reyhan kicked at a small rock in front of his chair.

"I would have more respect for these boys if they had a genuine complaint. We have neither taken their lands, nor displaced them."

"They want something for nothing. A share of the oil money or they make trouble. They're kids—seventeen or eighteen. To them this is a game."

"Extortion is a time-honored tradition all over the world." Reyhan turned his attention to the sky. It took a few seconds for his eyes to adjust to the total darkness, then he saw the thousands of stars twinkling in the heavens.

Beautiful, he thought. Mysterious. Distant. A world unto themselves. Much like Emma.

He shook his head. The point of his trip to the desert had been to avoid her, but if he was going to spend all his time thinking about her, then he might as well torture himself by being in her presence.

"I doubt they have a plan," Will said.

It took Reyhan a moment to remember what they'd been talking about. The teenage renegades.

"They imagine themselves to be characters in a movie," he told his security chief. "They will ride their purebred Bahanian stallions to victory."

Reyhan had no more patience for these boys. He'd listened to their grievances and investigated their claims. They had not been pushed off their lands, nor injured in any way by the oil production. Most of them were bored second sons from hardworking nomadic families. Unable to inherit, they didn't want to work to acquire their wealth. Instead they sought to take that which belonged to the people.

"Watch them," Reyhan said. "In time they will grow bored and go home."

"You hired me to keep the peace, then made it impossible for me to do my job."

"To date there have been threats, but no actions. They are afraid of you. I consider that doing your job."

Will was a former army ranger who had grown up on oil rigs in the Gulf of Mexico. His unique combination of knowledge and skills had made him a find. Over the past three years he'd worked his way up from the person in charge of security to Reyhan's second-in-command. There were those who disapproved of an American holding such a high position, but there was no one else Reyhan trusted at his back.

"The royal family has a centuries-old relationship with the nomads," Reyhan said. "Under normal circumstances, I would agree to your plan to simply round them all up and let them rot in prison for a decade or so. But the majority of these boys are sons of chiefs, and I have given my word that I will not endanger them without cause. Threats are not cause."

"As you wish."

The tall, blond American rose to his feet and headed to his tent. Reyhan watched him go. Will was frustrated, but he wouldn't say any more. Instead he would do his job. He would focus on the task. Did he know a way to keep a man from going insane?

Reyhan closed his eyes and tried to see nothing, but instead Emma filled his mind. Being apart from her had only made him want her more. She was like water to a man dying of thirst. Her light filled his day and without her, he was blind.

Not much longer, he told himself, looking for comfort and finding none. Just a few more days and Emma would be gone. Then he would be free to marry someone else. A sensible woman who would bear him fine sons. A woman he could respect and never love. A woman who was not Emma.

Emma found use for one of her fancy dresses two nights later when she was invited to dine with the king, Cleo and her husband, Prince Jefri and Murat, the crown prince of Bahania. Nerves rode a roller coaster through her stomach as she carefully applied her makeup, and she wished Reyhan was going to be around. With him at her side, she would find it a whole lot easier to make casual conversation with everyone else at the table. But she hadn't heard from him since he'd left and she was beginning to think she wasn't going to.

What if the two weeks ended while he was gone and she had to leave Bahania without seeing him again? She briefly closed her eyes and told herself not to think about it. If she had to leave without seeing him again, she would survive. Maybe it would even help her get over him more quickly.

Not that she had anything to recover from. It's not as if she was falling for him or anything.

After checking the mirror one last time and smoothing the front of the peach-colored cocktail dress she'd pulled on, she walked out of the suite toward Cleo's rooms. Cleo and her husband had offered to escort her to the dinner so she wouldn't get lost on the way.

"This is Sadik," Cleo said a few minutes later as she introduced her husband.

Emma wasn't sure if she was expected to curtsy or what. Wishing she'd asked Cleo in advance, she held out her hand and tried to look more impressed than nervous. "Your Highness."

Sadik—tall, darkly handsome and more than a little intimidating—smiled. "As you are a member of the family, I suspect first names would be allowed." He bent slightly and kissed the back of her hand. "Welcome, Emma. I'm not sure how you have been able to put up with my brother these past few days, but the fact that you have is a testament to your character."

She'd been expecting to shake hands, so the kiss startled her, although not as much as the gentle teasing. Were all the princes *nice* as well as good-looking and powerful? Was it possible?

"He's been very kind," she murmured.

"But a fool. Any man who leaves such a beautiful wife on her own takes his chances."

Cleo, lush and amazing in a dark blue low-cut gown, raised her eyebrows. "Sadik, are you flirting?"

He turned to her. "I am making our new sister feel welcome. You know there is but one woman in my world."

He spoke with an intensity and love that made Emma feel she'd stumbled into a private moment. She turned away, but not before she saw the way Cleo smiled at her husband. It was a smile of true contentment and security. In that moment Emma vowed she would find a man who would love her as Sadik loved his wife, and she would give her whole heart to him.

The three of them walked into the hallway.

"Jefri's fun," Cleo said, linking arms with Emma. "He's the youngest and has a great sense of humor. Murat is more stuffy. I guess it's the whole crown prince thing."

"Murat has many responsibilities," Sadik said firmly. "The weight of the country rests on his shoulders."

"He's also still single," Cleo told her. "Imagine marrying him."

"No, thanks. I'm having trouble dealing with being a princess, however temporarily. I wouldn't want to think about being queen."

"Someone's going to have to," Cleo said. "The king has started talking about Murat needing an heir. Not that there aren't hundreds of women lining up to volunteer."

"She will be the mother of his sons," Sadik said. "Not a choice to be made lightly."

"Exactly," Cleo said with a grin. "Now, if he was going to only have daughters, then he could pretty much marry anyone."

Sadik sighed. "You mock me, wife."

"Pretty much every chance I get." She looked at Emma. "It's a hobby."

Emma was still chuckling when they walked into the formal dining room. This was not the same dining room she'd been in on her second night in Bahania.

That room had been impressive, but small and intimate. This one was much larger, with arched windows and elegant tapestries.

The table itself would seat at least twelve, and judging by the chairs lined up along one wall, could expand to seat many more. The inlaid wood gleamed in the soft light of crystal and gold chandeliers. The floor was marble, the flatware gold and the plates appeared hand painted and antique. Equally impressive, there wasn't a cat to be seen.

Despite the warm temperature outside, the room was cool and a fire crackled in a massive carved fireplace. The king stood beside it, a drink in his hand. Two men stood next to him. They were both tall and dark, with strong features and lean bodies.

Do they know how to grow handsome princes here or what? Emma thought, trying not to give in to her nerves and panic. She just had to get through the dinner, then she could escape back to her room. No biggie. Besides, if Jefri and Murat were as well mannered as Reyhan and Sadik, she would be made to feel welcome. There was nothing to worry about. Really.

Emma had nearly convinced herself when the king turned and saw them. As he approached, she felt her knees begin knocking together. Telling herself over and over that he was just a man didn't help. Not even a little.

"Emma," King Hassan said as he approached. "How lovely to see you."

He squeezed her arm lightly, then turned to Cleo, whom he kissed, then Sadik. The two men shook hands.

"I heard you went to our marketplace earlier this week," the king said as he led her to the other princes. "Did you enjoy it?"

"Very much. The people were gracious and kind."

"A Bahanian trait," he told her, then he introduced her to his sons.

They were much like Reyhan, yet different. Murat was taller and more serious. Jefri smiled easily. Both welcomed her.

When a servant approached to take her drink order, Emma chose white wine because she didn't want to appear out of place, but she had no intention of actually drinking any liquor. Not under these circumstances. Back home her friends teased her about being a complete lightweight, which was true. One drink and she was giggly, two and the world got blurry. Better to keep her wits about her tonight.

"It is unfortunate Reyhan couldn't be with us," Murat said a few minutes later.

Emma noticed the king in conversation with Sadik and Cleo while Jefri had excused himself to take a quick call from America. Something to do with the new Bahania Air Force. She smiled at the crown prince.

"Another familiar face in this impressive gathering would be helpful," she admitted. "But he has responsibilities and I understand that."

"Many women do not."

"I can't imagine why not."

"They find reasons." He sipped his drink as he studied her. "Is it true you knew nothing of who he was?"

"Absolutely. I didn't completely believe it even after I was brought here. The whole prince thing isn't exactly a part of my regular life."

"The life you will return to in a few days?"

She nodded.

"Regrets?" he asked.

She considered the question. "One or two foolish ones."

"Why foolish?"

She motioned to the room. "This is fifteen light-years from where I belong. Reyhan needs to find a wife who will fit into his world."

"You let him go easily."

Was Murat criticizing or stating the obvious? "It's what he wants."

"And what do you want?"

Emma thought of her time with Reyhan. How he'd made her laugh and made her ache. Of how her heart fluttered when he was in the room. Of how innocent she had been all those years ago and how she'd let him walk away.

"I would like to go back and do things differently."

"Not possible," he told her. "Not even for a prince."

Jefri returned just then and dinner was announced.

Emma found herself seated on the king's left, with Prince Jefri next to her. Murat was across from her. She felt the sharp gaze of the crown prince settle on her more than once as the appetizers were served. She longed to ask what he was thinking and if he would say anything to Reyhan when he returned. Were the brothers close? Did they confide in each other? Did Murat know something of Reyhan's heart, and if he did, would that information please her or hurt her?

"The planes are being delivered next week," Jefri said, sounding pleased.

"All that training will finally pay off," the king said. "Are they being delivered to El Bahar, as well?"

Jefri nodded. "The people from Van Horn will be here by the end of the month to start the integration process."

Cleo leaned toward Emma. "Okay, you look confused. El Bahar and Bahania are starting a joint air force to protect the oil fields. Jefri, who has been a flying fool for years, is in charge. He bought a bunch of really fast planes. F-somethings. Anyway, Van Horn Enterprises is a private firm that trains fighter pilots."

Sadik sighed. "I'm not sure where to start, Cleo."

She straightened. "What? Did I get any of it wrong?"

Jefri looked at her. "You called me a flying fool."

"And?"

One corner of his mouth twitched. "Never mind."

King Hassan looked indulgently at Cleo. "She has given me my first grandchild. Little else matters."

Cleo winked. "You gotta like that, right?"

Emma nodded, thinking that they might be royal and rich and live in a palace, but at heart this was a family like every other. The knot in her stomach untied and faded away.

Conversation turned to current events and how they

impacted Bahania. Emma had long known that Bahania was an American ally, but she was surprised by the close relationship the king and Murat obviously had with the president and several leaders in the Senate.

They had just been served a delicious chicken dish when one of the servants approached the king and spoke into his ear. The monarch listened, said something back, then looked at Emma.

"It seems there has been a slight plumbing problem in your suite," he said. "A pipe cracked and flooded the room. Nothing of yours was damaged, but you'll need to spend the night somewhere else." He smiled. "I think we can find a spare bed."

She thought of the dozens of rooms in the guest section. "I'm not concerned about it."

"Good. I have asked for your belongings to be packed and moved. After dinner I'll escort you to your new quarters myself."

"Thank you."

The meal lasted another two hours. When it was over, Emma felt so full, she could barely move. The king made good on his word and walked her to her new room.

"I hope you're enjoying your stay in my country," the monarch said as they turned a corner and started down a long corridor.

"Very much. What I've seen is so beautiful. And everyone has been so kind."

"Even my son?"

She glanced at him. He was tall, with a slight graying at his temple. In his dark suit he looked both regal and powerful.

"Especially Reyhan."

"I was sorry he could not dine with us tonight."

Emma agreed, but didn't want to say that. "He has responsibilities."

"He takes them seriously," King Hassan said. "As do all my sons. But in Reyhan's case, perhaps too seriously."

She wasn't sure what he meant, but before she could figure out a polite way to ask, they stopped in front of a large door.

"You will be staying in here," her host told her. "I hope you will find the room to your liking." He smiled and left.

Emma opened the door and stepped inside. The quarters were larger than her own had been, but more spartan. There were no overstuffed sofas and lush paintings. Instead the room was filled with simply designed pieces in muted earth tones and the artwork leaned more toward sculptures with a few boldly colored abstracts for contrast.

She turned on several lamps and walked around the living room. Something about it made her feel…not uneasy, just odd. The room was almost familiar. How strange. Had she seen it when she and Reyhan had toured the palace? She didn't remember any guest rooms being on their tour. Had she seen one similar?

She walked into the bedroom. The huge bed rested on a platform. Massive pieces of furniture filled the space without crowding her. Again the colors were muted but not—

She froze in place. There was a book on a nightstand. An open book. Quickly she crossed to the closet and pulled at the double doors. Dark suits lined one side of the closet. Built-in shelves were home to shirts, sweaters and shoes. Her own newly purchased wardrobe filled the other side of the closet. She fingered the sleeve of the closest suit and knew exactly who owned it.

Reyhan.

The king had moved her in with her husband.

Emma sighed, not sure what to do with the information. Should she protest? Request another room? Was King Hassan testing her? Testing them? Even with Reyhan gone, she felt that she didn't belong in his rooms. They had never lived as man and wife. This felt too…intimate.

In the bathroom she found her cosmetics on the same counter as his shaver. Two bathrobes hung by the large glassed-in shower. As if they had always been together.

Not sure what to do, Emma decided she would stay the night, then speak with Cleo in the morning. Perhaps the other woman would know what was going on and what Emma should do about it. In the meantime, she would simply pretend all this was real and that this was where she belonged.

Reyhan arrived back at the palace shortly after midnight. The same demons that had driven him away had forced him to return. He had to see her, touch her, breathe the same air she breathed. The need inside of him had grown until he couldn't eat or sleep. He could only *want*.

He took the stairs two at a time. When he reached the second floor, he walked toward the guest wing. But as he approached her door, he slowed his step until he stopped several feet away.

What was he going to do? Break down the door and take her? He closed his eyes and shook his head. No. He would be strong. Just a few more days and she would be gone. He was back in the palace now. Within a few feet of her. That would be enough. He would retreat to the safety of his own rooms and figure out a way to survive until she was gone.

Retracing his steps, he made his way to the other side of the building and let himself into his suite. He shrugged out of his jacket and left it on the back of the sofa. As he loosened his tie, he walked into the bedroom, only to come to a complete stop.

He was not alone.

A woman lay in his bed. In the moonlight streaming in from the open French doors he could see a bare arm, the curve of a cheek and dark hair tangled on a white pillow.

His heart stopped for a full second, then resumed at a thundering pace. His body heated as blood raced down to his groin. He was instantly hard and ready to take.

Emma was in his bed.

Chapter Eight

Reyhan told himself to leave, to back out of the room before she awoke. As much as he wanted her, he couldn't have her. Not now, not ever. But he couldn't move. The passion was too strong. He could only stand in place and drink in her beauty.

He must have made a sound, or perhaps she sensed his presence, because she stirred, turned over then opened her eyes.

"Reyhan?" she asked, her voice sleepy. She pushed her hair out of her face and raised herself on one elbow. "What time is it?" She glanced at the clock, then back at him. "I've only been asleep for a couple of seconds. I thought…" She blinked. "Wait. What are you doing here?"

"This is my room."

"What?" She glanced around. "Oh." Her breath caught. "*Oh!* Right. I, ah, I had dinner with the king and your family and while we were eating someone came and told him that a pipe had broken in my suite. So he said he would put me somewhere else. Which turned out to be here. I thought it was weird, but it was late and I figured I would just stay here until morning, then straighten it out. I didn't think you'd be back tonight."

Of course she didn't. He hadn't told her when he would return. But he'd told his father who had most likely arranged for him to find Emma sleeping in his bed. While he was curious as to why his father wanted to tempt him with Emma, he was more concerned about the temptation itself. He had to get out of here before he said or did something he would regret. Before he gave in to the hunger consuming him.

"I'm sorry," she said, sitting up and drawing her knees to her chest. "I should have said something right away. I can go find somewhere else to sleep."

She started to climb out of the bed. He caught a glimpse of semitransparent fabric and sensuous curves.

"Don't," he said, turning away and staring blindly out the French doors. "Just stay there. I'll leave."

"But this is your room."

"Tonight it is yours."

Tonight and always, he thought, knowing he would never forget seeing her there. In the morning, when she was gone, he would haunt the rooms, searching for some hint of her presence, some clue that she'd been there at all.

"How were your meetings?" she asked.

"They went well."

"Did you really have to go, or were you just avoiding me?"

The softly worded question surprised him. The Emma he remembered would never have been so bold. He returned his attention to her and found her sitting cross-legged, staring at the sheets.

"I was avoiding you, but not for the reasons you think."

Her chin lifted and her eyes widened. "I don't understand."

Perhaps it was the night. Perhaps it was the ache inside of him, an ache that grew and fed on his soul. Perhaps it was the hint of sweetness in the air, the scent of which could only come from Emma. Perhaps it was madness. Regardless of the reason, he decided to speak the truth.

"I cannot be around you without wanting you," he said. "Rather than give in, I went away."

Understanding dawned slowly. The soft light of the moon didn't allow him to see her blush, but he imagined it. She swallowed, then shrugged.

"Oh. I, ah…" She cleared her throat. "You mean sex."

Her acceptance nearly made him smile. He wasn't sure if she was trying to act casually or if she was truly unsurprised by his admission. What had she learned in their six years apart and who had been her teacher?

"I prefer to think of it as making love, but, yes."

She tucked her hair behind her ears. "I guess it's

a guy thing,'' she said. ''I never understood all the fuss.''

He did his best not to react to her words, not to hope too much. ''Your lovers have not pleased you?''

Her nose wrinkled. ''I've sort of avoided the whole man-in-my-bed thing. It's not my style.''

Two warring thoughts invaded his brain and produced two very different reactions. First was pleasure and relief that she hadn't been with anyone else. That she was still only his. The second was stung pride that he hadn't satisfied her when they'd been together. He knew now that he'd been too intent on his own release, on claiming her over and over. He hadn't taken the time to pleasure her.

''Not that it's your fault,'' she said, interrupting his internal battle. ''I was too young. We went from kissing, to, well, you know, too fast for me. You were right about what you said before, that I wanted a schoolgirl's courtship with kisses and presents.''

So hard that he thought he might explode, Reyhan forced himself to walk to the chair close to the bed and sit down.

''You were a virgin,'' he told her. ''That fault lies with me. I was young and eager to take my bride. Too eager.''

She ducked her head again. ''Yes, well, it happens.''

''It should not have happened that way. The women I had been with before had been older and more experienced. They had been the teacher and I the student. With you...'' He clenched his teeth. ''I should have been more patient, more understanding.

I should have seduced you with slow kisses and soft touches. Only when you were begging for more should I have taken you.''

A shudder rippled through her body. ''That sounds nice,'' she whispered.

The slight quaver in her voice told him she was not unaffected by his words. The knowledge nearly propelled him to his feet and across the room to the bed. What would happen if he slid in beside her? Would she welcome him? Want him? Respond to him? Every cell in his body screamed for him to find out.

No! He could not. He knew the price of being with her again. A single moment of exquisite pleasure followed by a lifetime of wanting what he could not have. Better to not have her at all.

He forced himself to stand but not approach, and nearly shook with the intensity of his feelings. ''Good night, Emma,'' he said as he turned away. ''Sleep well.''

''Reyhan, wait.''

A rustle of sheets told him she had slid out of the bed. Her footsteps made no noise on the thick carpet but he *felt* her approach.

His blood boiled, his erection throbbed. It was more than he could bear and yet he did not turn around. He would not do this. No matter how much resisting cost him.

''Before,'' she whispered, her voice low and husky. ''When you kissed me. It was different.''

He thought of her passion, of how she'd clung to him, demanding as much as he. They'd fit together perfectly. Everything about her had called to him, yet he'd forced himself to pull back.

"It *was* different," he agreed.

"I'm not that child anymore."

Five simple words—an invitation to paradise.

He heard them and was nearly afraid to believe.

It doesn't matter, he told himself desperately. Taking her now, making love with her, would be a disaster. How would he let her go? How would he marry someone he didn't care about and live with her for the rest of his life? What of his future, his plans? What of being strong?

What of Emma?

Without thought, he turned slowly and stared at her. She stood only a few feet away, naked except for the diaphanous silk nightgown skimming her curves. Her long auburn hair tumbled over her shoulders; the curling ends lightly teased the tops of her breasts. Her eyes were bright, her lips slightly parted, her breathing rapid.

He told himself he could still resist her, and he nearly believed himself. Until she walked closer, raised herself on tiptoe and pressed her mouth to his.

The soft, gentle, chaste pressure undid him. It was as if the savage beast inside had been set free to prey upon the world. He grabbed her and pulled her close, wanting to touch everywhere at once. As his mouth settled on hers, he rubbed her back, her hips, then her fanny. He could feel the smoothness of her skin under the thin gown, but it wasn't enough. He needed more.

Tilting his head, he swept his tongue across her lower lip. When she parted for him, he plunged inside, stroking, exploring, needing. At the same time he tugged on the fabric of her gown, pulling it higher and higher until it bunched in his left hand. With his right, he stroked the now-bare skin of her hips, then slid up her back. She shivered and wrapped her arms around him.

He ground himself against her, rubbing his arousal against her belly. She flexed into him and moaned softly.

He let the nightgown fall back to her ankles and raised his hands to her shoulders. The thin straps slid down easily. He moved from her mouth to her jaw, then her neck, tasting her skin, licking, sucking, nipping. He bathed her long, slender neck with sensual attentions that made her shudder and cling to him. He bit her shoulder, then licked the wound.

The silk clung to her breasts, but one quick tug drew the fabric over her tight nipples so that it fluttered to the floor. Then she was naked.

Torn between looking and touching, he bent down and took her nipple in his mouth. He circled his tongue around the hard peak and she groaned her pleasure. She wrapped one arm around his shoulders and the other around his neck. Her fingers tunneled through his hair.

"Reyhan," she breathed. "It's too good. All of it."

Her words were like icy water thrown in his face. Reality crashed in on him as he realized what he was doing. Taking her hard and fast. They weren't even in bed. He was still fully dressed. Had he learned nothing?

Reyhan swore under his breath, which didn't bother

Emma nearly as much as when he stopped what he'd been doing. He straightened, leaving her nipples damp and achy. Everywhere he'd touched, she burned. Tension tightened her muscles and made her tremble. She didn't even mind that she was naked— not as long as he kept touching her.

"I'm sorry," he breathed.

She stared at him, at his dilated dark eyes and the firm set of his mouth. "For what? I liked it."

One corner of his mouth pulled up in a smile. "I'm glad you liked it but my plan was to seduce, not take."

"Taking works. Really."

"That is because you haven't been seduced. Come. I will show you the difference."

He led her to the bed and urged her to lie down. While she made herself comfortable, he quickly stripped out of his clothes, leaving only the briefs covering his arousal. Her interest in the long, hard bulge dissipated when he slid in next to her and pulled her close.

"You are so beautiful," he whispered into her ear right before he took the lobe between his teeth and nibbled.

Shivers rippled across her skin.

"You're soft," he continued as he kissed below her ear, then down her throat. One of his hands lightly stroked her belly.

"The scent of your skin drives me wild with passion. I ache to be inside of you. Filling you slowly, deeply, until your pleasure makes you scream your delight."

Scream? She didn't consider herself the type. But under the circumstances, she was willing to give it a try. Just the feel of his hand on her belly made her want to squirm. Up or down, she thought as he kissed her jaw. He needed to move that hand either up or down. Having it right there in the middle was making her crazy.

"The color of your nipples," he whispered. "Like a fully ripe peach. Open your eyes."

The unexpected request took a second to sink in. Emma opened her eyes and saw Reyhan lean over her breasts. As she watched, he touched the tip of his tongue to the tip of her left nipple. The combination of seeing and feeling was the most erotic experience of her life. She cried out in delight.

He circled her nipple, then drew it fully into his mouth. The gentle sucking had her arching against him. At the same time, his hand finally dipped south, slipping through her curls and between her legs.

She parted for him, catching her breath as he rubbed against her slick center.

This was nothing like before, she thought as tension filled her body. She ached with every fiber of her being. When he shifted his fingers slightly and found a single spot of pleasure, she nearly rose off the bed.

"Reyhan," she breathed. "Don't stop."

Thankfully, he didn't. He continued to touch her, stroking her, teasing, circling, as he worshiped her breasts. The combination made her mind go blank, her legs go limp and her breathing come in fast pants.

She couldn't bear herself enough to him. She wanted to be more naked, more exposed, more intimate.

Her wish was granted when he shifted so that he knelt between her legs and kissed his way down her belly. Part of her suspected what he was going to do while the rest of her couldn't believe it was really happening. She'd heard...she'd read...but before, he'd never...

He kissed her between her legs—an openmouthed kiss that made her tremble. Tension exploded inside of her as muscles tensed and collected. He found that one spot and licked it over and over until all she could do was dig her heels into the mattress and clutch the sheets with her hands. She tossed her head from side to side, tried to catch her breath, then gave up air completely as her release claimed her.

She hadn't known, she thought hazily as her body released and muscles contracted, that this much pleasure existed in the world. That she could feel so good, so right, so everything.

Her climax rippled through her and still he touched her, gentling the contact until the last drop had been wrung from her body. She opened her eyes and stared at him.

"I can't believe you did that."

He smiled. "Better than before."

"Miraculous. I've never..." She wiggled, feeling more than a little self-conscious. "You know."

"Yes, I know."

He sat up and removed his briefs. She barely had time to gaze at his arousal before he settled between her legs and kissed her breasts. She felt a shivery kind of ache all over. Suddenly there were more possibilities than she'd ever realized and she wanted him inside of her.

"Yes," she whispered, as he raised his head and stared at her. "Be in me." She reached between them and guided him inside.

He was large and stretched her in the best way possible. She felt filled, yet the need for more grew.

He wrapped his arms around her, drawing her close so they pressed together everywhere. She clung to him, urging him deeper.

"More," she breathed as he withdrew only to fill her again.

The rhythmic thrusting made her pulse against him. She couldn't get enough and she couldn't seem to keep control. She strained toward him, reaching, needing, wanting. She dropped her hands to his hips to pull him closer.

"Take me," she begged. "Oh, Reyhan, yes."

In and out, in and out. Tension grew again. She couldn't focus on anything but what they were doing. And then her body convulsed in release and she could only hang on as he took her to heaven and back. At the very end, when she was sure there couldn't be anything else, he shuddered in her embrace and called out her name.

Later, when the moon had set and they were both lying naked under the covers, Emma rested her head on Reyhan's shoulder. He was warm and relaxed next to her. She had the thought that things could have been awkward between them, but he'd made everything so easy and right by simply pulling her close.

As if he never planned on letting her go and this was exactly where she belonged.

Emma awoke to a bright sunny day and the feeling that she could quite possibly fly. As she lay in the large bed and relived her night with Reyhan, she felt herself smiling, tingling and fighting the urge to break out in song.

So *that* was what all the fuss was about, she thought happily as she rubbed her hand against the sheets where Reyhan had slept. Amazing how she'd missed the whole point before. Now she got it completely. Her only regret was that he hadn't taken her again and again, as he had on their honeymoon. For the first time, making love several times a day made perfect sense.

''We'll have tonight,'' she said as she tossed back the covers and stood. She was still naked, but there wasn't anyone around to see. After grabbing her robe from the foot of the bed, she walked into the bathroom and turned on the shower.

As she stepped into the steaming spray, she had the thought that night was really far off and maybe he wasn't doing anything for lunch. Or there was that massive desk in his office. The surface might be a little hard, but the space had possibilities. She was still laughing when she began to shampoo her hair.

Forty minutes later she made her way through the hallways of the palace. She found Reyhan's office with only a single wrong turn and practically beamed at the man in the foyer.

"Princess Emma," he said, leaping to his feet. "I'll tell your husband you're here."

"Thank you."

Emma continued to smile at no one in particular and practically floated into Reyhan's office. He hung up the phone as she entered.

"Is there a problem?" he asked, sounding both distant and stern.

"No. Of course not." She paused expectantly and waited.

He stared at her. A grandfather clock in the corner ticked. The silence grew.

She felt some of her happiness bleed away, and with the sensation came the chilling thought that he had regrets about what had happened.

After a few seconds, he rose and circled around his desk. "I'm very busy, Emma. Is there something you need?"

He spoke almost coldly, as if she were an assistant who had lingered too long. Trepidation clutched at her chest and she took a step back.

"I thought…" She swallowed. "I was just…" Mentioning her fantasy of a lunch break on his desk seemed impossible.

Who was this distant stranger? she wondered frantically. Where was the hotly passionate man from the previous night? What had happened?

He waited, watching her, giving nothing away. She remembered then that he'd tried to leave the bedroom and she'd been the one to stop him. Had she kept him against his will? Had he not wanted to make love with her? Had he done it out of obligation?

Her eyes began to burn but she refused to give in to tears. She was all grown up now, and she'd known what she was doing when she'd invited him into her bed. She'd *wanted* to make love with him. If there were consequences, they were her responsibility.

Pride squared her shoulders and raised her chin. She met his dark gaze. Maybe this was the moment to get answers to her questions.

"Why did you ever marry me?" she asked. "And once you decided to return to Bahania, why did you *stay* married to me? I don't believe it was because you were afraid to tell your father what you'd done. You fear no man."

"It doesn't matter."

"Maybe not to you but I want to know what's going on. You disappeared from my life for years, then you dragged me back here, played the charming host, then disappeared. Last night—"

A knock on the closed door interrupted her.

Reyhan frowned. "What is it?" he called.

His assistant stepped into the room. "I'm sorry, sir. I wouldn't have disturbed you except you and Princess Emma have been summoned by the king. He wishes to see both of you right away. It seems her parents have arrived at the palace."

"They can't be here," Emma murmured as she and Reyhan walked through the maze of corridors. "They don't like to fly. They never wanted me to. All our vacations were by car."

But here they were. As she followed Reyhan into a large reception room, she saw her parents standing with the king in an obviously awkward moment of silence.

When she came to a stop, Reyhan paused beside her. So far, he hadn't said anything, and she was grateful. This was going to be difficult enough without him taking on her family for withholding significant information from her for years.

In the second before they looked up and saw her, she studied them. Her mother was small and a little bent, her thick hair more gray than red, her father much taller and spare. They looked old, frail and out of place. Funny how all her life they'd seemed so powerful. She'd been afraid to defy them, to question the rules. Her only act of rebellion had been to fall in love with Reyhan and then run off with him, and she'd paid for that several times over. Now she saw they were just people. Older, out of their element and afraid for her. They had acted out of love, however misplaced, taking control because she'd never told them they shouldn't.

"Emma!" her mother shouted as she saw her. Both her parents rushed over and hugged her fiercely. Reyhan moved away.

"Are you all right?" her father asked. "Have they hurt you?"

"What? I'm fine. Everyone has treated me exceptionally well." She thought about last night. *Well* didn't begin to describe it.

"You shouldn't have left Dallas," her mother said as she brushed at Emma's sleeve. "You know you're not strong. Situations like this confuse you."

"I would think finding out you're a princess would

confuse anyone,'' Emma said, trying to step back, but
they held on tight.

Flanking her, they turned to the king. ''We've filed
an official complaint with the State Department protesting our daughter's kidnapping,'' her father said.

''Dad, no. I wasn't kidnapped. I'm here as the
king's guest to deal with my marriage to Reyhan.
You're seriously overreacting.''

''Am I?'' He looked at her. ''You up and disappeared, you lied to us about where you'd gone. For
all we know, they're brainwashing you.''

From the corner of her eye she saw Reyhan take a
step forward. Outrage darkened his features. She
didn't want to think about how much her father had
just insulted the king.

''I'm not being brainwashed,'' she said, then realized it was a foolish argument. If she was, would she
know?

''As your daughter's husband, it is my duty to care
for her,'' Reyhan said stiffly. ''I assure you, her safety
and well-being are my primary concern.''

''Some concern,'' her mother said tartly. ''You're
the reason she's here in the first place. If you hadn't
carted her off back then none of this would have happened. She was just a child.''

''I was eighteen,'' Emma reminded her. ''I loved
him.''

''You don't know what love is,'' her mother told
her, still glaring at Reyhan.

''You seduced her and then ran off,'' her father
added. ''What kind of concern is that?''

Reyhan glared at the older man. ''I attempted to

contact her on several occasions. You're the ones who kept me from her."

"Good thing we did. Who knows what would have happened if we hadn't?"

She would have come to Bahania, Emma thought. She would have been Reyhan's wife. They would have had children.

"This isn't accomplishing anything," she told her parents. "I married Reyhan and now we all have to deal with it. I don't want you interfering. You already got between us once. It won't happen again."

Her mother stared at her. "You said you were here to get a divorce."

"I am, but—"

"Then there's nothing to get in the way of, is there?"

"No, but—"

Her mother narrowed her gaze. "We'll be taking our daughter with us this afternoon. If you would have someone pack up her things."

"I'm not leaving," Emma said. "Not yet."

"Why not?" her father wanted to know. "You can't possibly plan to—"

"Silence," the king said.

His voice wasn't especially loud, but something in the tone got everyone's attention. They all turned to him.

He smiled at her parents. "You are my honored guests for as long as you would like to stay in Bahania. Or you may leave at any time, as may your daughter."

That surprised her. Reyhan also looked startled.

"The divorce," he said.

His father nodded. "That is a separate matter." The monarch paused.

Emma felt her inside clench in panic. Suddenly she didn't want to hear what King Hassan had to say. Was he granting the divorce a few days early? It made the most sense, but she didn't want him to. Things were too unsettled between herself and Reyhan. She needed to understand what last night had meant and why he'd been so cold this morning. She wanted to know what the fluttering when he was near meant. Was it just about sexual attraction or was there more?

Time. She needed time.

The king looked at her and it was as if he could read her mind. His kind eyes seemed to tell her that everything would be all right. To trust him. She took a deep breath and tried to relax.

"Despite Reyhan's request for a divorce, I am not convinced it is the right course of action," the king said.

"No!" her mother protested.

"This is an outrage," her father said.

Reyhan was completely silent and Emma felt only a sense of relief.

"It is my decision that Reyhan and Emma must get to know each other again. Something drew them together enough for them to impulsively marry. Was it a youthful prank or true love? Only time will tell. Therefore they must spend two months in each other's company. Not a day or a night apart. At the end of that time we will speak again. If they still both wish to divorce, I will grant it and their marriage will disappear as if it had never been."

Chapter Nine

Emma felt both relief and panic at the king's proclamation. Two months in Reyhan's company. If there were more nights like the previous one, that would hardly be difficult duty.

She glanced at the man who had married her. It was as if his expression were made of stone. She couldn't tell what he was thinking, nor could she see anything friendly or welcoming in his dark eyes. One thing she *was* sure of—he didn't look happy.

Without saying anything, Reyhan turned and left the room. Emma watched him go and tried to ignore the knot that returned to her stomach.

Beside her, her parents continued to protest.

"There has to be some legal court we can take this up with," her father said heatedly.

The king appeared more amused than insulted. "Mr. and Mrs. Kennedy, please." He opened his arms in a gesture of welcome. "You are honored guests in my country. I would ask you to stay here in the palace as long as you would like. Visit with your daughter. Get to know my people. You will find things very pleasant. As for your daughter—" he smiled at Emma "—she is a charming young woman. You must be very proud."

Her mother sniffed. "Of course we are. She's a very good girl."

Emma felt like a wayward puppy who had finally been pronounced housebroken.

"I do not wish to be unreasonable." The king turned to her father. "You are right—there are courts and laws. They state all royal marriages must be approved by the king. Reyhan defied me when he married your lovely daughter. Having met Emma, I can forgive his impulsiveness. Who could blame him?"

While she appreciated the compliment, she thought he was laying it on a little thick.

"This isn't her world," her mother said. "She belongs home, with us."

"She is a grown woman. Perhaps it is time for *her* to say where she belongs. In two months she will have that opportunity."

He beckoned someone from the rear of the room. Emma saw several servants approaching.

"Show the Kennedys to their quarters," he said, then nodded and left.

Emma's mother huffed. "Just like that. You have a life. Has he forgotten that? Responsibilities. A job."

Emma blinked in surprise. Honestly, she'd forgotten all about that. Her world back home. Funny how it had faded from her memory so quickly.

"You're right. I'll have to take a leave of absence."

"They won't like that," her father told her. "You've not even been working there a year."

Good point. "I'll have to explain things," she said, not sure how she was going to. Would anyone believe her? "If I do get fired, I'll find another job when I get home."

"A very cavalier attitude," her mother said. "You were raised better than that."

"Mom, I know you're worried. I appreciate that, and I know you only came here because you care about me. But I'm twenty-four. It's time to let me live my life my own way. If I make mistakes, then I'll recover from them."

Her mother's mouth dropped open, while her father seemed equally surprised. She took advantage of the silence and smiled at one of the servants.

"Okay," she said. "Lead the way." She linked arms with her parents. "You two are going to love this place. The rooms are amazing. And the views, even better than when we went to Galveston my senior year of high school."

Her mother sighed. "I don't like any of this, Emma. It's not you."

"I know. But from what I can tell, I don't have a choice. The king has to give his permission for a prince to get a divorce. So I'm stuck here until that happens."

Two months with Reyhan. What would that time bring? Would she learn to understand the man she'd married so impulsively? Would she be eager to leave when the time was up? Or would she find herself falling in love? And if it was the latter, would he love her back or would he still want to get rid of her so he could marry someone else?

Reyhan didn't return to his offices. Instead he walked to the garages where he took the keys for a Jeep and drove out of the city. An hour later, surrounded by desert, he stepped out into the warm afternoon and raised his face to the sky.

He wanted to yell his frustration, to rip and tear something. Anything. He wanted to travel north, deep into the inhospitable land and become someone else.

Two months. It was an eternity. How could he survive spending his days and nights with her? How could he be close to her and not reach for her?

Last night had been paradise. A miracle. When he'd left her bed this morning all he'd been able to think about was how much he wanted her. Having her had only increased his need. When she'd walked into his office, he'd held on to his control with every ounce of will he possessed. Just a few minutes longer and he would have snapped.

"I am Prince Reyhan of Bahania," he yelled to the heavens. "I am a man of power, of substance."

Yet in the presence of a mere woman he was weak. He would travel any distance, complete any task, risk life, limb anything, just for Emma.

He clutched the side of the Jeep. There had to be

a solution somewhere. An answer, a trick, a way to survive two months around her without going mad. He couldn't give in and take her into his bed. If he did, he would never let her go. And if she stayed...

He sucked in a breath as he considered the possibility. To have her stay was to love her. To give her his very soul. Then he would be nothing but a shell of a man. A spineless creature—a parasite.

No! That could never happen. Somehow he would conquer this. He would find the strength to turn away from her. To resist her. When the time was up, he would let her go. It was the only way. The alternative was unthinkable.

Emma went with her parents to the guest suite. It was similar to the one she'd had and even the ever sensible and conservative George and Janice Kennedy were impressed.

"You can see the ocean," her mother said as she stared out the large French doors.

"It's the Arabian Sea," Emma told her. "Bahania has some beautiful beaches. Tourism is an important industry."

Her father opened the suitcase one of the servants had left on the bed. "I can't believe they wanted to unpack for us. Like we're invalids or something."

"It's not that they thought you were incapable," Emma said. "It's part of the service."

"I've always done my own cooking and cleaning," her mother reminded her. "I never did understand those women who pay someone else to come in and clean their dirt. It's not right." Her mouth pressed together as tears filled her eyes. "None of this is right."

Emma took her hand and led her back into the large living room. Her father followed. When the two of them were seated on the sofa, she curled up in the wing chair across the glass-topped coffee table.

"We have to talk about it," she said.

Her mother pulled a lace-edged hankie out of her sleeve. "There's nothing to say. That man was trouble before and he's trouble now."

"Don't distress yourself, Janice," her father said gently. "We're here now and we'll make sure our girl is safe."

"I know. It's just... This place. It's so big and fancy."

"The palace is amazing," Emma said, trying not to get sucked into a familiar pattern of panic when she upset her parents. Knowing she made her mother cry was enough to give her a stomach ache for three days. But she couldn't keep giving in. King Hassan had been right when he'd said it was time for her to make some decisions about her life.

"All this is happening now because we didn't straighten things out six years ago," she said.

Her father sighed. "We went over this, kitten."

The familiar name made her stiffen. For years she's loved that he called her that, but now she wasn't so sure. A kitten was hardly a force to be reckoned with.

"You should have told me what was going on," she said quietly. "I had the right to know that Reyhan had tried to see me."

Her mother started to speak, but Emma held up her

hand to stop her. "If I was old enough to get married, I was old enough to know the truth."

"But you would have gone away with him," her mother wailed. "We would never have seen you."

"Is that what this was all about? Keeping me close?"

Her parents looked at each other, then at her. "We only wanted what was best for you," her father said. "We love you."

Why had she been afraid of defying them for so long? she wondered. They were just people. Misguided, maybe. She might not agree with their decision, but she believed they'd done what they thought was right. Their motivation had been selfish, but only because they cared about her.

"Emma, we should have said something about the money," her mother admitted. "It was such a large amount. It's not that Reyhan was bad, it's just that he wasn't like us. You were so sad. When you were happy again, we wanted to keep you that way."

Emma didn't know what to feel. Loss for what could have been. Although would she and Reyhan have had a chance all those years ago? At eighteen she'd barely been able to take care of herself. How would she have handled a husband, and maybe a child?

"It's done," she said, wanting to move on. "We can't change it and now we have a different situation to deal with."

Her mother sighed. "I can't believe the king is going to insist you stay here two months. That's barbaric."

Emma smiled. "You can call living in the palace a lot of things, but not that. Besides, I want a chance to get to know Reyhan again."

Her parents exchanged a look of worry and panic. "Is that such a good idea, kitten?" her father asked.

"I don't know. I loved him once."

"You were just a little girl."

"Legally, I was an adult," she said, silently admitting that on the inside she'd been a child. "But that's not the point. As King Hassan said, there's a reason the two of us ran off."

Her mother pressed her lips together. "We all know what *his* reason was. He was little more than an animal."

Emma thought of what had happened the previous night. A little more animal-like behavior would be fine with her.

"You two have loved each other for nearly fifty years. Don't you want that for me?"

"Not with him," her father said. "Can't you find a nice boy back home? Emma, you're only twenty-four. You have years before you have to settle down and get married."

"I'm already married. I'm staying the two months, and I'm going to take the time to get to know Reyhan again."

Her mother's eyes welled with tears. "But what if you fall in love with him?"

Would she? "It's a chance I'm willing to take."

"Oh, Emma. He broke your heart before. What's to stop him from doing it again?"

Good question. "I have to risk it. I'm sorry. I know

you want to protect me but this time you can't. I have to do it on my own. So I'm going to ask you to trust me.''

Her elderly parents stared at her. She sensed their misgivings and fear. Then they looked at each other and nodded.

''All right, kitten,'' her father said. ''If this is what you really want, we'll stand by your decision.''

''When he destroys you, we'll be here to pick up the pieces,'' her mother added. ''We'll take you home and you can move back into your own room.''

Talk about motivation to make things work with Reyhan, Emma thought. Still, she wouldn't let her parents sway her one way or the other. The king had granted her the gift of time and she intended to take advantage of it.

Emma spent the afternoon with her parents. She took them on a tour of the palace, the gardens and the chapel. They seemed to enjoy the dozens of cats more than anything. An hour before dinner, she returned to the room she now shared with Reyhan and called her supervisor back in Dallas. Fifteen minutes later she found herself on indefinite leave and accepting good wishes that it all work out for the best.

If only, she thought as she hung up the phone.

She leaned back on the sofa and tried to figure out what to do next. She was having dinner with her parents. There would be a more formal event with the king and several ministers the following evening, and a party later in the weekend.

''A whirlwind of social events,'' she murmured to

herself, trying not to feel nervous as she watched the clock and waited for Reyhan to return. However much he might want to avoid it, they *had* to talk, and the sooner the better.

Thirty minutes later, she'd given up trying to read her book. Sixty minutes later she was pacing the room with the intensity of an athlete training for an Olympic event. When the main door of the suite finally opened, Emma nearly stumbled in shock.

Elation, excitement and trepidation coiled together in her stomach as she searched Reyhan's face, hoping for a clue as to what he was thinking. There wasn't one.

"Good evening," he said when he saw her. "Are your parents settled?"

Not the words of a man overwhelmed by passion and desire, she thought sadly as she fought her own visceral reactions to being in the same room as the man who had taught her what all the fuss was about.

"Yes. They love their rooms." A slight exaggeration, but he was unlikely to press her. "How are you?"

"Fine."

He walked past her into the bedroom. She trailed after him, wishing he'd said a little more. "I'm having dinner with my parents tonight," she said. "You're welcome to come, but you don't have to. I know they probably make you uncomfortable."

Reyhan shrugged out of his suit jacket. "I would think the situation would be the reverse."

That he made them nervous? Probably. "Would you care to join us?" she asked. "Do you have to

because of what the king said?'' Days *and* nights together. She still wasn't sure what that meant.

He loosened his tie. ''My father's statement was
meant to keep me from taking an extended business
trip. We are not required to spend every waking second in each other's company.''

Too bad. She twisted her hands together. ''I didn't
know what to do about staying here. Should I? Do
you want me to move to one of the guest rooms?''

Reyhan pulled his tie free of his shirt collar. ''No.
Stay here. I'll sleep in the second bedroom.''

Supreme happiness crashed in and burned in a tenth
of a second. ''There's another bedroom?'' she asked,
because the alternative was to ask why he didn't want
them to sleep together.

''I have a small office at the other end of the suite.
I'll have a bed brought in. We'll have to share the
living quarters and the bathroom, but I'll make every
effort not to get in your way.''

''But I... But we...'' She swallowed and took a
step toward him. ''Reyhan, what's going on? Why
are you acting like this?''

He pulled his shirttail out of his trousers. Her gaze
dropped to his belt and she had the sudden fantasy
that he was going to get naked in front of her.
Wouldn't that be a treat?

His expression turned weary. ''It is only two
months,'' he said. ''Surely you can endure my company that long.''

''Enduring your company isn't the problem. Last
night...'' She cleared her throat. ''Reyhan, we made
love.''

He turned away and crossed to the French doors. "It will not happen again."

Stark words that clawed at her heart. "Because you don't want me?"

Because it wasn't good? Hadn't she pleased him? Last night she'd been so sure, but now...

Her throat tightened, as did her chest. Her legs felt heavy and thick, as if they belonged to someone else.

He bowed his head briefly. "Two months, Emma. That is all. At the end of that time, you can return to Texas where you belong."

And he would stay here, marry another woman and have children with her.

"But I thought..."

He turned to her. She'd never seen such coldness in a man's eyes before. Such rejection. "You thought wrong."

"I swear, there should be a law allowing wives of princes to lock their husbands in chains once a month. Just to keep them in line," Princess Sabrina said, grinning.

"Would you want to beat him, too?" Cleo asked as she reached for a slice of cantaloupe.

"Only when he really makes me crazy. Probably every third month."

"Works for me," Princess Zara said cheerfully. "Not that I'd ever want to hurt Rafe, but threatening him from time to time would make me really happy."

The three women laughed with delight. Emma smiled, knowing however big they talked, none of them was anything but completely in love with their husbands. She'd sensed it from the first moment they'd met.

Cleo had arrived that morning to invite her to lunch. "Without your folks," she'd insisted. "Not that they're not great, but you need a break."

Sabrina and Zara, both daughters of the king, although by different mothers, had been charming as they'd welcomed Emma.

"So you're the mystery woman Reyhan married," Sabrina said as she passed around a plate of tea sandwiches. She was seven or eight months pregnant and a beauty with dark eyes and dark brown hair highlighted with red.

Zara, equally pretty but in a more quiet way, looked like her sister. She was pregnant, as well, but not so far along.

"I don't consider myself a mystery," Emma said, which was true. Compared with being a princess, her life was pretty boring.

"Reyhan never said a word," Sabrina told her. "Not that any of my brothers are the chatty type. But a wife. That's a big secret to keep." She tilted her head and smile. "Then you appear out of the blue. Are you completely freaked?"

"Pretty much."

"I would be, too," Zara told her. "Sabrina grew up with all this, so she's used to it, but for the rest of us it's been a challenge."

Cleo laughed. "It's true. Zara resisted being a princess for the longest time."

"So did you," Zara reminded her.

"For different reasons. You were one by birth. Sadik wanted me to be one by marriage."

Emma was confused. "Didn't you want to marry him? You're so in love."

"It's complicated," Cleo told her. "A story for another time." She leaned over the back of the sofa in her suite and checked on Calah. "This is the best baby in the universe. She never cries, she sleeps like a dream and I swear she has an IQ of about two hundred."

Sabrina and Zara rolled their eyes. Emma laughed.

"She's *very* smart," Cleo said, sounding huffy. "You guys wait until your babies are born. You'll see what I mean."

"Sure, Cleo," Sabrina said. "I'm guessing we'll all be as goofy as you about our children."

"You mock me now, but just you wait."

"Watch yourself," Sabrina said to Emma. "There's something about this palace. It's pregnancy central. Be careful or you'll catch a baby of your own."

The three women laughed and Emma tried to join in, not that she was very successful. It was hard to joke when she'd just realized that she and Reyhan hadn't used protection when they'd made love.

She sucked in a breath and tried to stay calm. It had only been one time, she reminded herself. A quick calculation told her the day had been safe, relatively speaking. So she was unlikely to be pregnant. Based on how he was avoiding her, she wasn't going to be in a position to have a second chance at getting pregnant, either. Which was good. Right?

She *was* happy not to have to deal with an unexpected baby. Except she could easily picture herself with Reyhan's child. Holding him or her and overwhelmed by love. That would be wonderful.

She knew Reyhan wanted children, just not with her. Which made her wonder why. He'd been willing to marry her before. Why was he so determined *not* to be married to her now? She didn't think there was anyone else in his life. He'd said he would accept an arranged union. So she—

"Earth to Emma," Zara said. "Are you still with us?"

Emma blinked and saw all three women looking at her. "Sorry. I was lost in thought."

"I bet I know who was starring in that fantasy," Sabrina said teasingly. "It would be romantic if it wasn't my brother."

Emma felt herself coloring. "No, really. It was nothing."

As she'd never been a very good liar, she wasn't surprised when they didn't buy her story.

"Maybe there's more going on than we know about," Cleo said. "Which could be interesting."

"We'd love to have you as part of our princess sisterhood," Zara told her. "Think about it."

"Thanks."

She appreciated the invitation more than she could say. She'd always wanted a sister. But staying or not staying wasn't just up to her. Reyhan had a part in it, and based on what she'd seen so far, he couldn't wait to have her gone.

Chapter Ten

Two days later Emma accompanied her parents down to the stable. The king had suggested Reyhan take them out into the desert to show them some of Bahania's natural beauty. She was relatively sure her husband had agreed to the outing because he didn't have a choice. Ever since they'd shared that one night, he'd made it more than clear that spending time in her company was about as pleasant as root canal sugery.

What hurt her was that her feelings were so different. Since sharing a bed, she couldn't stop thinking about being with him in other ways. She wanted to talk to him, get to know him, laugh, tease, make memories. She wanted him to hold her close instead of stiffening every time she was near.

"Are you sure this is safe?" her mother asked as they crossed the stone courtyard leading to the stable. "Aren't there robbers and pirates in the desert?"

"Pirates are on the ocean," her father said gently. "However, we're going to have to deal with robbers."

Emma held in a sigh. She loved her parents very much but in the last couple of days they'd really started to get on her nerves. They weren't open to any new experiences and, despite the wonders of the palace, they kept talking about how much they wanted to go home. When she encouraged them to make plans they refused, telling her they wouldn't leave without her. The thought of two months in such close quarters made her teeth ache.

But that was a problem for another time. Right now she had to worry about the fact that Reyhan stood by the front of the stable, and upon seeing him she felt her heart rate quadruple while her thighs began to quiver.

"Good morning," Reyhan said as they approached.

He wore riding boots, dark slacks and a loose white shirt. Despite the short hair and freshly shaven face, Emma had the thought that he looked as dangerous as the pirates her mother feared.

But as appealing as she found him, he didn't seem to return her interest. He neither looked directly at her nor acknowledged her personally. He motioned to a large open vehicle—part roofless SUV, part topless van. There were three rows of seats.

"You'll be comfortable for our trip out to the oasis."

"Is it safe?" her mother asked. "Are there a lot of wild people and robbers on the loose?"

Emma winced. "Mom," she said quickly, "Bahania is a very civilized country."

Reyhan's expression didn't change. "The laws of the desert offer hospitality to all who enter. You will be welcomed by my people and treated as an honored guest." He motioned to the vehicle.

Emma's parents exchanged a glance before cautiously stepping inside. She hung back, wanting more than an impersonal trip with a man who was doing his best to become a stranger.

"I thought we'd be riding," she said.

He looked at her for the first time that morning. She felt the impact of his gaze all the way down to her already-curling toes.

"Do you know how?"

"I've had a few lessons." When she was twelve. "I'm a whiz on horses made of wood, but I can probably handle the real thing if he or she is gentle and doesn't think tossing me would be good for a chuckle."

Reyhan's dark eyes didn't flicker, not did his mouth even twitch. When exactly had he turned into a man of stone?

"Wait there," he said, and walked into the stable.

"Emma, what are you doing?" her mother asked fretfully.

"Reyhan and I are going to ride."

Both of her parents shrank back in their seats. "You can't."

"Sure I can. It will be fun."

Her father frowned. "When did you get so adventurous?"

She considered the question. "I can't give you an exact date," she admitted, knowing her change of heart had something to do with finding out nothing in her life was as she had first thought. Her parents weren't perfect. In fact they'd lied and kept the truth from her. Sure their actions had been in the name of keeping her safe, but she'd been an adult. The decisions hadn't been theirs to make. Not only that, but she'd been married for the past six years and hadn't had a clue. Information like that was bound to produce a change.

Reyhan returned, leading a beautiful white stallion. Emma might not know much about horses, but she'd heard rumors.

"Isn't he going to be too much for me to handle?" she asked, trying not to back up as Reyhan and the horse approached. Up close the animal seemed extremely large.

"He can have a temper, but he's very fond of the ladies."

The horse in question tossed his head, then seemed to give her the once-over. He looked large enough to pound her into the ground with just one hoof—the thought of which didn't exactly give her a warm fuzzy feeling inside.

"Great," she murmured. "A sexist horse. What's his name?"

For the first time in days, Reyhan smiled at her. "Prince."

"How appropriate."

She approached the powerful horse and tentatively stroked his nose. Prince stepped in close and rubbed his head against her arm, then bumped her side and exhaled.

"Is he flirting with me?" she asked, not wanting to know what the big animal would do if he lost his temper.

"Yes. He likes you. We'll ride out and take the Jeep back."

Reyhan murmured something to the horse, then moved to its side and made a step by lacing his fingers together. Emma remembered enough from her long-ago lessons to know she was expected to jump right up in that saddle. She sucked in a breath for courage and put her foot in his hands.

Not only was Prince's back about four hundred feet from the ground, the English saddle she settled in offered about as much protection as a handkerchief.

"There's nothing to hang on to," she said rather desperately as Reyhan handed her the reins.

"You'll be fine."

She would be maimed and possibly crippled, she thought, fighting fear. Reyhan disappeared into the stable, presumably to get his own horse.

"Emma, you can't ride that beast," her mother said. "It's not safe. Come down right now and sit with us."

The order gave her the impetus to stiffen her spine and smile brightly. "I'll be fine. We aren't going to go all that fast."

At least she hoped they wouldn't. It was a long way to the ground.

Reyhan returned with an even bigger gray stallion and mounted easily.

''The Jeep takes a longer route using the main road,'' he told her. ''We'll cut across the desert and meet your parents at the oasis.''

''Works for me,'' she said, thinking time alone with him might give them a chance to talk.

He waved off the driver and the Jeep pulled out. Reyhan gave her a few instructions, then watched her ride in slow circles. She found that her lessons from long ago came back to her and she quickly settled into the horse's rhythmic gate. After a few minutes, Reyhan led the way off the stable grounds and into the wild beauty of the open desert.

The morning was warm and brilliantly sunny. She was grateful for her hat and the sunscreen she'd slathered on her face. The hard-packed trail was easy to spot. She and Prince walked along behind Reyhan and his mount. When they went faster, Prince also picked up the pace. There were a couple of minutes of bone-jarring trotting before they settled into an easy canter. Reyhan pulled his horse to the side of the trail so they could ride next to each other.

The wind tugged strands of hair free from her braid. She tossed her head to get them out of her face and nearly slid off her horse. Reyhan shot out a hand and grabbed her arm. She managed to stay in the saddle, but only just. The slick leather seat suddenly felt smaller and more precarious.

''We will walk the rest of the way,'' Reyhan called as he tugged on his reins.

She slowed Prince, then glanced at the man next to her. "Sorry to be a bother."

"The fault is mine. You took to the riding so easily, I thought you were more experienced."

They walked side by side. Emma chose, then discarded several possible conversational openings. They all sounded forced and stupid, so she settled on the truth.

"I know you didn't want to do this today. Be with me and my parents, I mean. I appreciate you arranging everything and then coming along."

"It is important that you all enjoy your time in Bahania."

Before they left, she thought glumly.

"Seeing the desert will help you understand our ways," he said. "The desert is filled with tradition. For centuries nomads have wandered through the vastness of these lands. Thieves preyed on those using the silk road."

"Great. My mother was worried about being robbed."

He raised his eyebrows. "Those times are long past. Today those who live in the desert protect the oil fields to earn their living. A combination of the old ways and the new."

"Sounds like a good plan."

He shrugged. "There are those who do not wish to work. They want to take—much like the thieves of old."

She glanced around at the rolling dunes, the few clusters of scrubby plants. "Take what?"

"Money. They threaten our oil fields with disaster if we don't pay them off."

She caught her breath. "That's illegal, isn't it?"

"Yes. We know who these boys are. Most are second and third sons of nomadic chiefs. As they will not inherit, they are locked out of the family wealth. Instead of earning a living, they seek something more profitable and to their minds, easier. They play at being men."

"Are you going to have them arrested?"

He shook his head. "I have given my word to their fathers that I won't lock them up without cause. Mere threats are not considered cause, not out here. So we wait and watch. Sometimes angry young men grow up. Sometimes not."

"I don't understand," she admitted. "Why wouldn't their fathers want them to go to prison? What they're doing is wrong."

"To a man of the desert, there is no greater torture than to be locked away from the sun. I won't arrest anyone until he gives me a reason. This information does not make my head of security very happy."

"Hardly a surprise."

This was the longest conversation they'd had since they'd spent the night together. Emma wondered if Reyhan was thawing toward her or simply making the best of a bad situation.

"I'm sorry this is so difficult for you," she said. "Having me stay. Having my parents here. All of it."

"The time will pass."

Not exactly words to warm her heart. She wanted to remind him that a few days ago he'd wanted her

with a passion that had thrilled them both. That he
had kissed her and touched her. Remembering their
time together made her stomach clench and her body
burn.

"What if I just left?" she asked.

He continued to look straight ahead. "Nothing
would change. When you returned, the ticking clock
would continue. My father can be most stubborn."

She thought about how Reyhan avoided her as if
she had some disease he didn't want to catch. How
he barely spoke to her and never laughed anymore.
The stubbornness seemed to be an inherited trait.

They arrived at the oasis about an hour later.
Emma's parents were already there and rushed to
greet their daughter. Reyhan watched them, wondering at their anxiousness. She had been with him and
he would have died to keep her safe. Not that her
parents had ever trusted him.

He dismounted and moved beside Emma's horse.
Her mother glared at him as he helped Emma down.
Even with her parents watching and disapproving, he
noticed the warmth of her body and the way she
leaned against him while she regained her footing.

"So I have a way to go before I'm an accomplished
horsewoman," she said with a smile. "At least I survived."

He wanted to smile back at her and tell her that he
would be happy to teach her to ride. He wanted to
put his arm around her and draw her closer against
him. He wanted to kiss her and touch her and be with
her. Instead he stepped back and turned away.

"This oasis is not considered large. There are others deeper in the desert that cover several acres. But many families travel here because they can be close to the city while maintaining their old ways."

"Is it safe for us to wander around?" Emma asked. "Are there any things we shouldn't do? I don't want to offend anyone."

"You are an honored guest. You will be welcome." He looked at the small campsite set up around the pond of water. Children played with each other. The women talked together over the open fires, while the men tended the camels. Their arrival had been noticed, but his people would wait for him to make the first move.

"You have nothing to worry about," he said.

"Are you sure?"

He nodded, not surprised by her concern. One of the things he'd liked about her when they'd first met had been her soft heart. She cared about others—an unusual characteristic in the women he generally met.

Emma linked arms with her parents. "Isn't this fabulous?" she said happily. "Let's go introduce ourselves."

"They're strangers," her mother said. "We don't know if they speak English."

"Most do not," he confirmed.

"Then we'll have to fake it," Emma said, and pulled her parents toward the women.

He resisted the need to walk with her and claim her as his own by staying close. His presence was enough protection, he reminded himself. Even though she didn't need any.

He looked at the men hovering by the pen of camels. When he nodded, they approached, then bowed and offered greetings of respect. He recognized the oldest man, the chief of the small tribe, as someone who had ridden the desert with his father.

"Bihjan," he said, returning the bow. "I bring greetings from my father."

"I return those greetings and wish blessings on you and your family."

"And to yours."

The old man looked at Emma and her parents. "She is as beautiful as the sunrise."

Pride filled Reyhan. "My wife."

The old chief showed no surprised. "I see your blessings have already begun. You care for her."

Reyhan nodded rather than speak the truth—that *care* didn't come close. She was his life, his breath, and he wasn't sure he would survive without her.

"She will give you fine sons."

"If it is to be," he said simply, ignoring the tightness in his chest when he thought about children. He and Emma had made love without protection. He'd been so caught up in the moment, he'd never thought, never considered the consequences. If she was pregnant…

He cast the worry away. She couldn't be. If she were pregnant, she would stay forever, and being with her would destroy him. But to have a child with her…

He returned his attention to the chief. "You have been blessed with many sons," he said.

Bihjan nodded, his eyes dark with worry. "My

youngest son, Fadl, leads the renegades,'' he said quietly. ''I know what they do, what threats they make.''

''I have given my word,'' Reyhan reminded the old man. ''If their threats remain empty, then I will do nothing. Perhaps in time, they will grow up enough to rejoin their people and become honorable men.''

Bihjan sighed with relief. ''I had heard it was so, but I wanted to ask for myself. I know these young men try your patience.''

''My security chief's, as well. He believes they should be arrested and put in prison. I have explained that to be so confined is a form of death for men of the desert.'' He narrowed his gaze. ''But be warned. My patience has limits. If any of the renegades acts in the smallest way, if their talk becomes action, my retribution will be swift and severe.''

The old man nodded. ''As it should be, Prince Reyhan. As it should be.''

Emma loved everything about the oasis. The people were charming and at least two of the women understood a little English—at least enough for them to attempt to communicate. The children were beautiful and friendly and fun. She adored the dogs and the baby camels and the clever way the camp itself came together after being carted across miles of desert. Even her parents seemed to be having a reasonably good time, asking questions more than complaining. Maybe there was hope for them after all.

''They have invited us to dine with them,'' Reyhan said as he came up to stand next to her. ''I have accepted.''

Emma instantly glanced at the pen holding the camels and swallowed. "So, uh, what will be on the menu?"

Reyhan smiled. "Fear not. It's chicken."

"That's a relief. I don't think I could chow down on something I'd just petted and cooed over."

"I would not expect you to." He took her arm and pulled her away from everyone. "I told them you were my wife, without mentioning the pending divorce."

"Okay. That makes sense. The situation is complicated." She didn't know how to tell him she didn't mind him claiming her as his wife with no "but" tacked on.

"I wanted you to know," he said.

"Thank you."

They were called to dinner. Everyone sat around in a circle. Dishes were passed from person to person. Emma sampled spicy rice casseroles and tender chicken. There were flat breads and grilled vegetables. Two teenage boys played three-stringed musical instruments and a young girl with bells around her wrists and ankles danced for them.

"Can they afford to feed us like this?" Emma asked after a tray of honey-coated dates were offered. "I don't want them to starve or anything because they played generous host with us."

His dark gaze lingered on her face. "I appreciate your concern for my people. Do not worry. I have taken care of things."

She trusted that he had. Reyhan was a good man, a man she could admire. What would he say if he knew that she wanted these people to be her people, as well? That the more time she spent in Bahania, the more she liked the country and was confident she could have made a home here?

After the meal, several of the women rose and disappeared into one of the tents. A few of the men wandered off toward the camels. Emma started to rise, but Reyhan put a hand on her arm.

"There's more to come," he said.

"I'm pretty full."

"It's not food."

Sure enough, a young girl walked up and knelt in front of Emma. She held out her hand, offering a beautiful blue and red enameled necklace. Emma looked at it, then at him.

"I can't take that."

"You have to. You're their princess and they want to show respect." He leaned close and lowered his voice. "Don't worry. All that is expected is that you are enthusiastic and love everything. When we leave, the gifts stay behind."

"Good thing," she murmured as she noticed a teenage boy leading several camels toward her.

Still caught up in how Reyhan's warm breath had tickled her skin, she accepted the necklace, kissed the girl on both cheeks and thanked her warmly. Reyhan slid the necklace over her neck.

There were more pieces of jewelry offered, several bolts of amazing silk, four adult camels and one baby camel. The only gift she had trouble returning was a sweet puppy who licked her entire face and wiggled to get closer.

When she'd thanked everyone and carefully left all the smaller gifts on a blanket by the fire, she walked toward the SUV with Reyhan.

"They were wonderful people," she said. "Do the children go to school?"

He nodded. "They attend several months at a time, then return to their families. We are fortunate in that we can afford excellent teachers and modern schools that can meet the needs of children from the city and from the desert."

Emma thought about what Cleo had said—how she did charity work in her free time. Would that have been available to Emma, as well? Although she loved her job and knew she helped through one of life's greatest miracles, she was willing to admit to wanting to help on a grander scale.

Not likely, she told herself. Not when she was leaving and Reyhan was marrying someone else.

By the end of the week, Emma's parents had settled into life in Bahania. Emma was pleased to watch their attitudes slowly change from hostile mistrust of everything to pleasant acceptance. She would have loved to discuss the surprising transition with Reyhan but he continued to avoid her. So much for spending their days and nights together, she thought as she leaned close to the mirror and applied mascara to her lashes. They might physically be in the same palace, but they rarely spoke anymore. Reyhan worked impossible hours then disappeared into the guest room. The only time she saw him was at command dinners by the king.

At least tonight would be different. There was a large formal state occasion that was doubling as a welcome party for her parents. Reyhan had already informed her he was to be her escort. She would have been a lot more excited if he'd at least pretended to be happy about spending the evening with her. Instead he'd looked about as thrilled as a man facing the loss of both legs and an arm. She was determined to change his mind.

After finishing with her makeup, she pulled the hot rollers out of her hair, then fluffed the ends. After bending over at the waist, she sprayed her hair from underneath, then flipped her head to let the curls fall back into place.

"Not bad," she murmured as she finger combed a few wayward strands.

Next up was the bronze beaded evening gown. She slipped it on and pulled up the zipper, then stepped into her high-heeled sandals.

She studied her reflection and knew this was as good as it was going to get. If she couldn't dazzle Reyhan like this, it wasn't going to happen.

"Good luck," she whispered to her reflection, then walked out of the bathroom and into the sitting area.

Reyhan was already there. She nearly stumbled when she saw him in his well-tailored tux. His shoulders were broad and strong, his features lean and handsome. Her heart swelled with an affection she didn't want to name.

"You look beautiful," he told her.

"Thank you. You look great, too."

He held out a velvet-covered box, about ten inches square and only a couple of inches deep.

"For you."

She hesitated before accepting the gift and opening it. When she saw the contents, her breath caught in amazement.

A yellow diamond necklace lay on a bed of white silk. The graduated diamonds had to be at least three carats each in front, and nearly a carat in back by the clasp. Two clusters of yellow diamonds formed earrings and there was a white and yellow diamond bracelet.

Emma reached for the necklace only to find she was shaking too much to pick it up.

"I can't," she told him. "It's too much."

"You are my wife," Reyhan said, taking the box from her and setting it on the table. He removed the necklace and placed it around her neck. "Who would wear these if not you?"

"The next woman you marry," she said as he handed her the earrings. "You'll want these things passed down to your children."

As she spoke, she looked at him. Some emotion crossed his face but it was gone before she could read it. Awareness crackled between them and when he held out the bracelet to her, she wanted desperately to toss it aside and fling herself in his arms instead.

But she didn't. She let him fasten on the bracelet, then admired the fiery stones. She would wear these lovely things tonight but with the intent of leaving them behind. They were a part of his heritage and she had no right to claim them. If things had been different... But they weren't.

"Reyhan—" She touched his forearm, feeling the warmth of him and the tension of his muscles. "I want to mention something. About when we were together."

He didn't speak but a muscle twitched in his jaw. "There is nothing to say."

"Yes, there is. We didn't..." She cleared her throat. "When we made love..." She stopped and gathered her thoughts. "We didn't use any protection. I wasn't sure if you were worried about consequences. There aren't any. I wanted to reassure you that I wasn't pregnant."

"I see. You're sure?"

More than sure. Three days ago she'd gotten her period. "Positive."

He didn't say anything else as he led her to a large mirror in the dining room. He placed her in front of it and stood behind her with his hands on her shoulders.

"The jewels complete you," he said.

She looked at the elegant stones glittering at her ears and around her neck. They were lovely, but they didn't complete her. Only he could do that.

She wanted to know what he'd thought about the possibility of her being pregnant. Had he even considered it? Had he worried? Wondered? Had he hoped?

She had. Now that she knew for sure she wasn't pregnant she could admit that there had been times she'd thought it would be a good thing. That having a child together would be what they needed to connect. The truth or a schoolgirl fantasy? Now she would never know.

"Are you ready?" he asked, holding out his arm.

She nodded and slipped her hand into the crook of his elbow. They walked out of the suite together.

Emma had seen the formal ballroom on her tour with Reyhan but standing in the large empty space hadn't prepared her for the reality of seeing it filled with elegantly dressed people, sparkling lights and a full orchestra.

There were about five hundred guests, including several prime ministers and heads of state. A film crew working on an action movie in the desert had been invited, along with a former American president and a Nobel Prize winner.

Reyhan introduced Emma to many of the guests. She smiled, said little and reached for a second glass of champagne from a waiter circulating with a tray.

"Are you doing all right?" Reyhan asked quietly.

"Considering this is my first official function as a princess, I'm doing great. We'll ignore the butterflies in my stomach, my knocking knees and the nearly overwhelming urge to bolt for the gardens. I have to admit I'd feel a lot more comfortable with the king's cats."

Reyhan smiled. "You're charming and well-spoken. Everyone is impressed."

His compliment made her beam. Just then her parents walked up. They were actually smiling. Could this evening produce any more surprises?

"Kitten, you look beautiful," her father said. "Nearly as lovely as your mother." He kissed his wife's cheek.

Emma's mother dimpled. "Oh, George, you're just saying that." She leaned close to her daughter. "Isn't this party wonderful? We met that action star your father likes so much. Johnny Blaze. He was very pleasant, although his girlfriend looks thin enough to need Third World aid. And did you see the former president? He was very nice, too. Oh, and the king told us he's sending us on a cruise on his private yacht. We're going to explore the Mediterranean for a couple of weeks."

Emma nearly dropped her champagne glass. "You're going?"

"Of course. It's a once-in-a-lifetime opportunity. He said the boat's captain knows all the best places to take us."

Her father winked. "It will be like a second honeymoon."

Janice Kennedy actually giggled, then waved at Emma and Reyhan. "You two kids enjoy yourself. We have more famous people to meet."

Emma watched them walk off. "That was pretty amazing. I owe the king big-time. Not that I don't love my folks. I do. But they can be—"

"Oppressive?"

She smiled. "Absolutely. And a little judgmental. I hope they enjoy their cruise."

"I'm sure they will."

And she and Reyhan would be able to spend time together without her parents hanging around. The only trick would be getting him out of his office and paying attention to her. For that she would need a plan—and she would come up with one, just as soon as the champagne-induced fuzziness wore off.

The orchestra struck up another song, one that made her want to be in Reyhan's arms. She looked around and saw several of the guests dancing. They swayed to the music and laughed.

"You are more easy to read that usual," Reyhan said, taking her glass from her and setting it on a table in the corner. "Come. I will dance with you."

She was so pleased, she didn't bother to worry that he was doing her a favor. Not when he pulled her into his arms and held her close. If only the song could last forever, she thought happily.

Reyhan rubbed his hands against Emma's back and wished they were alone. Rather than dancing to music he wished to move with her in other ways. Perhaps it was the night, or how she looked or the invitation he saw in her eyes, but for some reason his resistance to her charms was weaker than ever.

He wanted her. More frightening than the desire was the truth that he wanted her in and out of his bed. He wanted to be with her, talk with her. He wanted to learn her secrets, discuss the future, name children and grow old with her. He wanted her to be his wife in every sense of the word.

He had the answer to his question about the baby. There wasn't one and he couldn't risk creating one with her. Yes, there was protection and it could be used, but that wasn't the point. He had escaped the possibility and he would be a fool to risk a pregnancy.

But he had always been a fool where Emma was concerned. From the first moment he'd met her that night on campus. She had smiled at him and he had been lost.

She swayed with him, sighing softly and snuggling close. She belonged, he thought. Whether laughing with his people in the desert or conversing with heads of state. She fit in. She made people feel at ease and never expected to be the center of attention. She was smart, kind and a woman of honor.

The fire always lurking below the surface flared to life and began to consume him. The need grew until he had no choice but to give in. He took her hand in his and pulled her toward a small alcove behind on of the decorated pillars.

"But the dance isn't over," Emma said. "Can't we finish the dance?"

Instead of answering, he drew her close and kissed her.

She melted into his embrace, parting her lips instantly and clinging to him. She stroked his tongue with her own and moaned softly. Her hands slipped under his jacket where she rubbed his back.

"Better than dancing," she whispered when he pulled back to kiss her jaw, then her neck. "I'll give up dancing for kissing you anytime."

He nibbled the sensitive skin below her ear and made her groan. She reached for his hands and brought them to her breasts.

As he cupped her full curves, he stared into her eyes and saw an answering passion there.

"Make love with me," she pleaded.

He knew how right it would feel. How good things would be between them. He knew she was wet to his hard, yielding and aroused. He knew he could claim her, mark her, make her his. And he knew the price he would pay if he did.

Without saying a word, he dropped his hands to his sides, turned and walked away. Emma's soft cry of pain made him pause, but only for a second. Then he resumed his stride and left the ballroom without looking back.

Chapter Eleven

Emma couldn't tell how much of the ache in her body came from her champagne hangover and how much came from humiliation. It wasn't just that Reyhan had left her alone at the party, it was that he'd kissed her and touched her, making her think he wanted her, and then he'd walked away. She felt both hurt and bruised, as if he'd been playing kick ball with her heart.

She curled up in the dining room chair and tried to work up some interest in the breakfast laid out there, but it wasn't happening. She'd taken a walk on the balcony encircling this level of the palace and that hadn't helped, either. Maybe she should shower and see if she could wash away the sense of having been a fool for a man who hadn't even noticed.

She stood ar.d stretched. The good news is her parents were heading off to have a good time. The cruise was leaving that afternoon. As far as she could tell, they hadn't witnessed her humiliation, so she wasn't going to have to talk about it with them. But that didn't mean she wasn't going to stop thinking about it.

She headed for the bathroom. What had gone wrong? One second Reyhan had been kissing her as if he'd really enjoyed it. He'd been the one to pull her into the alcove, he'd been the one touching her. Except she'd brought his hands to her breasts. Had he disliked her being aggressive? Did *he* need to be in charge?

She didn't want to think that was true. He'd never been weird about having to ''be the man.'' Not that she had a whole lot of sexual experience with him or anyone. Had she freaked him out when she'd—

Emma had been so deep in thought she hadn't noticed the steam and heat in the bathroom. It was only as she came around the corner and saw Reyhan stepping out of the shower that she realized she wasn't alone.

He was wet and naked. Water dripped from his arms and legs, from his hair. Droplets ran down his cheeks. Her gaze met his and she found herself unable to turn away.

In less than two seconds, she went from hurt and hungover to hungry. She wanted to touch him all over and have him touch her back. She was aware of his arousal growing, thickening. As if he was getting as turned on as she was.

She licked her lips. "What are you doing here? You're usually gone long before I wake up."

"I went riding at sunrise and came back to shower."

He was now fully erect. The sight of him made her midsection clench. He obviously wanted her, so why was he just standing there?

He reached out his arm. For one brief heartbeat, she thought he was going to pull her close. Instead he grabbed a towel and turned his back on her.

"I'll be done in a few minutes."

It was a very polite invitation to leave.

Emma dropped her head, realized the sudden burning in her eyes came from unshed tears and fled to her bedroom. She closed the door behind herself and leaned against it.

Ten days ago she'd considered the king's insistence that she stay for another two months a stroke of good fortune. Now it was torture—a prison sentence that trapped her with a man who wanted nothing to do with her.

Reyhan read his e-mail without understanding what any of it said. Instead of words he saw Emma's hurt eyes and the tears that had filled them as she turned away from him and fled the bathroom. Two hours and three meetings later, he hadn't been able to erase the memory of her confusion and pain.

He'd caused her that pain. No matter how much he wanted to escape the truth, it remained. He'd never meant to hurt her and the need to make it up to her was strong.

He instantly thought of returning to their room and offering her what they both wanted. That would ease the throbbing inside of him and hopefully bring her pleasure. But he couldn't risk it for himself and he wouldn't make her promises he did not intend to keep.

Determined to lose himself in his work, he returned his attention to his e-mail. An hour or so later, his phone buzzed and his assistant announced that Will was on the phone.

"There's been a change in circumstances," his head of security said as soon as Reyhan came on the line.

Reyhan swore. "What?"

"I'm holding Fadl."

Fadl was the son of a prominent chief. "What happened?"

"He was caught stealing drilling equipment. Two other men were with him."

Reyhan frowned. "Did he say why he wanted it?"

"He's not talking. I have a few theories of my own. He could sell it on the black market and make a few bucks."

"That sounds like too much work for him and his friends."

"Agreed. He could also sabotage it somehow and then return it to inventory. When the replacement parts were put into service, we could have a pretty impressive disaster."

Reyhan shook his head. Was that possible? Had the boys decided to act on their threats? "We're going to have to inspect all parts in inventory and anything put into service in the past few months.''

''I've already got men on that. I'm also rounding up the rest of his buddies. They've scattered so it may take a while.''

''Keep on it. I'll be there in a couple of hours.''

''Good. Maybe Fadl will talk to you. I'm getting nowhere.''

''I'll see what I can do. As the prince, I can make certain threats to his family he wouldn't believe from you. I'll be there shortly.''

''We'll be waiting.''

Reyhan hung up the phone and considered his options. While he had been willing to keep his bargain with the chiefs up to a point, the rules had now changed. If Fadl was stealing—or worse, sabotaging—then he and his friends had to be stopped. Being young and sons of chiefs would not protect them anymore.

He called his assistant into his office and made arrangements for his meetings to be rescheduled. Once he'd reserved the helicopter and told the pilots where they were going, he walked to his father's offices. The guards there waved him inside, where he found the king on the phone.

''Reyhan,'' his father said cheerfully when he'd hung up. ''What brings you to me this fine morning?''

''Will has detained Fadl, Bihjan's son.'' He quickly recounted what his security chief had told him.

King Hassan didn't look happy. ''Have they moved from making threats to acting on them?''

''That's what I plan to find out. Will is going to

invite Fadl's friends to join him in custody. We'll send a team in to search their camp. If they've already sabotaged replacement parts we should find evidence. Regardless, all the equipment will be inspected.''

''Which means shutting down production for a few days.''

Reyhan had already done the calculations. ''We'll be back online at the end of the week.'' He shook his head. ''There is also the possibility this was Fadl's plan all along. To get caught in such a way that we would have to shut down. But I won't take the risk. All the wells will be inspected.''

''What are the international ramifications?''

''Minimal. We'll issue a statement saying we're running scheduled inspections, and production for the next month will be increased to make up the difference.''

The king raised his eyebrows. ''But the inspections aren't scheduled.''

''They are now.''

''Good point. When do you leave?''

''As soon as we're done here.''

''I'm sure Emma will enjoy the trip.''

Reyhan stared at his father. ''You can't be serious. I am not taking her with me.''

''Of course you are. You already have their leader in custody and will soon have the rest of his men. She won't be in any danger. If you're truly concerned about her standing out, have her put on native dress. I'm sure she'll look especially fetching.''

Reyhan glanced at the sleeping tabby on the sofa in the corner and thought about throwing the creature at his father. But he recognized the stubborn look in the king's eyes and knew he didn't have a choice. Take Emma. It was a ridiculous request, and he refused to acknowledge the sudden pleasure he felt.

He left his father and headed for his rooms. At least Fadl's activities had been more passive than violent. Reyhan wouldn't have to worry about Emma walking into the middle of a gunfight.

He steeled himself, vowing not to react when he saw her. She sat on the sofa, reading and looked up when he entered.

"I have to go into the desert," he said. "I'll be gone a day or two. The king has suggested you accompany me."

Her green eyes were wide and unreadable. She looked both hurt and broken. As if her spirit had received one too many mortal blows.

That was his doing, he acknowledged shamefully. He'd been the one to reject her over and over. He reached for the phone and pressed three buttons. As he waited for his call to be answered, he wondered if there was some way he could explain so that she would understand and see this wasn't about her. Not really. His actions were about himself. Then he admitted he doubted that information would be of much comfort to her.

He made his request, hung up and returned his attention to her.

She hadn't moved, except to close the book. "Are they for me?" she asked, referring to the traditional garments he had ordered.

"Yes. I'll need you to wear them while we're at

the camp. I don't expect any trouble, but regardless, they'll keep you safe.''

''You don't want me to go with you,'' she said flatly.

''What I want isn't important.''

''It is to me.''

He stood behind a club chair and rested his hands on the back. ''This is business. There has been an arrest. I'm confident everything will go smoothly but as I am not completely sure, I would prefer you not be there.''

''So this is only about keeping me safe?''

He nodded.

''I don't believe you. Wanting me to stay is about more than that.'' She rose and faced him. ''I want to speak to the king and tell him you find my presence intolerable. There's no reason for me to stay here and both of us to be tortured. I don't believe that's his purpose. Once he knows there is no hope for a reconciliation, then he'll agree to the divorce and you'll be free of me.''

As she spoke, she squared her shoulders and met his gaze with a confidence that impressed him. The frightened little girl she had been was completely gone and in her place was a self-sufficient woman.

She stood before him, offering him his freedom and all he wanted was to pull her close and claim her as his own forever. He longed for her with a need that defied description and still he would let her go.

''When we return,'' he told her, ''we will both talk to the king.''

Light faded from her eyes, as if the last flame of

her spirit had been extinguished. Reyhan wanted to move closer, to touch her and tell her his reasons were not what she thought, but he stayed where he was and dug his fingers into the back of the chair.

"I guess I should pack a few things," she said tonelessly. "What do I wear under the robes?"

"Whatever will be most comfortable. The days are hot, the nights cool. Jeans or slacks will give you freedom of movement."

She nodded and headed for her bedroom. He retreated to his quarters where he quickly collected a few belongings. By the time he returned to the living room, the traditional robes had been left on the sofa.

Emma didn't recognize the woman in the mirror, but she didn't know how much of that had to do with the yards of fabric that covered her from head to toe and how much had to do with her bleeding to death from the inside out.

Reyhan wanted her to leave.

She supposed she'd known there were problems and that he didn't want to sleep with her again, but that was a far cry from having him practically jump with joy at the thought of never seeing her again. She'd hoped to shock him with her suggestion that she speak with the king and ask to leave sooner. Instead he'd agreed with her plan. He was going to get everything he wanted and she would spend the rest of her life in love with a man who didn't want to be with her.

Emma didn't know exactly *when* she'd fallen in love with him, or if it had been with her, buried for the past six years. Did it matter? More important than the how or when was the reality of losing Reyhan for a second time.

He escorted her to a helicopter. Nervous excitement at flying in one for the first time eased some of her heartache. She strapped herself in and picked up the headset Reyhan pointed to. When the engine roared to life and the rotors began to move, she understood that the headset was the only way they would be able to communicate.

"We're going about a hundred miles into the desert," he said into his microphone. "To the western edge of the central oil fields."

She could see his lips moving and hear the sound coming through her speakers. The helicopter rose.

Emma clutched the armrests as the aircraft zoomed up and forward, moving dizzyingly fast. The sensation was very different from a plane, but not unpleasant. She watched the edge of the city disappear under them, then there was only the vast stretches of nothing.

"A young man was arrested today," Reyhan said. "He was stealing replacement parts for the oil rigs. We're not sure if he planned to sell them on the black market or sabotage them and put them back into inventory."

"Faulty parts could create an economic and ecological disaster."

Reyhan nodded approvingly at her grasp of the situation. "Exactly. His friends are being rounded up and will also be arrested. The man we caught, Fadl, has been unwilling to tell us what he's up to. I want to talk to him and see if I can convince him to co-operate.''

She remembered what Reyhan had said about the nomads' need to be free. "Will he go to prison?"

"Probably. It depends on the seriousness of his crime. In this case, simply stealing would be a relief to everyone."

"An odd reality."

He smiled. "How true."

She turned away because she didn't want to smile back. She didn't want to feel that things were once again well between them. How could he act as if nothing was wrong?

She stared out the window and reminded herself that he had made it clear from the beginning that he *wanted* her out of his life. She'd been the one to forget that and try to change the rules. Was it his fault he hadn't agreed?

"There is a small camp of nomads by the oil station," he said. "They are friendly and you will be safe in their company. Even so I will assign two men to stay with you. Just in case."

"That's fine. Are there any cultural rules I should keep in mind?"

"No. Simply be yourself and they will adore you."

As I do.

He didn't speak the words, but Emma heard them. They hung in the silence between them as loud as the engine. She looked at Reyhan, but he was staring out of his window and she couldn't see his expression.

A trick of her own imagination, she told herself.

Nothing more. Her feelings for him weren't going to change anything and she had to remember that.

They touched down about an hour later. Emma saw the low buildings clustered together and the oil rigs beyond. To the left, a dozen or so tents were pitched close to the bubbling oasis. Reyhan had told her the pool was fed by an underground spring.

He climbed out of the helicopter first, then held out his hand to assist her. She took it and instantly felt the warmth of his fingers. Weakness invaded her, a weakness she had to learn to control and eventually conquer.

In time, she promised herself. She would heal in time.

Reyhan entered the interrogation room and stared at the young man sitting there. Fadl was all of eighteen, slightly built and sullen looking. The youngest son of a powerful chief. While he would not have inherited all his father's wealth, he could have made a good life for himself with the tribe. Instead, he'd chosen to take what he wanted.

"You have crossed me," he told the young man. "You knew that your father didn't want you harmed or arrested. He thought you would come to see the error of your ways. But I am not a foolish old man who still indulges a spoiled child. I am Prince Reyhan of Bahania and now we will play by *my* rules."

Fear flickered in Fadl's eyes. "That's a load of bull. You can't hurt me. You promised my father."

Reyhan allowed himself a small smile. "I agreed to let you run around and play at being a man until you broke the law. Which you did by stealing parts. Now the deal doesn't exist and you are mine.''

The young man squirmed in his seat. "I don't believe you.''

"Good. I will enjoy putting you in prison. Because of you, the oil rigs must be checked for sabotaged parts. That will cost my country hundreds of thousands of dollars. As I know you have no funds of your own to compensate me, I will take what I can out of your hide.''

Fadl visibly paled. "How did you know that's what we were going to do?''

Reyhan kept his expression impassive. He'd guessed correctly. Now he simply had to get the details from the boy and let Will deal with damage control.

"What made you think you could succeed?" Reyhan asked. "You know nothing of the oil equipment. You certainly haven't worked the rigs.''

Fadl shifted in his seat. "I don't want to go to prison.''

"You don't have a choice. The question on the table is for how long. Please me and I will make sure your time there is almost pleasant. Annoy me and I will find a particularly uncomfortable place for you to call home.''

There were several seconds of silence. In the end, fear won.

"It wasn't us," Fadl admitted. "Not really. A bunch of us were at a bar in El Bahar and we were trying to come up with a plan. This guy approached us. He said he'd been listening and that we were amateurs. If we wanted to make some big money, we needed to hire professionals. So we did.''

Reyhan's blood ran cold. He crossed to the door, pulled it open and yelled for Will to join them.

Fadl told them everything. The name of the man whom they'd hired, how many associates he'd brought into Bahania and how much Fadl and his gang were to pay them.

''We haven't put back any bad parts,'' Fadl said frantically. ''They're all in our camp. You have to believe me, Prince Reyhan. I swear. We were just after the money and this seemed like an easy way to get it.''

Reyhan stared at him with loathing. ''See if you feel that way after your stay in prison.''

Emma wandered around the oasis. Her bodyguards kept far enough away that she was able to forget about them. As she'd seen before on her outing with her parents, there were children playing and filling the afternoon with the sound of laughter. Several small dogs tumbled over each other in a game only they could understand. Women clustered together sewing and cooking and sending glances her way.

A little girl of about seven or eight ran up to her and offered a plate of dates. Emma smiled her acceptance and bit into one. Soon another little girl joined them, then another and another.

''I can't eat all these,'' Emma said with a grin as she touched the closest girl's smooth dark hair. ''But thank you for offering.''

A little boy tugged on her sleeve. She bent down

to his level and he pulled on her head covering. She reached up and slipped it down to her shoulders. All the children gasped at the sight of her red hair.

"I know. Not the usual thing," she said happily.

A girl reached out to touch it, then shrank away. Emma laughed.

"It's all right. It doesn't burn." She stroked her hair herself, then took the girl's hand in her own and brought it to the side of her head. The child touched her lightly, giggled and touched her again. The other children crowded close.

"My, my, my. Aren't you a pretty lady?"

At the sound of the male voice, the children scattered. Emma stood and turned, only to come face-to-face with two tall, armed strangers. Her bodyguards were nowhere to be seen.

"You're American," she said, trying not to betray her nervousness.

The man closest to her grinned. He had close-cropped blond hair and a tattoo of a snake on his forearm.

"Good guess," he said and stepped behind her. Before she could make a move, he had grabbed her and pulled her close, then pressed a knife to her neck. "And you're our prisoner."

"What the hell were you thinking?" Will demanded as he paced in front of Fadl. "You hired a man you met in a *bar*. Didn't it occur to you that he wasn't just a military consultant? Didn't you think you were getting in over your head?"

Fadl looked miserable, young and scared. "He said if we didn't do what he wanted, he'd kill us."

Reyhan stared at the boy. "You *wanted* to get caught," he breathed. "You need our help to get out of this mess."

Fadl nodded frantically. "Prince Reyhan, please. They're out of control. You have to help me. Help all of us. We're sorry. We didn't mean for any of this to happen."

"Of course you did. But now you've got a tiger by the tail and you don't know how to keep it from eating you." He looked at Will. "This is your area of expertise."

"I'm on it," his security chief told him. "I'll call in a team from El Bahar and—" he glanced at Fadl "—elsewhere."

Reyhan knew Will meant the City of Thieves, a secret city in the middle of the desert on the border with El Bahar and Bahania.

"I know the head of security there," Will continued. "Rafe Stryker and I have worked together before."

"Good."

Will started to leave, but before he reached the door, a man burst into the room. He ran to Reyhan.

"She was taken by two Americans. They shot one of the men guarding her and knocked out the other. They have Princess Emma."

Reyhan went very still and very cold. He looked at Fadl. "If she is harmed in any way, the desert will run red with your blood."

Chapter Twelve

"So how many millions are you worth, sweet-heart?" the man with the tattoo asked as he pushed Emma into the back of a truck.

The gag in her mouth made it impossible to speak, so she could only glare her rage.

"I didn't know Prince Reyhan was married or I would have planned this better," the man said with a grin. "Guess I just got lucky today. Don't worry. No one wants to hurt you. I thought those unhappy kids would be our ticket to the easy life, but they turned out to be all talk. When it came right down to doing the dirty work, they got scared. Said they didn't want to blow up any oil wells. So I figured I'd wasted my time. Then you came along."

Emma wanted to shriek her outrage. She couldn't

believe this was happening. If she could just get her hands loose she would claw her kidnapper's eyes out.

Her anger pleased her. It meant she wasn't going to be immobilized by fear. She had to stay strong so that when the time came she could escape.

The man fingered a strand of her hair. "I'm guessing your old man is going to pay through the nose to get you back in his bed."

A knife flashed. Emma jumped back but not before her capture sliced off a lock of her hair.

"Just so he knows I'm not bluffing," the man said, and slammed the door.

She found herself alone and in darkness. The hum of a motor and cool air blowing over her told her there was an air-conditioning unit. At least she wouldn't die of heat exhaustion.

Don't give in to the fear, she told herself. She had to stay strong. She had to be prepared. The men who had taken her weren't going to kill her. She was too valuable for that. They wanted money, and lots of it.

Feeling her way along the inside of the compartment, she found a bench seat and lowered herself onto it. Her hands were tied behind her. Ropes cut into her wrists and as she struggled to loosen them, her shoulders began to ache.

How long would it all take? She knew that however much Reyhan might want her gone, he wouldn't ever just leave her like this. She knew he would rescue her. But when? And how could she hang on until then?

Fadl shrank back in his chair. He looked far younger than his eighteen years. "I swear I didn't know," he said as tears filled his eyes.

Reyhan didn't care. "You are responsible. I should kill you now."

Will grabbed his arm. "Killing him won't help. We have a situation."

He glared at his security chief. "They have taken my wife."

"I know. We'll get her back."

Reyhan felt himself consumed by the fires of rage. He wanted to destroy with his bare hands. He wanted, at his feet, the broken and bleeding body of the man who had dared to take Emma, and then he wanted the opportunity to kill him a second time.

Fear lurked inside him, as well. Fear for her and what she must be feeling. Fear that she wouldn't believe he would move the rotation of the earth itself to get her back. He'd been so cold, had rejected her so many times. His efforts to convince her he didn't care had been too successful by far. What if she thought he wouldn't be bothered?

He clenched his hands into fists and turned to Will. "Find out how much they want. This is all about money." Will nodded and left.

Reyhan glared at Fadl. "Your attempts to play at danger have cost me something precious. You will pay, as will your entire family. The cost will bleed down through a hundred generations of your people."

Fadl hung his head. "I'm sorry," he whispered through his tears.

Reyhan walked out of the room. He needed to move, to act, to do something. Instead he could only wait for information. In the main security center, a dozen men worked phones and computers. His security chief walked over to him.

"Reinforcements will be here within the hour," Will said. "Troops are coming in from El Bahar and the City of Thieves. I've got my best computer guy working on a special kind of Trojan horse. Basically it allows the ransom to show up in the offshore account, but it's only good for ninety minutes. Then poof, the money isn't there anymore."

"That doesn't give us much time to get Emma back," Reyhan said, knowing he would gladly pay any price for her safe return.

"We set up the exchange so that we're face-to-face when it happens. We see Emma, we send the money transfer. They get notification of the deposit and they release her. It should only take about five minutes. That gives us the rest of the time to get the hell away."

"Do it," he said.

Will nodded. "Just as soon as they tell us how much. We should—"

A young man in uniform came running up. "Sir, we've heard. Sixty million in euros. I have the account number."

Will looked at Reyhan who nodded. "Agree to it."

The young man swallowed. "There's something else, sir." He glanced from Will to Reyhan and back. "A storm. It didn't look like much an hour ago, but now..." His voice trailed off.

Reyhan's chest tightened. "Sandstorm?"

The officer nodded. "It looks bad."

Reyhan stared at Will. "The helicopters won't be able to fly."

Which meant the reinforcements wouldn't arrive anytime soon and Reyhan couldn't fly Emma to safety.

"We could stall them," the young man said. "Explain that it takes time to raise that kind of money and—"

"No!" Reyhan's gaze narrowed. "My wife is not to stay with them one second more than necessary. Do you understand?"

"Yes, sir. Of course." He scurried away.

Will shook his head. "It's more risky without the backup but we can still make it happen."

"We have no choice. If necessary, I will fight them all myself."

The tattooed-snake guy who turned out to be called Billy pulled Emma out of the truck.

"Looks like this is your lucky day, too, sweetheart," he said as he helped her to the ground. "Your old man is going to pay up. Sixty million euros. Not bad for an afternoon's work."

She was stunned. Sixty million euros? That was close to sixty million dollars. An insane amount of money. She couldn't imagine there was that much wealth in the whole world. Reyhan couldn't pay that. Just the thought of it made her sick to her stomach.

"You look shocked," Billy said. "Don't be. These prince guys really have a thing about other men hanging around their women. Of course I thought he'd try to negotiate me down a little, but he didn't. I'm not going to complain. That's twenty million for each of us.''

She glanced around the camp. The sky had darkened and the air seemed thick, but she could still make out nearly two dozen men. She looked at Billy.

He nodded. ''I know what you're thinking. There's more than three of us here. But see, these aren't my guys. They're those kids who hired us. The ones who chickened out. So I say screw 'em. Me and my boys will be long gone with the money while these stupid kids take the fall. Good plan, huh?''

She nodded and wondered how she could get the information to Reyhan.

''Hold on,'' Billy said, and tugged at her gag. When it was removed, she sucked in a breath of air.

''Better?'' he asked.

She nodded, her mouth too dry for her to speak.

He glanced at the sky. ''There's a storm coming. Good for us, bad for them. They would have called in for help, but it ain't coming in the middle of a sandstorm. Come on, Princess. Your ride is this way.''

Emma followed the man. As she walked, she tried to figure out how long she'd been held in the truck. She would guess two or three hours at most. With clouds rolling in and covering the sun, there was no way for her to judge time that way. The air was so thick with sand that it was difficult to breathe.

Should she try to escape? If Reyhan had made a deal, maybe it would be better to go along with the plan. But she wanted him to know that the young men they had captured had nothing to do with the trouble.

* * *

"Be prepared," Reyhan told Will. "If things go badly and we can't get away in time, there could be a fight."

"Agreed." Will patted the gun at his side. "My men are ready."

Reyhan was also armed and determined. He'd given firm instructions that no one was to do anything until Emma was back in his arms. Once she was safe, their side would walk away.

"Is your team in place?" he asked Will.

The other man nodded. "They'll get behind the trucks and put on the tracking devices. Then when the storm lifts, we'll send in an armed contingent to take them." He grinned. "They won't know what hit them."

"Good."

Reyhan's first instinct was to punish the men immediately, but he had to think about Emma. Getting her to safety was his primary concern. The bastards who had taken her would be brought to justice. He would not rest until it was so.

He checked his watch, then stepped into the open Jeep. The vehicle offered little protection against the growing storm.

"It's time," he said against the wind.

Will started the engine and they drove into the desert.

Emma couldn't see anything. The sand was thick and hot and her face felt as if it were being scraped by sandpaper. She squinted against the windshield.

"How do you know where you're going?" she asked Billy.

He tapped the compass on the dashboard. "I'll find the rendezvous. Don't you worry, Princess."

She wasn't worried. Not for herself. Did Billy and his men have any idea about the danger they were in? Reyhan wasn't simply going to pay them, and if Billy thought he was, the man was a fool.

His two companions were in the truck behind them and the young nomad-rebels farther back.

"When will you three head out?" she asked casually, wishing he would untie her wrists. Her shoulders ached and her skin was raw.

"Don't even think you can bat your eyes at me and get me to spill my plans, Princess. You're pretty, but I'm not going to fall for it."

She shrugged as if it didn't matter, then stared out of the windshield.

Visibility had dropped to a few hundred yards. The road was covered with blowing sand and debris. She squinted as she thought she saw an outcrop of rocks in the distance.

"Here's the place," Billy said, stopping the truck. He took the keys and tucked them into his shirt pocket. "I'm going to leave you here, Princess. Tell me you're not stupid enough to try and escape into this mess."

"I'll stay here," she promised, knowing she would. Running now would be idiotic and suicidal.

Billy disappeared into the storm. Emma waited, trying to be patient, knowing Reyhan was close and wanting to run to him. But she couldn't be a distraction. He would have a plan and she didn't want to get in the way of that.

After what felt like a lifetime, but was probably only ten or fifteen minutes later, Billy opened the truck door.

"Show time," he said, and pulled out a knife.

He slit the ropes holding her wrists together. When she tried to move her arms, pain shot through her. She forced herself to ignore it and flex her arms until she could move them freely.

She saw Billy's two companions just behind him. They were equally scary with their close-cropped hair and multiple weapons.

"Climb on down," Billy said, motioning for her to step out of the truck.

When she stepped onto the ground she realized her escorts were the least of her problems. Sand attacked her like a giant angry beast. She couldn't see, couldn't breathe, could barely move. Grateful for the voluminous material covering her body, she pulled up her head covering and tugged the edges so she could protect her nose and mouth. Billy grabbed her arm and led her deeper into the storm. When they stopped, she looked up and saw Reyhan.

"I'm here," she called, trying to jerk free of Billy's hold.

The mercenary didn't let go. "Transfer the money," he yelled, then jerked his head toward his buddies. "Check the download."

The men pulled out small handheld devices. Emma strained to break free, never taking her eyes from Reyhan. He wore protective glasses and a heavy cloak, but she would swear he was staring right at her. She could almost hear his voice, willing her to be strong.

"Here it comes," Billy's friend yelled.

"What have you done?"

The fierce question came from somewhere on the left. Billy turned toward the man racing toward them.

"Shut up, kid. Stay out of this."

"No! You have kidnapped the wife of Prince Reyhan and now you ransom her?"

"Welcome to the games the big boys play. You and your friends were too much like girls to go through with your plans, so I had to pick up a little expense money elsewhere." Suddenly Billy was holding a gun in his other hand. "Stay out of this kid, or die. It's your choice."

Emma was so stunned, she nearly stumbled. "Don't hurt him," she demanded, pulling at her arm and suddenly jerking free.

Billy spun toward her. "Don't screw this up, sweetheart. I'll take you out if I have to."

"Emma."

She heard Reyhan's voice over the storm, over her fear and over the rapid pounding of her heart.

"Let her go," the first man insisted. He charged Billy.

Emma read the mercenary's intent before he ever acted. Even as he raised the gun, she flung herself at his arm, shoving him down. The gun went off.

The sound of the gunshot cut through the roar of the storm. Suddenly men where everywhere and bullets filled the air. Emma didn't know where to run or hide, nor did it matter. All she could think was that she had to get to Reyhan. Then something large and heavy crashed into her and she was trapped on the ground.

Panic flared. She couldn't breathe. She struggled until a familiar voice spoke into her ear.

"Be still. You are safe."

Reyhan. Fierce gladness swept through her and she wanted to roll over so she could cling to him.

More bullets cut through the storm. There were cries of pain, curses and the howl of the wind. Suddenly Reyhan was off her and pulling her to her feet. They were running toward the truck.

"Billy has the keys," she yelled to Reyhan. "In his pocket."

Reyhan didn't answer. Instead he circled around to the passenger side and shoved her inside.

"Stay down," he ordered. "Under the dash."

Then he was gone.

Emma huddled on the floorboards and prayed as she had never prayed in her life. That Reyhan would be safe. That no one else would be hurt. That they would all get out of this alive.

Time ticked by. Hours? Minutes? She wasn't sure. At last there was only the sound of the storm and she risked looking out the passenger window.

The three mercenaries were captured, sitting on the ground, their arms and legs bound. Several of the injured were being treated by men she thought must work for Reyhan. Relief coursed through her, making her weak and nauseated. They had survived.

After a time, Reyhan returned to the truck. "Are

you all right?'' he asked as he climbed in beside her and put a key in the ignition.

"I'm fine. Is there…'' She glanced out the window. "Are there a lot of injuries? My bodyguards?''

"A few. One of the mercenaries took a bullet to the arm. A couple of the rebels were shot, as were three of Will's men. None are fatal.''

"Good.'' She swallowed. "Was anyone killed?''

"One of the rebels. I knew him and his father. He was just seventeen.'' Reyhan looked weary and distressed.

Emma's stomach lurched. "Oh, God. It was my fault.''

"No.'' He turned on her. "Not your fault. These boys who wanted to play at being dangerous men brought this upon themselves. No one took them seriously, not even me. I knew their game and thought they would outgrow it. We were all wrong.''

He started the truck. "It's time to get you to safety.''

She was still stunned by the news that there had been a death. "I'm a nurse. I could help.''

"They'll be fine. Will's men are all trained in combat first-aid. He's very thorough. That's why I hired him.''

He started driving. She stared out the windshield and tried to come to terms with all that had happened in the past few hours.

"I'm sorry I was captured,'' she said. "I wasn't trying to make trouble.''

"The fault is mine. I shouldn't have allowed you to come here. I should have ignored my father.''

"Hard to do when he's the king."

Reyhan clutched the steering wheel more tightly. "He presumes too much and plays games with us all. This one could have cost you your life. I will never forgive him for that."

The force of his words stunned her. "Reyhan, he didn't know. None of us knew."

"Agreed. But it was a possibility."

He was acting as if he cared. This from the man who couldn't wait to divorce her. Thoughts swirled in her head. She felt exhausted.

He read her mind. "Close your eyes," he told her. "Rest."

"No. I want to stay awake and keep you company on the drive." The storm still swirled around them and made visibility nearly impossible.

"I know my way."

She supposed he would. This was his land, his desert. She leaned against the side of door and let her eyes drift closed. Maybe she would relax for a couple of minutes. What could it hurt?

Emma drifted off to sleep. She didn't know how long she'd been out, but she was awakened by a horrible crashing as the truck roared into what looked like the side of a mountain.

For a second, she was disoriented. Not sure where she was or why, she frantically glanced around. When she saw Reyhan slumped over the steering wheel, her memory returned and with it, panic.

Had they run off the road? Why had he driven into the rocks? She unfastened her seat belt and scrambled across the bench seat, then eased Reyhan into a sitting position.

His face was unscathed. She checked for bumps and bruises, but there weren't any. He hadn't hit his head.

"Reyhan," she called frantically. "Can you hear me?"

He didn't answer.

Why was he unconscious? She began to check for other injuries. First his shoulders, then his arms. She slid her hand down his side and drew them back when she felt wetness. Blood covered her right hand.

"No!" she whispered, horrified and afraid. The thick stickiness told her he'd been bleeding for some time. Reality crashed in on her.

"You were shot," she breathed. "Oh, God. It can't be." Hadn't he known?

She glanced around frantically. She had to get him somewhere that she could examine him. Maybe the back of the truck. But without a first-aid kit, what could she do? She didn't even know where they were.

He stirred and groaned.

"Reyhan? Can you hear me? You've been shot."

He opened his eyes. "It's nothing."

"You're bleeding and you passed out."

He blinked at her, then stared out the front of the truck. "We're at the caves," he said.

"At them? We're practically in them." She looked at the crumpled front of the truck. "I'm not sure it's going to still run. Are we close to the security camp?"

He shook his head, then groaned. "We're at the

Desert Palace. My aunt's house. Through the caves. We need to go through the caves.''

Emma wasn't sure if he was delirious or not. But if there was a house nearby, maybe she could get some help.

She stepped out onto the ground. The storm had lessened to the point where she could see the landscape around them. They were in some kind of small canyon with the front of the truck mashed up against a sheer rock wall. To the right was an opening to a cave.

She turned in a slow circle and saw nothing. Not a road, not a building, not a hint of life. They were truly alone.

The fear returned and with it a conviction that she wouldn't let Reyhan die. She couldn't. He might not care about her, but she loved him.

She crossed into the mouth of the cave. The opening was huge with the ceiling soaring up what looked like two stories. There was a small chest to the right of the opening and she crossed to it.

She opened it and inside she found flashlights, batteries, water, food and a first-aid kit. When she turned back to the truck, she screamed. Reyhan leaned against the entrance. He was pale, shaking and bleeding.

''What are you doing?'' she demanded as she raced back to him. ''Stay still. You can't lose any more blood.''

''It's about two miles that way,'' he said, pointing into the cave. ''You'll have to pull the truck into the cave, then help me walk the rest of the way.''

"You're not walking two miles anytime soon," she told him. "We'll camp right here until help arrives."

"Not likely soon, and there aren't enough supplies," he said, and winced.

She glanced at the food and water provided and knew he was right. The trunk provided emergency rations, not enough to live on.

"One thing at a time," she told him. "I have to get you bandaged up. Then we'll talk about moving you."

"We have to make the trip before dark," he said. "There's not much time."

Chapter Thirteen

Aware of the passage of time, Emma worked quickly. She pulled all the supplies out of the trunk and was relieved to find a blanket folded in the bottom. Once she had everything gathered, she helped Reyhan into a seated position.

His robes came off easily. Once she'd tossed them aside she could see the bloodstained shirt clinging to his torso. He barely hissed as she took off the drenched cotton, even when it pulled in places. When she was done, she examined the wound.

The bullet had gone through him. She had no way of knowing if anything vital had been damaged nor could she have fixed anything if it had.

Her emergency training came back to her and she worked quickly, grateful for her stint in the emergency room back home. Less than twenty minutes later she'd nearly stopped the bleeding, which meant she could finish bandaging the wound.

She was shaken, scared and ready for someone to rescue them, but she had a feeling they were on their own until she could figure out a way to call for help.

She crouched in front of Reyhan and smooth back his sweat-soaked hair. "I'm done," she whispered. "It shouldn't hurt so badly now."

"I'm fine."

She doubted that, but while the first-aid kit had plenty of bandages and antiseptic, there hadn't been any painkillers.

"Is there a cell phone I can use?" she asked. "Can I call for help?"

"In the Desert Palace," he said between clenched teeth. He sucked in a breath and rolled to his knees, then started to stand.

She clutched his arm. "You can't. We'll stay here."

"No. We go now. There's little time."

She glanced outside and figured they had about two hours left of daylight. Depending on how fast they could move, they had a chance of getting to the palace by dark. But it wasn't a sure thing.

"We should wait and go in the morning."

He looked at her. "You don't want to face what roams the desert at night."

Good point.

She collected their supplies and put them in the blanket, then knotted the ends together so she could wear it like a sling. She had them each drink some water, then she got Reyhan to his feet and leaned him against the wall. Finally she went out to the truck.

Surprisingly it started. She maneuvered it into the cave where it sputtered and died before she had a chance to turn off the ignition. So much for the backup plan of trying to find the camp via the truck.

She took one of the flashlights and handed the other to Reyhan. Then standing on his injured side, she took as much of his weight as she could.

It was slow going. She didn't want to think how much his side must hurt him or how weak and out of it he must feel from the blood loss. But he didn't complain, didn't slow down. He moved steady, at a pace that stunned her, turning left, then right, going deeper and deeper into the mountain, following directions only he could recognize.

There were hundreds of places to get lost, she thought nervously as they came to yet another fork in the path. Reyhan went to the left, passed three other trails, before picking the fourth.

Despite the distance they'd traveled, Emma knew they weren't going deeper underground because there were bits of light filtering through the rocks above. Although as time passed, the light seemed to get more and more dim.

"We're nearly there," he said, his voice low and raspy.

She stopped and urged him to lean against the wall. "Have some water," she said. "You're dehydrated."

He took the water and drank. His willingness to listen to her told her just how badly he'd been hurt.

They started walking again.

After about twenty minutes, Reyhan spoke. "There's a satellite phone in the office," he said. "Find it tonight and put it out in the courtyard tomorrow. There's a solar cell. It will take twelve hours to charge."

Twelve hours? That meant they couldn't call for help until tomorrow night. What if Reyhan was bleeding to death on the inside? What if the bullet had pierced his intestines or his spleen or…?

The path blurred and she realized she was crying. Blinking away the tears, she did her best to ignore the panic filling her and think about what was important. They'd survived this long. She could manage emergency first aid. Any crisis could be dealt with at the time. They would survive—she would make sure of it. She hadn't come this far and realized she loved him only to lose him now.

Nearly a half hour later, she realized the sun was definitely setting. Soon it would be completely dark except for the light from their flashlights. Her body ached from Reyhan leaning on her. She was tired, hungry and thirsty. If she felt this bad, he must feel a hundred times worse.

She was about to ask how much farther when he stopped and pointed. "There."

Emma peered into the murky darkness and saw what looked like a solid stone wall.

"It's a dead end," she said, fighting both panic and resignation. They weren't going to make it.

He glanced at her and raised his eyebrows.

"Do not believe everything you see. Go stand in front of the wall."

She made sure he was leaning against the rocks before shrugging off his arm and approaching the wall. She pressed her hand against the stones.

"Cold and solid."

"The bricks are a grid," he said. "Count across from left to right and down from top to bottom. Three over and five down. Push."

She blinked in the darkness, then did as he requested. The stone moved. Her heart nearly leapt out of her chest.

"It's working."

"Of course it is," he said, and gave her the next instruction.

So they went for a total of eight stones. On the last one, there was an audible click, then the stone wall swung in like a well-oiled door. The ground changed from uneven rock to polished stone and slowly sloped up.

"We are here," he said, and walked into the palace.

Emma followed him. Reyhan kept his balance by pressing one hand against the wall and holding his flashlight with the other. At the top of the ramp, they entered what appeared to be a basement or cellar. He turned a lever and the stone door swung shut.

"There is a short flight of stairs," he said. "On the main floor are several bedrooms, the kitchen and the office. You'll find the satellite phone in there."

He crossed the open area and headed for a flight of stairs at the far end. Emma was surprised that he barely limped. It was as if being in the Desert Palace gave him strength.

"Is there food and water?" she asked.

"Yes. No fresh food, but staples. And fresh water is always available. There's an underground spring."

He climbed the stairs, slowly only slightly toward the top. She saw blood seeping through his bandage and winced. "You need to lic down," she told him.

"Soon."

At the top of the stairs was another door. This one had a knob. He turned it and they stepped into a beautifully tiled hallway. The air was cool but fresh and there were still hints of sunlight coming in through large windows.

"There are battery-operated lanterns," he said. "Several in each room."

He moved down the hallway, pausing only to point out the direction to the kitchen, the placement of the office and where the wing of bedrooms began.

He entered the first one, made his way to the bed, sat down and passed out before he could put his head on the pillow.

Fear returned but by now Emma was familiar with the knot in her stomach and the tightness in her chest. She ignored it and went to work.

After setting down the supplies she carried, she found the battery-powered lantern in the room and clicked it on. Then she made sure Reyhan was comfortable on the bed and checked his wound.

The seepage from before had stopped, which was a relief. So far there was no red, swollen flesh to indicate infection. Was it possible they'd gotten off relatively easily?

Confident he was all right for the moment, she took

one of the flashlights and did a quick search of the main floor of the large house.

There were over a dozen rooms on this level and at least three staircases. The kitchen was huge and well stocked. Cold water gushed from the faucet. She found a propane-heated stove and oven, along with an empty refrigerator that probably needed a generator in order to run.

In the book-lined office, she found a case on the big desk that looked somewhat like a phone. She made a mental note to stick that outside sometime tonight so that it could start charging in the morning.

None of the four downstairs bathrooms offered a first-aid kit, so she returned to the kitchen and went into the pantry. Sure enough, on the bottom shelf was an assortment of medical supplies to supplement what had been in the first-aid kit in the case.

She collected what she needed and returned to Reyhan's room.

He hadn't moved. She checked his temperature, which was normal, then changed the bandage and decided to wait on everything else. If he regained consciousness, she would see if he could drink water and eat. If he didn't…she would face that problem later.

She returned to the kitchen where she dumped the old bandages and opened a can of soup. She ate it cold, too tired to bother with trying to heat it. After swallowing the contents and three full glasses of water, she made use of one of the luxury bathrooms, then returned to Reyhan's room.

He was still cool to the touch and there wasn't any more bleeding. She had no way to tell about internal injuries, but she was hopeful that he'd been very lucky and that the bullet had missed everything.

Weary behind words, she curled up next to him on the bed and closed her eyes. Just for a few minutes, she told herself. She still had to get the phone outside and figure out what she was going to feed him when he woke....

Someone stroked her hair. Emma felt the light touch even in her sleep and smiled. She was warm all over and rested and in just a second she would open her eyes and see—

Consciousness returned and with it the memories of what had happened the previous day. She sat up and realized it was morning and Reyhan was awake.

"Good morning," he said.

She stared at him, at his bare chest and the clarity in his eyes. His color was good. Except for the white bandage at his waist, she wouldn't have known he'd ever been injured.

"How are you feeling?" she asked.

"Good. A little sore, but otherwise fine. I am hungry and thirsty."

"Positive signs." She touched his forehead. "No fever?"

"Not that I can feel."

Suddenly aware that she was pressed against him and that they were on a bed, she shifted toward the edge then stood.

"Let me check your bandage. If there's no sign of infection, we can all breathe a little easier."

She removed the dressing. The wound was clean, the surrounding skin pale.

"It's already healing," she told him.

"Good. Then we can eat."

He swung his legs to the floor and stood. She hovered by his side, but he seemed fine. Strong and capable. Once again the prince and no longer the man who needed her.

"I would like a shower," he said.

"Me, too, but there's no hot water. At least there wasn't last night."

"The water heater needs to be turned on. I'll take care of that if you want to start on breakfast."

She nodded and followed him out of the room. He didn't even sway as he walked, she thought, amazed by his powers of recovery. As they passed the office, she remembered the telephone and collected it. Reyhan disappeared into a small room behind the pantry while she took the phone out into the courtyard and opened the case so the rising sun would charge the solar cell. Then she took a moment and looked around at the lush, nondesertlike garden in the middle of a three-story sand-and-stone house.

Plants bloomed and trailed everywhere. She couldn't name the various pink, red and white flowers, but she could inhale their sweet fragrance. Water trickled through several fountains and circled the garden before flowing into a stone-lined pond.

No doubt the underground spring was responsible for the flow of water. Emma sighed as she caught sight of a bench in the corner and a small grassy patch. This was a dream house—somewhere she could happily stay forever.

She left the courtyard garden and returned to the kitchen. By the time she'd put together a meal, Reyhan had returned with word that there would soon be hot water. He'd also started the generator.

"We'll have immediate electricity," he said. "We have to use it sparingly until the solar panels start working. Hot water will take an hour or so."

"There's nothing like a day in the desert to make one grateful for the little things," she said, smiling as if being alone with him was no big deal. As if she didn't remember how scared she'd been when she'd found out he'd been shot, and how much he'd hurt her, before they'd left, with his agreement that it was time for her to go home.

As she sat across from him, she tried not to stare at his features. There was no need to memorize his face. Their time together had changed her forever and she would never forget what he looked like. Even now, without a shirt, in need of a shave and less than twenty-four hours after being shot, he still looked masculine, powerful and very princelike.

Silence descended. She searched for a topic to keep the moment from being too awkward.

"Whose house is this?" she asked as she sipped the coffee she'd prepared.

"Mine. It belonged to my aunt. She left it to me when she died."

"This is where you came to after we got married," she said as the pieces of the past clicked into place.

He nodded. "I needed to be here for her funeral

service and then I had to settle her affairs." He stared past her, as if seeing into that long-ago time. "She and I were very close. My parents loved each other more than they loved their children. My brother Jefri didn't seem to mind, but I noticed." He shrugged. "When things were difficult, Sheza was there for me."

Simple words, she thought, reading the pain behind them. She could imagine a young, lonely prince, growing up in privilege, but without affection. The woman who took his parents' place would always hold a special place in his heart. No wonder he'd been devastated by her loss.

"I'm sorry," she said quietly. "I wish I'd known what you were going through."

He sipped his coffee. "It wouldn't have made a difference. I would never have let you comfort me."

"Why not?"

One corner of his mouth turned up. "I am Prince Reyhan of Bahania. I am not in need of comforting."

She leaned toward him. "I see. And who exactly buys into that line?"

"You would have."

"You're right. It's something a child would have believed. But I'm not that little girl anymore. Now I know better."

His dark gaze settled on her face. "You were very brave yesterday."

"Not really. At first I was furious at being taken hostage. I knew they'd try to get money from you. They didn't, did they?"

"No. We were able to cancel the transfer. My se-

curity chief had a plan to get the money back even if
the transfer had gone through. But if necessary, I
would have paid.''

''Nice to know,'' she said, not surprised, but still
pleased.

''You are my wife, Emma. I could not let you be
harmed.''

She didn't feel like his wife. She didn't feel like
anything except excess baggage.

''Thank you for saving my life,'' he said.

''Thank you for saving mine.''

''So we are even, which is better than one of us
being in debt to another.'' He smiled. ''You did not
expect danger to be a part of your visit to Bahania.
This experience must make you eager to be back in
Dallas.''

So much less than he thought. ''There are things
I'll miss about being here,'' she told him. Mostly him.

His smile faded. ''I'm sorry I hurt you when we
were at the palace.''

When he'd rejected her, she thought. When he'd
turned his back on her offer to make love.

''Yes, well, it's not a big deal.''

''I don't believe you,'' he said. ''It was a big deal
to both of us. There are things you don't understand.''

''Then explain them to me.''

He glanced out the window. ''There is a legend
that the spring that runs under this house is the result
of heartache. That a young man got lost in the desert
and wandered for days. He was nearly out of water
when he found a single blooming plant. So impressed
by the beauty of the flower, he poured his last drops

of water onto the parched leaves to give it longer life. Grateful, the flower became a beautiful woman. They made love but in the morning, the young man died from dehydration. The woman wept and her tears became a river.''

He turned back to her. ''The garden in the courtyard pays homage to them both. Some of the plants date back nearly a hundred years.''

''That's a very sad story.''

''It is a lesson. We must pay attention to what matters. The young woman possessed magical powers. She could have restored the young man first. Instead she took what she wanted and as a result, lost him.''

She shook her head. ''I think the lesson is to seize whatever love we can find for as long as we have it.''

''Perhaps you are right.'' He rose. ''The hot water should be ready soon. You may shower first.''

As appealing as a shower sounded, she had other things on her mind. Maybe it was stupid to take another chance on him and lay her heart on the line. Maybe she didn't have a choice.

''You don't have to let me go, Reyhan.''

He stiffened slightly and didn't look at her as he spoke. ''Yes, I do.''

''Why? Who is this other woman you plan to marry? What will she give you that I can't?''

''Peace of mind.''

Chapter Fourteen

After her shower, Emma decided to explore the rest of the small palace. Reyhan had settled in the library and after the cryptic end to their breakfast conversation, she wasn't sure what was left to say between them.

She had a thousand questions, but what was new about that? She'd had questions from the beginning— such as why had he married her in the first place and why had he *stayed* married to her? Asking why he had to marry someone else for his peace of mind was way down there on the "questions to ask" priority list.

She climbed to the second story and explored the amazing rooms. There was a large open area that had to be a ballroom, some kind of living room and four incredibly luxurious bedrooms that would rival the elegance of the famous pink palace in the capital city.

Even without any knowledge about antiques, she recognized the beauty of the carved furniture and the glittering gold leaf edging the chairs. There were dressers and armoires and four-poster beds with stairs leading to high mattresses. Amazing murals covered the walls. In one bedroom, she found a pumpkin coach and six horses, all made of crystal. In another there was a carved set of toy soldiers.

On the third floor were more spartan rooms, except for a round room in a tower. Stained-glass windows cast a rainbow of light on the marble floor. The room was completely empty except for a desk with a chest in the middle.

Curious, she crossed to the desk and opened the chest. When she saw what was inside, her breath caught.

There were pictures. Dozens of pictures, all of a young woman. In some she was laughing, in others serious. Sometimes she faced the camera, sometimes she hid her face. One had been taken while she slept.

Emma felt her heart constrict as she recognized a much-younger version of herself. Reyhan had taken these pictures while they'd been dating and then after they'd married.

Below the pictures were mementos from their dates, all the notes she'd written—and several detective reports. She flipped through them and read his messages to the company he'd hired to check on her for the first few months they'd been separated. He'd obviously wanted to know that she was all right. A few pictures of her had been included with the reports and they were as well-worn as the pages of the report.

"I don't understand," she whispered into the silence. Why had he done this? Why had he kept everything?

Had he been any other man, she would have thought—hoped—that he cared about her. That she mattered. But he wasn't. He was Prince Reyhan of Bahania and he didn't let himself care.

Or did he? Emma sank onto the floor and studied the detective reports more closely. Reyhan was proud. He would not give his heart easily, nor would he want it toyed with. Had he cared about her and had she not understood the depth of his feelings? He wasn't the kind of man who would marry on a whim. He'd chosen her—only her. Now he didn't want a divorce because he loved someone else but so that he could make a marriage of convenience to produce heirs. He didn't want to fall in love again—was that because he still loved her, or because the first time things had ended so badly?

She thought about all that had happened so long ago. How she'd hidden away from him, like a child afraid of being punished. How she'd let her parents convince her he didn't care because it was easier than confessing her guilty secret.

She claimed to be someone different from that scared young woman, yet was she any more willing to fight for what she wanted? If she loved Reyhan, she needed to tell him. If she wanted a chance at making their marriage work, then she would have to fight for him.

She tossed down the report and scrambled to her feet. She wasn't going to wait another second. They belonged together and she was going to help him see that. No matter how long it took.

She raced down the stairs. Once she reached the main floor, she called out his name as she ran from room to room. She burst into the bedroom he'd been using just as he stepped out of the bathroom.

He wore nothing but a towel, and both it and the bandage were white against his skin. Her throat closed as she remembered the last time they'd been in this position—how he'd rejected her. Determined not to be swayed by fear of rejection and his pride, she squared her shoulders.

"We have to talk," she told him.

His dark eyes burned with a fire she recognized. Her insides quivered slightly and her thighs trembled.

"No."

The single word didn't frighten her. He wasn't going to get his way—not anymore. This was too important to let his pride win. Of course if he really didn't care about her at all, she was about to experience the most humiliating moment of her life, but she had to be willing to risk it all if she wanted to win it all.

"I know you want me," she said, crossing the room to stand directly in front of him.

"Desire means nothing," he told her, turning his back on her. "It is simply a reaction."

"To all women or just to me?" She walked up behind him and placed her hands on his bare shoulders. "What happens when I touch you, Reyhan? I know what happens to me. My insides melt while my whole body starts to ache with a hunger I can barely control.'' She stroked the length of his spine. ''My breathing quickens. There is fire everywhere.''

His skin was smooth, his muscles unyielding. When her fingers reached the edge of the towel, he shuddered.

''You're so sleek and strong,'' she murmured, then pressed a kiss to his back. ''Straight to my curves, hard to my soft. Is it just me?'' she asked. ''Tell me.''

He turned on her with a roar that could have been anger or passion or maybe both. He reached for her and hauled her against him, apparently unaware or unconcerned about his bullet wound.

She was more than willing to ignore it, too, as he kissed her with a need that was even stronger than her own. There were no preliminarily kisses, no soft queries. Instead he took her mouth and claimed her. His lips pressed against hers with a pressure that had her arching against him.

More, she thought frantically as she clung to him and kissed him back. She wanted it all.

His tongue swept over and around hers even as he pushed and tugged at her clothing. She wore only a T-shirt and jeans, but they were too much of a barrier when all she had to do was tug at his towel to undress *him.*

And then he was naked and she didn't worry about her own clothing. Not when she could reach her hand between them and touch his arousal.

As her fingers closed over him, he groaned, then

swore and tore his mouth away. "Get these damn clothes off!" he demanded.

She looked into his eyes and laughed softly. "Impatient, are we?"

"I'll die if I don't have you now."

"Good. Because that's exactly how I feel."

She pulled off her T-shirt and kicked off her sandals while he worked on her jeans. Her bra went next, then she pulled down her panties.

The next second she was falling onto the bed and Reyhan was on top of her.

"I want you," he breathed. "Emma, I need you."

Uncontrollable desire tightened his features. She felt his need, because it was her own. She understood his dilemma even as she reached between them and guided him inside of her.

"You're not ready," he protested, trying to hold back.

She knew she was hot, wet and slick. "Yes, I am."

He plunged into her and they both cried out. Within seconds they were lost in a frenzy of sensation and wanting. She pulled him closer, wanting him deeper. He kissed her eyes, her cheeks, before claiming her mouth. She wrapped her legs around him and as her orgasm approached had to break the kiss to gasp for air.

"Reyhan," she breathed as her body stiffened before convulsing into release.

He continued to fill her over and over until the shudders faded. It was only then that he groaned out her name and was still.

She closed her eyes and let herself relax into his

embrace. Her need for him hadn't faded, only shifted. Now she wanted to be as emotionally connected as they had been physically.

Reyhan withdrew and rolled onto his back, pulling her with him so that she draped across his chest.

"We should not have done that," he said as he stroked her hair.

"Because you're worried about me getting pregnant," she said.

"That is one consideration. Eventually the odds will catch up with us."

They already had. Emma felt time shift and bend and suddenly she was eighteen, alone in her room and crying. Pain filled her body, but not from a physical source. Instead she felt the ache of being alone and so lost, she would never find her way back.

"What?" he asked, continuing to touch her hair. "Where have you gone? I see such sadness in your eyes."

She hadn't been sure she was going to tell him. What was the point? But now, suddenly she wanted him to know. Not to make him feel badly but so that he would understand more.

"I was pregnant before," she whispered. "From our honeymoon."

She braced herself for his violent reaction. She didn't expect him to get angry, but she knew there would be energy and demands for information. Perhaps even accusations. But instead he stayed on the bed, his fingers brushing against her scalp, his other hand tucked behind his head.

"What happened?"

A simple question, yet it was as if he'd unlocked a hidden door. She felt her heart shudder as the memories escaped and raced to the light of day for the first time in six years.

"The doctor said it wasn't uncommon to lose a baby in the first few weeks of pregnancy, especially for a young woman. He said there was probably something wrong with it and that was nature's way of making things right." She blinked to hold back tears, but still they spilled over onto her cheeks. "I was so upset when you left that I locked myself in my room at my parents' house and cried for nearly two weeks. I've always wondered if our child couldn't stand the thought of a mother who was so sad all the time."

"So you take responsibility for what happened?"

She nodded.

"I see." He cupped her cheek. "Perhaps our child didn't want a father who disappeared without word."

"You had nothing to do with me losing the baby."

"Neither did you." His dark gaze locked on her face. "So that is why you refused to see me. You were too upset."

She nodded. "That's a part of it. I was ashamed, too. And scared. I thought you'd be so angry with me."

He wrapped his arms around her and drew her closer until she rested on top of him and they could kiss. He brushed his mouth against hers. "Never. With the wisdom of hindsight I know that I shouldn't have left you behind when my aunt died. I should have brought you with me."

"I'm not sure that would have helped. I couldn't have handled the situation, or you. Not then."

One corner of his mouth turned up. "You think you can handle me now?"

"Yes."

"What makes you so sure?"

This was, as her father would say, where the rubber met the road. How willing was she to risk everything and lay it on the line?

"Because before I didn't know why you'd married me. I was young and scared and too inexperienced to know how to please a man. Everything is different now."

The humor disappeared as if it had never been. He started to sit up. Emma pushed on his shoulders, trying desperately to hold him in place.

"Reyhan, don't. We have to talk about it."

"There is nothing to say."

"I think we could talk for a lifetime and never say all the things we missed by being apart. Reyhan, why didn't you ever tell me you loved me?"

He grasped her by the waist and slid her aside, then sat up. That simple action warned her he was already slipping away.

"Why is it such a horrible thing to admit?" she asked desperately. "Is it because I was so immature? I know I couldn't be a partner for you then, but things are different now. We're *both* different. You loved me then. Couldn't you care a little for me now?"

He didn't speak, didn't move. She wasn't sure he was even breathing.

Frightened, and not sure how to convince him,

mostly because she didn't understand what she was fighting against, she tried to speak from the heart.

"I don't know what I felt back then. I was a kid. I keep saying that but it's true. I had a fantasy about love and marriage and what my husband would be like. You rescued me that very first day and I'm not sure I saw you as a real person. You were more like a superhero or something. But now I can see the man and he's a good and honorable person."

She leaned against Reyhan's back and wrapped her arms around his shoulders.

"You're proud and sometimes that's annoying, but I can live with it," she continued. "I want to stay here with you. I want us to stay married, to love each other and have babies together." She swallowed before confessing her most intimate secret. "I'm in love with you."

Reyhan felt each word. They cut him like knives. When he'd been shot the day before, he'd barely felt the pain, but now, with Emma, he was ripped apart.

Love. She spoke the words he would have sold his soul to hear. Words that would drive him to his knees with gratitude. But then what? Who would he be if he gave in to his love and desire for this woman? How could he be strong? How could he be a man if he was controlled by a woman?

"No!" he roared, and sprang to his feet. "Do not love me. I will not love you in return. Not again. I will not be crushed by the needing and wanting. I will not have you fill my head and consume the very breath from my body. I will not be made weak by all that I feel for you."

He glared at her, but she didn't flinch. Instead she met his angry gaze with a look so filled with love that he could have captured the emotion in his hand and trapped it in a box.

"It doesn't have to be like that," she said as she stood naked in front of him. Her long hair spread across her shoulders and teased the top of her breasts. "We can support each other, gaining strength from what the other gives. A team is better than a single man. I want to make you happy, Reyhan. I want to be the one person in the world you can trust with everything and I want to trust you the same way."

He knew what she asked, what she wanted. He knew the truth—it was better to be safe and alone. Better to walk away.

He started to do just that, but before he did so, he allowed himself one last look at her. He took in her beautiful face, the slight tilt of her eyes and the fullness of her mouth. He memorized the sound of her laugh and how she scowled when she was angry. He pictured her hair up, as she'd worn it to the formal reception at the palace.

His gaze dropped lower to her full breasts, the tight nipples that called to him like a siren. Wanting stirred, but he ignored it. Next he studied her narrow waist and the fullness of her hips. He felt badly about the child they'd lost, about the pain she'd suffered alone. Had she been recovering when he'd first tried to see her? Her father had said she was ill. Reyhan had assumed the old man was lying, but perhaps not.

They hadn't used birth control. Why hadn't he considered the possibility of her having his child?

A son, he thought with regret. Or a pretty little girl of five who ran through the halls of the palace and wrapped him around her finger as much as he would wrap her around his heart.

Standing there naked, with sunlight filling the room, Reyhan felt the weight of all he'd lost when he'd abandoned Emma, and the weight of it made it impossible for him to stand. He sank to his knees.

She was at his side in an instant.

"Don't let me go," she pleaded. "We've been given a second chance. Can't you see how rare and precious that is?"

He clung to her because she was as she had always been—his lifeline. He had tried to live without her. He had convinced himself a cold gray world was a safe place to be, but it was not living. It was an existence that offended those brave enough to reach for what they wanted.

"I am a man humbled by a woman," he said, taking her face in his hands and kissing her.

"I am the one who is humbled," she breathed as she kissed him over and over again. "I love you, Reyhan. For always."

"And I love you. From the first moment I saw you."

He drew her into his arms then carried her to the bed where he settled both of them on the tangled sheets.

"Stay with me," he pleaded. "Love me. Have my children, work at my side, fill my nights and my heart."

Tears spilled out of the corners of her eyes. "Yes. For always."

He wrapped his arms around her. Emma could feel the steady beating of his heart. His skin was warm against her own, both comforting and arousing.

There was much to discuss, she thought as she snuggled closer still. Where they would make their home—either here or the pink palace. How often she would be visiting her parents in Texas. What Reyhan was going to say when she told him she loved her work too much to give it up. While being a delivery room nurse would be difficult, she would have to find another way to use her skills.

Last, and perhaps most important, she wondered when she would tell him about the tiny life growing inside of her. She knew with the certainty that had served women well since the dawn of time that they had made a baby that morning. A child who would be the first of many. The new life was their promise to each other—that they would love with all their hearts. Having nearly lost everything, they would hold on to each other while nurturing a love as constant and endless as the desert itself.

* * * * *